CW00806871

"One of the best and wo~~r~~ author is people you've ~~r~~ their manuscripts. It lands that equation. I am deeply to read this fun, cheeky ~~...... ....~~ all my favourite things—cake, cocktails, travel and life-changing ideas. Here's to big ideas, adventure and a book that turns both into a fascinating tale."

Pam Grout, #1 New York Times bestselling author of E-Squared and 18 other books

"Fabulous! A starry-eyed ride across the jet-set publishing scene, set against the harsh reality of violence at home. Isabella May is the new Marian Keyes."

Venetia Welby, author of Mother of Darkness

"Kate Clothier took me on a journey of personal self-discovery and has encouraged me to re-evaluate aspects of my own way of life. She's my new heroine."

mariawyattwriter.wordpress.com

"Delectable, compelling and totally moreish"

N J Simmonds, author of The Path Keeper

"Kate could have been, is, or will one day be your friend. Her story will make you want to be hers."

Jaquelyn Muller, Author/Presenter/Columnist

"An outstanding, powerful debut. Isabella May somehow achieves the impossible, combining food, darkness, humour and spirituality in an absolute page-turner."

Beauty City International

"A perfect balance of wit, grit and Law of Attraction."

Eva George, author of Size HH

"A chic and compelling chick-lit read."

Books Beyond The Story

Dear Jeanette
may you always have your
cake and eat it... !

Oh! What a
Pavlova

Isabella May
xx

Isabella May

CROOKED
CAT

Discover us online:
www.crookedcatbooks.com

Join us on facebook:
www.facebook.com/crookedcat

Tweet a photo of yourself holding
this book to **@crookedcatbooks**
and something nice will happen.

For my three children: Carmen, April and William; the little loves of my life.

For Chris: the bigger love of my life. If you hadn't led us to the sea and the mountains, would this book ever have happened?

And in loving memory of Uncle Ronnie, who sadly passed away before this story was published, and was always partial to a Round Robin or two (our family's take on the Welsh Cake).

About the Author

Isabella May lives in (mostly) sunny Andalucia, Spain with her husband, daughter and son, creatively inspired by the sea and the mountains. When she isn't having her cake and eating it, sampling a new cocktail on the beach, or ferrying her children to after school activities, she is usually writing.

As a Co-founder and a former contributing writer for the popular online women's magazine, The Glass House Girls - **www.theglasshousegirls.com** - she has also been lucky enough to subject the digital world to her other favourite pastimes, travel and the Law of Attraction. Oh! What a Pavlova is her debut novel.

Acknowledgements

Writing a book is as complex as baking a cake, and there are many people to thank when it comes to acknowledging those who have helped, or inspired, the creation that is Oh! What A Pavlova.

So here goes...and my apologies to anybody I have unintentionally left out:

First off, a gazillion thanks to my long-suffering husband: 1) For listening to me rave on and on about my current word count/chopping of characters, and 2) For carrying our family afloat financially and enabling me to fulfil my dream. I would also like to thank my children for their never-ending patience as I have stared vacantly at a laptop screen while they asked me seven times in a row, "what's for tea?"

Mum and Dad, thank you for *everything*...and Mum, I have to thank you especially for consistently reminding me: "One day you'll be a published author, I just know it!"

Thanks also to my wonderful Nans, Margarita (Isabella) and Elizabeth (May) for being the two strong and independent role models you were, to all of us grandchildren. And thank you to all of my family members for their encouragement and promises to buy my book; now you will have to stand by your words.

As for my lovely friends, of which there are simply too many to mention: Lorraine Mace, Emma Wilson and Natali Drake, you guys are top of the list for keeping the rocket fuel burning in your very special ways. We were definitely destined to meet. Becky Lee, thank you for helping to shape my very unique sense of humour from a young age, as well as for those Sunday morning Cakey Days at the Mocha Berry Café. Sarah Hill, I am pretty sure you introduced me to Basel Biscuits, and Louisa Cox, didn't you and I used to have a 'thing' about Lardy Cakes? Well, both these fascinations undoubtedly steered me in the right direction...Lorraine Farmer, equally I have you to thank for many a cake and tea-filled afternoon. And Teresa Moult, Maiu Clark and Dawn Brierley, I definitely have you three to thank for keeping this tradition alive and kicking in sunny Spain! Vicky Bostock, you kept me saner more times than you'll ever know during many a stressful day at the office. Cristina Galimberti, thou hast been a constant deity of kick-ass girl power in your inimitable style over the years. Lisa Tenzin-Dolma, thank you for being you, for inspiring me not only to write, but for the creation of the gorgeous Glastonbury Tarot Cards, which you have kindly allowed me to feature in the book. Tracy Hails, Shoma Chatterjee, Maxine Byrne and Michelle Smith, you know why I am thankful you have all graced my path, our friendships at key moments have definitely led me to where I am today.

The Estepona and Sotogrande Writers' Groups have also been an amazing source of support (and patience...) as I often giggled my way through reading chapters aloud for their *mostly* constructive critique. I don't think I will ever be able to forget my first meeting at the Sotogrande group though, when a couple of rather opinionated ladies exclaimed: 'it's rubbish, we'd chuck it in the bin', upon me reading out the first page of my then *unpolished diamond*. Let this be proof to every aspiring writer: If you believe it, you WILL see it!

Jeannette Maw (of Good Vibe Blog) and Gary Temple-Bodley (of The Teachings of Joshua) have expanded my knowledge of the Law of Attraction tenfold, and I thank my lucky stars every day to have met these awesome dudes who keep me on my spiritual and quantum physics toes.

Crooked Cat, I thank you endlessly for your vision, for giving me the opportunity to get "Pavlova!" out there. Thanks so much as well to my Editor, Maureen Vincent-Northam and Designer, Anna Shepulova, for their expertise in helping to sculpt the finished product.

And finally, a very heartfelt Thank You to The Button Pushers and Naysayers. This story could never have happened without you.

Isabella May

Oh! What a Pavlova

The Noughties
The Decade from 2000-2009

A time when publishing contracts were signed at the book fair table; with a wink, an x-ray underwear scan all too often thrown in for good measure, and a sip of pretend champagne from a polystyrene cup. All hail those awesome, unfathomable Chinese print prices.

A time when Jamie Oliver still served up sugar and kept his views on breastfeeding to himself, Mary Berry's call to a bunting-strung, cupcake-fringed tent in a field was but a dot on the horizon – and we were all still madly in love with Nigella.

A time when women (and men) were being physically and emotionally battered…behind closed doors.

And the ley lines of Glastonbury continued to offer their timeless mystical wisdom, if only Kate Clothier was listening.

Chapter One

My infidelities had been set in motion some time ago, in Lyon during my Uni gap year, a mere three years into my relationship with Daniel.

I'd always dismissed my very brief fling with Pierre, the engineering postgraduate, as nothing more than getting things out of my system before settling down to married life. It colluded with the childishly sketched pictures of 'our future country cottage' that Daniel would send me, along with the lovesick letters which arrived in forlorn bundles begging me to always stay with him, have his children, cats and dogs. Even then it scared me sideways, the lengths to which he had water-coloured my life without as much as a consultation.

One Saturday I was whisked off to a ball with another English student friend. Both of us were stranded as teachers in a further education centre; a grey concrete jungle of nothingness, on the outskirts of the city. A mutual acquaintance just happened to be the not-much-older-big-sister of one of the engineering postgrads at Lyon University, securing us some much swooned over tickets.

The engineering ball was quite the grandest event I had been to at the time. Swarms of hot-blooded French men outnumbered the women four-to-one on the dance floor. The *Teenage Wedding* song from *Pulp Fiction* blared out and Pierre made his move: Quite from nowhere, quite a surprise, quite mmm. I played Ice Maiden admirably for a couple of verses.

"Je ne peux pas te baiser, j'ai un copain," I protested feebly every time he dived in for an intoxicating kiss.

Before long, I yielded to his charm; the heady scent of his expensive aftershave helping things along. As the night drew to a close and I discovered the meaning of a real French kiss, he inscribed his phone number the length of my inner arm in pillar box red *Chanel* lipstick, blunting my favourite make-up as he swept back his long model locks to concentrate. I felt quite the *tarte*.

But I was too stunned by my actions to care about Daniel, except for a brief spell a couple of weeks down the line when he had caught the Eurostar over to visit. He was a shadow of his former self, having eaten barely a thing since I'd left. Then the guilt caved in. Then I felt utterly wretched for cheating. I worried myself sick when he left, that the next time we 'met' would be at his funeral. It was enough to make me abandon my studies and the silly year away. What was I doing to him? It was my selfishness and insistence on completing my language degree that had driven him to the brink of anorexia. Remembering the words his mother uttered just weeks before my departure hadn't exactly eased my complex:

"But you're not really going to go away and leave him, are you, Kate? I mean, you'll jack Uni in and not abandon him on his own like this for a year, won't you?"

"Appellez-moi," Pierre ordered.

"Just you try to stop me from calling you," I said, hardly believing my luck.

I managed to wait a whole twelve hours, unable to think of anything else but that kiss and the fire it had unleashed in areas it shouldn't have. Then I called him, French script in hand, in case I needed a prompt and my throat froze over in pre-date silence.

Encounter *numero deux* was outside Lyon's Opera House, where romantic took on a whole new dimension. Dressed in my Little Black Dress, I searched for him up and down, around and around the grand steps; a wanton *mademoiselle* struggling to catch her breath as a vision of floppy golden-haired loveliness appeared in the distance. In his long black designer coat, he was other-worldly. And I wondered just how many forbidden trysts had there been on those very same steps, beneath the watchful gaze of a French October sunset?

We walked side by side, sneaking furtive glances at one another, trying to hide our beaming smiles. I desperately wanted him to put his arm around me, but it was too early. Besides, this was no date as such. He'd simply invited me over to his apartment. Obviously I'd taken a small overnight bag with me anyway – just in case.

When we finally arrived, after striding through some ridiculously posh parts, I felt like a glamorous Screen Siren, transported back to the heyday of Hollywood. The apartment belonged to a class one needed to be born into. As for the bathroom, I'd never seen anywhere as stocked from floor to ceiling with expensive French aftershaves. No wonder the boy smelt good.

We spent a wonderful evening chatting, laughing, kissing, watching films. He had the most uncannily identical music collection. Although *Radiohead*'s *'Creep'* raging across the sound system upon the flick of a hidden high-tech switch, was hardly the most appropriate of songs when things were getting raunchy, even if I adored Tom York's melancholic warble.

Something happened after the fading of that song.

It was then that I realised I had my arms around a *croque-en-bouche*, a rich tower of haute couture, the height of which was simply too majestic for a girl like me to scale. And it was as if my thoughts cast an immediate and irreversible spell on him too, reminding him that *I* – and not Radiohead's lead singer – 'didn't belong here'.

We finally retreated to the bedroom and he drifted off to sleep. I tried and tried, somewhat embarrassingly in retrospect, to weld myself into him, hoping to resurrect his libido, but all I got was a frustrating:

"Desolée, je suis bloqué…" followed by *"Il faut que je t'explique quelquechose…en fait, j'ai une copine. Elle s'appelle Chantelle."*

So he couldn't perform, because it had just dawned on him that actually, he had a girlfriend. And why did he have to say her name? I didn't care if she was called Pascal and wore a sailor's hat. Now I would cast scorn upon every future Chantelle I encountered.

"Oh," I replied, the bottom falling out of my world, "Oh."

But there was more to come. In fact, the whole thing was a farce. He'd also lied to me about the apartment being his: it was his parents'; they were simply in Paris for the weekend, so he wanted to feel like *un homme*, inviting a young English Rose over for a bit of romance. Was there anything about him that was real? I began to doubt he was even a student of engineering. The worst thing of all though was I'd been beached there like a whale until the buses were up and running again. It must have been two or three in the morning. And I definitely didn't have the fare for a taxi.

Somehow I slept remarkably well. It's not as if things could have got worse or there was any more of my dignity to lose.

Next morning I woke to an empty bed. What a relief to be able to slink off to the bathroom to reapply My Face before he spotted me. I could hear him already pottering about in some other part of his folks' lavish quarters.

"They must be absolutely minted," I said to my reflection, avoiding my disappointed eyes in the mirror by taking in the colossal tower of designer aftershaves and balms once again.

This was proper perfume; none of the cheap and cheerful stuff that I was used to. I cunningly opened a bottle, dabbing a hint on my wrists, as well as the pulse points of my neck – not that he'd be kissing me there anymore.

Just what had caused this sudden turnaround in his predilection for me? Surely Radiohead alone couldn't be held accountable. And then I remembered – the effects of the wine no longer clouding events; he had undressed me, taken in the contours of my body, and pulled away.

So I wasn't stick thin like his waif of a girlfriend (I assumed Chantelle was one of those enviable little things sporting a wasp's waist, anyway – Lyon, and the Rhône and Saône's banks, were overflowing with them), but I certainly didn't have a spare tyre either. Had that honestly been the reason he'd suddenly turned himself off? Or was it just that everything seemed safe, a bit of fumbling around, until, that was, we'd moved into the *dormitoire*? Whatever the reason, I didn't much care to think about it. He'd dented my pride and all I wanted to do was get myself out of there as soon as possible, back to my little sardine tin of a room to wallow under the duvet in self-pity and despondency, with a bucket load of chocolate and tea on tap.

I chanced to inspect myself a little longer in the mirror. Undeniably, I was a little jaded, but I still looked kind of cute.

Yet he hardly looked my way when I entered the kitchen, too busy percolating his gourmet coffee.

"T'as dormé bien?" he said, obviously feeling the need to pierce the air with some kind of sound other than that of the beans doing their thing.

I told him I had slept well, thank you very much.

"Tu veux quelquechose a manger, du café?"

I couldn't think of anything worse than eating in front of him. But when he handed me a *Mars* bar, I let appearances slide. Clearly that was his expectation of me, after all. And so the buxom English Rose chomped her way through its entirety, hastily swigged at her far too strong coffee and politely bade Pierre farewell – *sans bisou* – he'd had quite enough of those in the night.

The whole debacle was like taking five giant leaps forward and seven even larger ones back. The insignificant yet significant fling with Pierre shattered my confidence into mosaic-sized pieces. He gave me that first tantalising glimpse of a life – and a love – cut off from my puppeteer, and then he cruelly locked the door very firmly, threw away the key and rendered me hostage once more. I'd been depicted as fat and wholly un-beddable. I'd been deceived. And I'd developed a venomous hatred of svelte French women, scowling at them all on my forays in and around Lyon; that one of them might be her, the one who could turn him on.

Chapter Two
Seven Years Later

My Campari-lined stomach launched into full spin. How had I forgotten to call him? Seven every evening, my time, we'd agreed. Or rather he had told me: in no uncertain terms.

My hand was apparently disjointed from my body, shaking wildly as if somebody above was controlling my movements with invisible strings. The phone rang for what seemed like an eternity. Then at last his familiar Somerset twang echoed back at me.

"What time do you call this then?"

His voice shrouded me in a fog of dizziness and I wondered how I would cobble words together.

"Sorry, we've had to take cli…cli…customers out…" he hated it when I referred to them as clients "…and the waiter has only just taken everyone's orders."

It was only a small lie.

"I couldn't give a monkey's if you were dining with royalty. I'm s'posed to be the most important person in your life, and here I am slaving away, cooking me own supper after a hard day's graft," he said, before gathering his thoughts.

"I'll prick some holes in the johnnies. Put an end to all this gallivanting about for once and for all."

I held my stomach in and guarded it with a clenched fist, willing the pregnant image of myself away. He wouldn't dare, would he? I tried to reply but there were no words. As the years had taught me, sometimes that was the best way with Daniel.

"You enjoy your slap-up meal with your pen-pusher friends in Boloooogna tonight, won't you?" he said with his habitual sing-song. "Don't worry about me; I've got the dog for company."

I closed my eyes in anticipation of whichever of his catchphrases was to come. He granted me a couple of seconds of unexpected silence. A cute Italian student cycled by, wolf-whistling in my direction. Thankfully, the sound of a siren drowned out his approval. And then it came.

"You don't know you were born, girl."

"But…you shouldn't have to do any actual cooking…I bought you ready meals. And I've written out a list of instructions too, so all you have to do is switch on the oven or microwave – depending on which meal it is today – sorry, I can't remember what was on the menu for Wednesday…"

"No, 'cos she's too fuckin' busy to think about the man in her life, that's why. I'll tell you the gourmet experience Lady Muck's left me for Wednesday, shall I? Microwave Toad in the Hole." He paused again, presumably for effect.

"I've been toiling all day on the farm – not that you've even bothered to ask how my day was – and now I'm expected to tuck into this pile of shit? The Gloucester Old Spots eat better. 'Tis got right out of hand this so-called profession of yours."

I pressed the phone closer to my ear, desperate to hide the volume of his dialogue from the passers-by, fully aware that my alter-ego of an hour ago wouldn't even contend with this.

"I'm sorry. Next time—"

"Next time, my love? You'll be lucky if I let you go next time."

"But it's my job."

Silence.

The headlights and grilles on the passing stream of Fiats morphed into faces, mocking the beads of sweat that were forming at my brow. I cleared my throat in a bid to continue my defence.

"Next time I'll batch cook some lasagne," said my pathetic voice, "then you'll have something homemade."

"Hark at you and your Italian cuisine. You just don't get it, do you? I want meat and two veg; I'm a working man. And

11

you, you are a housewife to me."

"Ouch," I yelped, hopping unexpectedly to one side.

My toe began to throb and I found myself face to face with a short, rotund woman of senior years and a coiffured Spitz Volpino which peeped demurely out of her handbag.

"Attenzione giovane signora," she said with a look of utter contempt as I retreated further into the shop window.

"I really am sorry," I said, stooping to rub my toe and push out the dent from her angry heel, "I'll make more of an effort when I come back."

I grimaced at the self-portrait of the girl in the gingham-frilled apron who had made herself at home in my kitchen.

"It's just a few more days. And, if I get a pay rise next month, it'll make all of this worth it."

"I'm not interested in your money. I make my own." He threw in a surprise laugh. "Besides, you're contracted to work Monday to Friday, nine to five. It is now ha' past six on a Wednesday and I'm starving, hence why you should be back here seeing to me tea."

Gingham Girl cocked her head in agreement, wagged her finger and continued assembling her Stargazy Pie. I was lexicon bereft. Whose side was she on?

"You damn well make sure you call me on time tomorrow...or I won't be responsible for my actions."

I blinked away the not-so-distant memory of the rope he'd erected in the shed, and the perverse smile plastered on his face after he'd pushed me in there but two weeks ago so I could admire his handiwork dangling from the ceiling.

"Okay. Bye. Love you."

The puppeteer had taken over my mouth.

But Daniel had rung off.

I inhaled deeply. I exhaled deeply. At times like this I could see the appeal of smoking.

I turned to catch my reflection in the window. It was okay; no trace of harassment, nobody had heard what I'd said. I wiped my clammy palms on my denim-clad thighs. There, sweat gone, back to business.

Crossing the Piazza Maggiore to return to the others, I

slackened my neat pony tail, letting chestnut and sand spirals tumble down. It didn't go unnoticed.

I wanted to bottle that moment right there in the middle of the square: Kate standing at the centre of a compass, enchanting the men from north to south and east to west, for she was the real deal, the one I could sometimes tune into when I surrendered my years of suffering at the hands of the high school bullies to the past and entered another dimension. I ran my fingers through my hair feeling self-assured, knowingly so when Henry pointed at my half-drained glass, and signalled to the waiter for a top up as I sank back into my seat.

"Boyf okay?" he said with his Roger Moore face.

Annoyingly, he had that rare ability to raise one brow to the heavens whilst keeping the other perfectly still, as if trying to entice a bombshell in the flicks.

"He's surviving without me, just about."

That was the thing when you were living a double life; you learnt to lie with a straight face, to slip in and out of character as circumstance dictated.

I matched his grin, since that was also the thing with The Boyles; once they'd calmed down, Henry and his twin brother, Adrian – my un-identical bosses – metamorphosed into almost loveable rogues.

"What happens at book fairs stays at book fairs," said Steph with an elongated wink.

Just as well, because Kate Clothier had behaved like a fool, no matter how justified she felt in her mission to be spared a life of battering, preferably in the arms of a thoroughly decent looking man. Mercifully, my most recent escapade with the Joey-from-'Friends' Turkish barman round the back of one of the most prestigious hotels in Frankfurt, had remained a secret.

It was supposed to be true: whatever happened within the parameters of the four walls of a book fair, its surrounding hotels, bars and restaurants, must stay there; an unspoken rule – at least at *She Sells Sea Shells*. More often than not though, the gossip had wended its way back to the UK before the luggage could even be hauled off the conveyor belt at Bristol airport. Knowledge being power, the exchange of details with those left behind in the West Country was just too valuable to overlook.

But 18,526 words after my first sentence of the day, I was finally free. No longer was I accountable for tempting an editor into bankruptcy, or sympathising with the unsolicited critique of the multitude of faces I'd greeted with staged enthusiasm. And for the rest of the evening, at least, no longer was I accountable to Daniel.

"Cheers, guys," Henry's voice boomed.

Clink, clink.

A cluster of Champagne flutes, a shot glass filled with pale lemon liquor, and my own tumbler loaded with a heady medicinal re-fill of Campari, blood orange and rustic shards of ice, tilted skywards in a remarkably steady fashion. Some of our gathering had been polishing this routine since lunchtime.

"Cheers, Henry," I found myself chanting in unison with my colleagues.

"Guys, call me Hen at book fairs, guys," he said, grammatically incorrect as ever.

The homely fragrance of focaccia momentarily scented the air, wafting over from the café just beyond our line of vision. For a moment I was biting into its quilted dough, before my daydream was tainted with wafts of smoke, mostly emanating from our table, and the red fury of Daniel's face as he stomped about in a kitchen in England. A warm breeze carried my nightmares away to another congregation, where a huddle of Japanese editors supped long drinks and fiddled incessantly with their cameras. Talk about a stereotype, I smiled, granting myself permission to unwind.

Clink, clink. Henry's glass was airborne again.

"Can we quit the endless toasts please, Hen? My Campari's getting cold."

"Hey, it's all in the spirit of team building, Katherine. How can you drink that revolting stuff anyway? Don't they put beetles' shells in it?"

"Mexican beetles' shells, actually. Cochineal, gives it its glowing colour," I said with another smile, knowing how unappetising those around me found the ambrosial concoction I noted I was drinking a little too fast.

With the first day of business over and my conscience prickled with guilt, I needed to get nothing short of sozzled to entertain the notion of an evening with a pair of Boyles, even in one of my favourite cities.

Henry and Adrian's tri-annual expectations had driven us to the threshold of despair. Nine hours of back-to-back meetings, clients lamenting over late deliveries and air freight demands, had become something of a regular occurrence when the buyers had me, face to face, unable to escape their wrath.

Then there was the unfortunate incident of the wobbly shelf falling on a South Korean client's head mid-negotiation, killing all hope of the sale and almost him. I'd been torn between feeling downright negligent for the shoddy stand workmanship, perturbed by the thought of any broken bones, yet also wanting to snort in pig-style chortles, just as certain members of the company had so shamefully done.

I pulled my focus back to the now, alternating between the desperate wrestle with my chattering mind, and the warming marmalade magic of my tipple. Why wouldn't it take the edge off for more than a few seconds? Damn Daniel for consuming my thoughts, although I had to concede, imagining his anger from afar, sure beat imagining him acting on his ever increasing declarations that he'd take his own life if ever I left him.

But suppose calamity struck with the microwave? He used it so rarely that the house could be cinders already. And what if my portioning still left him hungry? He was, as he often reminded me, a hard worker – a cider farmer and part-time peat cutter by profession – although the farm was actually his Uncle Ted's, and his loyalty a misinterpreted quest for inheritance. Yes, Daniel had acted well to carve himself the role of surrogate son.

Hindsight was futile, I decided. If I had to pay for it when

I got back, then so be it. It was my own fault for not being more organised.

"Erm garcon, one more for the road here, gracias," said the newly-highlighted Henry.

The waiter looked perplexed, but headed off to the kitchen anyway, returning with a spontaneous tray of limoncello. Henry and Adrian knocked their shots back together as if rounding off a five course feast, and then Adrian's eyes glazed over, a clue that before long his I'm-at-a-book-fair-and-I've-been-let-off-the-leash persona would be putting in an appearance.

"Here, discard of this will you," said Daisy, passing me two full glasses behind the shield of the menu.

"Pssst," I whispered to Steph, nudging a queue of glasses her way.

Steph expertly tipped their contents at the roots of the soon-to-be-merry olive tree, potted behind her.

Oh no, the dishwasher.

I'd spent so much time labelling the food, stacking it all neatly in the fridge, and allocating the helpings of dessert, that I'd forgotten to explain how to use it. He couldn't really be expected to wash up by hand, not after a long day of manual labour. I'd just have to pray I could pacify him during tomorrow evening's call, or the next evening's, or the next. It was something of a mystery how kitchenalia remained a foreign species to Daniel, whereas the appliances residing in the lounge had not.

"May we join you beautiful ladies and uh...dapper gentlemen?" said a frolicsome Antipodean voice without waiting for an answer.

I jolted, having not perceived anything or anyone creep up on me from behind. Sebastian nuzzled his chin in at an interesting angle on my shoulder, as if he were some kind of human jigsaw puzzle. Accompanying him was the ever smirking beaming-eyed Gary, aka She Sells Sea Shells' Product Manager – which was basically when he could be arsed.

They pulled up a couple of empty chairs, at which point it

was decided that eight at a table designed for the use of four, wouldn't go. So it was left to Steph to 'man up', pushing tables together, giving everybody a little personal space.

Sebastian started to comb his desperately-in-need-of-a-trim peroxide locks with his fists, reclining in his seat and letting out a long Aussie 'ahh'. He turned his back on everyone to realign with the fading rays, shades slipped over eyes; nothing new to note on the lack of social skills front. But the bags, hmm, they did seem a little more prominent this year. Then again, he still had it in the eyes of some, particularly those who were unhappily married. Before I knew it, even I was twisting loops in the ends of my hair.

Oh quit it. You're practically married and Sebastian is a colleague – albeit a timely reminder that at this book fair I wasn't just after another potential bedpost notch but the final piece of proof, the final scrap of evidence in the final category of men: the George Clooney range. A night with an older man would be the absolute conclusion that I can attract, start a new life, and leave Daniel behind.

Gary had also taken to combing. He patted down his stubborn auburn waves with strange robotic actions, before bringing glass to lips at exactly the same moment as Sebastian. What was it with men buddying up in twos and imitating one another with tribal conduct? I was mesmerised and once again found myself creating extra ringlets whenever either of them looked my way.

Thankfully, my Czech customers waved across the square snapping me out of it.

"Invite them over for a drink, Kate."

Great, here we go.

"We can discuss up-coming projects with them," Henry said, fidgeting in his fresh Hawaiian shirt, now dressed up for the evening with a beatnik rope pendant, and slashed so far to the waist that he looked like he was off to a disco.

"I think they're probably a little tired of talking shop."

"Argh, you need to be more of an entrepreneur about things, Katherine...spot the opportunity for pitches even out of hours. That's the difference between a salesman and an amazing salesman."

"Saleswoman – last time I checked, anyway," I said, slightly taken aback at the level of sexism that was still going on in the twenty-first century, but not entirely surprised. Still, I was determined not to rise to it. No point adding to my current stress levels.

"Look at how Adrian and I set up when we just happened to be sat next to somebody on that Chinese junk during our backpacking trip around Asia, who just happened to have connections with printers in Singapore, which just happened to be the best factory ever, helping us create a highly profitable publishing business. It's fate. We could do some good business in Czechoslovakia."

Adrian nodded in agreement.

"Czech Republic, Henry. And I have a meeting with them tomorrow. Fate might work for you" – Daddy's fountain of money would be closer to the truth – "but this is foreign rights we're talking about."

"She's right," said Daisy, my sidekick and rock, without whom I've no idea how I'd deal with the craziness that was my career, "two hands to pass and accept a Japanese business card; don't get offended if the Southern Europeans snatch pop-up books out of your hands, and Czechs don't do cold hard literary sales."

"The Three Pernickety Rules of Foreign Rights," said Steph, "which is why you'll never see this chick selling them." She took an irritated drag of her roll-up with one hand and gave some kind of *Prodigy* style ravers' move with the other. Which I didn't have the heart to tell her was probably slightly more in fashion ten years earlier.

The liquorice all-sort of the top floor of the office (on account of her selling English language stock), Steph was quick-witted and acid-tongued, which when coupled with her jet black hair and turquoise eyes deep as pools, made her oh-so-dangerously-mesmerising to men, whom she was accustomed to eating for breakfast and spitting out by elevenses.

Steph had an inbuilt sense of vogue, an enviable

refinement allowing her to carry her voluptuous frame with confidence. Self-confessed and light-fingered, she was a Domestic Goddess where all things cake decorating were concerned. Her other hidden 'talent' – not to make light of the tidy profit from eBay – she'd struck up a bartering system with the office receptionist, consisting of free postage in return for hand-iced wares – was her rumoured fortune telling. Although, evening get-togethers for this were constantly being cancelled when she received a better offer from her higher calibre, senior ranking groupies, her relationship with Daisy and myself being purely narcissistic.

Yet despite it all – don't ask me how – she and I, we worked as friends.

Daisy, who certainly never made three a crowd – and was matching our pace, albeit herbal brew to alcohol – trailed at our coat tails in a bizarrely unconfident way. I guess her lack of self-certainty, despite her ability, reminded me of myself at home. It fuelled my office persona into being anything but pathetic. For much as I loved Daisy, she was prone to the most wobbly of putting-herself-down moments.

And then there was me.

Physically, I suppose I was growing into myself. It had recently dawned on me that I finally understood which colours suited me best, which cuts of clothing accentuated my figure and, perhaps more importantly, which did not. At times this sudden appreciation radiated like a halo, attracting opportunities, new friends, and male interest in equal measure.

My corkscrew curls were said to be resplendently chestnut (and sandy, if I got my highlights booked up on time); they settled just above the line of my bra strap. My chocolate eyes were generously adorned with long black lashes, and my face framed with thick dark brows – the type that when plucked correctly made me almost pretty as a picture, but hadn't always been so advantageous to my ranking, particularly at school. I was petite, but attracted a tummy effortlessly. My love of food (or more accurately, cake – I was Somerset Junior Baker of the Year in 1995), and tendency to gravitate towards it in times of seeking solace, had fuelled me to become ever-so-slightly-obsessed with my weight.

"How's business anyway, Sebastian?" I said, desperate to change the subject, hands welded to my frosted glass for fear of imitating a heated roller once more.

He was back in present company, our blissful suntrap but a distant memory, as all around people started to pull on their jumpers. And the Italians were now kitted out in scarves and gloves.

"Ah yeah, look, you know, we had a slow start to the year, but it's picked up again, can't complain…" his voice trailed off, absorbing the loyalties of the twins, who'd honed in at the mention of all things meaty and transactional at the Melbourne-based branch of our company which Sebastian ran.

A muffled ring tone pierced the air. My blood ran cold and waves of panic gripped at my throat. Gary dived into his pocket, averted his gaze from the table, and muttered dialogue that could not be caught. I grabbed at my drink and swallowed the last of its thick bitter comfort.

"I think we'll start having regular meetings when we get back," said Henry, quelling my trembling hand with an almost welcome diversion.

I don't think I'd ever met anyone more like one of those 'Jumble' biscuits of my childhood; you never knew quite which combination you were going to bite into. And today he was decidedly walnut, still in the shell.

"Yeah." He sniffed at the air suspiciously. "Katherine's reaction to my sales technique makes me think you could all use a little tuition on how to think outside the lines."

I was sure he'd meant to say box.

"I forgot to say," I said, feeling my eyes expand to the size of saucers – well, if the tribal thing worked for the men, "Pederson China will be on the stand tomorrow. You remember what happened last time?"

They all remained silent.

"What? How can you not? Twenty of them showed up, falling head over heels with everything."

"We'll need to get more chairs," said Adrian, raising his brows to such a height that his nut-brown sheet of hair took on the appearance of a flattened wig. It was far more consistent in colour than his brother's dappled locks, as to be expected being the twin who took the extra day to emerge from the cocoon, yet it was he who seemed to burden himself most with the stress of running a company.

"Steph, Daisy: you can organise that tomorrow," said Henry, clearly not as spellbound as I'd hoped.

"Just a minute there," said Steph with a look that only she could conjure up, "what do you think the rest of us are going to be doing, twiddling our thumbs? You'll have to find some other minions."

"There's no need for that, Stephanie. We've all got to muck in. Right, Kate, since it's your meeting, you'll have to sort it."

I was furious. And he could quit alternating between my full and shortened name whenever he saw fit.

"Oh, I see. So no chance either your good self or Adrian will be free? Hmm, let me check the schedule."

I bent down to the floor, hauling my chronically overworked file onto my lap, papers jutting out at all angles.

"It's no good doing that," said Henry, raising his hand to his mouth a little too late to catch the dribbles that had escaped in protest. "We've got lots of off-the-cuff arrangements that won't be included in your timetable."

This produced a male chorus of laughter.

Idiot, everything that came out of his mouth was counter-intuitive to making money.

"Henry, we're a team. We'll all sort the chairs tomorrow, one way or another," said Steph. "Anyway, Gary will be loafing about."

"I will not," he said with his routine squeak, eyes dancing between heaven and earth to avoid Steph's accusation, call now over.

"Well, what exactly are you doing here? You can see the printers in Malaysia; you speak with them every day on the phone. This is just a holiday for you: admit it."

Once again, I was grateful for the shift in attention. The lure of a career overhaul was gaining momentum.

"Guys, let's all chill out and get some grub in our bellies." Sebastian had grown visibly tired of the commotion.

Once the idea had been put out there, thoughts turned with little persuasion to feasting. It was virtually impossible to eat a bad meal in Bologna, so I was happy to go with the majority, as long as it wasn't *Gigi's* with its unashamedly harsh lighting, perfect for illuminating blemishes and stray facial hair, but not so perfect when you were on the hunt for a man.

After raucous debate we un-unanimously opted for trying our luck at *Osteria de Rizzutti*.

"Can't believe you've outvoted us, ladies," said Sebastian, "that Mexican was amazing last year; re-fried green beans to die for…and those nippy little tequilas, man."

"When in Rome…" Steph threw him a glare of snobbish proportions.

She was Welsh Bara Brith was Steph. And that was no stereotype just because she came from Swansea. Spicy, speckled, soaked in strong tea overnight and best eaten thickly buttered. How I wished I had her instant wit – and cake icing skills.

Daisy yanked a map from her bag, straightening it with her coaster as if she were ironing her smalls. Sebastian sniggered. He clearly regarded her as the most curious of souls. I would have to agree, much as Daisy was a friend. The eldest of the females in the party, the most retiring in a boisterous crowd, yet her eccentricity often gave off a completely different impression, especially on the days when she wore her *Hello Kitty* tights with matching scarf and beret to work.

"Look, there's a Via de Rizzutti," she said, tracing her finger along Bologna's twists and turns. "Surely, if it's going to be anywhere, it has to be there."

We followed her lead, not quite managing to exit the Piazza without the men giving their expert opinion on the genitalia of the Fontana di Nettuno. Sebastian and Henry even removed their flip-flops, dipping their feet into the fountain's waters.

Not so long ago, you'd have been subjected to torture for that. My face lit up as I imagined them with arms tied behind their backs, winched up to the point of dislocation by the powers that be.

Gary's mobile buzzed yet again. Was he rigging it or what? Such an oddball that guy, forever scurrying off to talk in private, yet those lips barely moved. And I couldn't help but notice that Sebastian now seemed entranced by him, too.

Steph and I trailed a few paces behind them all. We passionately discussed the books that had got the best reception, and as we passed the trattorias that hopscotched their way across Via Indipendenza, Steph needed little encouragement to commence our unquestionably immature, but hilarious – you had to be there really – counting-how-many-men-are-looking-at-us game. I would love to argue that its origination came from Steph's vain tendencies. Then again, I could hardly deny my fixation with getting a regular dose of male feedback. But the difference was Steph was expectant, whereas I was eternally grateful.

"Remember where this little game led us last time?"

"No, where?" I was curious.

"Memory like a sieve, the Italian brothers..."

I blushed. Then the guilt hit hard and I quickly imagined I was standing beneath one of those giant raindrop showers, cleansing my sins with a cast iron loofah.

"What an evening."

"Let's make a pact right here and now that we don't revisit it," said Steph with another of her winks.

We quickened our pace, only to slow it right back down to catch the scent on the air. Pretty little Amaretti morsels capped with snowy icing sugar peaks, and Torta di Riso di Bologna – the city's take on rice cake, selling out by midday the eve of Good Friday – streamed out the doorway of a bakery.

"Mmm," I said, fluttering my eyelids. "How can Daisy pass this lot by without as much as a drool?"

"She's a boring twig who exists on green tea and goji berries, Kate; that's how."

Steph tossed her hair over her shoulder like a scarf and we reluctantly carried on.

We passed the Hotel Pandolfi, and I couldn't help but think back to those early Sea Shells days. Working life had been so much simpler during Silvia's reign (the former Governess of foreign rights), and with it, admittedly, my behaviour.

One evening, released from Silvia's protective wing, Steph and I had been left with The Boys.

"Tick tock," Sid had said, looking solely in Steph's direction as we'd made our entrée into the bar for pre-dinner cocktails with our male escorts. Her high-waist boot-leg jeans, the sequined camisole that peeped invitingly out of her suede jacket, and her patent heels, were explicitly to his liking. Calculated to precision as usual, and causing me to feel quite the underdressed nerd.

Daniel of course, would have been furious at this double date, although in reality he'd nothing to fear; Sid only looked vaguely kissable when I was trolleyed. And Piers, well he was Millionaire Shortbread, one bite and your temples ached from sugar overload.

Although similar ages to Steph and me, a different set of genitals and a glut of cash rich US clients, meant the guys magically commanded salaries, perks and company credit cards to match – their gold flexible friends taking a hammering throughout the city's bars. And for Sid this was the perfect opportunity to woo The Diva. In spite of their tumultuous relationship, he'd secretly had Steph in his sights for years. Of course he'd never have admitted to it, mainly since she petrified him. But as with most publishing activities of the extra-curricular kind, alcohol loosened one's inhibitions around one's co-workers; something I didn't deem at all necessary when it came to him.

"How are those Mickey Mouse accounts of yours doing?" he'd say with a snigger.

But of course, whenever he needed to glean some crucial

information, it would be quite different.

"Looking good, looking real good in that skirt, Katy Baby..."

Translation: I need to pilfer your client database.

Yes, he put me in mind of that twenty-strong queue of kids who'd flocked to befriend me just before the French GCSE exams at school.

"Which questions did you get, Kate? Oh, and what are the answers while we're at it? Promise I'll be your best friend, invite you to my next house party, chick..."

With 'Clothier' virtually top of the list, those oral exams had been a farce. By the time I'd disappeared into the broom cupboard with the examiner, the rest of the class had figured there were just four papers, all being used in succession.

"Good old Caterpillar Brows!"

Thank goodness I'd outgrown my naivety.

Similarly with Piers, I could see beyond that Golden Boy facade, unfathomably impenetrable to everyone else. Outwardly pleasant, that was as may be, but he also had one of those I'm-a-cut-above-and-wouldn't-want-to-be-seen-in-your-company-amongst-people-I-know airs about him. And he was constantly panning the vista for fear of being caught out accompanying a less than perfect woman.

A woman like me.

Friday morning had sneaked up on us all too quickly, with Steph and Sid at some point merging into a single being. I was just relieved my evening of treadmill-talk with Adonis was over. I'd spent too many hours physically mapping that face at the bar. And he'd seriously cramped my style. Who was going to attempt to chat me up when they thought I was with him? Self-centred git, I needed to milk every opportunity I got.

"Where's a taxi rank when you need one?" I raised my arms to the heavens as if somebody up there might care to produce one upon request, instead of the distant rumble of thunder.

Something else turned up instead.

"*Ciao, Bella.* Hey beautiful lady, how're you doing? Jump

on. Let me take you for a ride. You look bored with these boys."

An uber-confident lad pulled up next to Steph on his machine. Apart from the initial introduction, and the fact that he was instantly magnetised, nobody had the foggiest what he was trying to say at one hundred kilometres an hour in regional Italian.

Except Sid.

His nostrils flared in defence accentuating his amphibian features.

"No grazie," Steph smiled back with far too long a flicker of her lashes. "I'm just enjoying a nice walk home, thank you."

But her flirtatious decline had been far too inviting for the Bolognese to give up without a fight.

"You heard the lady. Move it." Sid was enraged, although an argument had neither developed, nor needed to.

"Hey, idiot, you're going to regret what you just said." He roared with laughter and his bike joined in with excess throttle as both sped back towards the city centre.

"Thanks, Sid. You nearly got us mown down then, mate."

Piers, like Henry and Adrian, wasn't one for strife. The drizzle spurred him into bird-like preening, and he busied himself re-slicking invisible stray hairs into place with his pot of gel.

"I am not having that jumped up little shit talk to a woman in my company like that. And…and…it wouldn't have been any different if it was Kate."

Sid slurred his words as if he'd been mulling over whether they were in fact true. He waved a drunken finger in my direction, giving me an affirmative nod.

"Gee, thanks, my hero."

"Why did you have to do that, Sid?" Steph beamed serenely as we walked on.

But he'd barely opened his mouth to respond, before a revving engine screeched up from nowhere beside him. The none-too-happy youth riding it signalled the pummelling he was going to get with his heavy-duty bike chain; his leather-

26

gloved fists clashing together hard and fast in a repetitive punching motion. And this time he had a friend in tow.

Piers vanished into the night. So us girls had to somehow fight his best friend's corner now?

Meanwhile, Sid just stood there chewing hard on the corner of his lip, ruminating, weighing up his rather limited options, deciding quickly there were none.

"Okay, easy, boy."

He surrendered, hands in the air and stumbled backwards in defeat.

But The-Jumped-Up-Little-Shit was having none of it. He'd called his mate out for support after all. And he'd got himself a weapon. He might as well stretch this one out; have a little fun and games.

I was beyond terrified. What could we do to intervene except continue to offer our apologies for Sid's behaviour in English, and try to stagger back to the hotel with him, each supporting one of his unsteady arms? All the while, I was sure I could make out Piers. Someone had been standing in the safety of that haberdashery shop doorway anyway, texting his latest girlfriend against a twee backdrop of knitting wool. The guy was not only the definition of vanity, but the ultimate coward besides.

The cocksure offender began to circle us, firing on his bike, whilst his sidekick had taken command of the massive chain, swinging it in giant barbaric loops; the pair of them wittering away to one another in undecipherable, but hysteric-fuelled Italian. How I wished the larger than life Italian teacher at college had been more concerned with passing on knowledge of street-talk. Fusilli and orechiette were hardly going to get us out of this unscathed.

"Look, I'm sorry, bud," Sid said, clamping his hands together in prayer.

He'd gone downhill fast, was now verging on paralytic. Just like excess rosewater in a cake, the boy didn't know where to stop.

We tried our best to steer him to the zebra crossing, heading back toward the main thoroughfare of the

Indipendeza, outmanoeuvring the youths until we were out of harm's way. But our pursuers continued to hound us, and as soon as we reached the pavement's edge, the chain-clad ally shoved Sid into the road. Cars hurtled in both directions, forcing him to lose his balance, skidding dazed and confused in those pathetic patent loafers, for all their designer credentials.

I ran straight into the oncoming traffic to help him to his feet, followed swiftly by Steph in two spur of the moment adrenalin bursts. It was foolishness, but we recognised he was in grave danger, and barely aware.

Horns hooted all around, brakes slammed and screeched, and then, as if on cue, a siren rang out. The *carabinieri* were closing in.

"Great," I said. "A night in the cells; how the effing hell am I going to explain this to Silvia?"

It was all very well for the rest of them. They only reported to a couple of clowns who'd see the funny side. Not that there was anything remotely side-splitting to see at that moment; although there was a high chance that could literally happen with the sudden impact of a car unable to stop itself, ploughing into one, two or all three of us. We were stranded in an aquaplaned road in a country that didn't exactly take heed of stripy white lines.

I imagined Daniel visiting me as I lay mummy-like in an Italian hospital bed. No, that was not going to happen. Heaving Sid to the side of the road, I blinked his dark brooding face away.

The two thugs started to ride away, tired of the game, leaving just a guilty party of drunkards staggering about in the road; nobody to blame but themselves for the tailbacks of traffic.

But Sid got a new lease of life. Somehow he broke free from our grip, tearing through the night. And for a moment I was in the scene from *Bridget Jones's Diary* – although sadly it wasn't going to be the dashing philanderer, Mr Grant, who'd be returning to battle it out for Steph's affections.

"Come on then," Sid bellowed, determined to provoke the

youths some more.

Observing that the carabinieri were way in the distance, they took him up on his noble invite. But this time there was no messing around. The sidekick had only to lean forward from the back of his seat, striking Sid square in the right eye, and knocking him clean to the floor. Blood seeped instantly from his nose, covering his once pristine shirt.

Piers was nowhere to be seen, whilst the angry witnesses directed the police toward Sid, Steph and me – not before we'd managed to haul him onto the grassy bank of a quaint fountain-topped roundabout, making for quite a sight. Steph busied herself patching up Humpty, propping him against her shoulder, dabbing blood with tissues as best she could, coaxing him back to some sort of vague reality.

The police were furious. Sid had caused one tremendous jam; a couple of cars had even been pranged. Huh, nothing new in Italy. But Steph and I were evidently shaken, and fortunately for us all, this bought their reassurance; we really had been terrorised, we weren't just a bunch of stereotypical Brits on the lash.

***

After ensuring Sid was tucked in bed with all the force of a straightjacket, we returned to our room next door; two parents who could now reflect on their son's thoroughly mischievous behaviour.

"What an episode," said Steph, hanging her upper half out the window, inhaling deeply on a cigarette.

"I'm staggered," I said, lying flat on my bed in a star shape. "We were so lucky. It could have been a very different ending, locked up behind bars, in a hospital bed, or worse."

"I'm never going out with them again…and as for Piers… what a joke."

We pulled on pyjamas, thought briefly about removing all traces of streaky make-up, then flunked on Steph's bed instead nursing thick, over-sweetened, room-service hot chocolate. We were in desperate need of some bolstering;

sleep would have to wait, even if we were in desperate need of that too.

No sooner had I raised the burning cup to my lips, than there came a rap at the door. My heart stampeded.

"You don't think reception have been given a report by the police do you?"

I was rooted to the spot.

"I doubt it," said Steph. "Then again, I don't know a thing about the protocol here. As long as we don't get ourselves turfed out! I'll go…"

She rose from the bed reluctantly, cocoa still in hand.

"What the hell is this?" she said into the empty corridor.

"What is it?" I decided that whatever it was, it wasn't interesting enough to move for.

"You've got to come and see for yourself, I don't think I can even…euh…," she strained, "lift it."

I made my way to the door, refusing to relinquish my cup of hot comfort. "Oh my…but…how did that get there?"

Before either of us had time to even think about reporting the fact that a dignified, slightly dashing Roman head and shoulders was staring disconcertingly at us outside our door, the phone pierced the air. I sped across the room to answer it, petrified in case it was the police wishing to further interrogate us after all.

A strong Italian accent on a male of about sixty – I guessed so anyway – ranted passionately, no doubt gesticulating in sync in that dramatic way in which only the Italians are masters.

"I am calling from reception and I am notta very 'appy at all. I have reason to believe, further to a sighting that has just been made in the corridor of the third floor, that you 'ave stolen our priceless antique statue from reception and thrown it outside your room. I 'ave called the police and they will be knocking at your door in about twenty minutes to charge you with attempteeeed robbery. We 'ave never had guests behave so terribly. You must pack your things and leave this hotel immediately."

This couldn't be happening: it would be one thing to face

Silvia in the morning, but another altogether when news of this filtered back to my home town of Glastonbury.

"What?" said Steph. "But we haven't taken anything and put it outside our door. They can damn well show us the video evidence, because unless I'm completely mistaken – and yes, I have had a few drinks tonight – we hobbled back up here, one on either arm of Sidney, unlocked his door, gave the evils to his room-mate, threw Sid on his bed and then came back to our room for a tame hot choc."

Tears pricked at the back of my eyes and I began to sob. It wasn't just the alcohol. Daniel would crucify me if I got a police record. And my God, if he found out I'd been out with other men…well, it just didn't bear thinking about.

But first I'd have to face Silvia and the shame of losing my career – although, at least Daniel would be hunter-gatherer again.

The knock was so startling when it finally came that I let out the whimper of a small animal.

"Go away. We're in our pyjamas," I said from behind the safety of the door. "Anyway, we don't know anything about this statue that's gone missing. B…but we did look outside our room earlier…and we noticed there was something further down the corridor, outside of room forty-five…kind of looked statuey. So they must be the culprits…who decided to frame us—"

"Haha." A peal of laughter thundered through the wood. "You really think we'll fall for that?"

Steph shook her head in disbelief. "You're a bloody muppet, Kate. It was only Sid." She marched to the door.

"Well…well…maybe it was the phone line then that made him sound so pissing Italian."

Damn him for fooling me. He had no idea what a mess I was thinking he'd got me in back home.

I assembled my very best frosty glare as I walked to the door ready to give him some verbal abuse. But Sid's hue had turned from Scarlet Joker to the boy who'd been experimenting with his mother's talcum powder; mouth wide open, pupils bouncing in every direction for an escape route.

31

"Cosa sta succedendo qui?" the voice of authority demanded.

Sid pivoted to make a futile run for the stairs, but the police were too quick. The Tall One wrestled him to the ground, The Short One pinned back his arms; handcuffs clicked firmly shut.

Chapter Three

"Number 49 over there, he's badly failing to disguise it, his woman's definitely suspicious, it's all in the twist of her mouth, but hell yeah, he's clocked us; can't keep his eyes on his way ahead. Ah, haha…"

"What was that?"

"Thought you were playing along? You're in a world of your own again, Kate Clothier."

I clutched at my ribs and shivered myself back to the present. The market stalls of the back streets may have been alive with infectious haggling; negotiation may have been life, book or banana, every side street may have revealed something beautiful, left-wing political, wealthy and culinary. But three years on and all I could think of was revenge.

How could events have been interpreted so differently? Henry and Adrian had practically wet themselves when they'd stumped up the bail. Silvia's reaction had been slightly less forgiving: sales trips were limited to two for the rest of the year, and at book fairs her team were under strict curfew. As for Daniel, his response had been in a league of its own. Unfortunately, I hadn't been first to the post the morning the letter from Bologna's police department arrived in Somerset.

***

"Three bottles of your best red to get us started," Henry shouted at the waiter once we finally reached the Osteria.

Money definitely didn't buy manners.

It all came rushing back to me now. I'd definitely eaten here before. Lanterns from golden ages hung either side of the archways, so that the myriad wines classified like a library, shone with intellect. Even above our table, giant oak barrels pouted from the partitions, and ancient bottles perched themselves high up on shelves.

"Best place for them with the Boyles in residence," I said to nobody in particular.

"P'ah. You can un-weld yourself from Sebastian for a start, Gary. Boy, girl, boy, girl round the table is what this party needs."

"It's not the festive season yet, Adrian. We can mix it up later," said Steph.

We'd all grown used to Adrian. The more he drank, the looser that tongue, which had threatened international relations round the dinner table on more than one occasion: the heritage of the Germans and the colonisation of New Zealand being its fields of expertise. And when he wasn't offending a nation, he revelled in playing ridiculous games of the 'who-would-you-shag-out-of-everybody-in-the-company-if-your-life-depended-on-it' variety.

Always funnier when we questioned him, I smirked.

Adrian smiled back, sidling up to Steph anyway. He was all too happy to play submissive boss if it meant a chance thigh stroke or two against that black leather pencil skirt.

By the time we were seated, I was just relieved I'd been designated the remaining place opposite Daisy, my perfect dining companion. But, as I was soon to realise, you couldn't have it all.

In the same way you couldn't choose your blood family, it was impossible to go anywhere after business hours without bumping into your book family either. I chanced upon the back of the room and cringed as I spotted a sea of familiar second cousins once removed from way back when: the British all-male brigade of a European print house. They reciprocated, high-fiving me in the distance, and I swore I overheard a 'whoop whoop', bringing back un-cherished memories of the evening I'd partied with them in my *Lady in Red* number, getting the dress code totally wrong whilst every other woman had been in jeans.

And then seconds later, the cheeky Osteria produced

Luigi. Of all the possibilities in the joint, he and his brother took their places at the intimate table reserved for two, inconveniently situated just an arm's width away. I squirmed with embarrassment.

Steph's eyes burrowed into me, and I peeked over the tower of breadsticks to acknowledge her expression.

"Go on. You know you want to. He's loaded even if he hasn't got any hair," she said.

It must have been a year since I'd last seen him, but Luigi still had those emotional puppy dog eyes, that with a full head of hair and a fuller face, might have given him quite the sought after look of an Italian Stallion. He was a moneyed-mid-thirty-something – courtesy of Daddy's publishing emporium – and insatiable to pin himself down a woman. He'd never have spoken to me in the words of Daniel. Why couldn't I at least try to fall for him?

His eyes glowed perceptibly as he noticed the table of girls to his left, with his gaze resting firmly on my upper half in his emblematic 'this is fate' stare. I raised my glass of Prosecco in a demi-toast, hoping it would suffice, preventing any further ideas. Carlo, his shorter weightier brother, had a mop of bouncing ebony curls which must have been quite a tease for his elder – although he was minus those affectionate eyes and had a decidedly hooked nose. The *fratelli* made numbers 78 and 79, yet financial inheritance aside they'd sadly made no lasting impression of desirability.

The antipasti eventually arrived, a confetti-strewn potpourri of colours. Waxy layers of ham produced just a few train stations away; giant coal-coloured olives balanced in earthenware bowls next to their green cousins, mozzarella, tapenade and an extremely moreish rocket pesto.

I could happily dive into the tableau of bounty along with the others indulging in garlic-doused dishes devoid of disdain. Daniel had developed a mounting dislike of it over the years. And what a revelation to learn that actually, life really did carry on, even if we had to wait forty minutes for our mains.

But I felt so guilty too, for revelling in the luxury, for

getting a kick out of our childish tally nearing one hundred.

I swiped at my red, taking great gulps to ease my conscience.

"So, Gary," said Steph, "tell me, when am I going to receive those mock-ups you've been promising for the last nine months?"

"Um…they'll be in next week," he said.

"What, what, what?" said Henry.

Gary reached for some schiaciatta, repeatedly faltering with one hand and dipping back into the bread basket again with the other in a hokey cokey *a mano*.

"You've been saying that for the last few months," said Steph, eyes glowering. "The customer's had a reprint order for the new design sitting prettily in my in-tray for the best part of a year."

"Come now, Garth. Is that true?" Henry slammed down his glass in an attempt at amateur dramatics. "Let me talk to the plant as soon as we get back if that's the score. We can't afford to keep clients waiting around for aeons like this when Stephy has an order."

Stephy? And since when was Garth the full length version of Gary?

The waiter lovingly – conveniently for Garth – set our bowls of delicate truffle-filled pasta before us, breaking with tradition and starting with the men.

"You're casting pearls before swine there," said Steph.

"No, I'm afraid I'm not letting this one go." A suddenly distinguished Henry patted his lips with his serviette between mouthfuls. "That could've been one of my VIP customers, couldn't it? The girls are trying their best with their smaller accounts."

Daisy's mouth formed a defiant 'O'. I filled it with a voluntary forkful of my pasta.

"So, new ideas?" said Henry, clearing his throat. But there was no reply. "So…I was having a shower earlier this morning—"

"Eugh. Spare us the details, purlease," said Steph. "We're trying to eat."

A unanimous fit of giggles filled the air.

"Are you going to listen, or not? As I said, I was showering this morning – the shower as it happens, is a really good place for new ideas—"

Laughter interrupted his flow again, but this time Henry decided to ignore it.

"We're going to start making board games"

"That's it?" said Steph.

"We'll keep it simple to start with. You know, Snakes and Ladders, Ludo…I"

"I like it, I like it. Might just be the catchpenny of the century, mate."

Brown-nose. It's a crap idea, Sebastian, and you know it.

"We're a publisher, Henry, not a toy manufacturer. And what about our backlist?" I said. "It's the bread and butter of our sales and we're shamefully hiding it away in the cupboards this book fair. Look at all the reprints we've sold for you around the world."

"We'll turn it into a board game," Gary snorted, dabbing pretend tears with a serviette.

"He's got a point," said Henry. "Word of the day, Kate: diversification."

I scowled. The times I'd thought to call in Lord Sugar, or one of *The Dragons* to talk some sense into those who were supposed to be running this excuse for a company.

And then that divine image of me serving cake behind the counter of my novel-stuffed bookshop cafe popped into my head.

One day. Like when I'm forty.

Although any such establishment would definitely not include a 'Gary' – aka those hideous Coconut Macaroons you bite into with so much expectation, only to be disappointed with dry flakes of nothingness.

I bathed in the daydream for a second or two before a noise from my bag trilled reality. I rooted around desperate to locate my phone. He never called, but that didn't mean I could rest easy. I flicked the lid of the mobile open.

'Babe, I'm sorry,' it read. 'I've got a lot on my plate, that's all. Miss you. x'

This was odd after the tone of our recent conversation. And he never texted when I was abroad, it cost money. I guessed I must have really upset him this time.

He was probably sat by the fire with Clover, our dog, and those Eeyore-grey thoughts he shared from time to time. The contrast suddenly seemed unforgiveable.

I sensed the band that had just set up at the other end of the room would start a woeful little number on the violins if I didn't change my current thinking, and was even grateful for the nonsense Henry couldn't seem to stop coming out with.

"So, guys, now we're all together, I'm going to use you as my guinea pigs. My sounding board, if you will."

"This sounds ominous," said Steph.

"Just hear me out," Henry said, palms pushing up against something that was invisible to everyone except himself.

"Are you sure you don't want to discuss this with me in private first, brother dear?" Adrian sneered, helping himself – and himself alone – to more wine.

"We need some European offices, and I was thinking…we ought to have one in each of the four corners." As if to dissolve any confusion, he gestured at the angles of the room with his fork. "So, we'd have an office in Prague covering Eastern Europe – see, that's another of the reasons I wanted to get chatting with your Czechoslovakian clients, Katherine…"

Czech bloody Republic!

"…one in Lisbon, as that's about as far west as we can go…"

I tried to refrain from creasing up. An image of Henry mounting a world map, mulling over the relevance of mini Madeira, flag pins and a magnifying glass at the ready, stubbornly refused to disappear. I was sure I wasn't alone.

I turned to Daisy, shielding my frown. Henry was getting giddily carried away, potentially sabotaging the credibility of the company, and the future of foreign rights. My head pounded, crying for time out. I gave her the nod and we vanished to the restroom; a timely interval from the panto.

As we peered into a tiny mirror full of cracks, we were something straight out of a trendy black and white coffee table book. And at certain angles, a two-headed snake, twisting and turning to check our reflections were to one another's liking. A legendary establishment this may have been – the ornate sinks certainly suggested it – but really, a broader piece of glass was called for.

"So, how was Daniel?"

"Yeah fine." I coughed away my nerves at her question, "You know…same old. Not particularly happy he's had to cook." I proffered the shortened version of his conversation.

"Really? I'm so lucky I don't have that problem with Scott," Daisy giggled a little too heartily.

Scott, Daisy's boyfriend, ran a large supermarket, spending most of his mealtimes in the canteen. The notion of him scurrying around in an apron, scratching his head trying to fathom out the kind of childish step-by-step instructions I'd left Daniel, was unthinkable.

"Packing my case was one thing, but getting the house shipshape before I could leave, making sure he'd be okay, that was another." I rolled my eyes with more than a hint that all men are from Mars.

"Can he not sort himself out for a few days? Get a takeaway here and there? Make do with beans on toast one night? He is a grown man."

I felt myself grow awash with a strange defence. Pointing out his flaws was my job. It came as a real knock when others took a pop, like they were disapproving of my taste in men or something.

Maybe all of this would have been fairer if I'd zipped back in time, chosen a different degree, something that kept me by his side. But this was the path I'd taken; it was hardly my fault that a Foreign Rights Manager needed to be on a plane every six weeks for a sales trip or book fair. Admittedly, the constant flurry of faces and places could be a dizzying and disorienting ride, sometimes my feet didn't even know which country they were standing in. But I adored my job.

Oh, stop over-thinking it, Kate.

I pulled myself together. It was part of his personality. That was all. Everybody had their quirks.

"The thing that really got me today," I decided to change the subject, "had to be the constant questioning over profit."

I recalled how the Boyles had continuously scrutinised my margins, scurried to their tables, digits clambering over their calculators to do the Maths: was my sale lucrative enough to pay for their kids' school fees, wives' hot tubs and general feathering of their Marbella villas?

"Forty-two per cent after shipping, Kate, that's giving it away."

Adrian had come out with that little gem.

"We're not a charity. We've got to hit the bottom line: base is loaded," Henry had said.

If I'd heard that 'base is loaded' crap once, I'd heard it a hundred times in the past twenty-four hours. It was getting highly annoying now, but he'd committed it to memory following a night at the American Bar the previous year, having scoffed the fattest greasiest burger.

This was the dangerous part of our job. In the book fair bubble, the twins were marbles on the loose; collaring customers, attempting to unlawfully sell titles, quoting the wrong prices, and shaking on deals before the dotting of the i's, crossing of the t's and the signing of any legally binding contract.

"They're a couple of kids in a sweet shop, eyes bigger than bellies, capitalist cartoon characters so caught up in making money that the concept of the book evolving from a tree has quite possibly been lost on them altogether."

"Ha. I couldn't put it better myself." I giggled at Daisy's literary image.

"And don't get me started on the rationale behind naming your company after a tongue twister. Nothing like helping your overseas customers out…"

"Come on. We'd best get back to Steph. Goodness knows what's been going on since we've been away."

Things really had taken a turn for the worse. Alexandre De Camps, who neither of us had previously spotted, was rollicking about on the table. The main buyer for one of our significant French partners; there was never a dull moment, and not necessarily to his merit. In times gone by he'd been quite the charmer, reducing some of my female co-workers to beetroot-cheeked mush. Clearly, in his era, he was the crème de la crème of Parisien heartthrobs. But as with all good things, one needed to know when to call it a day. M De Camps, who had by now at least re-connected feet with floor, was scanning the room for a little light fandango partner.

"Please no," I said to Daisy.

The four-piece band that was playing on the makeshift wooden stage had instinctively (having no doubt been threatened that 'the plug will be pulled if the French guy doesn't get his arse down off the table') slowed the tone right down, lurching from their rendition of *The Gypsy Kings*' greatest hits, straight into a mellower number by *Sade*.

But it had little effect, he was on the prowl. I pretended to detect a new text on my phone, my best endeavour to look occupied. The rest of the female diners were turning away in their drones too, not wishing to encourage his game. Daisy seized me by the arm and we charged back through the narrow aisle to the safety of our table. The rest of the company were by now in absolute fits. They could see what we couldn't: Alexandre haring down the room after the both of us at breakneck speed, about to have his fill.

"Ooh, I'd recognise that poised posterieur anywhere."

He rested one hand on Daisy's lower back, dangerously close to her bottom, whilst the other unravelled its way outwards in anticipation of a Viennese Waltz. Daisy was an involuntary spinning top, until little by little the band's instruments broke off into silence, a random out of sync toot from the trumpet signalling the end of '*No Ordinary Love*'.

A young waiter helped a disoriented Daisy straighten up, guiding her back to the table, whilst an embittered head waiter ushered Alexandre to his abandoned plate, lectured him in hushed tones as to his inappropriateness, and requested that he remained seated if he wished to continue to be treated as a customer. The fellow countryman dining with him was no doubt familiar with the extravaganzas of his insufferable friend, but no better acquainted for it. The pair decided to move on. And the band picked up from where they'd left off, if a little gingerly at first.

"Great dancing, Daze."

Adrian whistled, hair poking out in all directions. How it could transform itself from a lifeless bed of matter to a mad professor in need of a good spritz down during the course of a dinner, never ceased to amaze. I'd struggled for a while to class Adrian as cake. And that's because he wasn't. Rather he and his hair were soufflé – and about as unpredictable as my one and only attempt at it.

Daisy flushed.

"Yes, well, I didn't seem to get a whole lot of choice in the matter. Let's get out of here," she said, "before my customers put two and two together."

"I think you're safe, Daisy," I lied, "everyone will have been so half-cut themselves that they'll not remember any of this tomorrow."

I reached for my mobile phone to take stock of the time: another text from Daniel. Crap, I should have stayed more alert. I would read it a little later when prying eyes were farther away.

***

Back out into the balmy night, people could be labelled in two distinct groups, those from the heat and those from frost-bitten shores. All traversed the city snappily in summer holiday clothes or winter woollies.

'Our men' were out in front this time, making great strides into the darkness. And before long, the porticos of Via Indipendenza came into sight once again, recurring like a colossal hall of mirrors that stretched as far as the eye could see. The pace was slower, people unhurried. Although the street was uncluttered, Henry, Adrian, Gary and Sebastian could no longer maintain lunar leaps and bounds, and found themselves restricted to daintier footwork instead, darting in-between lovers, companions and lone men like a procession of bobbing dragonflies.

"Ah the *Baglioni*," said Daisy.

"Know it well do you?" Henry shouted backwards having eavesdropped on our conversation.

Thank God he never got involved in our expenses.

"Oh, we were taken there once by a client, a few years back," I lied – again.

Actually the girls and I had dined there on more than a couple of superfluous occasions, which just so happened never to have included the Boyles. Yes, the Baglioni's restaurant still had to be one of the most prestigious gourmet dining experiences of my life. A far cry from my local *Giovanni's i*n Glastonbury, where the waiters used to corner us as fourteen year old girls, chancing on a grope as we indulged in a spot of underage cider drinking over our pizzas. And for sure, unlike the best a small Somerset town could produce, the Baglioni didn't jazz up their supermarket-purchased economy deserts with a squirt of aerosol cream, claiming they were homemade and adding on a five times mark up.

This kind of fine dining, where the menus hadn't even shown the prices; drinks had been decanted with military precision, and food had been served with serious aplomb, was exactly the type of thing Daniel would have snubbed. But sometimes I had even started to feel worthy of five waiters per table, each suave gent unveiling a panoply of courses from the silver cloches they were guarding. I liked to feel as if I was dining in a museum, the exorbitant wine slipping down all too congenially as the frescoes adorning the ceiling of the former Palazzo regarded me from above.

The echoes of Ricky Martin greeted us long before the electric pink and white honeycomb lights of The Piano Bar could be seen, such were the acoustics of the arches.

"Earth to Kate," Daisy was almost shouting.

"I was miles away there, sorry."

I couldn't be bothered to recount my daydream, and as much as his earlier apology had offered some respite, I really ought to check Daniel was okay.

I opened his latest message and the capital letters screamed the new direction the dialogue was taking:

WHERE THE HELL HAVE YOU PUT MY WORK OVERALLS?

I gulped. Fortunately, the girls and their longer legs were a couple of steps ahead of me. No wonder he couldn't find them. I'd put them nowhere. They were still lining the washing basket, no doubt reeking of bonfire from the time he'd last been wearing them.

The alcohol made me laugh the seemingly far-removed triviality off into the evening air. He had plenty of others. There was nothing so spectacular about these, and if he really needed them he could call his mum, give her the honours. I loved the courage Campari gave me. Three or four of its ruby marigold mixes – plus wine – and I was oblivious to whatever Daniel had to dish out on Sunday night.

Little by little, matchstick people grew larger; equally pervaded with alcohol, spilling both themselves and their drinks into the passageways as they attempted to groove. Among them would have been numerous wannabe and had-been Piers and Sids. The male sales side of the industry was awash with them, even if the boys themselves had since moved on to more 'serious' enterprises of their own.

"Poor locals," I said. "They must witness this every time there's a *fiera* in town."

The Piano Bar was a tradition embedded firmly in the top ten of Corny Things to do in Bologna. Whilst the melange of confection and liquor was a feast for the senses (Steph was already cooing over the Zuccoto Semi-Fredo, mentally noting how she could re-create its perfection), the clientele were mainly tragic, brash or both. For a woman, it was a dodgy place to be. People were packed concertina-tight across the width of the bar, so that for someone as petite as me – and sadly we're definitely only talking height – it could take several hours to wend your way through the maze of conversations. Bottom pinching wasn't unheard of, pickpocketing either.

But for all that, there was something so compelling about gradually making your way up the stairs, drink in hand, to the famed lounge to feign sophistication whilst something wretched was being hammered out on the keys of the electronic organ, and an overenthusiastic, glitzy, blue-rinsed lady belted out a number from the golden ages, warbling pitifully whenever she hit anything higher than a top E.

As Henry handed me the umpteenth mixer of the evening, I turned a little too quickly, bashing straight into a tall middle-aged man.

"Hey watch it," he said, flicking drips of liquid marmalade off his rugby shirt.

Oh, okay maybe he wasn't quite middle-aged. I quickly decided that for a Silver Fox, he wasn't all that bad looking either.

I felt a sharp tap on my back.

"It's nearing midnight," said Daisy, as I turned to see my well-meaning colleague had started tapping at her watch as well. "We really ought to head back to the hotel. The morning only heralds Day Two, after all."

Thanks, Daisy. That was close. I chanced to look over my shoulder, but thankfully he'd gone.

Steph and I followed the advice of our elder, ditched our glasses and turned to say our snappy farewells to the men, who were far too inebriated to understand what our plans were anyway.

"Ah choof off then, why don'tcha?" said Sebastian, at which point I don't think I'd ever seen him look more like Eton Mess. "Talk about boring…it's not even officially Thursday yet. Geez, guys." He pointed at Henry and Adrian. "You two really need to train your staff to last the distance."

We snaked our way to the exit where Silver Fox stood, running his fingers through his hair whilst chatting with a group of men. Something told me – and my pulse – it would be impossible to slip past undetected.

"We meet again," he said, as I chanced to unsuccessfully squeeze past him, my bust making more than ample contact with his shoulder.

"Hey, I'm so sorry about earlier," I said with a giggle. "My boss will insist on topping me up every five minutes." I was too merry to wonder whether that came across as a sexual double entendre.

Silver Fox, amused, seemed to have forgotten the soaking already. And I sensed that all too familiar book-fair-affair-twinge in my stomach as he studied me intently and his grin widened.

"So, I'm guessing you're a PB?"

I ignored yet another sharp tap on my back and gave him my 'excuse me?' face.

"A Publishing Babe," he said, laughing cheekily.

Christ, how corny.

"Steph's managed to hail us a cab, Kate. Time to say goodbye to your friend," said Daisy, revealing my true identity.

"Well, that's you told. See you around…Kate," he said.

"Maybe you will," I smiled, emphasising my final word far longer than was necessary as Daisy tugged me out the doorway.

But the fresh air seemed to sober me immediately. As we sped back to the hotel, and Steph and Daisy pondered our four male colleagues' likely actions over the encroaching hours, I lay my head against the taxi's window, saddled with remorse.

You can't keep doing this to him.

Chapter Four

The week passed by. The numbers dwindled. There may have been more opportunities for sneaky breaks to soak up spring's solar rays, but I always found this part of the fair so depressing. Like being at a party you'd looked forward to for so long then in the blink of an eye it was over, fever pitch gone until the tempo cranked back up again for Frankfurt book fair in October.

I hastily packed the last of the boxes ready for shipping back to the warehouse, trying with all my might to think of anything but the likely fanfare I'd receive from Daniel. Counter display units were falling apart at the seams, and the boxes I was hemming everything into had seen better days.

The others had disappeared to return borrowed shelves, demand a discount at the book fair office for a long list of faults, and most crucially, to bring back a tray of steaming hot coffees. They'd be a while.

I totted up the likely successes of the fair perching on the single remaining cabinet of the empty shell of the stand, where I was waiting for Spitty Steve and his wooden wheelie pallets. He was a cuddly teddy bear of a guy, over-friendly in a non-sexual way, but he had a rather hapless spitting impediment.

I hope he doesn't start on about the Dubai show again, I winced. The Ds and Ts were the worst.

I thought about Venice instead; that amazing light spilling across the waterways of the city, the happy-go-lucky gondoliers and the seemingly permanent carnival atmosphere. That was the other great thing about being left to my own devices to run a department: command of the travel budget.

I'd been obsessed with seeing every dot on the globe since I was a young girl, and my first overseas trip to The Canaries didn't fail to disappoint. It was there, aged eleven, that my penchant for languages was born. Barely able to enter a corner shop without being mistaken for a local *chica*, I'd be greeted with alien dialogue that I longed to decode.

Justifying a journey to Bologna and back via Venice had been all too easy. I had only to show Rupert, our Finance Director that the flights were seventy-five per cent cheaper and all was approved.

I picked up a first words book that had somehow strayed from its box, marvelling at the fact that our hard work had seen it published in twenty-four languages.

Twenty-four!

And then my stomach flipped.

Strangely, it seemed to take a few seconds before my brain caught up. Jake (aka Silver Fox from a few nights ago) – I now assumed that was his name anyway since referencing him in the exhibitors' directory, having noticed him all week on mostly one stand – hurried past. We exchanged another long, mutual attraction kind of a look as he hurtled down the aisle with his trolley bag, undoubtedly full of top secret book samples, mostly low end drivel; the company he worked for being even more mass-market than our own.

"Bye, see ya," he said in a broad Yorkshire accent.

Oh. Did he sound like that in the bar?

I'd really expected something a little classier to come out of his mouth when we finally got chatting, as I knew we surely would. I shook my head at my snobbery; a bit rich from a West Country lass.

Yes, he definitely has to be early to mid-forties. Come to think of it, he's the first Silver Fox I've ever found myself gushing about.

I shook my head at my haughtiness once again.

Yeah, and you discovered your first grey strand at the tender age of twenty-one…

Even now at the other end of the decade, I had to take bi-annual trips to cover my flourishing badger streaks –

something Daniel liked to make merry about whenever the mood fell upon him.

I pretended to straighten the labels on the boxes, concluding that he couldn't have been looking at me after all. What was I thinking? I poked my head round to the booths either side of mine. Not a soul to be seen, definitely no sign of a semi-attractive woman. Okay, then maybe he was saying goodbye in that northern inflexion, but probably only because he felt sorry for me.

And then he reappeared just as I was gawping.

"This is really embarrassing." He covered his eyes as if willing away a migraine.

You're not kidding me.

He smiled with that I'm-so-going-to-get-you-in-bed-in-the-end look about him.

"I've forgotten my passport."

He disappeared, reappearing again within moments, passport clutched firmly in his utterly capable-looking hand.

"Look, I hope I'm not speaking out of turn here, but it's pretty damned obvious that you've ah, well, you've clearly got a thing for me, and I um…I think you're pretty damn hot too. How's about we go out to dinner next time?"

"Well…okay…get erm youuuu!"

I took a couple of steps back, trying not to look fazed, wishing Steph had been parked outside in one of those giant white vans like you see on TV, drip-feeding invisible one-liners into my hidden mic. Anything would have been an improvement upon that last sentence.

My blood rushed to my extremities in all directions. I hadn't expected him to approach me, let alone to be so forward. I didn't know the first thing about him. And anyway, how could he be sure I wasn't married?"

"You're definitely not married."

Oh, so he was a mind reader too.

"Trust me, I've been there – three times." He laughed as if multiple marriages were the norm these days.

"Well, you really are the charmer. And I suppose you say that to all the ladies?"

49

"I've got to go." He smirked. "Taxi meter's running. Dinner next time though, definitely." And he winked, vanishing around the corner.

Before I could even begin to process our dialogue, I spotted Daisy battling to regain symmetry. A blinding flash of sunlight streamed through the greenhouse panes of the roof, making it difficult for her to see where she was heading. I cut across the aisle, aiding her balance by taking my own caffè latte, which I then managed to spill all over the tray and our three pain aux raisins.

"What's up with you, Kate?"

"Me? Nothing, nothing." I giggled. "Whoops, how clumsy." I dabbed at the pastries pointlessly with a serviette, butterflies on overdrive in my stomach. "Where's Steph anyhow?"

"Oh she's not far, loads of complaints in that office. Hey, as soon as Steve's done his thing, what do you say to us getting an earlier train to Venice? I, for one, can't wait to get out of here."

The juicy neon Campari sign hugging the shore in the online ad for our hotel was waiting to welcome us, after all.

"That's the best idea I've heard all day," (well, the best sensible one anyway), "and it's going to be fab this time round." I felt a shiver at the memory of the Old Dear who'd prodded Daisy with her umbrella spoke, when we'd tried to board the water taxi, just as the heavens had opened. "I promise."

"Hey, none of that was exactly your fault. But yeah, I would prefer to arrive without resembling the character illustrating Force Eight of the Beaufort scale as per the *Ladybird* Weather book. That Lido hotel you've been raving about sounds out of this world."

I'd pocketed a small fortune selling off the books that didn't need to go back to Bristol whilst the girls were off-stand. As soon as Steph was back I divvied up the proceeds.

"This is our treat," I announced. "To be spent in Venice or at duty free – preferably not on fags, Stephanie, but definitely before we get back to England."

Steph and Daisy grinned widely, stashing away their neat bundles.

And I tried. Oh I tried... not to imagine undressing Jake in the lift on the way back to his hotel room after dinner in Frankfurt in six months' time.

Chapter Five

"Just look at how this place has gone to rack and ruin."

I'd scarcely wiped my feet on my own doormat, much less put down my bags and flicked on the kettle. His old-fashioned clichés had beaten me to it. Butterfly-inducing Jake and that excitable tingly feeling were already long gone.

Daniel shunted me as if I were a train and I knew exactly what was coming next when he gave the main road behind me a cursory glance. But it wasn't like there had been the merest sign of civilisation when I'd walked up the path, he really needn't have bothered.

He grabbed me painfully by my striped silk scarf, dragged me into the kitchen and pinned me against the American fridge. Clover, who would normally be leaping and bounding all over me, quickly burrowed her head back into her basket in response to the pitch of his voice. My toes curled, as if they might somehow claw the floor open allowing it to gobble me up.

Oh to be back in Venice.

According to my guide book, the Venetian tourist 'unwittingly became part of the scene'. That was one way of putting it – now as much as then.

Thankfully this time, for some unknown reason, he loosened his grip, tugged the scarf from my neck, discarded it to the floor and added a well-targeted spit.

"One: you never once called me on the hour. I waited and waited by the phone, finishing work early purposely. Two: you've been off cavorting with all those collar-and-tie types, oblivious to your responsibilities back home. And three, woman…number three is this: you've been getting way above your station."

I lowered my head and let him say his piece.

Maybe this ten minute rant had done him good, made for a peaceful evening. It looked promising when Hyde became Jekyll anyway, letting me heave my own cases up the stairs; letting me make him a brew, letting me tend to his supper while he counted his monthly Toby jug and taxidermy sales.

I sometimes wondered how I could ever have mistaken Daniel for Black Forest Gateau when we'd first met. He was Marble Cake through and through; tumultuous, twisted, and wholly unpredictable.

"Food's ready," I said a short while later.

He wasn't in the mood for chat when he finally joined me at the table, still so engrossed in the receipts of his hobby that was fast overtaking the house, that he hadn't even noticed what was on the menu.

"So, what do you think?" I said with a tentative smile as I admired my land and sea creation on a plate.

He poked at the tuna as if raking leaves in the garden, then gathered a sticky cluster, sniffing at his fork. I could already see the scorn creasing his face.

"Do you like it?"

His answer came by way of a lifted elbow, which didn't stay airborne for long, but smashed loud and hard on his plate, showering it and its contents across the floor. My knees buckled in reflex and everything I'd previously tried so hard to control seemed now to be spinning dangerously out of control. Delicatessen morsels covered the flagstones, resting on their tiny shards of china like some kind of Heston Blumenthal deconstructed micro-meal mosaic.

Why did I always push my luck?

"Look what you've made me do, silly bitch."

I trembled. If I kept my cool, I knew there was the remote possibility it would blow over quickly, just like earlier. He hadn't quite got everything out of his system. That was all.

"Why do you insist on being somebody you're not? T'wasn't so long ago and you'd be anybody's if they took you out for scampi and chips."

"Nice compliment," I muttered under my breath, as I bent

53

to retrieve the jagged remnants of my favourite plate. I knew I shouldn't have said it, but whilst the thought of him transferring abusive language to action scared the hell out of me, he'd also royally pissed me off. I may as well have brought him back a box of frozen crispy pancakes.

"What was that? I hope you're not bleedin' well answering me back. You won't do yourself any favours winding me up. You should know that by now."

I shuffled, keeping my head down, cautiously making my way to the bin. The last thing I wanted was for Clover to cut her paws. The dog ventured a few steps out of her basket, smelt the air and swiftly retreated with a whimper once she'd felt the cold hard lob of Daniel's slipper across her left ear.

"Get in there, you stinking mutt." He lowered his voice into that canine growl of his own, a sign to both his subjects that he meant business.

My heart was lead. I vowed to give her one almighty cuddle later.

"I'll um…I'll rustle up something else then. It's not a problem."

"Right'o," he said. And all was eerily calm as he got back to his calculations, the past few minutes erased.

Chapter Six

I locked the door and sank into the bath tub. A hippo, I wallowed in my bubble-topped river, safe for now. The sight of my stomach parting the foam reminded me of a mountain peeping through the clouds – and that I'd massively over-indulged. I'm not so sure Jake would have found me 'pretty damn hot', after all. I tried to meditate the early evening's negativity away, but my head was too busy playing over Daniel's rage and Clover's whimper. I still hadn't got to grips with the affirmations in my latest Self-Help book anyway.

Talk about an anti-climax.

It was enough to make me flash back to our group dismay when we'd reached our thoroughly in need of a facelift Venetian hotel. Half boxed-in wires had dangled out of every orifice, and the corridor to the bedrooms had resembled the one from *The Shining* – so much so that I'd had to shield my eyes for fear of a child trundling past on a trike.

"I guess my impulse to discover new places isn't always such a healthy thing," I'd said with a sigh.

Daisy and Steph looked thoroughly unimpressed, although both claimed to be too exhausted to care. I could only hope the little restaurant we were heading to would offer something in the way of ambiance to make up for it.

A haze of tea lights redolent of a muted scene of conviviality from one of Nigella's cookery programmes, greeted us from across the courtyard. Happily, once inside, this was backed up by the kind of fragrance that sold houses to dithering purchasers. It appeared I'd redeemed myself.

As I mulled over the scramble of culinary terms trying to decide whether my soul screamed out for the simplicity of gnocchi or a good hearty steak a la Gorgonzola, I knew it was time to share my brewing thoughts.

"What if we set up on our own?" I said, peering into my glass to avoid Daisy's predictable body language. I was sure I detected the note of berries and plums in my first sip of wine. I was getting better at this tasting charade.

It had been on my mind for a while now, and why not? Our jobs really did seem to encompass it all; accounts, production, even commissioning new projects when Gary wasn't quick enough – which was all the time.

"We'd be a force to be reckoned with," said Steph, fingering the solitary ice cube from her water glass and plonking it in the ashtray. Kind of pointless given the fact she was an avid smoker.

"Yeah but—"

"Not the yeah-but-chestnut, Daisy. We're running a company within a company and being completely taken for granted. Would it be this way if we were men?"

I decided a pause at this point would be appropriate; a chance for Daisy to digest.

"All we don't have is the money. But surely a bank would prop us up? How else do people get started? There are companies who'd give their left and right bingo wings for our department's turnover and margin."

"I'm not saying you don't have a point," said Daisy, readjusting her impressive collection of rings on her piano player fingers. "I just don't think I'm suited to it. I need the stability my salary gives me. Okay, the twins are complete pains in the backside, but I also have so much more to learn before I'm at a stage to go solo – even with you lovely guys. No harm in dreaming though—"

She shuffled her perfectly straight cutlery to signal the end of our discussion.

"Well, I won't give up on you...or my pulling the crowds in from all angles café-stroke-book shop idea," I frowned as I raised my glass in a lone toast.

"Us...running a café and a bookshop? Oh, well, I didn't realise that was quite what you had in mind." She chuckled. "You do come out with the funniest things, Kate. I suppose I could whip up some of my vegan Quark, Loganberry and Pine Nut Cheesecake as a contribution though."

"Please don't, it sounds foul," said Steph.

"That's right, make a mockery of my ideas," I said. "I can take it."

I put my hands against an invisible piece of mime artist glass and pulled an offended face.

"I'm totes up for it," said Steph, "especially if it means proper cake with sugar in it, but changing the subject slightly, what do you make of these rumours that Henry and Adrian are buying up part of an industrial estate outside of Bristol?"

"It's just another colossal waste of money if you ask me," said Daisy.

"Isn't it funny," I said, "how they can find the money to invest in a warehouse, new office buildings besides, yet they can't seem to find it when it comes to their grossly underpaid staff?"

My wine glass had become an experiment for centrifugal force.

"It's like sure, we do get some travel perks, but only because we're savvy enough to milk the system. But none of these things pays the bills. When I've come back from a cosmopolitan sales trip, staying in luxury hotels, being taken out to dinner in all the best places in town, and then I have to get out my credit card to pay for the car to go through its MOT, well, there's something a little bit wrong with that, don't you think?"

"Then you have idiots like Gary surfing car websites all day. The number of times we've lost sales because of that guy's incompetence," said Steph.

"There was absolutely no reason for him to partake in this fair," said Daisy, playing once again with her rings. "He's wasted company money with a flight to Paris, a first class Eurostar ticket to Brussels, and another first class train ticket to Milan. Then he apparently jumped in a taxi all the way to Bologna, simply to litter the stand."

Gary had woven his way snuggly onto the production floor courtesy of the UPS parcel he was delivering. Just like many an employee who'd similarly snuck in off the pigeon-roosting streets of Bristol, leading to a top-heavy business with not enough seats for bottoms.

"And how about Sharon popping in for her three mornings a week?" said Steph. "Most of which are spent on the phone to her kid's nursery, or buying up M&S's entire middle-aged clothing range."

"Do not get me started," I said, still swirling my glass by its stem.

"And I've heard the figure that Piers and Sid were getting back in the day," said Daisy, snapping a breadstick. "If that was three years ago, and the economy is growing, then the company needs to move with the times, pay us all what we're worth."

"I think we're basically saying," I said, "that out of the entire company, we are the most disproportionately paid."

"And we haven't even got onto what the Boyles must be pocketing." Steph took a swig at the dregs of her wine before granting herself an immediate re-fill.

"Then there's Hayden in the Singapore office. He has to be on a packet," said Daisy.

"Hmm, to be fair though, he does work crazily long hours – Saturdays too."

I sprang to his defence. And I hoped that was just the wine I could feel flushing my cheeks because I'd assumed I'd long forgotten about that fairground attraction.

Anyhow, the fact remained: most employees were paid a small fortune in return for very little. The days I felt I could no longer support that, were fast outnumbering the days when I was indifferent. The only person who seemed to understand our true value was Harold. And he wasn't even an employee, but our token Agony Uncle, who appeared from time to time to partner up with the twins for special projects.

"It's not like we got to experience the good old days and the infamous Kenyan Safari trips either. Nowadays, the twins can't even be arsed to dish out Christmas cards. And, here's food for thought..." I shuffled in my seat in a bid to untangle the wedge my knickers had created, "...do you realise that when they did, the one never checked with the other, and the cards would be duplicated, so everyone would get a double wodge of—"

"They never," said Daisy, eyes wide in disbelief.

"See, this is why I am suggesting we set up on our own. Something's gotta give."

Steph, who was now attacking the olives, bit at them angrily. I knew we weren't just three women complaining, there was huge disparity and it needed to be addressed, at least if the company wanted to keep hold of its most productive staff.

Every sip and chew sharpened our philosophy. Every single project we launched would come to its eventual fate.

"Fairy tale or jigsaw book – they'll all end up as fuel for a bonfire, be chewed to pieces by a dog, or crayoned to within an inch of their lives," I said.

"But we are making a difference," said Daisy. "I mean look at your Caribbean order, Kate. Those Papiamento books were the very first in the schools of Aruba which had previously been one hundred per cent Dutch. What a milestone for those kids."

"Yeah, I s'pose when you put it like that—"

"There's always a chance that one of our little stories brought to life in Germany, Mexico or Japan, could in some way help shape the thoughts of future revolutionaries."

"Now that's a worrying thought," said Steph.

"We could be selling nuts and bolts, oil, or false eyelashes," said Daisy, "but no, we're selling books, wonderful, wonderful books!"

***

The island of Murano was the perfect antidote to the fair. The back of every slightly distinguished man was Jake, knotting my stomach into balls of anticipation, until one by one they turned around. Add to that the meagre pickings of a hotel breakfast, and just the sight of extra-terrestrial, lurid green cakes wedged into the corner of a bakery window added to my rattling stomach. We'd seen the oddities everywhere, although quite what they contained was anybody's guess, since they never seemed to be labelled.

"Perhaps with good reason." Daisy looked on in dismay.

But I could halt my curiosity no longer; neither did I much care what I was eating: it filled a hole. Naturally, Steph joined in too, although having a distinctly more refined taste in all things cake, she opted for the Venetian Zabaglione.

It also seemed fitting to pay mainland Venice one last visit, this time thankfully, minus the rain. Despite Murano's laid back aura, there were only so many glass and bead shops one could handle in a day, without bulldozing into a pièce de résistance. All three of us were nursing a hangover, although it had to be said, there was method in my madness, the green cake had definitely taken the edge off mine.

Pottering around Venice was fun, as was the fabulous art of getting lost. We abandoned the map, caring not a jot that our flight was early evening; that getting back to the airport alone would involve another blessed water taxi and bus fiasco. We marvelled for hours at the miracle of coffee (Daisy at chamomile tea), and indulged in the art of anthropology, mostly of the male of the species.

"It shouldn't work, yet somehow it does." Daisy was awestruck by the guy in the daffodil yellow tank top with Rupert Bear checked trousers, who by all accounts was a coffee and cigarette addict.

And since her cautious influence couldn't bring us to spontaneously jump into a gondola (oh, was she ever true to her wholesome and practical Muesli Muffin self on this trip…hangover aside), we made do with our senses instead, imagining all of the hidden corners the bloke with the boat could have shown us. If Venice was a stage, as so often described, then we were the extras in its chorus line, sharing our role with the vibrant washing lines overhanging balconies, the pigeons, and the *vaporettos*.

"How much more colourful can life get?" I said aloud as I attempted to pose in contemplation on the cute chair which randomly happened to be abandoned on one of the many bridges we'd crossed.

Daisy stood behind me in a snapshot in time, clutching at a bouquet of Christmassy-red chilli peppers to which she'd earlier treated herself. Steph snapped away at us in her enviably natural style, equally at ease behind the lens as she was in front of it. There was nobody but the three of us, and the golden cracks in the clouds which offered an early taste of sunset over the canal.

"Shit, our flight," screamed Steph, almost dropping her precious camera into Venetian H2O.

Time had ceased to exist for so long that I was tempted to wave my friends away, rooting myself to that chair on the bridge, eager to see who would step on the scene next.

But the holiday was over.

And my bath water was cold.

It was time to face reality, mine being a lunar landscape and the volcano who ruled it. Worse still, I knew that an eruption of a scale I'd never quite seen before was imminent. Nine years with Daniel had taught me a lot, and I was about to pay the price for having abandoned him.

Chapter Seven

I laid my mock rocks on the cake table. I doubted I'd partake in their consumption. I was still feeling sick.

Baking was usually an act of salvation, something for the weekend. The rise – and sometimes the fall – of something golden in the oven put me in blissful creative flow. Today's Rock Cakes, my go-to hefty time-capsules of the eighties, were essential après-fair sustenance. With the mountain of work to be scaled in the coming week, the team needed to draught in all it could get.

Last night was unexpected. Not totally, something was always simmering away beneath Daniel's skin. But, it usually took a lot longer for me to wind him up to this point. Somehow it felt different this time. I had the sinking feeling we were working our way to a crescendo which try as I might, I would not be able to stop.

I could see he wasn't happy, but it wasn't like I'd never been away. And it wasn't like I'd never cooked him a continental meal.

I trotted downstairs to the office kitchen making for the kettle. Birds twittered their early morning anthem outside the window. I loved having the place to myself in the mornings, notwithstanding the accounts crew, but their tales of woe were several floors away.

It had been a while since my salary had overtaken Daniel's, I realised as I scoured the shelves for my mug. But it was becoming clearer that the role of breadwinner was not something he was prepared to step down from without a fight. Another week on his own had obviously given him too much time to think. He'd taken on the appearance of somebody who'd overdone it in the sun last night; eyes narrow and venomous.

It was an innocent enough mistake on my part. I thought the little luxuries I'd brought him back from the over-priced deli at Venice's airport would have made a meal worthy of accolades. Now I just felt plain stupid. I should have anticipated his mood, bought some meat on the way home. A steak wouldn't have taken long to pan fry. Surely I should have figured out by now that when it came to the culinary, he liked what he knew.

I popped a tea bag into a chipped mug, the only one that was clean, and tutted. Somebody had pilfered my favourite again. It couldn't have been washed up since Friday. Caked-on hot chocolate coated its circumference. Yuk. *Whittard* at lunch time it was then – and I'd soon tag on a scout around *Karen Millen* too.

Above all, I hated it when Daniel hurt Clover. What had she done to deserve that attack? I felt the burden of my own shame; the shame of not being able to reach out and scoop her up in my arms, or call the RSPCA to rescue her and set her up with a better life.

"So," he'd said after I'd emerged squeaky clean from my bath, "after a week of fending for myself, you plonk a bit of tuna fish on a plate with some bleedin' rabbit's food and you expect me to be grateful?"

"I can't believe you just did that," I'd said, tugging at my earlobe. "It cost me eight Euros that tuna. It's preserved in olive oil in glass jars...not like the kind we get in the supermarket here in a little tin."

And then having taken in his unimpressed look, I wished I could eat my hapless words.

"What are you even doing spending eight Euros on a jar of fish? You're useless with money; spend it like water while I'm back here putting a roof over your head, clothes on your back."

"I was working too," I whispered.

"Work? That wasn't work. But I'll tell you what is: you can clear this lot up for a start, and then you'll need to see to cleaning that there kitchen floor that didn't get tended to before you went away."

Remarkably, he knew where the cleaning equipment lived and was now a javelin thrower in an Olympic stadium. My reflexes, tested so often to their limit, caught the mop by its handle, only just sparing my head.

"I'm off out to the Chinese. I'll get myself some proper grub," he said a little too calmly.

So Chinese got the stamp of approval.

He stormed out the house, not before marching back to the table to swipe at a Young Farmers' brochure – something I'd definitely not spotted lying there of its own accord – leaving me shaking, but also somewhat relieved that he hadn't taken things further. All I had to do was tidy up, give the floor a superficial wash before he got back to inspect it, then some kind of normality could prevail.

I hoped.

The office fridge smelt suspicious. I swung the door open reaching for the milk anyway and instinctively shut it again. "Green," I screamed. I pinched my nose, ventured back in, grabbed it and plonked it on the sink for the guilty party to deal with. Then I bounded two at a time back up the stairs to the office to swipe my bag. There was only one thing for it: *Starbucks*. With any luck I'd make it out the building without playing waitress.

But even on the streets among the throng and singsong of early morning workers, I just couldn't stop myself from replaying the sequence of events. The pictures flashed back through my head, a frustrating reminder of a movie reel demonstrating how dire my life was.

I'd barely wrung out the suds from the mop when I'd detected the frenetic screech of his breaks outside. And the frosty atmosphere had taken up residence once more as he'd angrily, sloppily eaten his food, hardly letting it touch the sides.

Once he seemed calmer, I decided it was best to apologise.

"You're right. I should have made you something meaty. I promise I'll be more inventive tomorrow."

"Well, just think on," he said, correcting the spacing

64

between his smallest Toby jugs lining the living room shelf. "There'd be women queuing up round the block to be with me if I was back on the market tomorrow. Why do you think Stella has that look of regret whenever we run into her?"

Funny that. I would have called any look from his ex an evil, green-eyed glare at me.

"I meant to say though…I didn't pay for the tuna. It was work's money. Sometimes there are perks to being away, I can put things on expenses," I said, thinking it might smooth things over.

Then with the air of a magician I picked up the abandoned bags of souvenirs from the hallway, hoping to further redeem myself. I conjured up balsamic vinegar hailing from none other than the quintessential home of all things balsamic: Modena; there were lollo rosso seeds, extra virgin olive oil too. Finally, out came my trump card, an elaborately handcrafted Easter egg. I knew I was taking a risk on the latter since he'd shunned 2003's Easter gift from me, turning mockingly to the mass-produced variety instead. But when I'd seen it on the counter of the confectioners, I'd almost wept at its beauty.

"What do I want with all of this muck?" he snatched at the seeds turning them over and over as if trying to decode an enigma.

I just couldn't understand it. Didn't they say the way to a man's heart was through his stomach?

"Well…I…uh…thought the seeds would be perfect for your vegetable patch. You're always going on about how we should eat seasonally, be more self-sufficient—"

"With something English, yeah, not this fancy stuff. These poncey trips abroad have changed you."

My face fell, until Jake and his cocky swagger swam randomly back into my thoughts – a welcome break – but I could only hope that they weren't transparent.

"Okay, my fault. Well, I'll keep some of it back for me then…" the egg sprang to mind "…and I'll take the rest to my parents."

"See, there you go again. Why can't you just give it all

away? The only thing to my mind that's gonna put paid to all of this is marriage and babies. You say not till thirty, but if this malarkey carries on much longer, Kate, I'm gonna have to play dirty…" he laughed with a sparkle in his eye that once again suggested he'd resort to foul play – and that he'd gained some sort of intellectual brownie points for rhyming prose.

You dare. First, you'd have to actually get me in the mood.

He was lucky if that was once every eight weeks, and even then purely out of duty. For some reason, I couldn't stand to be touched by him.

As for Jake, right now I'd happily un-wrap his red velvety layers. And not of the cupcake variety either. Jake was most definitely a slice: a chunk, a hunk of cake. Wasn't that the term?

I knew it was wrong, vastly unfair to Daniel, but Jake was fast becoming a necessity. And I had to marvel at the fact my selective memory had already overlooked his marital history.

On my quest for coffee, I passed The Brizzle Tea Shop and returned to the present, wrapping my cardigan tighter around my curves to keep the chilly morning air at bay. The chintzy cups and saucers in the window twinkled their reflection of spring sunbeams, giving a false impression of the warmth I'd enjoyed in Bologna. One of these days I'd have to go in to sample the Bristolian Seed Cake.

But no sooner had I marched past its Enid Blyton-esque display, than I was back in my living room all over again.

"Fire up the box, good girl, match is about to start."

That's how he'd greeted me after I'd cleared up the scraps of his takeaway. I was accustomed to being second-in-line to the TV but the normalcy after his outburst was verging on ridiculous.

"Stick the kettle on while you're up as well. I'll have me evenin' cuppa now."

He lost himself in the game while I flitted around the kitchen waiting for the water to boil. The exchange in tempo was strangely palpable, as if the kettle and I were trading energy. My heartbeat steadied itself and I felt my blood cool whilst the kettle took on the fury of my previously throbbing pulse, until the clouds of steam emerging from its spout signalled a climax.

I rested his mug on the coffee table and joined him, numbing myself in front of the incessant on-screen chatter, my best attempt at the old 'quality time' routine.

"So...ah Daisy, Steph and I had a meal together last night and we got talking..."

I started hesitantly, hoping to pave the way for my brainwave. His eyes were transfixed on a sitcom – his tolerance for the half-time chitchat of the match commentators being zero. At least by breaking the news while he was operating on a selective hearing basis, there was every chance he'd tell me to go for it.

"Well, you know how I've told you we pretty much run our own business within the company?" I paused, waiting for recognition. It didn't come. Interpreting this as a good thing, I pressed semi-confidently on. "The thing is, we already utilise every required skill between us, and we have a joint love of books, coffee – okay, Daisy's more of a herbal tea girl – and cake, so we thought perhaps we could set up on our own—"

"You're getting above your station again," he said with more than a hint of hysteria.

I jumped and silently screamed at myself for being so dumb, for not reading the signs (of which he'd been giving plenty). I could only put it down to tiredness – and my hormones flying all over the place at the prospect of a not-too-distant-future fling. My mouth was so disengaged from my brain, living in a wishful thinking bubble of its own, letting my thoughts fly out as incessantly as a machine gun. I was asking for trouble.

All the while he stayed glued, demon-like to the screen, making for an uncomfortable stillness which hung between us until the programme wound up with the crumbiest of endings.

"I've never heard anything so ridiculous."

And I decided, unconvinced by his random and somewhat

delayed retort, to leave it like that. Put it on the backburner, forever.

"If you spent more friggin' time doing something productive around the house, rather than sticking your head in the clouds, I'd be a happier man. Look at this," he stood, running his fingers along the top of the television, "there's dust everywhere."

I saw this as my cue for redemption and scurried to the kitchen to track down a duster. It wasn't that I'd been ordered to clean it right now, I reassured myself. I wasn't being submissive. Sunday night was just never a good time for confrontation. The slog of the working week ahead never did much for Daniel's mood.

"Silly Little Women, how could the three of you run a business?" He lay there pointing at new patches of dust from the comfort of his stopgap bed, quicker than I could keep up.

The giant Starbucks muffins which usually jumped out at me begging to be guzzled at my desk with a milky coffee, churned my stomach by the time I made it to the front of the queue. Those rock cake 'casualties' I'd binged on last night and the ticking time bomb thought of him stabbing the contraceptives, brought on a nausea that had me wondering if I was already with child.

But then it would have to be The Immaculate Conception.

Chapter Eight

"You're not going. I don't trust that mate of yours Carys. She's always had a bit of the old slapper about her."

Daniel made no secret of his discontent, inciting hatred for hatred's sake.

"Anyway…" he chopped his hand through the air, "…we have a family meal planned."

First I'd heard of it.

"But she's getting married. Why would she be doing anything she shouldn't on her hen night? She's found the man she loves," I said, exasperated at his misogynistic crap.

"She's trouble through and through, that one. Wouldn't surprise me if you two have already been up to your tricks when you were at Uni."

I hadn't as such, yet I certainly couldn't deny the thought hadn't entered my head.

Perhaps it was no wonder he had Carys-based issues if I was really honest. After Daniel's Tuesday visits, when he'd race straight up to Bath fresh from work, Carys would phone me at her designated time slot:

"Coast clear, doll?"

Twenty-seven minutes later the doorbell would ring, and I'd be hopping about trying to squeeze into a sultry little number, twirling through tornadoes of cheap eau de toilette to a backdrop of *Alanis Morissette*. We'd catch the last bus of the evening to Milsom Street, club until three, and somehow still manage to haul our bedraggled selves into the eight am History of Algeria lecture.

It was the official start of my double life, and strangely, it didn't take long to create my new identity. I quivered at the thought of the repercussions if he'd ever found out about those student shenanigans, tame though they may have been.

"You are allowed to be happy," Carys had said over sea-blue cocktails one night.

"I am happy." I almost had myself believing it too. "He's a few years older, that's all…says he's done with the going out scene."

"Kate, he's twenty-two. Doesn't that strike you as a bit, you know, oddball?"

Yeah, it did. Course it did. But still I managed to convince myself that I, in fact, was the freak. I just needed to live a bit, do some catching up. It wouldn't do him any harm not to know what I was up to and then everything would be rosy; I'd have purged myself of all this fun and 'Sex on the Beach' with friends.

Truth was, there were no men involved – yet I couldn't exactly help it if they wanted to dance around me either, I really did try to pretend not to notice. Only in the second year were there a couple of male friends, and then purely in the form of flatmates.

Strangely Daniel didn't mind.

He'd more or less vetted them, perceived them all to be geeks. Little did he know about my penchant for the tall athletic Nick, but nothing was ever to materialise there – despite a kind of half-baked mutual attraction – hardly helped by the evening I hurled his work placement clothes into a muddy puddle in the garden because he'd left me in a nightclub on my own. Me, ever the stubborn Taurean and he, the unforgiving type, no further words were uttered between us.

In a sense, I felt I'd had a lucky escape with that one; a second chance to make things right, to rectify the disloyal behaviour of my wandering eye.

Then again, Daniel was hardly struck on my first year flatmates either. He constantly referred to them as 'toffs'. Admittedly, one of them did hail from Hooray Henley and rowed boats. But he made me feel so wretched for living with them, so awkward about it all, especially when he refused to walk through the kitchen – where they'd be gathered, sipping

Prosecco – to use the bathroom, peeing instead out of my sash bedroom window and into the garden. Just because we were country folk, didn't mean we needed to behave like farmyard animals.

Heck, it wasn't just Carys, all my friends were Scarlet Women.

But this was to be the first time he'd dished out a resounding 'no' upon me seeking his say-so. Maybe if I'd never asked for permission, did what I wanted anyway, I'd never have created this begging situation?

I couldn't use the banality of a family meal as a get out clause. Carys had been a firm friend for years. I waited for Hen Day, pretending I'd be there; then feigned bedridden flu, something I hoped would at least be a little more credible and not return to me like karma. Daniel had turned me into a fraud. This wasn't the way I wanted to treat the precious few people in my life.

Invitations to anything from anyone dried up after that. Friendships fell by the wayside. What was the point in asking somebody to be somewhere when you already knew their answer? I couldn't hold it against them. I felt rotten to the core for constantly having to invent excuses and let people down.

But the thing was: Daniel didn't used to be this way. Slowly, imperceptibly, he'd mutated into a lone wolf, cutting himself – and then me – off from the outside world.

"All 'friends' are fair-weather-friends; they'll only let you down. Anyways, I should be your best friend, not some woman from Wales who you hardly see anymore. Get your priorities straight."

His overbearing nature began to intimidate me so much that I no longer had the will to argue. And so The Family Meal was as choreographed as ever. The dialogue followed the same old pattern with Daniel's sister – who he irritatingly referred to as Sissy, on account of his childhood attempt at saying 'sister', portrayed as The Gorgeous Slim Creature.

"Go on, Hannah, you really ought to treat yourself to the Chocolate Fudge Cake. You need some fattening up," his mother would chivvy her along into ordering something other than lemon sorbet for dessert.

"Look at this!" Daniel would hold her arm aloft for our fellow diners to see, just like that scene from *The Nutty Professor*, "What a catch…Sissy's toned to perfection, not a wobble in sight."

And Sissy would indeed be lapping it up, compliments flying across the table quicker than she could keep up with them. They'd talk at length about her job at the outdoor swimming pool, her 'budding modelling career', and the three times she was voted Glastonbury's carnival Queen – as well as yacking for hours on end about Daniel's farm chores and his relatively few and colourless pastimes. Then they'd round the evening off by pouring over childhood stories which had been regurgitated time and time again.

"Ha, d'you remember that time down West Bay when you had a strop and threw your picnic in the sea, Daniel?"

I swore they were plotting conspiracies against me. Any time I opened my mouth to say anything they'd find one more tale. I'd feign interest over the hours, furtively loosening my belt under the table, feeling bloated and enormous whenever The Stick Insect gnawed on her lettuce leaves, or the calligraphy on the dessert board reeled me in.

A Sticky Toffee Pudding and a dollop of the West Country's finest clotted cream later, and I'd be unzipping my flies as well. How Sissy would gloat as she finished off with her sparkling water. She and her radar vision knew all right. Her orthorexic deprivation and the pleasure to be derived from said scenario were the highlight of her treadmill-disciplined week.

Hannah 1, Kate 0.

But definitely not a size zero…

Chapter Nine

"Pass me the gravy would you please, Daniel."

"My pleasure, Audrey," said Daniel to my mum as he handed her the cow-shaped gravy boat. He smiled as he watched her top her roast potatoes with Dad's gleaming, award-winning red wine infused sauce; the very sauce he loved to slag off for unnecessarily undermining *Bisto* when we were behind closed doors.

Mum couldn't resist a quick bite before the rest of us had loaded our plates.

"You've done it again Trev," she shouted through to Dad who was still pottering about in the kitchen. "I'm pretty sure you could take me to The Ritz and they couldn't produce anything finer."

Simon, my older brother sniggered.

"Well, this is nice, isn't it," said Mum, looking around at the circle of faces before her as she balanced fork and knife on her plate. "It makes a lovely change to have both my dear children here." She raised her right eyebrow at Simon who would usually make it his mission to come up with any excuse not to join us every other Sunday.

"And I suppose no sooner have your feet touched down after Bologna," she turned to look at me with her what-ever-next face, elbows propped on the table in exactly the manner she'd brought me up insisting they shouldn't be, "than you'll be off to London book fair, won't you?

"That's right," I said, refraining from touching my plate until Dad was seated. "And not long after that it's Warsaw. It's just the way it is at this time of year in my industry."

"Poor Daniel, it's a lot for him to run a house as well as being up to his neck in work at the farm though," said Mum.

73

"I mean she gets her itchy feet from me, no doubt; once Simon turned thirteen that was it; the Canaries, Malta, Crete, you name it, there was no stopping us. But still, the amount of travel they expect you to do with this job is something else."

"Yeah," said Simon, guzzling down two whole roast potatoes aided by his chunky fingers, "women need to know their place."

"Arse," I flicked a pea and smirked when it landed in his wine glass.

"Katherine!" Mum was clearly far from impressed by my table manners. "No, Simon, that's not what I mean at all and you know it." Mum narrowed her eyes. "It's no wonder you don't have a regular lady, coming out with remarks like that. Anyway, as I was saying, it's just that, well, you know, one day when babies come along…then it's not so conducive to happily married life, is it. One of you has to take a backseat career-wise."

"Yeah, well, let's not forget, Mum, I'm not even twenty-six yet, okay? Plenty of time for all of that in the future," I said, unable to think of anything worse.

"I'm very proud of her and all that she's achieved actually, Audrey; wouldn't have it any other way," said Daniel lifting his glass of red. "She's a role model to other women at the end of the day. Why should it be the female of the species running around cooking, cleaning and washing? I'm all for equal opportunities, me." He rested his glass back on its coaster and switched to his cutlery; one hand piercing a fork into his pork chop, the other carving around the fat as he focused with precision.

I felt a short sharp kick to the shin as he loaded the chewy, unappetising slither into his mouth in a near perfect impersonation of Hannibal Lector.

Just then Dad walked in providing a timely decoy from my very public shiver to the bone, a tray full of stuffing in his oven-gloved hands. "I can't believe you lot are tucking in without me, and without this."

"Oh, Trev, I told you not to bother with that. If we were

eating roast chicken, yes, but pork chops and stuffing? Good job you're not a chef at The Ritz after all," said Mum.

Daniel chuckled. "Load me up, Trevor." He bent to pick up his napkin, expertly pinching my calf with his free hand as he straightened himself back up again. "I'll help you get rid of it."

My foot pushed into the carpeted floor, big toe rubbing away at the coarse fibres beneath my sock to take my mind off the throbbing of my lower leg.

"You're a star, Daniel. I say, he's a star that one, Kate. You wanna keep hold of him."

My family laughed and raised their glasses to Daniel and his chivalry. I swallowed hard in a bid to halt my tears in their tracks.

The rest of lunch was a blur of niceties, head nodding, and gossiping about the neighbours' extra car which was 'infringing driveway rights'. What had it come to? Now he had the power to petrify me in this, the very family home I'd grown up in; damned if I did, damned if I didn't, I was an endangered species even before my parents' eyes.

Chapter Ten

My clients could be divided neatly into two groups: friends and boring, the latter occasionally bordering on foes. I attempted to vary the monotony of my words in my meeting follow-ups. Some clients welcomed a little light-hearted banter in their exchanges:

"Hope the weather is turning spring-like there in Helsinki/ Cape Town/Sofia. It's tipping down here…"

With others, prattle of any sort other than business, was a definite faux-pas. And, as seemed to be happening more and more frequently, some clients were taking it upon themselves to send their own unique follow ups, unnecessarily complicating everything.

As for Steph, her days were largely taken up scouring dating websites.

"What about this one?" She was in stitches.

What was the point in looking? The ill-fated, prêt-a-love men she was asking us to rate were being ripped apart based on looks alone. Nobody's opinion would be taken seriously anyway. Only Piers' bit on the side, was qualified enough to give advice on whether any of these guys were designer, rich and golden enough, that her friend should adorn one of their arms.

"We really don't have time for staring at online dating sites, Steph," I said, frustrated at having everybody's train of thought interrupted for the hundredth time.

I hardly dared look up from my computer for the sheer volume of emails, but also because in hindsight, I knew I could have worded my outburst a little more sensitively. From the icy silence that hung in the air, I sensed my statement had been a bit red rag, but heck I may as well carry on now I'd started.

"We've done nothing but mark men out of ten for you these past few days. Why don't you just go with your gut? It's not like we'd be with you on the date, it's what you think that counts."

"Okay then, I will. What do you know anyway, stuck in a tired life-sentence of a relationship?"

"Hey, that was uncalled for—"

"Truth hurts sometimes, Kate."

"Okay. I see where this is headed." I rose from my seat and placed my hands on my hips, despite Steph's desk facing the wall. "We've clearly had too much time in one another's pockets. You can pick on somebody else for a change. I...I... need to grill Sharon over these seemingly non-existent new titles for Frankfurt, anyway. I'll leave you to it."

I stormed out, extremely annoyed that anybody except myself dare analyse my relationship. What business was it of hers? Unlike Steph, at least I could hold one down.

Production communication was something to be carried out in writing, on the phone at a push, but face to face, that usually equated to desperation. Damn Steph. Now I had the thrill of The Peacock's cutting remarks.

Sharon Peacock's inadvertent criticism and instantaneous dispatch of disparaging emails to her blue-checked-uniformed production boys (a bunch of groupies headed by Gary) who sat before her like a clan of limpets bowing down to their Goddess, was somewhat notorious. With their matching shirts, opinions and coy giggles, her underlings were the epitome of a herd of sheep. I could deal with her one-to-one, but give Sharon an audience and she revelled in her role of headmistress, orchestrating her little puppets, petrol to an otherwise clapped-out old banger.

"Oh it's nothing, private joke," she'd say with upturned mouth amidst the brouhaha of female-pitched cackling.

Of course I knew different, it was bound to be something about my choice of outfit that day, my hairstyle, or both.

But there was no getting away from it. It really was time to see Sharon in person. Passing Daisy in the kitchen as she patiently waited for her nettle tea to infuse, I had only to ask once and she kindly agreed to come along as my source of moral support.

I knew I was setting myself up for a fall in my striking red, cut above the knee, figure-hugging dress. But it was tasteful, conservatively covering me up to the décolletage. Gok would approve. Whereas the same definitely couldn't be said for the tame cotton shirt Sharon had sucked herself into, the tell-tale signs being the stretches under the armpits and the expanding gaps between the buttons, which retracted with every titter. Mind you, even this was a slight improvement. Not so long ago she had a thing for those tragic animal jumpers; the jet black market-stall ones embellished with bits of glitter and holograms of wolves.

"Adrian's decided we're re-jacketing these to present them as a new series." Sharon shoved a pile of omnibuses at me across the desk and continued to type as I stood like a waitress.

"But that's illegal," I said. "We can't sell something again in the same market, just because it has a new cover: the content's exactly the same."

"We can and we will. You'll just have to work with what we've given you." She sighed in the manner of an extremely wooden actor. "I've got enough other stuff going on; foreign rights do not take priority."

This was a new one on me from The Peacock. This was hankering-after-a-fight talk.

"Okaaay, I can see I'll have to take this up with Adrian," I said, hands on hips for the second time that morning. "If we don't have enough new material to sell at Frankfurt, we won't make our budget, simple as. I'm only trying to ensure that our side of the business contributes in its full capacity."

And then I partially regretted my words. I seemed to have the knack for irritating people today, in fact, taking Daniel into account, every day.

"We're all trying to do our jobs, Katherine!"

Before I could find any further ammunition, Adrian shuffled in. He made himself at home beneath the supposedly minimalist brightly coloured canvasses hanging on his wall. Maybe the less is more effect would have worked, had it not been for the overbearing world clocks which had all run out of batteries, and his infamous shot at one-upmanship graduation portrait that forever baffled the passer-by. Through all the sweat and swotting, he must have visualised himself hanging on that wall someday, his strained smile baring the teeth of a dog; a constant reminder of his IQ to Big Brother. Perhaps I was missing a trick in my own home.

"How can I help?"

Bubbles of laughter abounded. At first, it seemed the production boys were in cahoots over Adrian's stray cowlick. But it didn't take long to figure that Sharon must have sent a flurry of words about me. Unperturbed, I opted for Plan B, wondering why I hadn't chosen to do so sooner.

"Right then," said Adrian, "that's settled. You can have your own budget and commission your own projects. I'll discuss the figure with Rupert and confirm it by email."

"Seriously?"

"Seriously, if you can make me more money, I'm all for it."

Daisy and I jumped up and down exchanging high fives.

"Yes," I cried, looking in Sharon's direction and adding a slightly pathetic 'woo hoo', once the moment had decidedly passed.

One-up-woman-ship!

Chapter Eleven

It was a wonder we had a stand at London at all.

Gary, ever the expert at finding a reason not to be at his desk, had sensibly ducked for cover as Jason had given the un-friendliest of the two possible 'V' signs to the 'trumped up git', who'd repeatedly turned them away from the VIP car park in their shiny white van. But Jason was having none of it. He'd driven to a nearby fancy dress wholesaler, returning a couple of wigs later, so they could attempt to get into the Olympia exhibition hall again.

"Ee'll never recognise us this time," he'd apparently cackled wildly, whilst the trembling Gary obeyed the orders of She Sells Sea Shells DIY man, placing the ginger mop on top of those perfectly parted curtains.

But it didn't quite have the desired effect, and they'd found themselves and van relegated to the far-side car park, shunting frames and arches into the hall for several hours in the rain. The experience had left Jason with a nervous energy that either needed to be dissipated, or threatened to end the show before it had even started.

I had always been drawn to London, I could picture myself working there – someday. I knew it was more than plausible, having twice been offered a position in the Big Smoke. But my sense of duty to remain within an hour's radius of Glastonbury, no matter what opportunities glittered after graduation, put paid to that. I often pondered how my life might have turned out had I been allowed to take a different path. I'd felt equally excited for Daniel and all the opportunities he could have had to make those big bucks he'd always dreamt of on his beloved stuffed animals, as well as his Tobys; cutting out the middle-men who wheeled and dealt his stuff onto the London markets anyway.

"Our lives are here, in Glastonbury," he'd said, as I was hunched over the stove one evening attempting to make risotto without burning the pan. "If you love me, you'll not keep pushing this further."

Defeated, I'd continued to ladle and stir.

"I don't see why you have to put London on a pedestal all the time. It's nothing but a shitty, overrated rat race at the end of the day, all those good-for-nothing ex-public school boys in their suits, and the big wigs dashing about on th'ick sweaty tube."

I loathed the way he accentuated his linguistic mannerisms once suitably riled up. Farmer-talk made him sound dense; made me wonder what I saw in him.

"You've got a good life here. You still get your travel bug catered to, what wi' work. We're off abroad – not through my doing – I'd rather see a bit more of our own stunnin' country, but still, we're off on foreign holideeys a coupl'a times a year. What more do you want from life?"

There was no point harping on about it, he'd made it clear.

The train broke to a halt at Paddington returning me to the present. This was where my book fair officially began and ended. I was two different people stepping off, and then back onto that train again. In a moment I would emanate the highly spirited Eartha Kitt in that infamous black and white Catwoman-esque pose: *The girl has hit the town.* Yet on departure, I'd have about as much get up and go as a sloth. For as much as I'd hoped and dreamed, I hadn't quite been whisked off my feet by my elusive soul mate. Better luck next time.

Being here all over again gave me a keyhole glimpse into the buzz I'd have on the doorstep of the shoebox I'd rent. London in my twenties, it just felt so right. But it also paralysed me with fear. And first I needed to rectify things with Daniel, make him happy again. Beneath the bitter layers, there was a compassionate man.

In another couple of years, when I have a bit more publishing experience, then I'll bring it up again, I told

81

myself – and when I'm a size eight, just in case he does end it. Life was always going to begin when I'd slimmed down to that Magical Eight.

Confined light struggled to stream in through the fleur de Lys archways of the station. I could have hailed a cab, but opted for the tube. I wanted to be one of them, a local, and sighed with a sense of belonging. Here I was just a number weaving my way in and out of everybody else. Nobody knew I had been the most unpopular girl at school. I didn't go around wearing that badge like my clothes.

I finally reached the Hammersmith stop then headed straight for the hotel reception, careful to avoid the social trap of the open-plan bar. The receptionist confirmed I was the sole member of She Sells in residence. Well, the others were cutting it fine then. I got an alarming vision of conducting everybody's meetings on my own as I crossed the foyer to the lifts balancing folders and bags like a circus acrobat. I quickened my pace upon spying the bearded pervert who had consistently 'undressed' me and Steph every morning in the dining room during last year's book fair. And then the hostile key card to my room delighted in playing silly buggers, illuminating any colour but green, resulting in a return trip to reception, fortunately pulled off once again incognito.

Once I'd eventually carted myself and my belongings into my new abode, I smiled with the realisation that I had the monopoly on the mini bar. I extracted the solitary bar of chocolate, stashing it away for personal consumption as the week rolled on.

Steph was on unusually good form when she did show up, all smiles as she laid her case on her bed and began to unpack. As was now becoming a polished routine, she'd met a new man Saturday night.

"What's his name then?"

I tried not to appear only half-interested.

"Dave, Dave Difford, I think he said. Bloomin' lush, although his nose did get in the way now and then—"

"Woah, too many details there, Steph…"

There was only one thing worse than when Steph was after her eponymous dream man: the replaying of their first encounter over and over. Shame on anyone who forgot the first drink he bought her or the song they'd sucked one another's faces off to. My chocolate guilt evaporated in a haze.

"C'mon, I can't face spending the evening in after such an amazing weekend – no offence, Kate."

"None taken," I said, mentally scrubbing off the tea tree mask I'd intended to trowel over my face before an early night.

***

We honed in on a Cockney boozer a few streets away, all good fun for the first couple of rounds. We'd even been chatted up by some fairly decent looking guys.

"So, you're a publishing exec? Ooh, very posh, did ya hear that, Kris? We're in the company of some seriously educated ladies."

"You're doin' a show down at Olympia? Yeah, I reckon we'll be able to come over on our lunch break. Greg and I have, ahem…what you might call offices down the road. I'm sure we'll be able to take off an hour or two, treat you both to an afternoon champers up on the landing at that snazzy bar."

I revelled in the attention. And I'd hardly made an effort tonight. Steph though, was still lost somewhere in imagination with Davey D.

But by the time we'd emerged from the basement loos to indulge in round number three, it was to find ourselves in a perilous brawl. Quite what had happened in the five minutes we'd been absent was unclear, however we were now smack bang in the middle of a Tarantino film set involving the guys we'd been drinking with. Men of all ages, shapes and sizes, flew in all directions, fists clashing mid-air, beer glasses hurtling.

"We've got to get us the hell out of here." Steph said the obvious.

83

Except the doors were blocked.

"Hey, watch what you're doing!" I screeched at a heavily tattoo-sleeved punter who'd accidentally banged into me, causing me to take the brunt of an airborne pint.

Steph smirked.

"And you can stop that too," I said, wiping beer from my cheeks. "I could've been glassed there."

"Sorry, honey. I know that was out of order." Steph struggled to control the lines at the sides of her mouth. "It's just…you're looking more rat than woman now."

I threw her a look of disgust.

"Come here, let's get ourselves back down to the bogs and dry you off."

Steph linked arms with me and led the way as my previously neat braids dripped into hops-infused witchy points.

We were met by a gaggle of women (and a couple of token men), who were livid at the way their innocent local had been sacrificed by a group of cocaine dealers. Sisters in arms, they led me to the dryer, coiffeuring me as best they could, whilst Steph continued to unhelpfully howl with laughter. She'd better not be filming this on her phone for a certain TV show, was all I could think.

I thanked everyone for their generosity, and then at their advice, we chanced upon making our escape through a fire door, up some ropey iron stairs and out onto the pavement where it was lashing it down; transforming me back to my former rodent-like glory.

Sirens began to roar in between the raindrops. As we turned the corner to the front of the building, Decent Looking Man One and Two were being arrested and marched into the van along with a number of other suspects.

"I guess we won't be toasting over bubbly tomorrow," I said.

Country life and cocoa curled up next to Daniel really didn't seem so bad an existence.

***

Bleary-eyed expectant queues waited in that patient British way to be let into the showground. Some had evidently started a little prematurely on the social scene; their wave of optimism was touchable.

Steph and I had now been joined by Daisy. We were greeted by a sea of book fair stands, where the customers would soon become boats, bobbing about, mooring themselves up every now and then to fish amongst the rich – and not so rich – literary pickings.

"I'm not 'appy" Jason also greeted us as we sashayed our way down the red carpet, making our way to the stand. It was a worryingly large one this year. Goodness only knew how it was being funded.

"Nice to see you too," said Steph.

I was glad this was a lightweight exhibition for Daisy and me. Steph was already stressing over her packed schedule.

"It's twat features over there," said Jason. "And he was doing it all day yesterday too."

The guy in his sights was circling our stand, as would a vulture regarding its prey. One of the most iconic characters in kid's publishing, he reminded me distinctly of The Penguin from *Batman*. Like a child poking with a stick, he was revelling in his role of wind-up merchant.

Knowing how Jason's mind operated when he was suitably charged, everybody made it their business to distract him.

"Hey, Jase, have you seen those new games of 'Snap' we've been told to try to flog?" Steph decided market trader language might get her there quicker. "Who in their right mind is gonna buy 'em? The lids don't stick, the cards look like they've been made from tracing paper, and the design absolutely sucks."

"Yeah, they're awful all right. We had a load in the ware'ouse last mumf, doubt we'll shift any of them," he said in a trance, unwilling to take his eye off the target.

"I'm gonna swing for him in a minute. Th'ick bloody Desmond, or whatever his name is, prancin' about on our stand like he owns it. How dare he come onto our premises stealing our *ideals*!"

But Dudley Finch continued to pick up books, turning them over cover to cover with the kind of false disdain that spelt plagiarism.

Daisy went next. I wasn't surprised. From the corner of my eye, I swear I'd seen her tearing down a board from the back partition wall.

"Help me, Jason, quick; the shell from our logo is hanging by a thread."

"Why's it doing that I wonder?" Jason glared at Dudley who was now rummaging around car boot sale style. "I bet ee's bin knockin' into it, the utter cheek. Sorry, Daze, but he's doin' my 'ed in now. Me and Gary had a run in wiv him last year on set-up day as well."

I'd heard about that. So the rumours were true then. Holy moly! It hadn't ended prettily.

"Want some more?" said Jason, louder than was the social norm at a book fair.

Dudley took the threat as his prompt to evaporate a little too late. Jason had already seized a skipping rope (the latest idea in Henry's plans for 'diversification' being the retro toys range), jumped him from behind and flung it around his waist in a manner which took me straight back to primary school and playing horses.

"Ger' off me!"

"Ger' off? What part of the world do you come from?" he jibed. "Pass me a piano book, Gary."

Gary hovered, unsure where to look next.

"I said pass me the piano book."

Gary did as he was told. Jason raised it high in the air; an over-enthusiastic child about to belly flop into the pool with a float, he aligned the chunky plastic keyboard with the bald patch on Dudley's head.

Clunk.

"Ouch. There was no need for that. I'll call security."

"I am security, former bodyguard for the Lakota club in Bristol, mate. Now piss off out of here. And if I find out your new projects have even a smidgen of a similar design, God 'elp you."

Nobody was more relieved at the finale of the drama than I was. I had visions of the stand being obliterated in one fell swoop. It was never wise to cross Jason, no matter what one's status in the hierarchical chain. Every male in the company had worked that out in lightning speed the evening he'd challenged the twins to an arm wrestle on hotplates at the local Thai.

Most of the work arguments hinged on the book fairs, none more so than being assigned to the 'lowly' task of packing up. Sid in particular used to morph into frog persona, purposely setting up meetings instead.

"Can you pass me back those books, Sid? I've got to box the stock up to go back to the warehouse."

"Fuck off, I'm having a meeting," he'd shouted in front of his entourage of male Indian clients.

I didn't welcome the buckling at the knee reaction it brought on, something I'd assumed was only inclined to happen at home. None of the others had been about, and not one of those men had stood up for me.

I'd chuckled silently as Sid pilfered a Rock-a-bye Baby book from my hands, oblivious that his very behaviour was re-enacting the historical background of the nursery rhyme, which served as a warning to those who put themselves upon a pedestal that, in the end, they were bound to fall.

Then having delayed us by at least an hour, he sped back to Bristol in his company Mercedes, leaving us three girls – who could've all quite neatly squeezed into it – to hail a cab in the torrential rain at rush hour. The queues outside the fairground were monumental. Skirts were rolled up creatively, a case of desperate measures or pneumonia.

I'd downed two giant whiskey and oranges when we finally made it to the station.

"I am going to kill him when we get back."

That was of course if I didn't get slaughtered first. He didn't have to face the wrath of Daniel for being late.

It wasn't quite the pinnacle of beatings when I did reach Glastonbury, but he definitely let me know it wasn't acceptable for him to wind up on the doorstep of his mother's house, begging to be fed in my absence.

I wanted to lift up my top and show him the bruise where Daniel had repeatedly pinched me – and could have done for the following twenty days, such was the marking. I could barely bring myself to look at Sid from that day on.

And what was it with the males of the company turning to pathetic book fair slush? If they weren't gormlessly crowding a non-celeb Z-lister promoting her latest omnibus of revelations, they were darting after the heavily 'papped' Page Three Girl as we'd left *The* saintly-diamond-stained-glass-windowed *Ivy* after dinner. Then the men were full of praise for my ingenious choice of venue. Oh yes.

It was no stereotype to say most of the company's males tripped themselves up with the slightest of effort, falling neatly into the wolf-whistling builder category; the crowning glory of which had to be chez Peter's.

Steph and I knew what to expect. Well, kind of. At least we'd assumed the lap dance and topless waitress side of things took place well behind the red velvet curtains. Silvia had been with us then. She'd chatted animatedly in the taxi all the way there, no doubt imagining we were heading off to a sophisticated London bar after our pleasant dinner; a couple of convivial drinks to round off the evening. Clad in black polo neck and sensible cream mackintosh, never had a woman worn so many clothes at *Stringfellows*.

"You're 'avin a laugh," the Spaniard retorted to the doorman at his twenty pound fee to hang her coat, which she insisted on keeping firmly buttoned to the throat.

A haze of stunning ladies with curves and contours in all the right places shimmied across the floor, bearing trays laden with meagrely-filled glasses, leaving as little to the imagination as their outfits. A clone of Peter Stringfellow (we assumed it must have been his cousin) busied himself patting a derriere here, adjusting a bra strap there, whispering sweet nothings into the ears of some, air-kissing others. Males in business suits straddled high stools at the bar, some having lost the ability to coordinate mouth to glass already, caught up in their very public fantasies.

Henry looked decidedly out of his depth.

"This is disgraceful, Sebastian. How could you bring us here, especially when we're out with the ladies?"

"What, d'ya mean, Hen? You knew the score," said Sebastian, who'd flown over especially.

"I absolutely didn't."

For once, I thought Henry probably meant it.

Adrian was a statue, his eyes twinkling like we'd never seen before. But it was our German client, Hartmut, who came into his own. He'd been a little on the smutty side throughout dinner, the wine always seemed to encourage those eyes to direct themselves mid-way up a woman's physique. He whisked off his tie in no time, fashioned it into a lasso and attempted to lean seductively against the bar to round himself up a flock of buxom girls, all the while sporting the most obsequious of grins.

For Silvia – who was now more than welcome to keep her beloved German sales market, thank you very much – enough was enough. She stormed out of the club, an extremely anxious Henry trotting along behind.

"I have never been so insulted."

"Me either, Silv. I had no idea, promise—"

"Don't you fucking 'Silv' me. Get me a taxi back to the hotel immediately. What kind of a man takes a woman to a strip club?"

A heated husband and wife-like argument erupted onto the streets of SoHo, possibly the only time I had felt sympathy for Henry, who was verbally mashed.

Steph and I, satisfied we too had fulfilled our own curiosities, were not far behind, although Steph couldn't resist a quick call to Sid. He and Piers had pulled their usual swanning in and out of an exhibition with great importance stunt.

"Uh, are you sure that's wise, Steph?" I tried to snatch the phone from her hand.

"Mate, none of this is exactly going to stay under wraps. Might as well give the office a head start…"

Chapter Twelve

"I've handed in my resignation."

"What?" I almost dropped my latte mug. "Because of the…you know…the Stringfellows thing?"

9.01 the following morning and the entire office had been au fait – Chinese whisper-au fait – with the evening spent in Peter's bar. Poor Silvia would endure weeks of jokes and taunts.

"No." Silvia shook her head. "I mean, yes, of course that was the night I totally lost my respect for those effing Boyles. But it's not just that. I'm a highly educated *madrileña*. I can't work with this chaos any more. I have my reputation to think about."

"Oh, I see," I said. Clearly Silvia felt I had some way to go to reach my own, that Glastonbury wasn't quite up there with prestigious Madrid.

Three years to the day, I'd been a lost soul. What would I do and how could things possibly carry on? I'd sensed something was up when I'd been taken out for coffee – and cake.

I'd love to call her a Churro, a Spanish Windtorte or a Yema. But the sad fact of the matter was Silvia never ate cake. Ever. So if the C word was involved, it was sure to be serious, for Silvia would never condone the use of anything sugar-coated, other than to soften a blow.

"I'm having a baby."

"I'm having another baby."

"There's no pay rise, Kate. I'm sorry, the twins say there isn't enough in the pot, but…do you fancy doing Warsaw Book Fair this month?"

It was always the same cafe, same cake – carrot, because

at least something in it was healthy – and same comfy sofa.

I knew I had to get assertive quickly after Silvia had broken her latest piece of news. The chances were Henry and Adrian had some very whacky ideas about the future, and who would be sitting on that departmental throne. I needed to intervene quickly, remind them I'd coped miraculously during both of Silvia's maternity leaves; times when just about every delivery had screwed up. There was no real difference, except this was permanent.

But I would miss Silvia too. For all her quirks, for all her boquerone and gazpacho lunches, and for all her outbursts of 'what a pavlova' and 'let's get this out of our hairs' what I hadn't been taught by that powerhouse of a woman, simply wasn't worth knowing.

Still, I purposely allowed things to get a little more slapdash under my care. Everything mysteriously became a little more productive that way. What did it matter if a customer's carton markings arrived a week late? And would everything really come to a grinding halt just because the printer had sent uncorrected blueprints again?

A new laissez-faire way of running this multi-million pound department was essential. It was that or a breakdown. No amount of organisation was going to change the workload of the factories or speed up a Spanish customer in those last throws of Costa del Sol daydreams before they shut their office down for August. Since I'd attached my very own pair of oversized dream catchers to my office windows, I'd felt strangely reassured that things were being taken care of in the vast, incomprehensible, invisible realm.

Not long after Silvia had left and my prayers had been answered in the form of Daisy.

And not long after Daisy had appeared, Daniel had been whipped into a sufficient enough fury to slap me across the face, push me on the couch and threaten to smother me with the brand new furry *Habitat* cushions…as my African wood-carved Three Wise Monkeys looked on.

Well, with the exception of the 'See No Evil' figurine.

Perhaps it had something to do with my pay rise.

Chapter Thirteen

Celestial light streamed through the clouds in perfectly diagonal lines revealing a patchwork quilt of farmland in every shade of green and brown, as the plane peeped through the slots in the giant cotton wool balls to begin its descent. I never quite understood how Warsaw was nestled amongst it.

Taxi drivers approached new arrivals outside the airport's entrance. Curiously, they always seemed to drive everyday cars devoid of cab signs. Oh well, I'd just have to take a gamble again, head into the sunset with the closest definition of a normal-looking Skoda driver.

But when my selected chauffeur and I hit the city and belted back out the other side, I feared I'd made a costly mistake. Why couldn't I 'do a Daisy' and stick with good old public transport? It dawned on me I knew nothing about the man to whom I'd entrusted my life. He probably didn't speak a word of English, nor I a word of Polish. My pulse galloped as I tried to cajole him back towards civilisation.

"We're kind of going the wrong way."

"Yes, I know. There was big traffic, just wanted to avoid any hold ups."

"Yeah? Well don't worry, this is company money. I can pay you one hundred Zloty, please let's go back to the city…"

Somehow, after many minutes which felt like the longest of my life, *The Bristol* slowly came into sight as we neared Nowy Swiat's iconic hotel. I'd definitely be getting the bus or train back to the airport, no matter how many muscles were pulled in the process. I tipped the driver heavily, grateful to be alive.

This was exactly the sort of incident I'd stopped recounting to Daniel. He'd never been one for my accounts of dodgy men. Not long after we'd met, I'd had the misfortune of a double weekend of drama.

One Friday I'd decided to lay flowers on my grandma's grave. I always drove home at the end of my University week, since Daniel wouldn't entertain us spending a weekend apart. Trailing behind me from the main road to the cemetery, off the beaten track, was what could only be described as a man possessed at the wheel of a pick-up truck. By the time instinct kicked in, I'd reached a T junction where I did a speedy U-turn, followed swiftly by my pursuer. Fortunately for me, quite out of nowhere, an oncoming motorist was driving so leisurely, that I'm sure in hindsight he was a road patrol angel.

I flagged him down, and the lunatic behind me span an instant one hundred and eighty degrees; fumes billowing, rubber burning as he vanished into the ether. I only wished I'd had the gumption to memorise his number plate, for the reality was: the women before and after me, they might not have been so lucky.

By the following weekend I'd just about stopped sweating, yet I started to wonder if I had 'victim' printed across my forehead. A customer approached my checkout with his shopping while I was doing the Sunday shift at work, repeating my name over and over; just a bit of light-hearted banter it had seemed...that was until the crazed fanatic came sprinting across the empty car park at 'clock off'.

"I don't mean to scare you, just let me have a chance. I thought we could go on a date; get to know one another properly..."

"Help!" I shrieked. "Help!"

What would you know? Once again, some invisible force must have been looking out for me. A couple of elderly gents appeared from nowhere, I guessed they'd heard the wild bellow of my lungs.

"Oy, leave the young lady alone!"

Sprightly they may not have been, but their warning was deterrent enough, sending him scarpering into the abyss –

well, behind a hedge and beyond.

"Oh, thank you. Thank you," I cried.

"Not a problem, luvie. Now mind how you go."

From then on I took them at their word, minding how I went, everywhere I went. In fact, I simply grew scared of going anywhere alone, day or night. I wanted Daniel to jump in his car, to stop at nothing in the hunt for the men who'd terrorised his precious girlfriend.

"It's all in your head," he said, one eye on a giant bag of salt and vinegar crisps, the other on picking his toenails. "Why would anybody take a shine to you in that hideous work uniform anyway?"

And so, for argument's sake, I too had agreed. Perhaps I had imagined it? Maybe he was right? It was a totally unflattering uniform, as far as uniforms went.

***

Far better to sell off the Warsaw stock than truck and sail everything back to England, I decided, as I queued to spend the profit on a return train ticket to Krakow instead.

The previous year I'd squandered it on a coat and boots in one of the department stores opposite the exhibition. At least this was a little more cultured. Okay, it wasn't technically my money. But that long sought after pay rise three years after I had not only kept the foreign rights department afloat, but transformed it into an ever thriving part of the business, left me peeved. All I was really doing was evening things out. Plus, I'd call in on a shop or two, check out what was hot in the Polish book trade. In any case, my frivolity was nothing compared to the time Sid ordered two hundred pounds worth of shots (shots which nobody wanted, shots which remained on the flippin' table) in a Frankfurt bar.

After the drabness of Warsaw, the countryside unfolded to reveal cherry blossoms marching up and down the rolling fields. I drank in the views of farmsteads, animals and pastures. I tried in vain to imagine the trumpeter in the tower. I hoped I would catch him just as he blared out his pomp, and if I could do so whilst sampling whatever Krakow had to offer in the way of coffee, cake – I'd heard the *prierogi* were out of this world - and people watching, all the better.

Lest as the endlessly picturesque parade of photo opportunities sped by, it occurred to me that it was becoming impossible to ignore the progressive feeling that something wasn't right.

On paper I had it all: the hardworking boyfriend, the sprawling thatched cottage with country furnishings to match, a degree and a sports car. Then there was the joint disposable income permitting three foreign holidays and a city break every year, and the career that sent me around the world. So why was I so unfulfilled, so desperate for the attention of every moderately good looking man? Daniel reminded me constantly that I couldn't do better than him, that nobody else would put up with me. Surely I should just be thankful for what I had and come back to my senses?

But I was insatiable, continuously on the hunt. I'd drive top down in my cabriolet (weather permitting, and sometimes, weather not), lapping up every opportunity for mirror contact. On foot or at the wheel, I sniffed out pedestrians, on-coming drivers, males stuck in traffic jams. Nowhere was off limits when you were seeking out an affair.

Even on the short stroll from car park to office, I'd check my reflection in every shop window. And my make-up bag took pride of place in the ladies' at work, so I could perfect myself every couple of hours, keep that wretched oiliness at bay. Occasionally somebody would remove it, report it as 'lost property', rendering my palms sticky, labouring my breath. I would have to choose my time with care to snatch it back from the harbour of reception, where the do-gooder had placed it for safe keeping: thanks a bloody lot.

A Waltzing Matilda ring tone invaded my daydream.

"Mrs P, how the devil are you?" its recipient answered, before quietening his voice.

I don't know many Aussies, but crikey, did it ever sound like Sebastian. I shook my head and smiled. London this year had certainly been a tamer affair without his influence.

My make-up nightmare soon had me rummaging around in my bag, checking I really was armed with mascara and friends. Phew, yes, there they were; I'd learnt my lesson.

Since there was nobody sat at my side, I couldn't resist a quick peak in my super strength mirror, just in case an unruly hair required plucking. All was fine and in place, except just as I was about to put it away, a crest of bleached locks with a mobile phone glued to its ear, was reflecting back at me. There was no way it could have been Sebastian, of course, yet I hadn't been imagining it a few moments ago, that voice coming from approximately four rows back was mighty similar. I strained to tune into the conversation but all I could catch was the tail-end of sentences, so that phrases like 'give them an ultimatum', 'in disguise' and 'I'll sort it for you' wafted down the carriage.

Ten minutes later, the train chugged slower on our approach to Krakow station and I was already up and heading for the doors, eager to prove myself right or wrong.

But Sebastian's double had vanished.

Chapter Fourteen

"You're travel obsessed. Have you forgotten you've got a house here that needs tending to?"

A Dickensian woman dressed in a coal-hued skirt, round-toed boots and an Amish shawl flashed through my mind. I was starting to realise that really was the kind of dark-age matrimonial towing of the line he expected of me.

"Sissy wouldn't play a stunt like this. She's quite happy with Tenerife once a year. You're just like she" – he meant Stella, the ex – "used to be, always gotta be doing something better than The Joneses. What's the matter with you?" he said, implying I forsake such frivolity.

"I just want to see something of the world. Mum's coming too. Dad seems fine with it—"

"Well, your mother ought to know better at her age. You're peas in a pod, egging each other on, running up credit card bills instead of saving for the future: our future. You ought to be thankful for what you've got here." He out-stretched a finger, almost spinning full circle to showcase his material goods. "You've got it all ass backwards, I'm tellin' you. New York isn't real life. You'd better get used to things being very different when you get back." He laughed sadistically. "I've had to put up with enough of you buggering off."

And so Daniel wasn't exactly thrilled at my flash of inspiration to spend a long weekend in The Big Apple to celebrate my twenty-sixth birthday.

"A hundred and ninety-nine quid for a return flight, you say? That'll buy me a fence."

I tried in vain to convince him that it would be a romantic getaway, the perfect opportunity to spend time together; anything to ease this Rite of Passage. I knew booking the flights without his permission was a risk, a big one at that. But at such a bargain price – sadly due to nine-eleven – even he couldn't deny me the trip.

Never had the contrast between us been starker; him with his thrifty sensible ways, me with my longing to explore, and penchant to do so extravagantly.

***

I'd seen it a hundred times or more on the silver screen. Now I was there in the flesh starring in my very own movie. Even as the aircraft taxied to its resting place until the next flight shuttled passengers back to the less exciting side of the Atlantic, I could already trace the Gotham outline of that great city through the condensation of the porthole. America had always been the place other people went; well not anymore. After years of dreaming, I'd finally made it.

We'd set out with good intent ordering oatmeal for breakfast on Tuesday, but by Wednesday we'd gotten into the swing of pancake stacks drizzled with glistening, woody maple syrup and washed down with not one, but two and a half coffees – the po-faced waiter would insist. Just heaving our lethargic bodies out of our booth and across the chessboard diner floor past the shiny chrome columns and back onto the hurly-burly of the streets was an effort. Each of us would become so engrossed in the eavesdropping of an innocent diner's conversation; all those entangled lives beginning their days with a hearty breakfast, or a skinny latte.

For four nights and five days, New York waltzed, quick stepped and pasa dobled with me. Maybe cities were supposed to be effeminate, but New York was a definite male in my book. He spun me around until I was dizzy, yet still hungry for more; he took the lead and exhilarated me. Come the neon-bright lights of sunset, he wined and dined me, pouring me glammed-up, hourglass Piña Coladas at *The Waldorf Astoria*'s bar; making me promises I knew he would keep if I chose to call him home.

Yes, the glitz and glamour of the American Dream lived

up to all of its hype. We succumbed to all things touristy and pre-requisite; The Statue of Liberty, Empire State Building, Macys, and the over-priced but essential horse and cart ride around Central Park.

I pictured myself arriving as an immigrant at historic-laden Ellis Island, gazing up in awe at that great female icon of the free. The appeal of starting a new life, albeit bewildering, was evident in the black and white photographs housed in the island's museum. All those brave unshackled souls quite literally left everything familiar, most without anything guaranteed to go on to. No job, no home, no family and no friends. I regarded them from my present day stance with more than a tinge of envy. They'd had the dogged determination and conviction to see their dreams through.

Later, wending our way from Battery Park and up to Wall Street, we paused briefly at Ground Zero. Both of us were divided as to the appropriateness of viewing the site, especially when the nation was so knee-deep in raw grief. But ultimately, we wanted to pay some kind of personal respect to those who'd lost their lives. The heart-warming placards and pictures shone out like little rays of light upon the dark mesh of the wire which cordoned off the senseless crater in the ground. But the bleakness, the perpetual chill in the air, the sense of apprehension, of people looking over their shoulders, was still very much apparent.

'You can destroy our buildings, but you can't destroy our foundations', read one of them. It resonated so deeply, that for a moment, I selfishly wondered if it was trying to tell me something too.

Lunch consisted of a greasy pizza slice on-the-go, followed by the gravitational pull of our clogged-up arteries to the nearest donut outlet. We were in good company. Wall Street's bankers and traders were also pigging out on their daily excess of saturated fat – well, judging by some of their stomachs anyway. They slouched in pecking order over the counter atop wobbly stools after a stressful morning of number crunching. And who could blame them? If *Krispy Kreme* was on tap near my house, I'd gladly partake after a bust up with Daniel.

New York embodied the perfect marriage of success and happiness; it didn't matter where I looked. South Street Sea Port harked back to the heyday of the city's maritime greatness; the flowing Hollywood lettering etched on Radio City smacked of the joy of holiday-time – Eggnogs in the snow, woolly reindeer jumpers, and a little upbeat Sinatra on the wireless; the Willy Wonka-esque, spring flower display at Macys was good enough to eat; and what didn't fit inside the level living spaces of New York apartments and zigzags of external iron staircases, was simply stored outside. There was a solution for everything. I'd even seen John MacEnroe rehearsing for *Saturday Night Live* on the *NBC* studio tour that afternoon…then watched it on TV hours later from just a few blocks away.

***

I was petrified to leave the gift shop at the top of the Empire State building, but so glad I did poke my head out the door and almost faint at the power of the wind and the fragility of the railings; a man was on bended knee proposing to the love of his life.

"See, anything can happen here." I smiled at my mum. She had no idea I was privately scheming to relocate.

That just has to be a sign I'm meant to live here someday. I mean, what are the chances of witnessing a proposal?

Looking tentatively down, to the left and to the right, I was struck by the Germanic organisation. Streets were lined up like a circuit board in a computer. People were ants, except here they all had the potential to become Queen Ant. The treadmill experience was virtually impossible to detect, because from rich to poor, everyone had blind faith in their own American Dream. Everyone knew they could make it, right? Even at Times Square, I could sense the throng of pedestrians intuitively exploding into one cheesy, mass show-stopping dance at any given moment where everyone – me and Mum included – just happened to know the moves.

100

That's how enchanted I'd become. And I wouldn't have batted an eyelid if the giant toy soldiers guarding *FAO Schwarz*'s store boogied along too, commanding the ruthless banana-yellow cabs to an abrupt halt.

On the penultimate afternoon we'd gone to watch none other than *the* Antonio Banderas on Broadway. I had to pinch myself. This was all so surreal; me, Plain Jane Kate Clothier, seeing a Hollywood icon in the flesh. Daniel, who'd no doubt have half his fence erected already, seemed so insignificant.

I ran out of film on my disposable camera just as Antonio's hypnotic-self posed for the perfect snapshot spread across the bonnet of a car a mere three metres away.

"Not to worry, we'll come again." Mum winked.

Melanie Griffith emerged from their stretch limo, hands on hips, one of her cowgirl legs tap-dancing away impatiently.

I felt a mutual affiliation with Antonio just then and couldn't help but wonder who was wearing the trousers in this relationship? I supposed most women would have to be the same, married to The Beautiful One. My chest puffed in and out releasing the sadness of coming so near yet so far, and Antonio gave us a final wave before being escorted away by his wife.

I tried not to think about the fact that I too, would soon be back with my decidedly less glamorous other half.

***

"Those eyes of yours, they're perfect, darlin', but if you use some of this purple mascara" – yeah, along with the seven other products you've already convinced me I can't possibly live without – "it'll bring out that gawgeous hint of hazel in them…"

"But I look like an owwaal," I complained to Sandy, almost forgetting myself and impersonating her American twang.

"But honey, it's good to look like an owwaal."

They trained them well with the chat-up lines in the Beauty Hall at *Saks*.

Still, maybe Sandy had a point. Longer lashes to flutter were all the better to hypnotise the right man with…just as long as Daniel didn't notice.

In New York it seemed anything could happen, after all. The question was: could I be that brave in my own life?

Chapter Fifteen

The house was empty when my parents dropped me off from the airport. Daniel was still at his Sunday auction, hadn't come in until just past midnight with yet another box full of jugs and a hideous stuffed guinea fowl. We exchanged the briefest of greetings at dawn as he left for the farm; one clocking on, one clocking off.

I couldn't help but think it was strange that he'd let me get away with it. I'd been expecting some kind of recoil. Stranger still, he hadn't noticed my pretty bird of prey eyes as he'd dressed for work – then again, most of the mascara was smudged across the pillow.

Maybe he's loosening up, I thought cheerfully.

And then I spotted the Times Square peanut butter chocolate I'd bought him, relegated to the top of the swing bin; a statement that spoke louder than words.

'Waste not, want not," I said, as I broke myself off a generous chunk.

To be fair, he had remembered it was my birthday. He'd left a card slanted against the TV, two hundred pounds stuffed inside with a spider-scrawled statement:

"Buy yourself something nice, luv Daniel."

It was a lot of money. Certainly there was a credit card bill it would go some ways to covering. But where was the warmth? A wrapped bacon sandwich would have contained more sentiment. On the bank notes, her Majesty's and Charles Darwin's heads and shoulders seemed to rise and fall in mockery:

"We're only money, young lady. What the Dickens did you expect?"

Switching on the computer instead, I scanned the seven

hundred and thirty-nine messages of my work inbox. But all of them could wait.

I trudged upstairs to the bedroom, snuggled under the duvet; birthday treats, remote control and celebrity gossip mag to hand. The latter would go perfectly with the *Jeremy Kyle* debate about the mother who'd been accused of having an affair with her daughter's boyfriend.

Hours later and half in slumber, I wondered if I'd really heard the front door slam or was it just part of my dream. A pair of military drumming, steel toe-capped boots quickly revealed the answer. Holy shit, I hadn't predicted him returning with this vibe.

"What the hell do you think you're doin', you lazy cow?" Daniel bellowed upon reaching the doorway and viewing me at my leisure.

My jet-lagged brain woke with a start, working overtime to hatch an excuse for eating *Maltesers* in bed. There were more appropriate places for a sugar blow-out, I'd grant him that, but I'd crossed several time zones, and generally, on a birthday, anything was meant to go. His nonchalance angered me at first, but I soon thought better of retaliation.

"I'm just having a birthday chill. Want one?" I offered up the half-eaten box and popped another of the chocolates in my mouth as if to justify my inactivity.

But he was already on the bed, yanking me by the hair with one hand, the neck with the other, and smashing me down onto the Turkish rug – as pointless as a postage stamp cushioning my face against the jaw-breaking wooden floorboards. My words became melted dribbles as I tried desperately to force something out to save myself. Shiny chocolate balls cascaded in the air, before spilling across the floor, rolling off with an agenda of their own.

How the wheel of fortune could turn. A day ago and I'd scaled the heights of the Empire State Building. Now I found myself squinting face down at oriental carpet patterns, until he'd flipped me onto my back, cupping my throat with his shovel of a hand, and all I dared look at was the uneven plastering around the alchitrave. This really smelt like the end. My pulse was all over the place.

"I've had a guts-full."

Hoping his words would calm him, I chanced to quickly glance at him, but all I could see was that deranged pulse of his pounding his veins, rendering his temples cartoon-like. It only served to heighten my desperation. He was foaming at the mouth, eyes locked in a degree of white rage I hadn't quite driven him to before; something altogether more unhinged.

"D'you hear me? I said I've had a guts-full."

Yeah, I heard him. And I'd had a gut-full too. I feared his next move, imagined myself clicking my heels together twice in a fleeting *Wizard of Oz* inspired moment. But it did nothing. The Dorothy in me may have been ready to go home, but Kate was still in the room.

His hands pressed tighter and tighter around my neck, so that I had to fight harder to win my breath. He knew I was slightly asthmatic, wouldn't have the advantage of hearty lung capacity.

'Beg for mercy and surrender. Beg for mercy and surrender. Beg for mercy and surrender…'

A tiny voice – I guessed it must be my 'higher self' since discovering 'she' existed in a recent personal development book – clamoured to be heard. It seemed ridiculous. I was sure it was just another part of my brain somehow diverting, panicking itself into inventing a last resort coping mechanism, but I certainly wasn't in a position to dismiss it.

Over and over it whispered, growing slowly louder, more assertive, until it became so deafening, I feared Daniel could hear it too. I was desperate to cry out the words I was being told to put into practise. If only I could persuade him to loosen his grip. Kneeing him in the genitals crossed my mind. It might spare me in the short term, but would surely finish me off in the end.

The wisdom of the voice took over again. It was almost screaming:

'You'll survive this one with his hands at your throat, but it'll be the last. Next time he restricts your air flow, he will murder you. Promise you'll never put yourself in this position again. Promise you'll get out.'

It was definitely the worst I'd ever suffered at his hands, which were squeezing ever harder. I had to agree with this mysterious voice. How naïve had I been, thinking I knew the limit of his games? I didn't know him at all; his mind was a labyrinth on acid.

"My f...fault, so...sorry, love y...you..., c...cook you st...steak for tea."

Oh dear God, save me, I prayed in my head hoping somebody up there would be tuned in to my particular plight, amongst the excess of heinous things currently going on out there. I wasn't ready to die today. Life was just beginning.

'Hang in there. He'll stabilise soon.'

I knew I couldn't be imagining this voice now. I'd never have said the word 'stabilise'. I quickly came to feel I could trust it – whoever and whatever it was. Even in my sudden life and death situation, I'd quite like to stop and have tea and cake with it. Actually, yeah, tea and cake would be nice.

'Well, just keep thinking tea and cake then, Kate. Visualise yourself sat down with your favourite cake, a cuppa in hand. All is calm, all is well. It's like I've said, he'll stabilise soon. He's scared himself he's taken it this far, you see...'

I did as I was told. I closed my eyes, concentrated hard and imagined myself in a Cornish tearoom, pouring fragrant lapsang from a flowered teapot, even though I couldn't stand the way it coated my tongue. And the ritual of cutting that Saffron Bun into bite-sized chunks, that was helping too. Perhaps I could kindle his interest by saying I'd do some housework, I thought as I saw myself tucking into a morsel.

'Anything's worth a try,' said The Voice.

I wasn't sure how much longer I had, how many seconds remained before he exerted that extra surge, cutting off my oxygen flow – regardless of The Voice reassuring me I'd survive – until there was nothing but darkness, and whatever happened thereafter.

How dare he play God like this, deciding if I'd live or die?

I was an intelligent woman. People like me didn't get

themselves caught up in stuff like this. But it was too late for questions. The one thing, the only thing I hadn't thought to say before; the thing I had never ever wanted to say to him came out of my mouth:

"I n…need to be a h…housewife to you…"

"Come on, spit it out, woman."

"I…r…realise th…th…that n…now."

"Yeah? Bit late for that. I might just want to finish you off, haven't quite decided yet." He laughed, relishing his dictatorship.

"I…pr…promise I'll ch…change if y…you g…g…give me one m…m…more ch…ch…chance."

My teeth chattered the words. I closed my eyes again, tried to blank my mind. I had no idea what was going to happen next.

Seconds passed and I felt him loosen his grip. I could have sworn it was solely wishful thinking. But one by one, his fingers and thumb really did uncurl themselves. I peeped through my eyelids, taking in the disgust on his face.

"You're not even worth my effort," he spat at me, before stomping out the room, leaving me strewn like an abandoned toy.

'Told you,' said The Voice. 'Now leave.'

The relief was instant, even if there was no guarantee the torture was over. So was the pain. It seared inside causing me to hack away in agony. What had he done to my windpipe?

I heard him rushing around in a stupor downstairs, pulling phone lines free of sockets, bolting windows and doors. My spine tingled. I was locked up with a madman on the loose. How foolish I'd been to shun suburban life.

Gingerly, painfully, I heaved my weary body upright; scared to sit in case he should freak out that I wasn't playing dead and repenting adequately for my sins, yet petrified too to stay lying still. What if he thought I was feigning injury, making things look worse than they were?

Whatever I did and whatever I said, Daniel always knew the way to twist it. He was King of manipulation. I could only hope this interval was giving him chance to reconsider his next move, for fear of his own destiny; one behind bars if it went any further. Surely, even he in his vehement state of mind acknowledged that.

My primeval instinct was to run for help. But where was the escape route? I'd had one for every room in the house – some unavoidably resulting in a broken leg – but now they were all useless. It was all very well in the early days when he was still living at home. I could threaten to scream then, or dangle one of his blessed bulbous-nosed jugs out the window.

I'd have to be a contortionist to get out of here, I realised in full on horror movie terror.

Even if I managed to secretly call the police, what could they do without proof? The marks had probably started to fade from my neck already. They wouldn't arrest him, not without witnesses. Heck, what he'd done wasn't even a recognised crime – he'd actually have to kill me for that. It wasn't as if Clover could stick up for me, telling them it had happened to her as well. They'd simply caution him; a little slap on the wrist sparking even more outrage.

"We'll have no more of this nonsense," he said, stepping a little too calmly back into the room. He'd been so quiet creeping in like that, I'd almost screamed.

I hardly dared to breathe, let alone reply.

"You'll do well to remember: you're nothing without me."

I pretended to let his words de-sensitise me. I had to be an actress from now on, let him think he was in control. I could finally see through him, see the way that he'd brainwashed me all these years.

"I didn't hit you, anyway. You haven't got any marks, it wasn't anything serious. Don't go all quiet on me, giving me the guilt trip. You're making this out to be a lot worse than it really is."

I supposed I ought to agree, let him celebrate this apparent gas-lighting victory, purely through fear of retaliation though, nothing else.

"Yeah, I know," I managed in a gravelly voice.

***

I woke the next morning to the smell of freshly cut grass. The buzz and hum of a lawnmower lulled me back into a trance-like sleep; the kind blissful lie-ins are made of.

And then I remembered.

An acute discomfort struck my head. My throat was arid. I couldn't have had a drop of fluid in over seventeen hours, was famished; empty after the pool of tears I'd silently wept into my pillow. It was all coming back to me now. He'd left me to 'think on' about my behaviour while he de-camped to the living room. He may as well have locked me in the bedroom since he'd made off with the master key to the window, putting paid to 'any silly ideas' of tying sheets together to make a fireman's pole, I supposed.

I'd been under house arrest for hours now. It was nine-thirty in the morning – according to the alarm clock anyway – and who knew what he'd done to that?

Oh my God, I haven't even called the office.

An eerie noise hollered up the stairs, disrupting my theories and thoughts, bounding along the narrow corridor to the bed.

"I'm off then," it said. "Unc wants me in a bit later today so I've just cut the grass…Now then, I don't expect to find you lolling about in bed all day. This house needs a thorough clean, and I'll be wantin' me tea be six sharp. We're all forgotten about, what wi' last night's stupidity, aren't we? Don't go doing anything you'd regret. Phone work up like a good girl, fake a sickie today and get yourself back on track. You were bang out of order. All you got was what you deserved…and you were lucky cos' some men wouldn't have stopped at that."

"Wanker," I whispered, in case he'd bugged the room. Then I laughed pitifully (as soon as I had visual proof that his van had driven him far enough away, despite all the correct and corresponding sounds). He was the ultimate technophobe; I could have said Arsehole, Fucker and Twat besides.

I hobbled slowly down to the kitchen. Banana Bread called (after the most life-giving litre of water), the perfume of over-ripe fruit and vanilla whisking me back to the safety of childhood; party-strung, pastel-hued bunting; a time and place of all things good.

Sugar-fuelled, I spent the day cleaning. There was something quite cathartic about it today, like I was physically removing all traces of the virtual mess I'd got myself into, because who would believe such a far-out story anyhow? His behaviour in front of family and friends was exemplary, I acknowledged, as I sprayed polish along the windowsill. He was revered, idolised for being the charming, hard grafting gentleman. Heck, if my grandma could knit a pattern for the dream man, it would be him. He made people laugh; he outwardly expressed his support for me – well, to my side of the family anyway. He was sensible, careful with money and oldie-worldly. He even kept hens. All of this and the term 'wife basher' didn't quite go together.

"What a rare young breed in today's fast-paced society," they'd say.

Only I saw the gender inequality and discrimination, I realised, as I buffed up the wooden frame of his trio of stuffed rats, determined as always to avoid eye contact with the disgusting creatures. Only I spotted his stern eyes darting across at me in a crowded room. Those looks had a language of their own, as damaging as any fist.

Chores completed, the computer beckoned. It seemed to want to show me all the flats it had for rent in Bristol. I wasn't sure why. It was a crazy, crazy idea. But I whiled away a couple of hours anyway clicking, mentally storing figures, terms and conditions. I wondered if this was how it started for Shirley Valentine when she planned that trip to Greece. It wouldn't be long now before I too, started talking to The Wall.

He'd petrified me yesterday. I'd continued to tell him what he wanted to hear when he'd returned to the bedroom, forcing out conditioned sentences like sandpaper against my throat:

"I'll put you first now, babe, career and travel second."

I had to outsmart him, rely on my ego now the

110

enlightenment of whatever that was had disappeared.

Those eyes had been so sinister last night. Seeing me like that when he'd spent all day exerting himself, clearly piqued. That wasn't to say the past events hadn't been hideous enough in their own right. He'd bitten and kicked, punched and slapped, pinched and restrained. He'd lobbed various objects inducing various degrees of pain. Perhaps if Mother Nature had given me more of a helping hand when it came to my memory, I would have left him by now. But only the tiniest of flashbacks intertwined so that all I could recall of historical events was an isolated lunge, or a solitary punch extracted from autopilot moments locked in time.

Funny too how the air magically cleared itself after a particularly tempestuous session; whenever he realised he'd tipped me dangerously close to the edge, whenever his head wasn't cloudy with the urge to be violent, I noticed he would sweet talk me into oblivion.

Indeed that's exactly how his return on this occasion played out.

"Let's go on holiday. Anywhere you like. How about a cruise?" he said, not long after he came home from the farm.

He couldn't be serious? Not after the brute force of this attack.

But he was.

"Here," he said, depositing a holiday brochure on my lap. "I want it all booked up by the weekend. Get choosing…"

Chapter Sixteen

The next Saturday he rose with the cuckoos; another Young Farmers' meeting for him and another round of stuffed animals to dust for me. But I could hardly contain myself as I over-enthusiastically waved Daniel off; home alone for hopefully a copious amount of hours. First though, I really needed to whittle down my in-box. I'd hardly made a dent in it since New York.

My usual routine would be to raid the cupboards, fridge, or both, to see what little nibbles I could find to keep me company. But I opted instead to nurse my lukewarm cup of tea, somehow firing up the computer without it made me feel semi-naked, a smoker in a pub in the 'good old days' without a cigarette.

At first glance it seemed empty, just a few round-robin messages from printers, which were unnecessarily involving an increasing number of company employees. I scrolled through them quickly, frowning where applicable at the highly strung-out excuses given for delays. Then something caught my eye: an email from Hayden.

I recalled the jesting we'd shared Friday morning over the legendary Jorge Pacheco, whom he'd sarcastically dubbed 'the most important man in Argentina', in a bid to trivialise the supposed haughtiness of one of my clients. It was something I could definitely see his point of view on, yet naturally, I would always side with a company who'd put in a large order and so expected delivery on time. I wasn't sure if it was just my imagination running wild, but Hayden really seemed to enjoy catching me out, going backwards and forwards with a tide of remarks lately. The messages tended to fly in at the end of the day, a bit like the last bulletin on the news to end things on a lighter note.

What was also notable was the way he seemed to prioritise replying to my utter nonsense, whereas Daisy and Steph often had to press him day after day for answers on urgent enquiries. Granted, he'd been a bit of a wonder to me during that trip to Singapore with Steph, but that was a couple of years ago now, the quirk of a time and a place.

His sudden attention gave me a glow. Quite why, I'd no idea. The guy was hardly your conventional pin-up. The baker in me would assign him Gingerbread (minus the icing); sometimes crisp, sometimes chewy, with that unexpectedly doughy on the inside personality. He was a spicy bite, almost always pulling off the shrewd businessman gig, except when he relaxed enough to undo those currant buttons and let his resemblance to actor Will Ferrell come out to play.

Indeed, it was getting harder to deny that I was – just a little bit – charismatically attracted. *Enigma* playing on the stereo in the background hardly helped. Before I knew it, I was typing back to him in response to his need for a deep powerful massage to help soothe his ligament injury.

"I could do that. I have very healing hands, you know. Then...maybe one day, I'll let you give me a massage in return...in the bath. Lots of bubbles...whilst I seductively pop cherries into my mouth..."

I read it back, howling at how terribly mushy and promiscuous my message was. Then I deleted it.

Five minutes later, having resorted to half a Chocolate Brownie for courage, I was at my desk again, reviving the very same overly-suggestive statement. I put it down to the current Martha Beck Self-Help book I was dipping in and out of. I'd become ever more curious about them since hearing The Voice. And since Daisy, of all people, had loaned me this particular read which recommended I take a risk every day, followed immediately by a reward, I decided in my case, if I really did go through with this utterly mad idea, the treat would have to feature before and after the deed.

"What's the worst that could happen?" I said, checking all around in case Daniel had secretly snuck back in and was hiding in the corner, ready to throttle me. "Hayden will think I'm a little crazy, true. But he was the one who embarked on all of this. He's blatantly trying to instigate the subject of a massage here. Why else would he mention his need for a 'deep, powerful' one? He must fancy me just a bit... On the other hand, I do have to work with the guy, although thankfully we're on separate sides of the world. It's not like it's ever going to turn into an office romance. Oh sod it. You only live once, no point in reading this book and not practising what I preach."

SEND

"Oh bloody shit, what have I done?" I rolled my head back to stare aghast at the ceiling then twirled non-stop in my swivel chair in a state of disbelief and nervous laughter.

There really needed to be a cancel button to retrieve provocative messages as they soared off into cyberspace; a kind of last chance are-you-sure-you-really-wanted-to-send-that key for blithering idiots who'd got too carried away with the fact they were hiding behind the mock shield of a computer screen. Would I ever have said any of this in person at the photocopier, or queuing in the communal kitchen waiting for the kettle to boil?

Would I, heck!

I was supposed to be a professional, and now I'd just committed the ultimate faux pas, tumbling headfirst into the pitfall of sharing more than just my office-based frustrations. At least neither one of us was superior to the other – although Hayden would beg to differ. Yes, we were equals, and to me, that made it ever so slightly more acceptable, as I clung to anything for an excuse.

The entire weekend was spent pacing. Just what would be facing me Monday morning when I switched on my computer at work? Why did I have to put myself out there like that? It wasn't as if I didn't have enough drama to contend with. What if he let it slip in conversation? Or worse still, by way of a forwarded 'Hey, check this out...did you realise how easy Kate is' type email to Gary, or one of the other production guys? I'd committed a sack-able – and at

114

the very least, disciplinary – act of wrong doing.

It wasn't the first time something like this had happened though (although the computer-based scenario was a new one on me) because three years after Pierre in Lyon, came Marco in Frankfurt.

"Stay away from Marco, he and Sara have a mutual thing," said my boss at the time, Diana. Although, whatever this thing was, it appeared solely to be happening in the space between Sara's ears.

But Marco was no cookie cutter heartthrob. If he meant losing my job, frankly, this man was a risk worth taking; that one more last fling before my impending nuptials, something I'd become increasingly unsettled about since Daniel's cousin had got hitched at the tender age of twenty-two. I shuddered at the memory of Daniel's mother grinning and announcing:

"It'll be you two next."

Justification aside, Sara – my colleague in my first publishing job – was in a very different situation to me altogether; married with three young boys. Plus she was older, presumably wiser. She shouldn't have been fostering these feelings.

The chemistry with Marco was palpable and there was nothing I could do about it. He was, quite simply, Boston Cream Pie; layer upon layer of lip-smacking exquisiteness. He was also a marketing exec – by all accounts a bored one – having joined the family business after college. Based in New York, but Italian born (the son of a fading but wealthy politician), his Manhattan twang crossed with mellifluent, Italian, dulcet tones, was utterly compelling. This sudden surge of attention came as a gargantuan and much needed bolster to my self-esteem. Well, surely I had changed then? Surely I was no longer the misfit of my school years? Pierre could take his chocolate bar and frankly shove it somewhere unsavoury.

"I bet you're an amazing sales woman...sell me this..." his eyes danced with mischief, clearly thinking other very naughty things as he handed me a risqué-titled: Teddy's

Bedtime Stories book.

I was speechless, unfortunately not colourless; a flush of hot pink staining my cheeks like some kind of ground-breaking blusher.

"I hope you're coming out tonight?" His tone was insistent, his words fact.

I barely recall how I'd replied.

He slipped his number under my folder. And I almost tripped on my chair leg, before shuffling my notes in preparation for my next meeting, trying in vain to look business-like, anything to disguise my giddy fifteen-year-old self who longed to jump up and down on the furniture.

"Call me," he said. And when no one was looking he whispered:

"I don't want to be stuck with the oldies on my own every night…"

As luck would have it, Diana did announce we'd be going out that evening with his company. Suddenly I was petrified. Not only did I have no idea what I was going to say to him, I also lacked the necessary industry jargon for such an event. And to top it off, this was my virgin encounter with Greek cuisine (the package holiday in Crete all those years ago hardly counting).

I spent the evening pretending I couldn't feel his muscular thigh doing overtime against my hip; a brief interlude here and there when he stopped to pour me more wine, or to look deep into my eyes, the pupils of which must have expanded to reveal moons that could seduce the most reluctant of werewolves.

Then as dessert was in full flow – the sweetest and nuttiest of baklavas – and the company had become ever more lively with the promise of dancing (and who knew what else) to follow, The Interlocutor dragged her chair over to our side of the table, creating a wedge between our intimacy. Sara proceeded to flaunt Marco a reel of almost identical snaps of her three sons, which he did a very decent job of expressing interest in. Then, sensing the way events could pan out, she announced to me in particular that we should, "All be having

116

an early night: no dancing mid-week."

I, quite the grounded teenager, had no choice but to concede. Sara may not have been my boss, but she was also too high-profile to disagree with. It was an incredible disappointment, but even I acknowledged that I needed time to think. There was no doubt in my mind that Marco would stop at nothing to pursue me, and of course I wanted to reciprocate, but I had a boyfriend back home. He was good to me. He loved me. He'd spent so much money on me over the years. Everybody could see that. Sleeping with Marco would be a betrayal of the greatest kind. Up until now my adventures had seen me entangled in nothing more than a kiss, a little fooling around. That was one thing. But sex, pure unadulterated sex; that was quite something else. I needed to be sure about this because there would be no going back once the deed had been done.

The following morning I was sure. His intent to undress me, to have his way with me right there and then in the aisle of that great football-sized pitch of an exhibition hangar, as I queued for coffees for Sara's clients, sealed my fate. I went into limp ragdoll mode; limp ragdoll with a pulse of one hundred and forty beats a minute.

"See you tonight," were the three words he whispered into my ear.

And he was right; I didn't see him again until dinner at the Steak Haus.

This time however, Sara made certain to be in charge of the seating, positioning herself conveniently next to Marco, grinning incessantly.

The footsy was slight at first, slowly building in intensity and meaning. I sensed little trickles of pleasure flowing from my feet, ever and steadily upwards. It certainly felt like this was emanating from Marco's expensively-heeled feet anyway, but who knew? Whoever was doing it was clearly well-rehearsed.

I thought better of returning the compliment, just in case Sara was trying to catch me out with her stilettos, or worse still, the senior print rep with the handle bar moustache sat the other side of Marco. Chancing upon my 'lover's' direction for a cursory glance, he licked his lips, and I knew without a doubt. The tender-crumbed lamb in its glorious red-currant jus, jammed itself obstinately in my throat, wasted on me in more ways than one. I reached out panic-stricken for some water, before all manner of spluttering could ensue, retaining my grace and composure once more as I dared to smile back becomingly.

Like a toddler with a first set of cutlery, I played about with the various courses all evening, pushing them around the plate. Getting food from fork to mouth was hopeless when you were concentrating on the serious business of being turned on. His self-certainty and intuition paled all former encounters into comparison, marking the end of my vanilla experiences; I'd reached graduation.

After much speculation and wrangle as to how the bill should be split, Marco was, an hour or so later, holding me extremely close on the *Maritim Hotel* dance floor.

"I want to do really bad things to you. You know that, huh?" he whispered insatiably into my ear, brushing my neck just a little with his lips, leaving me in no doubt as to how delicious a trail of kisses would feel when he planted them there later.

"And I want you to, too. Really I do...but I have a boyfriend. I shouldn't even be dancing with you. You're a dangerous man—"

"And what of it? I don't see him here, do you? Nobody gets hurt. I'm leaving for New York in the morning, baby. It would be a crime not to spend the night together. Who knows, the world could end tomorrow."

A temporary fear set in, which kind of helped to mask the incredible cheesiness of his pulling technique. I wasn't sure I was cut out for all this male attention, much as I craved it. I'd always enviously watched other women handle these situations with ease, but I was still struggling to get my head around the apparent magnetising effect I was having on someone of Marco's calibre. Maybe his eyesight was failing him? Could it be he was seeing some embellished version of a Kate instead? What if he 'did a Pierre?' The increasingly likely thought of him casting his eyes over my naked body was positively stomach-churning.

His calm pursuit left me under no illusion that this was more than a glossy performance. And like any of his women past, present and future, I soon put my inadequacies to one side. If I did have some inexplicable lustre about me, well, I couldn't help it. Resistance was futile. I was Lilliputian putty in his hands.

Sara's grin had become a scowl, even if she was pretending to engross herself in the after-hours chat of the printers. She signalled over to Marco, as if harbouring a boat to shore.

"I'm leaving now, Kate," she said, suddenly portraying herself as quite the sensible retiring boss. Since Diana had already gone back to the hotel, I supposed that technically, she was.

"Okay, are you sure? Take a taxi, won't you?"

I had a lot of respect for Sara on a professional level, even if the hierarchical power games sucked. She'd really got my back up after my request for a pay rise was declined, the money – and the rest – paying for her brand new company BMW instead just a couple of days later. But I still didn't want her walking all that distance alone at night.

"I think I'll stay actually…"

I hoped against hope she'd be reasonable. It was obvious I was enjoying myself.

"Marco will walk me back," said Sara in a ha-didn't-see-that-one-coming-did-you kind of a way.

"Great idea, I'll come back now too, I think," I said, double-crossing her. Sara was furious, her attempt at being a killjoy hanging in the balance.

"No, Kate, you stay. You're having such a good time."

"No, no. I really ought to follow your lead, get some beauty sleep. It's late, after all." I glanced at my watch and just about made out a time of one-twenty am.

"Well, Marco you should stay here then. There's really no need for you to escort us now we are two."

"I don't think so," Marco's voice was authority and Sara knew she'd been double-rumbled. "Let two beautiful women walk the dark streets of Frankfurt to their hotel alone? Not a chance." And he winked at me as she turned to snatch her coat and bag from the back of the chair.

The long walk was filled with awkward elongated silences and sudden attempts at the fakest of chat. But we finally reached the hotel, where Marco pecked Sara goodnight on the cheeks, in the fully-embracing Italian way he had been brought up on. With Sara's back to me, and enviably locked into his warm body, I signalled to Marco: 'Five minutes', stretching my fingers out wide in case he misinterpreted the time, 'meet you down here outside'. I hoped he was as good at reading lips as he was at caressing them. My rebelliousness shocked me to the core.

Sara remained evasive in the lift up to our floor. But I was so angry at her. How dare she continue with this nonsense? She was almost old enough to be his mother – well, technically if she'd had him as a teenager.

We air-kissed goodnight and then I waited and waited.

Finally, the sound of rainfall next door suggested she was in the shower. It was safe. I hurried back down to the ground floor and out into the chilly autumnal air; a child running downstairs to tear apart her presents on Christmas morning.

What if he wasn't there?

But my heart leapt as I detected his muscular frame leaning enticingly, expectantly, against the wall. And thank you moon light, there was no need to further enhance those piercing blue eyes. He took me by the hand and we bolted to the elevator, kissing greedily as we unleashed the desire we'd had to keep bottled over the past few days. But I was very strict when we got to the corridor of my floor. Sara was far too close for complacency; we needed to creep about with the delicacy of mice performing a ballet, contain ourselves for just that little bit longer.

***

So this was why they inserted those trademark fireworks in the films of old. I smiled in the dark, trying desperately to remember all the words he'd murmured in Italian as we'd made love, so I could look them up later, devour their meanings. And then the cruel bells of his alarm rang out at five am, waking me with a start. It was over before it had barely begun. Time to catch that damned early flight back to his life in the US of A.

I wrapped myself in my quilt and trailed it behind me like a princess for one final smooch goodbye at the door before the plug was pulled on the fairy tale.

"You can be my book fair affair," he said, stroking my face tenderly. "See you in Guadalajara, baby."

Guadalajara book fair: getting there was going to be a project and a half. Even Daniel would think that sounded a little too exotic to be a plausible venue for business.

Oh God, Daniel. How I'd really betrayed him this time.

Still, I couldn't help but flop back on the bed clutching the pillow where Marco's head had rested; gathering in the scent of him, looking forward to doing the same again that night. No way will housekeeping be changing these sheets.

Breakfast was uncomfortable at best.

"Lots of activity going on in the corridor last night... sounded a little like lovers running up and down, fooling about...did you hear it, Kate?" Sara's eyes were a power tool let loose. But buckling at her probe was not an option.

"You look tired and emotional today, sweetheart," she continued. "Yeah, you've got real bags under your eyes. Don't think I've ever seen you like this. Has last night taken its toll?"

I knew she knew the double entendre was understood. And I knew there'd be no slamming back of tequilas and romancing over burritos in Mexico. So I mentally erased the image of Marco massaging sun cream into the small of my back there and then. Pity, we'd had that rooftop pool all to ourselves as well.

"Really? I didn't hear a thing; must've been in the land of nod as soon as my head hit the pillow. Bags? Oh, I've forgotten to use concealer. Do you have any on you?" I said, almost too quickly.

The sun had set and risen again by the time I opened the front door, crossing the threshold of my parallel lives. My pores oozed guilt and reproach, lies and deception. Remarkably, Daniel didn't notice a thing.

But Sara never forgot, not even years down the line when we'd bump into each other at a book fair.

"Meant to say, Kate, I heard from Marco the other day... yeah, he's living the Canadian dream now, Banff National Park Ranger, beeeeeautiful girlfriend as well, so loved up the pair of them...I hear wedding bells...the tiny pitter-patter of —"

"How lovely for him, sorry can't stop," I'd said, marching quickly to catch up with Steph.

I'd always known our circles would never overlap again, our last correspondence taking place during nine-eleven, out of concern he was unharmed more than anything else.

Whilst I couldn't deny his devastating good looks and how the scene we'd created beneath the sheets played over and over like a tape on heat, it was what it was: a one night stand. He was a charmer; a charmer with a girl ready and waiting in every port of call, which didn't even begin to offer a plausible alternative.

And that's why I'd stayed with Daniel; tried to make it work, because he was all I knew.

Not long after joining She Sells, I even felt quite at ease telling my colleagues about my flings.

"Do you think maybe Daniel isn't the right man for you?" the office receptionist quizzed over group Pimm's and lemonade on Whiteladies Road one lunch time.

"How do you mean?"

"Ah, well, the um infidelity thing—"

"Oh that? It's nothing serious," I replied. "It's just what happens when you get together so young. Of course I'd never do that once we're hitched."

What I couldn't understand was why there weren't more people doing what I was?

122

"So, uh, when will that be? Should I get myself a hat?" she raised her left eyebrow, retrieved a floating strawberry half and plonked it into her mouth.

"Not until my late thirties. At least."

I guess what nobody understood was the flings were scientific experiments allowing me to test out his theory that nobody else would put up with me, I couldn't get better, we were meant to be together for ever and ever. Amen. Whilst the evidence to disprove him might have compelled, all my studies had so far created was an embroidered reality. Once the cheating was over, my head would berate me, whilst my heart would scream out for more.

The book fairs were balls, and me, Cinderella – well, Cinderella *Apprentice*-style. But unlike the rose-tinted version, nobody came to Somerset knocking at doors with glass slippers. Marco had simply kicked mine under the bed during the throws of passion. And so, once again, I remained a prisoner in my own home.

But what Marco had unearthed in me; that was hard to shake off. The ego had longed to gorge on him, whilst the soul silently knew he was on a pre-programmed mission from the Universe, and no amount of intervention from Sara could have kept us apart.

If I could score somebody like him, then there had to be something greater out there than my relationship with Daniel. Marco was the adult embodiment of the guy everyone fancied at school, the guy who wouldn't have touched me with a barge pole.

From then on there were various snogs and shenanigans, predominantly taking place – though always discreetly, I had to be mindful of customers – at book fairs. A tale of two cities, my entire life was planned around Frankfurt and Bologna. When else would I be surrounded by so many men under one giant roof?

Bristol may have been north of the county, but it was hardly far away enough for a little hanky-panky, although to say I hadn't weighed up some of the male quarry at work would have been economical with the truth.

Alas, all fell short, although I'd admit to a very occasional fancy to Adrian, usually only an occurrence at the Christmas party. Hell, even Gary, Sid and Henry had pricked up my antennae at certain points in time.

And then strangely enough there was Hayden, who prior to now, come to think of it, prior to that visit to Singapore, had merely glittered momentarily on the Christmas tree like everybody else.

Chapter Seventeen

Monday morning arrived too soon and proceeded to unfurl just like any other. I had even begun to think that my email couldn't really have been sent, that it was just a figment of my imagination, or perhaps there had been technical issues with the internet at home? I was convinced by two pm, a little disappointed even, when there had been no correspondence from Hayden. And then I remembered that (in one sense) I hadn't been quite so foolish after all. I'd sent the message from my personal address; nobody at work would be any the wiser.

My hands shook as I registered the reply had winged its way into my private account. I hadn't even contemplated what he might come back with. What if I'd got this all terribly, terribly wrong? What if my promiscuity had scared him off? Maybe his flirtation had been part of some hilarious pre-planned joke courtesy of the production team. There was only one way to find out:

"Next time I see you, I'll be expecting it then, Ms Clothier…"

A grin worked its way from ear to ear, catapulting my stomach back onto the rollercoaster ride it had endured all weekend. I gasped. Daisy looked over, wondering who was responsible for the latest book-related blunder.

"Oh, it's nothing. Just some more corrections to the Danish cover text for the animal board books. Should've seen it coming…"

I switched my personal email off and tried – in vain – to concentrate on the shipping issues that lay strewn across my desk. But naughtiness fizzed through my veins and I was soon logged back into my inbox.

'Your place or mine?'

And then I deleted my reply. I don't want to appear too keen too soon, best not inflate his ego.

I switched back to my work messages instead. I needed to check on the status of an order that was due to leave the warehouse in Malaysia at any moment anyway, so I decided a hint at his muscular pains as a little ps. at the end of my work-related message, would be an appropriate way of maintaining the status quo.

Hayden, it seemed, was rather enjoying playing this game. Each of us got the hang of it beautifully within a couple of days. Comments, innuendos and even mini role plays were flying from one side of the world to the other.

What had I started?

"Well...let's just put it this way: I'm glad the delivery guy has left, that little excerpt went straight to my erogenous zone... You really know how to give a man the desired effect."

As the weeks whizzed by I was finding it harder to keep tabs on the stuff that mattered. One morning in particular it occurred to me that I had not only given the okay to print to the wrong order, but directed another consignment to be shipped to Bilbao instead of Barcelona. I seriously needed to get a grip if this was going to be a regular thing. And the emails had to go through just one address, or the other.

Sometimes his something-for-the-weekend replies would be too tantalising to leave until Monday, as saccharine as pre-revamped *Mills & Boon* as they may have been.

"...I take in the contours of your curvaceous breasts, nipples erect, and I can wait no longer. I lead you to the sheepskin rug laid before the fire and make love to you over and over as you scream my name...until you are spent."

Occasionally, I'd pen something on paper at home, stuff it into my bag and then type it out first thing at the start of the new week back in the office. Even at that un-godly hour the fiction turned me on. But more often than not, his scenarios getting ever more complex, I preferred to read them over and over at home on my private computer – when Daniel was out,

126

of course.

Except one Sunday, I'd inadvertently taken living on the edge to the extreme. Daniel had said he was going to a YF meeting, but had – inaudibly – returned home unexpectedly, and not solo either; a 'friend' – who I could only assume he'd picked up from Young Farmers – was in tow. They peered at me together through the window as if I was one of his taxidermy curiosities. One of Daniel's hands shielded the reflection of the light-filled room that was streaming out at them into the garden. In his other hand he held an axe. Occasionally he sold antique tools, and must have brought it in from his van to polish up. But no matter what its origin, at that precise moment in time, Red Riding Hood was sat before not so much The Woodcutter as The Axe Murderer.

Accompanied by a buddy or not, I was dumbstruck. Did I hope they couldn't make out the font that made plain my intended deeds to my 'lover'? If I carried on typing, feigned innocence, surely he'd assume I was engrossed in the usual overtime from a heavy week of work. Or did I go with my reflex, which was to just shut the machine down before I got my head hacked off later?

I smiled sweetly over my shoulder, swivelling my seat so that it blocked the page of infidelity, hoping the 'T' signal I was making with my hands, might distract them both from attempting to squint at the description of me wearing a lacy black bra and thong with matching suspenders.

"Yes, please," said his lips. Daniel's mysterious friend gave me the thumbs up too, and I prayed to God he wasn't imparting his knowledge of my on-screen alias. I may have laid eyes on him for all of twenty seconds but dodginess emanated from his pores.

They headed toward the shed and I swiftly turned everything off and practically ran to the kettle, pushing my shame to one side for the rest of the day. Daniel was computer-illiterate anyway. Even if he did get suspicious, he could only just about switch the monitor on, no chance of him navigating my words.

But this had got too close for comfort. It was time to stop.

Chapter Eighteen

I liked to feel in control as I 'penned' my erotica – even if my fingers, hovering indecisively, about to connect with the keyboard, said something quite different. The killer heels would make an appearance, as would the seductive underwear which never saw the light of day with Daniel. Once I had even dared myself to wear my cream zip-up, figure-hugging dress, all but commando beneath.

"How can you get away with that?" Steph had asked one day, incredulous.

"Excuse me?"

"I can't even make out your knicker line."

Time to reign in my libido too.

But lately I couldn't wait to start the office day. The lyrics of *Snow Patrol* captured my feelings, propelling the car with rocket speed to Bristol. They conspired to talk to me, sending secret messages about my hopes, dreams – and torment. Or maybe it was just that I'd recently seen them live at Glastonbury Festival and was getting a little bit carried away.

I'd even baked a batch of rainbow-coloured psychedelic cupcakes for our day trip to Glastonbury – which was really in the village of Pilton. It was my first foray with food colouring – excluding my recent disaster; a red velvet, cream cheese frosted, triple-tiered masterpiece (the kind of creation best left to Steph) which had stained everything in sight. A state of inner happiness had taken hold of me, the flow of my 'art' lifting me high above Daniel's views on the world.

"If it's got tits or tyres, it costs money," he'd earlier said to Mikey, his farmer friend who'd perused me through the window.

He'd turned up to repair the ride-on lawnmower, as well as

loaning Daniel his monster of a camera so he could take pictures of his ever-increasing collection of Toby jugs for some nerdy magazine or other. Mikey had grinned with seedy eyes at that suggestion – as in your face as the assault to the palate when you realise you've bitten into a catastrophically acerbic Lemon Drizzle Cake.

"I've made them for the picnic," I said, refusing to acknowledge Daniel's look of disapproval as I put the finishing touches to the icing.

"What are you wasting time and money baking those things for?" he hissed. "You knew Sissy had sorted food for us. I told you s'mornin'. Why are you trying to get one up on her and purposely disobeying me? You're bloody obsessed with baking."

"I don't think they'll be very practical, Kate…and the saturated fat in them, well, that's not something I'll be happy to eat," snubbed his sister, Hannah, triumphantly. I followed the mirage of her voice to the hallway where she appeared like the Lady of the Lake, rolling anoraks into tight sausages. She stashed them away in her waterproof bag with more than a hint of a smirk on her face.

I'd forgotten she had her own key at Daniel's insistence.

"Hi Hannah." I decided to be welcoming, holding as steadfast as I could to my rapidly diminishing optimism. "Well, if you change your mind and get into the party spirit, I'm sure Lizzie and I won't have eaten them all." I grinned childishly.

"Don't be stupid. Sissy's gone to a lot of trouble to pack us up some decent tucker. You can leave the fairy cakes behind; do your waistline a favour. And what makes you think you're meeting up with that Lizzie anyway?"

"Leave my cupcakes behind to go stale? I don't think so. Lizzie and I will eat them while *Muse* play this afternoon, we'll share them with the crowd."

I was furious at his snipe, especially in front of his sister. I wouldn't starve myself to look perfect for him, or anybody else.

"You are not wasting money on food to hand out as

freebies to others: Number One, I don't hold wi' it, charity starts at home. And what are you doing meeting up with her: Number Two?"

I chose to ignore his first remark, heartless git.

"She has a day pass. I told you about it this morning. I'll only be an hour or so."

"What are you trying to say, my love? Now I can't remember the threads of our conversation? You must be getting a touch forgetful," he said in a voice that was disproportionately calm when one considered his accusation. "No, you never mentioned any such thing. We'll stick together. How would it be if me and Sissy wandered off with friends?"

Just because you don't have any to wander off WITH...I said to myself silently.

"But then Liz will be on her own," I said, impressed at my assertiveness. "How awful would I be if I left her there with all of the weird and wonderful festival characters? No, I arranged this a while ago."

Hannah raised her eyebrows and commandeered the pine table, laying out the sort of paraphernalia that left me wondering if we were Snowdon bound instead.

It was impossible to go to the festival without her. I winced at the unappealing salad, rye pitta bread and calorie-controlled apples she'd lined up ready to be re-packed. We were going to a festival, a venue that celebrated life, the gloriousness of being; somewhere you were meant to let go, treat yourself to freshly-cooked noodles in a box and ice cream from the *Ben & Jerry's* van, if that's what the stomach desired.

"Right, before I forget, there's a selection of anoraks here too," said Hannah.

"Ah, you're all right, thanks. I've got my wardrobe sorted."

I would not be seen dead in one of those hideous khaki cagoules.

"You'll wear it if I have to squeeze you in it myself," said Daniel trying his on for size.

"No, I won't."

This was stupid. I'd pay for it later one way or the other, but I was not being moulded by Hannah as well.

Perhaps this year's event coincided with a full moon? The temptation to rebel was somehow too compelling. I may have had to kick about with a group of people I'd rather not have, but none of them could dampen my spirits. Glastonbury was supposed to be the antithesis of conformation after all, and I would revel in that, if only for the one short day.

I disappeared upstairs to boldly braid my hair as would a St. Trinian's girl, interweaving coloured ribbon for extra effect. Then I pulled on black leggings and a multi-coloured artisan tunic.

"What the hell do you think you look like?" said Daniel, again a tad too calmly when I reappeared. But the eyes were a giveaway. He was seething at being shown up by his woman, who was comically disobeying commands.

"I'm dressed for a festival," I said. "And if I can't have the freedom to do that, I'm not going."

"Huk." He excreted something unsavoury from the back of his throat in my direction.

"You're an embarrassment to us all, a right stinky hedger."

He stomped over to the coat pegs, grabbed Clover's lead and let out a high-pitched whistle, eyes sharp as daggers.

"Walk, now."

Clover's ears unfolded themselves, her tail was alert and wagging, she trotted to his side.

"We'll be ten minutes, Sissy. I'll let her out in the field to do her business then we'll make a move."

The door slammed with a ferocity that could have, should have, shattered windows.

"Put it on, Kate." Hannah proffered the anorak once more. "You really do wind him up something chronic. It's all so unnecessary, so childish, so—"

"Do you honestly think I am worried about a little rain after the crap I have to contend with via him?" I heavy-handedly patted the sausage of an eyesore into her chest. "You are not my stylist, sweetheart. But thank you anyway for your concern."

There, I'd said it. And I'd said it like I'd never said it to her before. She was intelligent enough to translate that. She was also loyal enough to grass me up.

**

It was all a bit fake on the other hand, this being a hippy and finding yourself malarkey; a three day orgy of pretending to be somebody else because you were wearing a rainbow, still stinking of a mixture of last night's joss sticks and dope, and walking round with a 'Hi Mum, It's Steve!' banner. The confluence of the ley lines did little to silence the mobile phones, conversations about office politics, gas bills and shellac nails. So, I too could only mock myself for my ethnic disguise as I feigned adoration of track number four of one of the awful fringe bands on one of the smaller stages. It would be a wonder if Lizzie actually recognised me later.

I trooped around to wherever 'Sissy' decided we should head next, inwardly sulking in one of those fine misty rains that deceptively chilled to the bone. At times the idea of vanishing into the cosmos with a bunch of complete strangers overwhelmed me. I could easily have blended into the most unconventional of gatherings. Daniel would never have found me, and I'd have had a ready-made entourage, a human shield, for protection.

But I trudged obediently to the *Scissor Sisters* gig instead, which despite the weather and company, was one electric disco treat on a stick. I'd recently bought their album, almost worn it to dust on my journeys to work, and although most of the lyrics were far from romantic, the lilting tones left me bizarrely hankering for Hayden's touch.

"I'm off to find Liz," I said.

"Have fun." Hannah even seemed to be smiling; then again she had mysteriously permitted herself an Alcopop.

"Yeah and don't be late at the meeting point," said Daniel.

I smiled for the first time that day. My spirit soared. Even the stomach-turning whiff of the pungent holes masquerading as loos couldn't deter me.

Lizzie looked fabulous as she waited on the outskirts of the CND stage. She waved excitedly in a floppy Andalucian sunhat, lacy white shirt, cut off denim shorts and muddy wellies. We hugged and suddenly the whole world seemed to hug – or maybe it was just that I had drunk too much cider.

"Show me, show me," she said.

I panned the horizon; once, twice, once more for luck: all clear.

"Okay, so these are the latest. What do you make of them? A bit of fun, or do you see a deeper connection?"

"Hang on, Kate, give me chance."

Lizzie buried her head in the emails I'd grabbed in a fluster from my bag.

I tried not to read her body language as she absorbed the words. She seemed gripped though, now that had to be a good thing. My stomach flipped as I waited for the verdict, taking in the sea of tents all around and the ocean of people ebbing and flowing before us. The Tor reminded everyone to look south west every once in a while, taking stock of the mysticism and beauty surrounding the music, mud and drugs.

"Aw, it's pretty poetic," she said, before sinking her teeth into my vivid cupcakes and giving them the thumbs up, "but I still don't understand what you see in him." She stifled a giggle.

"Hey, he has got a certain something…and bucket loads of charm." I felt myself melt at my own words.

"But what if Daniel finds out?"

"He won't. It's just a bit of harmless fun anyway."

"Really? Hayden's words make him sound rather smitten. I'm not sure he ever came across to anybody like that when I worked at Sea Sells, I mean She Sells…"

Good, I thought; right answer. Although I kept it to myself as I later made my way back to the others via a bin.

***

Radiohead were up next. Their music always made me

feel strangely empowered, despite the haunting melody of 'Creep' taking me right back to Pierre's pied-a-terre. Tonight they stirred up all kinds of swirling quivers in the pit of my stomach, as I tried for the umpteenth time not to wonder how Hayden would respond to my latest message.

Hannah gnawed on an apple in a way which so reflected my pondering that I couldn't help but feel paranoid. Or perhaps my cider had just been laced with something else?

And then what do you know?

In the distance, I spotted a familiar figure rocking and rolling in the crowd. He was hard to distinguish at first, but then I realised it was none other than a totally off his head – and there was no way on God's Earth it could be by means of alcohol alone – Gary.

So that's how he spends his leisure time; who'd have thunk it?

Gary, in a rusty-coloured tea cosy hat and kaleidoscopic T shirt, it was a bombardment to the senses all right. Presumably, he was attired beneath? His torso upward was all I could make out of him in the crowd. Talk about a dichotomy: here was the absolute opposite of the squeaky clean Little Boy Blue image he so innocently transmitted at work. Then again, maybe even the school-uniformed one needed an alter ego sometimes, stepping away from convention to centre himself. It did cross my mind to take a suitably bribe-worthy snap, but as Daniel would undoubtedly accuse me of adultery, I thought better of it.

Several hours later, as I was being dragged across the kitchen floor by my hair, as Daniel's booted foot connected with my thigh and I curled into the foetal position, Matt Bellamy's caution interspersed the ringing in my ears:

"You will be the death of me…you will suck the life out of me…and our time is running out…"

And much later before sleep finally caught up with me in the spare room, Muse continued to play round and around in my head.

Chapter Nineteen

I was safe now. I was at work. Monday had come to the rescue again. The bruise smarted but at least it had come out quickly.

Thank you, arnica.

My follicles were on edge, then again, I didn't wear my hair down nearly often enough.

I switched on the cute bakolite radio for company – anything to drown out the 'leave him' chatter that was engulfing my mind with an alarming frequency. It was blissful to stare out the window listening to a faraway presenter's voice, or a soul-stirring track, putting the internal clutter to one side as the thick cotton wool clouds sped over the Georgian rooftops. Like a mother who had risen before the children to enjoy an undisturbed coffee with the papers, I revelled in this peaceful morning ritual of contemplation.

Every other day (at least) there would be an email full of flirtation – sometimes slightly more suggestive banter – from Hayden, often in response to something I had sent, but not always, sometimes he initiated too. I savoured those words from him. I lived for them. They unthawed me whilst teasing me. They challenged me and they comforted me. I hung on his every sentence and full stop, longing for the phone to ring at that early hour, for it might just be Singapore. Yet I dreaded it in equal measure, nerves causing my stomach to rise and fall, jumbling the contents of my hastily eaten breakfast.

Here in the safety of the office nest I could toy with ideas and scenarios, re-arrange and re-live them, edit and extend them, letting them linger deliciously in my mind. I re-read messages past; picked them apart and analysed them incessantly, scoured them for hidden meanings, for the three words I hungered for.

When it was my turn to let him know where the story was going next, reality would usually come crashing down as the troops marched in, forcing me to pull myself together and set a good example. But he was never far from my thoughts and nobody; nobody at all in that building knew of our secret.

I glanced at my watch hardly daring to believe it was twelve o'clock already. My stomach rumbled wildly, and I finally succumbed to the temptation I'd been successfully ignoring all morning, darting over to the fax machine and inconspicuously helping myself to a wodge of the giant Jenga puzzle of tray bakes. The cake table was fast becoming dangerous – something only I seemed to be producing the supply and demand for lately (Steph and her fancier fare having a more hectic social and love life at the moment). But lunch would be taking a backseat, I justified. It was hideously busy. The phones had scarcely been off the hook, so the latest frenzy of rings wasn't anywhere near my radar, particularly as I was also battling to send a contract through to a stubborn Russian fax number.

"It's Hayden for you," said Daisy.

The hot sensation I was only too well acquainted with these days, prickled my veins, colouring me crimson and my legs almost gave way. But not before the grainy buttery chunk of Flapjack lodged uncomfortably in my throat.

Damn.

Why was he still in his office anyway? It had to be nine in the evening there. I began to get giddily carried away, believing he had even sacrificed after-work pints, all for me; the icing on his cake.

Daisy looked concerned. I was still spluttering; red-faced and paralysed at the fax machine.

"Just a minute Hayden, Katherine is pigging out on cake and it seems we have a minor catastrophe. I'm just going to give her the Heimlich manoeuvre…and a glass of water."

"Thanks, Daze," I snapped, guzzling at the water a little too quickly, almost repeating the entire episode.

Great, what a fabulous image he must have of me now.

I skulked back to my desk, wondering how I was going to turn this on its head, maintaining at least some kind of Screen Siren prowess. I melted as soon as I heard the gravelly and suggestive intonation of his voice.

"Heimlich manoeuvre, hey? Mmm, I wouldn't mind giving you one of those—"

"Slight problems here, yes..." I said, before he interrupted me with a provocative chuckle.

"So she's sexy and powerful, sassy and beautiful, yet as fallible as us all...cake before lunchtime; who'd have thought it?"

"In the words of Shakespeare: "Tis an ill cook that cannot lick *her* own fingers," I quipped, having no idea where my quick-witted comeback had come from.

It threw him into a momentary spin and then I said: "They're my cakes. I'm quite a skilled baker you know—"

"A woman of many hidden talents it seems..." he paused for breath. "...I'm much more a savoury man; you'll rarely catch me eating anything sweet. I do have a certain weakness for cherries though."

I blushed profusely. I wasn't expecting him to bring that up.

Somewhere deep inside, right there with the receiver pressed as close as humanly possible to my ear, I knew this was as good as it would ever get with Hayden. But he brought such a new dimension to my life. In my desperation, I'd gambled my very last chip on him. Pierre and Marco, they'd simply attracted me. Their honeyed good looks and Garden of Eden temptation were mere infatuation. Yet Hayden wasn't anybody's conventional definition of handsome – at all. And so this primeval gravitation toward him went deeper than the surface, encompassing those grown-up subjects I had constantly laughed off as a hormonal teenager; personality, sense of humour, a certain *je ne sais quoi*.

Meanwhile, the further I fell for Hayden, the further Daniel was carving out 'Our Future'.

Chapter Twenty

"This could be us soon," he said rubbing his hands together as he studied the menu.

We were grouped on a table with the handful of young couples on the cruise, one of which was a pair of doe-eyed newly-weds.

I was mortified; the words Daniel and honeymoon did not belong in the same sentence.

I hadn't wanted to go, although naturally, I'd felt more than a twinge of motivation at the list of places I could get a feel for in just one week. There was something impossibly romantic about waking up in a different port of call every day – if you were with the right person that was. Still, no doubt about it, my old-head-on-young-shoulders guy blended in nicely with a mainly retired crowd, who'd insist upon ejecting one another off the coach whenever they arrived at the destination of the daily excursion – and claiming their seats with beach towels on the way back.

Then again, there was the added bonus of a cooking, ironing – well of course, I still had to master the cabin's fold out trouser press – and housework free week.

His seven days, in contrast, were spent in one stifling, drawn-out moan about all the fast-paced cities we'd visited. His critique of everything foreign was ungrateful at best.

Barcelona was too gritty.

"See how lucky you are living in the open countryside, rather than holed up in one of these shitty city apartments hanging your washing on a tiny balcony like these poor sods, looking out onto a road full of exhaust fumes," he'd reminded me earlier in the week after a whistle-stop tour.

The irony there was I'd have snapped the arm off a local

letting agent (in fact I'd already made a mental list of the Barcelona-based clients I could approach for work). I'd brush up on my Spanish, take a few intensive courses and *olé*, my new life would be born.

Indeed, the more I fell in love with each metropolis, the more it seemed he wanted to keep me in a cage like his blessed poultry.

Monaco was too stuck up.

"Too many people flashing their overpriced cars about for my liking: if you've got money, why d'ya feel the need to brag about it? Keep it to yourselves…"

And Corsica was too wild and rugged.

"Yeah, it's pretty and that, but it's all a bit excessive – and too many mountains. Th'ick there grass could do with a good mow down too."

I spent that day snapping as many perspectives of the scented forest *maquis* as I could, intermittently grazing on the coarsely-chopped pistachio and honey nougat from the family-run factory we'd just toured. I'd definitely have to 'whip' some up for our next W.I.P (Work in Progress meeting).

"No, I don't want another piece," he'd barked. "I'll pull me fillings out with that shit."

On to Florence which only triggered him to shower more nuggets of unwanted negativity.

"Tis' too pretentious here, too intellectual, you'd need a Fine Art degree to take an interest in all of this fancy malarkey."

Well I didn't have one of those either, but how could he not appreciate the architecture? And if nothing else, how could anybody dismiss that tiramisu from lunchtime? In all my Bolognas, I had never tasted anything so divine.

And then there was Rome.

"Tis' way too hectic here. How can people be expected to drive?"

The cruise's only redemption seemed to be the slower pace of The Vatican – with the exception of the thousand-odd milling tourists inside the Basilica.

Once back in the cabin for a rest, having walked several miles around the The Colosseum, The Spanish Steps, and The Trevi Fountain (where I'd kept my wish about Hayden to myself), I couldn't wait to remove my flip flops. Tell-tale red marks warned of the queue of blisters about to erupt.

I flopped onto the bed, closed my eyes and hoped like mad that he wouldn't interpret this as an invitation for any kind of intimacy, something I had prided myself on getting away with for six weeks and counting.

"I'm just gonna have a quick shower, then go up on the deck, find myself a chair and sit down with me book," he said.

Happy days.

"Okay, well I think I'll have forty winks, all that walking has taken its toll."

I was optimistic I'd also laid the foundations for an early – equally non-physical – night.

The hum of the air conditioning and trickle of the shower blended together to soothe my passage to sleep. Not before my attention turned to Hayden. I wondered if he was missing me. Maybe he was composing something right now? I was so tempted to send him a postcard. But that was too dangerous. I held his image close to me like a security blanket instead and felt myself falling into the beginnings of a sweet light slumber. But no sooner had my mind begun to drift, than an inky nebula attacked it.

At least if the violence was regular, had an ETA like my precious cargoes of books, I would know where I stood. In my typical, serpentine style, I also acknowledged a mutual pity for Stella, the girl Daniel had dated through his late teens and into his early twenties. I had always felt such a strong dislike towards her in the past. But I was realising I may have misinterpreted her revenge-filled glares at me in public after all. Perhaps they were glares at Him; glares for all the years of mind-bending, guilt and coercion.

Stella, like me, was younger than Daniel. Too young at that time to have realised what she'd bought into, and probably too scared to run; not knowing any different, not

140

realising how the dynamics of a healthy relationship played out. Ultimately, she and I, we had that much in common.

My work phone, which I had brought with me (but pleaded with Daisy and Steph to only call me on in an emergency), was ringing red hot through the inside pocket of my suitcase. I sprang to my feet to silence it, just as he emerged from the ever flimsier looking plastic door attaching bedroom to bathroom.

"Why's yer phone goin' off? What the frick's going on?" His temple creased to reveal a demonic mono-brow, catching me completely by surprise.

Water dripped everywhere forming shadowy circles on the carpet. He shook his hair as would Clover after a dip in the River Brue. I had, by now, in my newfound flustered state, fumbled around for the phone in the deep pocket. I wouldn't have dared answer it with him being so choked up about the interruption. But he misinterpreted me, assuming I was going to take the call. He wrestled the phone from my hand, pinching me hard on the arm in the process; then slammed it against the wall.

"Fuck you, you lying bitch. And fuck those morons you work for." Spittle flew from the corners of his mouth. "We're on a fucking cruise."

He crouched to retrieve the phone from beneath the bed where it had slid, and lunged at me with it firmly in his hand. His strike caught my temple with a pain so excruciating, it was all I could do to hobble to the bed, sink my teeth into the pillow and try not to scream.

"You're a fool!" said The Voice. "As if you haven't been here before…"

I shut my eyes tight and pushed them further into the pillow as I continued to sink my teeth into the fibres, fully aware that he might use this as a smothering opportunity. Yet the danger of a shriek expelled seemed to pose, momentarily at least, far more of a threat.

The last time I had to get the make-up out was the first time. He was usually much more careful about where he aimed his attacks when he threw objects.

141

Here we go again: Gadget Cover-Up Incident Number Two.

Some years back, I don't know, maybe six, or nine months into our relationship, he'd slung the remote control at me in exasperation. I'd messed up the alphabetical order of his CDs – *Jamiroquai* after *Kanye West*. Although it had smarted at the time, it wasn't until I chanced upon my reflection hours later that I realised just how visible the mark in the middle of my forehead was. I'd used half a bottle of concealer to disguise the bruising, so I could still work my shift at my part-time job.

"Had a fight down town last night, Kate?" my supervisor had asked in concern.

"What this?" I'd patted at the heavily made-up area. "Oh, no nothing like that...but I, um, I did have a few drinks, walked straight into the, uh, the fridge door when I was rifling around for something to stop the munchies... You know how these things can easily happen," I'd giggled nervously.

That was the ludicrous thing: I was sure it was a one-off at the time, just one of those things. And as he'd reasoned with me after the event, I had asked for it.

"You promised me no work while you were away, promised me," he shouted again then turned and stepped back into the bathroom, almost breaking the door with his slam.

I rocked the pain into submission and gradually unclenched my teeth. Another narrow escape, how many more would I get away with?

"Indeed, how many more?" The Voice echoed back.

Oh, just leave me alone. You don't understand.

Like a house that has been doused with burning sage, I knew, courtesy of my flippant instruction that was the last I'd hear from her: I was on my own now. I'd been bestowed with a tenderised meat look to go with my Captain's Dinner attire for the grand finale, and there were still two days left to go on what was turning into the cruise from hell.

The rest of the early evening was spent listening to the

grandiose, manipulative, needy and apologetic outpourings of love I was all too accustomed to in the aftermath of his aggression.

"I'm nothing without you."

"I love you, babe, you mean the world to me."

"I just wanted this holiday to be perfect; quality time on our own. It's not my fault I don't like sharing you with the office."

I sent him off to dinner alone, faking sea sickness – not difficult since we were in rocky waters – clutching my pillow as if it were a giant teddy bear.

I realised the one and only comfort I had to hand was hiding in the bottom of my bag: a pack of amaretti biscotti bought earlier that day in Rome. They were meant to be a souvenir for Mum and Dad, but every bite of their soft, crumbly, almond liquor-tinged centres seemed to numb his malefic reign – momentarily anyway.

***

Through the porthole window the next morning, I could make out the dinky Mediterranean windmills of Mallorca. The ship hugged the coastline and slowly sailed back into its starting point of Palma, where the impressive cathedral perched cosily above the harbour, overlooking the throngs of cruise ships. The charming cafes and restaurants were waiting to greet them and the rest of our ship's passengers as they disembarked before their transfer to their week's siesta in a four star Magaluf hotel.

I could only thank God we would not be joining them.

And the neatly lined up stripy deckchairs on the layers of our liner perceptibly stretched and elongated their frames in readiness for the next onslaught of over-zealous holidaymakers.

I could only hope they'd have a bon voyage.

Chapter Twenty-One

Santa pop-up books had already loaded their August vessels at port in Singapore, yet if I'd seen two consecutive days of sunshine in Bristol all summer it would have been a miracle. It was such a sluggish month, a time to get round to tending to all of those boring, rainy day jobs, since most of my Europeans and Scandinavians had their backsides planted firmly on sun loungers.

But whilst Hayden's recent chain of emails still had all the predictability of Mills and Boon – particularly Volume Two of the sheepskin rug, open fire, and secluded Swiss lodge adventure – I sensed he was now definitely as invested as I was.

And it wasn't just 'sex'. An underlying friendship threaded through the literary traffic. It was just like having a real physical relationship, and all the 'getting to know you' stuff that went with it – just without having a real physical relationship. It was the strangest, most ridiculous thing. Neither of us could stop. Or perhaps it was simply that neither of us was prepared to give the other the last word.

'You really are a cunning linguist, aren't you?' he wrote at the end of a lengthy exchange of Malay puzzles and French proverbs. He, delighting in showing off his moderate (it had to be said for the length of time he had now resided there) language skills.

I wasn't quite sure what he implied by the 'cunning' part, or why he seemed to pleasure in finally enlightening me. So I ran to the study that evening, car keys still jangling in my hand, and made straight for the dictionary. My heart thudded as I flipped through the translucent pages for the start of the CUNs, and despite the fact I didn't have an audience, the definition it gave for 'cunnilingus' induced rouge to my cheeks that could have been bottled and sold for millions. I slammed the book tightly shut for fear of a peeping Daniel.

I hadn't even realised there was a word for doing that.

How I wished I could re-live that summer of two years ago. No not because of this latest revelation. But because, well, who knows how things would have turned out between us knowing what I knew now.

The Far Eastern Odyssey had started out as an invite to Steph from an overseas agent; nothing more, nothing less.

"Why don't you tag along?"

"Who me?" I totted up markets and clients on three fingers. "But I don't really sell a lot to that part of the world."

"Exactly," said Steph.

***

"So this is what they mean by humidity," I'd said against the thrust of a nearby jet engine, as I'd emerged behind Steph onto the aircraft steps a few weeks later.

Singapore had greeted us like a hairdryer. And culture shock and familiarity had descended upon me with a loud and confusing bang. I'd found myself in a land where I couldn't even begin to decode the language, yet trademarks of the colonial past abounded. I knew all of this would be waiting, I'd read the guide book of course. I knew I could also expect tea-time G and T and polo, should I feel inclined, but witnessing it first hand; this blending of east and west, was so uncanny.

Home was a small, one bedroom (and one bed) apartment, nestled in a seriously high rise building on a mountainous incline in the Outram district next to Chinatown; typical of She Sells Sea Shells when it came to adequately catering for the women. I doubted Sid and Piers would have stood for this.

"Aha, it's the English ladies." A short, smartly uniformed man startled us, as we set foot inside.

Freddie had the widest and sincerest of smiles. He directed

145

us swiftly to the lift, giving the full breakdown of which floor every single button would take us to. There were thirty-eight.

"Never ever press all button at once: lift break," he said, cupping his mouth in a poor attempt to disguise a guffaw, as if he had seen it come to pass and involve the emergency services too many times.

Even on our most drunken of escapades, we would somehow manage to remember this.

When we finally reached the door to our apartment, Freddie handed us each an over-sized bunch of keys. Quite why we needed so many was never made apparent.

"Right," he said, before we had even set down our luggage, "we do demonstration now." He marched past us to the toaster. "Put bread in, press down, wait." He drummed his fingertips on the cheap-looking worktop and then shouted: "Bread pop up. Got it?"

"Yeah, thanks a lot, Freddie, I think we'll manage now," said Steph, slouching on the worktop, eyeing up the bottle of wine on top of the fridge.

"Oh, no, there's much more to show."

The trio of fans; telephone, cooker, lights, blinds, light inside the wardrobe, extractor fan, water, TV, remote control and air conditioning were next.

"Oh wow, just look at this view," I said, opening the window to take in the riot of activity down below.

"Come back!" cried Freddie. "Never ever open window, especially in typhoon, you near top floor, girls."

Steph scowled at me for I had given him the perfect excuse for a window safety demonstration. I prayed that we wouldn't be experiencing any wild weather.

Just as Freddie was about to leave – and Steph was about to dive towards the alcohol – he decided it was best to run through everything again, double checking all had been understood, further to which he insisted upon a demonstration of the correct way to use each appliance, by both of us.

A cool refreshing shower followed by a long drink at the nearest establishment could not come quickly enough. We were already late to meet Hayden.

"He's left a message on my mobile to say he's waiting for us in a bar on Club Street," Steph yelled through to me in the bathroom.

That's right, you make sure you're all glammed up first, why don't you; sink yourself into the red, and I'll go out looking like I've been dragged through a hedge backwards.

I hopped back out of the shower, pulling down the flimsy rail and curtain with me.

"Bugger."

"How much longer, woman?" Steph shouted again. "Now he's saying he'll have burger, chips and beer waiting for us; nice of him to remember I'm a veggie...and we might be there a while, apparently they're showing an England match tonight."

Great.

I de-misted the mirror with my old scrunched up knickers, re-coated my mascara, and attempted to step into my dress – something which had become nigh on impossible with the humidity already coating me in sweat again. A thirteen hour flight to endure the antics of the same over-paid and inked up, matching diamond-earringed buffoons on TV, as I could at home.

***

I detected his impatient silhouette long before we reached him. Hayden could easily have masked as a lover awaiting his fashionably late date. The evening sun basked him in a golden aura, which surprisingly enhanced his tightly-curled hair and sea-green eyes. This unexpected vision almost stopped me in my tracks – just a little, anyway – especially when it was my turn to be kissed. Had he ever looked that appealing at Christmas parties past? I mentally re-pulled last year's cracker with him, re-sensing that excessively laden with rum Christmas Pudding. No, I didn't think I'd seen him in this light before.

A market trader weaved through us with his pushcart,

balancing an impressive tower of boxes.

"Steady how you go there," said Hayden, offering him a reassuring pat on the back.

"Shouldn't you be fluent in Malay by now?"

Nice one, Kate, great way to make an impression on your host for the evening.

"I'm semi fluent…wouldn't want to upstage you too much too soon," he said adding a grin.

"No chance of that: I'm multi-lingual," I muttered, trailing behind Hayden and Steph, who were engrossed in best buddy banter already, oblivious to my presence.

Plucked from production assistant obscurity, Hayden's luck had come in five years ago. Like a toy in a penny arcade grab game, Sea Shells had honed in with claws on their latest recruit. No ties, no relationship to take with him or cut loose from. Since boarding that plane with a one-way ticket, he'd barely been back.

"Sorry, ladies, I was starving," he said, smiling widely and gesturing at the remnants of his chips as we reached our table. "I don't think I've had chance to take a lunch break all week. But I knew you'd both be homesick West Country girls, so I've ordered jacket spud and beans. Will that do you?"

"Blimey, you take us to all the best places," said Steph.

But I couldn't wait to guzzle something, anything down. That familiar zombie-rendering jetlag had possessed me already and something told me this was going to be (I wanted it to be, anyway) a long night. As ridiculous as it sounded, Hayden was growing on me, and quickly – so much so that I realised I couldn't think of a single line of conversation.

"So what do you think of Arsenal's line up this year, Steph?"

"Midfield: useless; they need a new manager, new strikers, new investors; goalie's shit hot though."

"In more ways than one I'm sensing, right?" he ribbed her playfully.

What was it with Steph and men? I loathed football, was especially loathing it right now for making me re-enact the

148

Shrinking Violet School Girl, but I was beginning to loathe Steph and her bloody timeless allure even more. Couldn't Hayden see she didn't have the foggiest what she was talking about?

"And what about you, Katherine? What are your thoughts on this season's performance?" he winked unexpectedly.

Did he just flirt?

I drained my glass of Singaporean beer, basking in the attention as the fizz worked its magic.

"I'll tell you what I think," I paused to flick my hair. "I think this is all a bit of a comedown watching football in a distinctly British pub teeming with ex-pats; we may as well be in The King flippin' Billy."

"The voice of authority has spoken." He arched his brows with a look of genuine surprise.

"Yeah," said Steph, "we've flown halfway round the world, we want to see Asia, not the footie."

"Then it seems I've been outvoted, I'd best go settle up."

The moon had apparently traded places with the sun when we stepped outside onto the street. I swayed next to Steph, already a little wobbly on my feet, half-mindful of the fact I needed to let Daniel know I'd arrived safely, but equally too half-cut to care. I was a continent away from all of that now I realised, smiling trance-like, despite staring at a row of alien carcasses hanging upside down in a traditional meat shop.

Hayden re-appeared, wedging himself between us so we were all linking arms. And I succumbed to the embers in the pit of my stomach, watching with wonder as the neon lights reverberated up and down Singapore's buildings to reveal a tightly-packed fusion of nightlife.

"You'll love JoJo's," he said, "quintessential Singer's experience. Not to be missed."

My mind rushed to Daniel from time to time as I strolled along the streets with Hayden (and Steph). The alcohol was great for shrouding reality though, and I was soon imagining we were a couple on a date, as I mentally flicked her off his other side and into one of the rowdy bars.

"I can see why you like it here," yelled Steph through the

raucous JoJo's crowd once we arrived.

A hearty outburst of Canto pop bop-bopped out the doorway and I grimaced at the skimpily-dressed girls who were strutting their stuff on the bar top, stopping only to pour yards of ale into punters' mouths as they concurrently copped a load of their cleavages.

"Go get yourselves a table near the dance floor and I'll pull in this round."

"Betcha will, you dirty boy."

I chose to ignore Steph's kick to the stomach remark, mainly because it shouldn't have had the remotest effect on me, and rightly or wrongly, I sensed Hayden would have a little more class. I placed my bag on top of a stool instead and commenced a safe side-shuffle on the dance floor (grooving had never been my thing) – a couple of arm flicks thrown in for good measure whenever an upbeat piece came on.

Yeah, so you might win hands down when it comes to the bump and grind, I thought, glaring at Steph and her rhythm; the alcoholic mix and lack of sleep somehow invoking a bizarre feistiness. But just you wait until we move onto the karaoke.

Steph beamed at me, oblivious to my thoughts, and I shot her back my flakiest smile. A willowy blonde cut past us, boyfriend – and a bag just like mine in tow, and Hayden dodged the crowd, skirting individuals and groups alike, making his way to our table, glasses bunched together like a giant posy in his hands.

I glanced over to the stool top, then back again at the girl who was fast tracking it to the toilets.

Stool top, girl, stool top, girl.

"She's got my bag, my money, tickets, passport…my make-up!"

"What are you on about?" said Hayden with more than a twinkle in his eye as he studied me. "Have a dance, nobody's got anything."

I pelted across the dance floor after the girl and tapped her hard on the shoulder.

"You must be mistaken," she said in her Canadian drawl following my heavy-handed grab of the straps, "this bag is mine. Maybe you have one similar…"

"Yeah," added the boyfriend. "I mean, there are so many black patent bags around in this style these days. Easily done though, we forgive your mistake."

They span – a little too quickly – on their heels and headed towards the front entrance to the bar leading onto the street, whose presence threatened to turn my belongings into not so much a needle, but a bag in a haystack.

It turned out that theft of the cosmetic kind produced in me a surge of energy I didn't know I had. I launched myself at the girl and a tug-of-war on the dance floor began, with Steph and Hayden somewhere in the middle, making pathetic attempts to pacify, apparently none-the-wiser as to who was the bag's owner anyway.

Finally, I seized it, only for the boyfriend to intervene.

Yeah? Bring it on.

There was no way I was letting the strength of an extra body – male or not – put me off. I continued yanking away at a strap (I couldn't quite clutch at both), contemplating getting catty, if that was what it took. As soon as it was back in my possession, I could open it up; put an end to this craziness with my passport photo.

One final tug and it was mine again.

"Oh, I'm so sorry. It was yours after all. You know, these bags they have such a similar, almost common look to them —"

"I'll give you common," I heard myself breaking into Somerset. "You're nothing but a thieving bitch."

"Give her a break, Kate. It was an innocent mistake… anybody can see that."

"Yeah, these things are easily done," said Hayden.

I sat in a sulk at the window, feeling like my fifteen-year-old self again after my brother had pilfered my entire CD collection, and my parents had refused to believe it. I slammed my glass onto the table and rifled through my things, checking everything really was still intact.

"By the way…your boss Sharon's been in touch," Hayden smirked, not before clearing the head of his pint. "She wants a daily written report from me on the two of you. Seems she thinks this trip is a bit of a jolly. Can't think what would give her that idea."

"What the fuck?" I said, as he lit a cigarette and took a deep drag.

Sharon wasn't my boss. I reported directly to Henry, Adrian – or both – whoever screamed loudest on any given day.

"I'm just passing on orders. We can always embellish a little if need be, but we'd best do as we're told."

"But Adrian OK'd the trip. There's nothing to tell, other than a write-up of the potential sales once we get back," said Steph banging her glass down now as well.

"I'll tell you what it is, shall I?" I said. "She just can't stand it that we're somewhere a little bit exotic with an excuse to put on some heels. Well, you know what? She's had her time. She's a different generation now, all married up and domesticated with her kids, cats, and mumsy jumpers. She should have jollied about a bit more herself when she was younger, then perhaps she wouldn't be so bitter."

I reached to take another large swig through the ample number of straws, knocking my glass and Steph's onto the floor instead.

"Muppet," said Steph.

"Geez," said Hayden, relinquishing his smoke to the ashtray, "you are in a pickle."

He wiped a drop of the blue cocktail from my chin and peeled back the strands of hair doused in it. I frowned to disguise my delight.

"First the handbag, now you're breaking glasses. You really don't think much of Sharon, I take it?"

"I hate her, absolutely bloody well hate her," I continued with my crusade. "She's like a Cut and Come Again Cake, or, or…an earthworm, you chop it in two but it just keeps growing and growing and…" Hayden almost spat his drink out at my analogy. "Basically, that woman owns like 0.001%

of the Boyle Empire, a grain of sand of Sea Sells, I mean She Shells, I mean—"

"Yes, I think we know what you mean. And you'll find she owns quite a bit more than that. A word of advice where Sharon's concerned: tread carefully…even on earthworms —"

"Just you let me finish." I went to collar my glass only to remember I'd broken it.

"I'm pretty sure you have," he said, attempting to disguise his laughter with a curled fist. "There's only one thing for it: noodles and tea."

He led Steph and my extremely reluctant self, next door to another of his 'favourite places'.

"It's just like being back at school," I shouted, plonking myself on a long wooden bench in the canteen, resigned to the fact that I knew too little about this city to take the customary sightseeing lead. "Except they're much nicer here than they were at my school…did I ever tell you I was bullied?" I felt I was slurring my words now. Steph's head shake and piercing of my eyes with her characteristic warning glare reconfirmed it.

"Pull yourself together. Hayden and I are going to end up carrying you home at this rate."

"And I haven't given a fireman's lift round Chinatown for quite some time," he said. "Steph's right. You can't sit there either; that's somebody else's jasmine tea, Kate."

"Oh, yeah," I said slowly inhaling the fragrance of my grandma's summer garden. I let Hayden pull me along to the opposite table, waving an apology of sorts to a puzzled punter.

'You do look after me, don't you...?' I half-told, half-questioned him, feeling my heavy eyelids flutter.

***

"You'll never know what you missed out on in the morning if you don't come back to mine tonight," I was being harassed by a pokey-nosed, Kiwi flight attendant an

153

hour later, after I'd consumed what seemed like half my weight in noodles – which admittedly did hail from the heavens – and Hayden had recounted tales of city life, pricking our ears up with accounts of staff past (and present) frequenting hostess bars.

Somehow I had semi-sobered up.

We were now in Eddie Bongo's; a lively, unsophisticated American-themed establishment, complete with disco and fake palms – the kind of place a tee-total would require an OBE in patience. Allegedly, it was also the haunt of the world's cabin crew.

"I'll take my chances," I said to the persistent flight attendant.

"Why are you so entranced by your Mr Curly anyway?" continued the Kiwi. "He has a girlfriend y'know, been telling me all about her. He's not interested in you in the slightest. Me on the other hand…"

I wasn't used to this, I didn't welcome it, neither did I think I had sprayed myself with catnip.

Flight Attendant Guy retreated like a clockwork toy on re-wind into the smoke of the dance floor just as Hayden made his way back to the bar from the gents. He turned to look for me, his eyes illuminating, just as I too sensed once again the inexplicable magnetic pull between us.

"Has that guy been giving you trouble?"

"N'ah, he's just being friendly. But on the other hand…I mean, just for argument's sake…if you could kind of pretend that we're, y'know…together, he'd probably piss off."

Hayden smiled and if I wasn't mistaken, looked deeper into my eyes. I willed my lashes to stop fluttering as I sidled closer to him at the bar, trying in vain to ignore the hint of musk, sandalwood and yes, jasmine again.

Meanwhile, Steph's silhouette could just about be detected in a cosy corner, embraced by a tall dark stranger – who Hayden assured me was perfectly kosher, and Flight Attendant Guy continued to look my way, tilting his evidently miffed head from side to side, performing some questionable dance moves to *Madonna*'s *Vogue*. Hayden,

154

arms stretched out strong and wide, obediently took this as his cue to envelope my shoulder in a semi-embrace.

So this was how it felt to be looked after.

We danced and chatted all night, as if our bond had been that strong forever. But when at last we clambered up the ski slope linking the underground bar with the outside world, I was completely freaked out. Double decker trams cut through the iron grooves in the streets ferrying early bird workers across the city, and the sun dazzled blindingly into my face.

"Fancy breakfast?" Hayden whispered so softly into my ear that I was sure I detected a brush of the lips besides his invitation.

The ungenerous splash of light did little for his pallid complexion and I guessed mine didn't fare much better either, although I supposed I couldn't have looked too worn around the edges to be at his personal request for an intimate early – or late – table for two, sharing coffee and croissants, or whatever the custom here was.

"Um," I glanced at my watch, almost on the brink of fainting – as much through shock at his sudden transformation, as weariness, "I kind of feel like the evening's over…can't think of doing anything except diving into my pillow." I yawned, initially for effect, but then I couldn't seem to stop. "I'm sorry, some other time maybe."

I tried not to detect his face falling as he hailed himself a cab, whilst I was most definitely back in a pumpkin on wheels.

***

Eight hours later, Steph and I made our way via the metro to the office, factoring in a hideously over-sweetened cookie munch courtesy of a western imitation outlet. It did little to energise, or to stop me worrying about what was lying ahead.

The best tactic would definitely be to pretend nothing had happened. Nothing had happened. Except some kind of bizarre connection, which I sternly reminded myself, must have been a figment of my imagination anyhow. I forced away dawn's stark image of Hayden's pasty face and 'permed' hairdo and, once again, he really didn't seem so appealing.

"I'll play hard to get with Miles," Steph said, recounting the details of her evening with Hayden's ex-pat friend yet again as we emerged from the MRT station at the Central Business District. "Don't want to give too much away too soon. I'll wait until you fly home, Kate, yeah that's what I'll do."

"That's really not necessary, Steph. I'm more than happy to have a night in on my own."

"Who knows, he might ask me to stay at his for a couple of nights," she sighed, the chignon holding the hair off her neck looked as fresh as if she'd just stepped out of a salon, and despite the sweltering temperature too. How could she create such an effortless look without eyes on the back of her head?

Hayden's head on the other hand, was ground down to business when we arrived; so much supposedly so, that he didn't register either of us for a whole two hours – and only then at my insistence.

"Um, sorry to interrupt, I can see you're busy but—"

"It'll have to wait. I'm working through some important figures," he interrupted me back without raising his head.

I bit my tongue to break the temptation to retort. Rage consumed me.

How dare he?

And he hadn't as much as acknowledged the fact I was positively smoking in my favourite red office dress. This sudden change in behaviour was absolutely staged, it had to be; he obviously knew he'd been a little too affectionate last night. And what a bugger, he looked good again, surprisingly good on little sleep.

Why didn't I let him take me to breakfast?

I decided to credit myself with a little significance, dialling through to Bristol for some 'business' chat. Everybody would have arrived by now; there would definitely be urgent things that needed my expert attention, hot potatoes to toss into his frosty lap.

"I'm, um, sorry to disturb you again." I'd returned to his office twenty minutes later, immediately despising myself for apologising. I was after all, only doing my job, "but I really do need an answer on these fairy tale book delivery dates for the Finns, Turks and Russians: why the hold-up at port?"

"I'll get round to calling the shipping agent."

"Can't you just—"

His phone rang cutting me off with the efficiency of a knife.

I stood speechless before him, feeling my anger rise again as he listened intently to the mystery voice, fiddling with the spiral loops of the telephone cord, swivelling his chair from side to side impertinently.

"Great, thanks very much for nothing," I managed to mumble.

He might be Top Dog in this office, but I run foreign rights, and damn him, I'd tuck this dispute up my sleeve for a few surprise fireworks later on tonight. We were all going out again for a proper dinner this time – or so he'd promised. I'd soon get what I wanted.

Just as the working day was drawing to a conclusion, I thought I was seeing a mirage: Hayden finally approached us.

"Steph, Kate: I think it's probably time you earned your keep. As you know, I'll need something concrete to report back to Sharon after Day One."

He smirked teasingly, yet only at Steph.

I can read you like a book. You've done well keeping your distance all day…but I'm going nowhere, well, until Taipei and Seoul on Friday. And tonight the wine will be flowing – or the beer in your case – you won't be able to keep this charade of yours up for long.

"And what exactly would that involve?" I heard my outer voice shake (and my inner voice retreat into the bushes) as I made it my duty to reply.

Pull yourself together.

"Well, since we're going out somewhere nice to eat tonight…and this time on the company, I'll expect you to

157

overhaul the meeting room's display cabinets...it's only right."

I burst into a round of unimpressed giggles.

"Something you'd like to share with us?"

"No, no." I dismissed his question with my hand as if his statement was suddenly completely acceptable.

"S'pose it's fair dos," said Steph.

You wouldn't be saying that if you'd been cold shouldered by Smiley Miley – or whatever his name was from last night.

I glared at Steph's perfect, annoying hair-do, vowing to take the scissors to it if she sucked up to Hayden once more.

He'd vanished already and could be seen head down once again, flipping through mounds of paperwork.

I tutted aloud and flipped my hair, just in case he looked up at that moment. And I would stick my bottom out extra seductively too while I was at it, re-shelving his stupid books indeed. Why did he find me so goddamn repulsive today? It was like working alongside a blinkered horse.

We worked tirelessly for the rest of the day, until Geraldine entered the building in the most dramatic of fashions, announcing she was 'going to kill Hayden'.

We'd heard unconfirmed reports of her diva-like behaviour before, but, wanting to give her the benefit of the doubt and assuming they'd been embellished, we had no real preconceptions of Hayden's other half. We were witnessing it now all right. Not even stopping to say 'hello' much less acknowledge us full stop, she marched into his office, where he, mid-phone call, was left with no option but to put the promptest of endings to his conversation.

"What are you doing here? I told you I'd meet you in the restaurant with the others at seven-thirty."

"I have been fucking calling you and fucking calling you on your mobile for like an entire hour, you haven't even picked it up, you twat."

Hayden pulled the door to his office to, and rolled the blind down in a pointless attempt to masquerade his girlfriend.

"My shoes aren't back yet from the repairers."

Steph let the pile of books she was previously transporting from old shelf to new, clatter to her feet. It was somewhat symbolic given the subject of Geraldine's 'catastrophe'.

"…I need a new red pair. I told you I needed the money this morning and still the transfer's not in my account. I cannot go out like this…wearing these bloody flip-flops with these pants. It looks crap. I need money. Now! I've seen some designer ones in the mall back in Orchard Road. I wanna get them, before the last couple of pairs disappear."

"Oh, right, and that really warranted me cutting short a hugely important conversation with the factory, did it?"

"If you had just answered your shitty mobile, I could have told you that already, like a whole hour ago. You're a moron. Work always comes before me."

"Geri, if you hadn't already noticed, we have visitors over from the UK office. Tone it down a bit, yeah? You're giving a really bad impression—"

"What do I care about those girls out there? They work for you. I'm your woman. You need to start treating me like one."

"Did you just?" I mouthed to Steph who had become my reflection in a mirror and was silently saying the exact same thing, with the addition of a plethora of expletives.

"Oh, come here, baby…"

Hayden beckoned to her, his voice softening in forgiveness. If I squinted I could just about make out the pair of them entwined through the gap in the Venetian blind. One white flag and all was calm again. I didn't want to think about the making-up style kiss they were inevitably sharing and returned to the job in hand.

Steph looked at me, and I looked at Steph, matching her horrified expression once more. "Biyaaatchhh," she mimed, her hands mimicking claws spitefully digging into something.

I was stunned. That wasn't cranky, or narky even. It was downright vicious. I'd go as far as to say Draconian. Bloody hell, it even made some of Daniel's outbursts look a little subdued. Hayden didn't need this woman, surely? A guy in his position with the world at his feet; a businessman, an expat in Singapore making money hand over fist. Sure, she was attractive, I had to begrudgingly give her that...attractive with a hard, edgy, unsympathetic face; the kind of trait which painted a creosote veneer over any remote beauty.

He certainly wasn't one to relinquish control so quickly when it came to business. No wonder he had warmed to me so quickly. We had listened to one other, something I was sure never went on in his excuse for a relationship – just as it didn't in mine.

It didn't quite kill me to see the pair of them together. But it did leave a nasty taste in my mouth. I reasoned it was not only because of the way Geraldine had mouthed off at him, but her querulous comments about the food, the drink, and the service, which continued to litter the table all throughout dinner. Would she have behaved the same way in front of the Big Cheeses from the factory? Henry and Adrian even?

The only mitigating factor was the news that had just come through from Daisy about a colossal pop-up book order for a German supermarket; that soon got Hayden's attention. Ha, Geraldine and her needs were momentarily on the backburner.

"So what's their absolute deadline?" he said.

"Delivery end of October."

"I might be able to push for mid-November, but no, October's a no go…"

"We'll have to put it to them. All depends on the supermarket's campaign, time-slots, that sort of thing," I said matter of fact, refusing to commit to his suggestion.

Just as I was getting into my stride, my mobile called my bluff. My hands turned to jelly, the wine and rice, and whatever else was in tonight's concoction of duck, spare ribs and spring rolls, swelled like an ocean in my stomach.

A bag this big and still I can't find a bloody thing, I cursed silently.

Desperate to hide my panic – and desperate, in all senses of the word, to create some Steph-esque 'allure' – I excused myself from the table, hoping to pull off mysterious-and-constantly-inundated-with-attention-but-wouldn't-you-like-to-know-from-who.

There was really no need. Steph had probably filled in the gaps by the time I'd made it to the doorway.

Finally, half-trotting, half-rummaging, I dodged a party of diners weighing up the offerings of the outside menu display and flipped open my phone, bringing it and my bag simultaneously to my ear in a look reminiscent of a perpetually frazzled mother of four.

"Tis me," Daniel announced.

"Hi, babe," I cringed. I would never say anything remotely like that, but I was an actress at the moment – for the benefit of point scoring against Hayden's ego anyway.

I eyed him up through the window. Yeah, he saw that. I'd throw a beamer of a smile in now…and another in approximately twenty seconds.

"Is it next Thursdee or Fridee you'm back?"

Christ, never mind smiling, the Somerset in this delivery was enough to make me laugh – hysterically.

"Neither, it's next weekend. I, um, I did write it on the calendar, as well as the diary; hope that's okay?"

"Tis'nt ideal, babe, no," he said. "But I understand. It's work. They best be giving you some days off to make up for it, or extra time pay."

"Well, um," I chanced to glance through the glass at Hayden who caught my gaze and promptly put his hand on Geraldine's thigh, "it doesn't uh…" I turned my back to him, facing the road was preferable to witnessing his grand gestures of 'lurve', and coughed the image away, "it doesn't quite work like that, but I'll see what I can get."

"Yeah, you should. They're taking the piss with your good nature otherwise."

Oh, the irony of that remark coming from him.

Right, well, this'll be costing me an arm and a leg. Cheerio for now. Love you."

"Yep, you too," I said through clenched teeth and twisted fingers which had crossed themselves of their own accord.

Despite the fact he was gone, I couldn't face sitting around

161

that table and all its fakery. So I stood watching bikes, trams and cabs hurtle past, having a pretend phone call with a pretend lover. The fumes, the rush and the onslaught of boisterousness strangely soothed; perhaps because unlike Daniel, unlike Hayden, unlike just about everyone right now, they were real.

Then I began to fret about my psychotic behaviour. This was nonsense. I was blowing a simple night out in Singapore out of epic proportion.

Fast forward a couple of hours and perhaps my paranoia was justified…

"Who's for pool?" At Geraldine's insistence we rounded the evening off with 'competition'.

"Steph, I'll pair up with you," said Hayden. "You look like you've knocked a few balls about in your time."

"Cheers, mate, I'll take the compliment."

"Geraldine, you can play with Danny."

Danny was second in command in the office, good looking but quiet, so much so that if he'd contributed to a single conversation since we'd met him, I'd be stunned. For once Geraldine seemed happy enough with that.

And I guessed I'd be sitting this one out then with my glass half-empty. Cheers indeed.

**

Twenty-two hours in Taipei, the second leg of The Far Eastern Odyssey, were over before they had started. Seoul, leg three, was a whirlwind too.

Literary agents were the quickest route to selling foreign rights into South Korea – their offices often doubling as bedrooms. It didn't seem like such a bad thing to me, I would have loved to stay overnight in my own office back in Bristol – ghosts downstairs laying tables with heavy silver cutlery and all. Daniel couldn't touch me there amidst the solidarity. Even the likes of Gary were a buffer.

The last afternoon in Seoul was spent in a temple, whose intricate rafters and cherry blossomed trees, made a hauntingly magical contrast to the mammoth TV screens advertising all things modern and bling in the distance. For a second or two, Hayden was selling aftershave. But on closer inspection, it was just Will Ferrell. Man they had something similar going on.

***

When I returned to Singapore, Hayden had drifted perceptibly further away once again. If he'd uttered but two words to me in the remaining couple of days, I'd have been incredulous. His farewell – and apparent gratitude for my help around the office – was a far cry from the friendly hug I'd been met with on Club Street just last week.

A simple 'see you' complete with matching hand rise was as good as it got when I announced I was leaving for the airport. His colleagues enveloped me warmly, as if attempting to mask the twinge in my stomach as Hayden chanced to look up at me before becoming seriously busy once more. He hammered away at his speed dial, pen in mouth. I could sense the cogs in his brain doing overtime to consider the words for his upcoming dialogue – as opposed to being given the slightest inch to contemplate anything else.

I closed the door, hauled my suitcase (which Steph, who was accompanying me to the underground station, sensed I had lost the energy to navigate and seized the handle of) and walked away from something which, try as I might, I couldn't put a finger on.

With every step I took to the check in desk, I scolded myself for not extending my itinerary. Adrian would hardly have protested given that he'd let me come this far. Staring in a trance at the departures boards, I sipped watery iced coffee and mulled over my options. The exciting lists of destinations clack clacked every thirty seconds, revealing another flight had taken off. Couldn't I go anywhere else? London might be calling, but I didn't have a clue where I was supposed to belong – or with whom.

Later, as the plane commenced its ascent, I resigned

myself to thirteen hours seated next to an inquisitive Singaporean boy who was being sent to English boarding school for the first time.

"Do you like David Beckham?" he said, fascinated that I was from England too.

"No, I don't. But we share the same birthday."

"Oh? Wow. How about pasta, do you like that?"

"Yes. Yes, I do. I really like pasta," I replied to his final words to me for the entire flight.

An indescribable feeling washed over me. I'd left something behind. This time it wasn't just my Cinderella shoe.

Chapter Twenty-Two

Deflated balloon syndrome reigned supreme. The twinkling lights of England's shores gleamed through the breaks in the blanket of cloud that seemed to permanently cover my island home.

The Far East had been one noxious adventure, already rendered little more than a distant dream – ever more so with every mile I travelled closer to the cottage. And when I thought again of Steph over there in the heart of the action, it was with more than a streak of jealousy. Just hours ago we'd clung tightly to one another, cementing the kinder side of our friendship as the train doors parted to invite me in. But she'd be coming to the end of a Saturday night of partying on the town with Hayden and friends, now. No doubt in Miles' bed.

I tried to tease my journey out, unnecessary but welcome tea breaks at the motorway services gently assuaging me back into the real world. Until unable to put it off any longer, I entered the humdrum abyss of Glastonbury High Street. Just five minutes more and I'd be home.

The Weirdos were lined up on their benches outside St John's church. But hang on, wait, wasn't that a new piece of Banksy street art spewing across the pavement? The wares of the magical, mystical crystal shops glistened with temptation; Aladdin's caves ready for business tomorrow morning. A ubiquitous tractor chugged by, more than likely trudging back from the yokel pub from whence its driver had been drinking. A pile of straggly youths tumbled out of The Backpackers. A couple of dealers exchanged *gear* (yes, I was driving that slowly) just as I approached the top of Benedict Street. Nothing had changed.

The contrast of the past twenty-four hours was never more

evident. I didn't belong. Certainly, this was the place of my roots – the ancient Isle of Avalon and all that. But what could it offer? If I wasn't working at She Sells, what would I have done with that coveted degree? What use was there for French and German, a smattering of Spanish, here in Glastonbury? A tour guide at the Abbey Ruins, maybe? That didn't warrant the sacrifice of four years of study.

The world had never felt more like my oyster, and yet paradoxically, seemed ever more out of reach. The constraints of my relationship had cemented me firmly in the candour of small town mentality. Sometimes this having a taste of the exotic was the worst thing of all. I still had to come back. And nothing ever happened here. People stagnated, year after year; ageing, gossiping, weekly grocery shopping, maybe a package holiday to Majorca in August if you were lucky…and that was your lot. The streets were etched with invisible demarcation lines so that one knew one's place. Houses and gardens conformed, conspiring to be like the rest of the flock.

But more than anything I was scared of who would be waiting to greet me when I did reach that front door. Would I get Jekyll? Or would it be Hyde? This was the longest stretch he'd had on his own. Due to the time difference and cost – even on company money – I couldn't really go to town on phone calls, and his composure during our last conversation was plain unnatural.

The demons of an education at the town's St David's came back to haunt me too. Steve Ellis, now how could I forget him? The pin-up boy who'd accused me of goofily spying on him through the window. It wasn't me. It was never me. It was funny how I had acquired a sudden army of friends when he moved in across the road. They'd all pile in to 'listen to music' in my bedroom, screaming in teen-pop hysteria, hiding behind the curtains because Steve was bare-chested and on the move. I had a badly-timed knack for standing there completely gormless, all traces of friends long gone. I'd then have to face the music next morning at tutor group when he'd reduce me to a pile of rubble along with his sidekick, the gangly Tony Chant. How fair was that? Ever since The Ellis clan had moved into the grand Edwardian house on the posh side of the road, even my bedroom was no longer a sanctuary. How I'd begged my parents for net curtains! But they'd said they looked old-fashioned, didn't go with the double glazing.

I shivered at the hurt some of these memories still contained as I braked gently at the zebra crossing, letting out an almighty sigh as a trio of skateboarders whizzed themselves before me in safety.

Thank goodness there was no social media back in the day, or mobile phones. Kids today really had it tough, I acknowledged with another lengthy breath.

I remembered how my spirit had soared in the second year. A letter circulated announcing the Austrian ski trip. But it turned out to be just another spate of bullying to add to the scrapbook of yesteryear. Nobody would sit next to me on the coach, nobody would sit next to me at the dinner table après-ski, nobody would pair up with me at ski school and nobody wanted to share a room with me. The two girls I was kind of friendly with shunned me to snog their way through the boys instead, leaving me to retreat to the background like a gate-crasher. All fine, dandy and quite forgettable on a day trip, but not when it had gone on for a week.

Hockey was another sport where I promised talent. I was nifty with the stick, had even been awarded a trophy in the annual house matches. Okay, it was largely for scoring a goal after being accidentally walloped across the windpipe and floored for fifty-nine seconds, echoes of 'is she still breathing?' all around me as I came to, yes; but it was also an accolade achieved through merit.

I recalled the moment when I was presented with my prize on stage. There hadn't exactly been much applause, only adding to the beetroot shade of my already self-conscious cheeks and re-confirming my unpopular status, this time for the entire school to see.

Yet in an institution which permitted its pupils to select their own squad, there was never much chance of me making

Team GB. It enraged me to reflect on the un-bureaucratic ways of the school. Just about everything was a popularity contest, only to be won with a pair of honed thighs, snake-thin lips and flawless skin.

"Miss Lacey?" I plucked up the courage to question one day. "I always seem to be cast in the chorus line. I mean, I'm not ungrateful, but I'd love a few lines to read out, to feel like I'm progressing. And I can sing. You know I can sing…you stood by me listening for ages when you came to check out the choir."

"Yes, but you're too shy, sweetheart. I'm sorry."

"But I can be whoever I want to be when I'm acting, anybody but shy Kate… Please, oh please."

"Sorry, Kate, it's a 'no' from me. But the chorus is important. It's the backbone of the production. Why, without the chorus line, there is no school play."

I stopped auditioning after that.

Just about nobody at that school wanted me to excel. Or so it seemed. I didn't stand out from the pack. I was soft-hued and timid. And so they wrote me off as just another statistic in the system; a brighter than average bit of data for sure, but I was never going to set the sky alight. Even when I completed my English coursework a whole two months ahead of schedule, and asked Mr Willis for advice as to how to improve it, all I got was:

"You won't get it from a B + to anywhere near an A, that's just how it is."

I twiddled my thumbs. I played games of paper consequences with my friends. I apparently hadn't the potential to set my sights higher.

Yes, your face either fitted at St D's, or it didn't. And mine most definitely fell in the latter camp.

Unfavourable, excommunicated, doomed and outlawed I may have been, but college was on the horizon, the light at the end of the tunnel in sight.

I'd already proven a hit with some of the lads from the neighbouring town of Street. Still, the boys of St David's wouldn't touch me; despite growing out that hideous fringe and the sideburns to match, despite investing in tweezers, despite waxing my legs, despite the retreat of the blessed zits, despite spending my pocket money on Body Shop make-up, and even despite amply spritzing myself in the potently glam yellow and white California beach-striped, Beverly Hills eau de toilette.

Born again, but my school tormentors soon tracked me back down in the Promised Land, where they introduced a brand new breed of attack: Dan Portillo and the chip throwing incident in the college canteen. The thunderous, belly-aching laughter seemed to linger there taunting me whenever I passed. In the end I avoided it altogether, walking the safe rim of the college's buildings just to get from French to German.

And after I'd committed the ultimate treason by snogging the best looking guy in college at Caroline Slocombe's party – despite both of us acknowledging he'd probably never be interested in looking at me or her…if indeed he even turned up…and if he did, well then, fair was fair, whoever got him, got him – my social life as I knew it was over.

Sam Baldwin could have told me that he had a girlfriend at the time. The entire establishment conspired to detest me, so much so that lunchtimes and breaks were either spent locked in the toilets eating something highly calorific, or swotting up in the library.

By the time my path crossed with Daniel's, I was more-or-less destitute of friends, confidence and hope. I could see it now on this trip down memory lane. This was the reason I'd pinned my existence onto him. I'd been swept up in his pursuit. To be idolised like that, told I was beautiful after years of believing the contrary; that was something I'd never wanted to lose, even if love had never come into it. He'd been my knight in shining armour back then. Older and more mature, he had money and a car that could take me places.

And with such a lack of self-esteem so like had continued to attract like: weekends and evenings after college had called for a part-time job as a checkout girl. How my geography teacher, Mr Watson and my maths teacher, Mr

Carp would look down at me across the aisles! I'd failed them, under-achieved. I wanted so desperately to tell them what I was doing:

"A levels in French, German and Spanish…and then I'm going on to University, to study to be an interpreter. I'm going to make something of my life."

But they never came to my till. All I could do was helplessly listen to the beep-beep as I scanned tins, packets and bottles – more than occasionally being scolded for going too fast, or not handling somebody's honeydew melon with enough TLC.

Like Daniel, all Glastonbury ever did was try to knock me down. Small wonder I despised the place; myths, legends and all. It should have contained nothing but happy childhood memories – certainly there were all the usual suspect family ones – but the town and Daniel's small-mindedness had done nothing but plant my roots firmly in unyielding Arthurian soil.

And then I felt dreadful, if not a little ungrateful too. As I rounded the corner onto Beckery, making my way home out into the open countryside and the starry night, I realised there were a lot of things I loved about the rural-ness of it all; the complete one-off-ness and chaos of the place. There really was nowhere else quite like it.

Only in Glastonbury could you find a bookshop shelving every title from shamanism to transcendental meditation and then pop next door to the quaint tea rooms to read about faeries whilst feasting on a traditional cream tea, putting your hand up and miming 'Awwrriigghh' to Norman the Egg man and his re-stitched bag, as he trundled by his their eggshell grey Morris Minor van.

Once you'd digested that, you could amble a few steps to a delicatessen to arm yourself with a litre of *Scrumpy* by recommendation of The Wurzels, and a block of the finest quality Cheddar to accompany it; all fuelled up for the incense, oil and candle trail. Here you could wonder in awe at the Harry Potter-esque specimens stocked in the medievally-styled shops; the Holy Grail of all things essential oil and herbal, before ruminating over the contrast of your purchases at arguably the best fish and chip shop on the planet. Should you still feel the pangs of hunger, the organic vegan cafes that fringed the High Street offered a plethora of hemp breads and spirulina-based smoothies. Still uninspired? You could become a Pagan for the day, go visit the Holy Thorn or Arthur's remains.

And was there ever a more iconic and magical sight than the Tor moor-side? Her familiar bumps and contours running the length of her mound at sun set with the Brue beneath her becoming but a trickle, embraced by pale willows. That mysterious celestial quality of light only seemed to capture the ancient tower and the hill she guarded. One day presenting a canvas of lush velvet grass dappled with the occasional shadow, the next transforming her into a sombre Goddess frowning upon her subjects.

And how then would it be if everyone were to have the same idea as me; grand plans to jet off to a new life somewhere more exciting, running from their woes? There wouldn't be any locals, any roots anymore. How out of kilter! And wouldn't I just encounter the same things elsewhere anyway? I reasoned with myself, remembering as with the culture and beliefs of the very place I'd just been, that life was indeed a harmonious balance of yin and yang; half of this and half of that. Hadn't my steadily growing mountain of Self-Help books taught me that much?

But by the time I'd reached the driveway I'd turned full circle on myself once again. Why couldn't Mum and Dad have sent me to Crossfields, the town's private school? I doubted my experiences would have been the same if only I'd been educated there, where order and discipline prevailed.

Was it any wonder my current life was in such a mess?

I hadn't addressed any of the emotional baggage of the past. It was time to heal and move on. As I pulled off the roadside and parked in the garage, I vowed to do just that, as of tomorrow.

***

"How was your trip, babe? I didn't want to wake you but I figured it's better jetlag-wise if you're up and about in daylight hours," I couldn't quite believe what I was hearing…or seeing through my sleepy eyes. Daniel approached me with a mug of tea as I propped myself against my pillow in bed. I rubbed my eyes, and then again a little more frantically, certain this was nothing more than a hallucination.

"Yeah, it was good," I said as the memory of Hayden and I walking arm in arm down the street re-surfaced. "Hard work though, and a really long and boring flight, glad to be back, missed you too." I smiled and reached for the handle, conscious of the fact this may all just be a horrible act, that he could at any moment decide to douse me in the hot liquid as some form of punishment for my lengthy absence. Not to mention that the tea could be poisoned.

"I've gotta run. Unc's called me in early this morning. Shit loads to do. See you later." He planted a kiss on my head and I braced myself a second time. But nothing, I'd got away with it, apparently.

Work granted me a day in lieu and thank goodness, there was so much to learn. First off, I found a suitable hiding place for the two books I'd purchased on a whim; the books that would change my life – if only I could master their words. Then I moulded myself into the sofa, stretching my legs for the odd tea and biscuit break, or to double check Daniel hadn't nipped back from work unannounced whenever I perceived an engine loitering on the main road.

I nodded in agreement at the recognition of myself in some of the pages and shook my head woefully at other passages of reflection.

"How can me being angry and wanting revenge on somebody who made my life hell at school," I said aloud, "have anything to do with them being a mirror image of myself? How can I see my own reflection of my unwanted traits in others? This is insane, poppycock."

Enlightenment was light years away.

Chapter Twenty-Three

That was then.

Two years later and this summer's wanderlust only seemed to take my itchy feet to the kitchen, either to bake cake or eat it. One Saturday afternoon Daniel arrived home early from yet another Young Farmers shindig without the faintest trace of a sound. I was engrossed in reading my latest book on Fear, digging away at a tub of luxury ice cream, blissfully oblivious to the fact I was about to be caught out.

"Hey, Fatty, what do you think you're doin'?"

The intrusion of his Bart Simpson-mocking-Homer vocals sent half-eaten tub and spoon flying.

"Please don't do that to me, I hadn't even realised you were back yet," my dribble of words became the perfect doormat to his standard critique of the so-this-is-what-you-get-up-to-behind-my-back variety.

I pulled a tissue from my sleeve and tried not to feel his eyes as they scanned me from stomach to thighs, matching the intensity with which I had finally managed to scoop out the much yearned for cheesecake chunk, which sat in my lap: Exhibit A in the prosecution.

"You should be more like Sissy. She doesn't pig out on this that and t'other." He clung to the door frame, whose width ironically wasn't far off Hannah's miniscule waistline. "That's why she's in such good shape, the perfect eight to ten."

I have no frigging desire to be an eight to ten, I lied inwardly.

I got down on my hands and knees, put the lid back on the pot and then stood to return my 'guilty pleasure' from whence it had come. I tried to slide past him and into the

173

kitchen where he was still eccentrically gripped to the door's wooden frame, but he blocked my passage, leaning diagonally across the portal so that my only choice was to get back down on all fours like an animal, crawling to the freezer. But there was simply no point in arguing, not unless I wanted to risk a pummelling. The house was His Kingdom and, on a good day, when I could bear to play by His Rules, things would usually blow over quickly. He was master of moving the boundaries, de-sensitising me so slowly, so imperceptibly that it had taken me this long to see it. If only he'd have used the chat-up line:

"Come back to mine, we can get to know one another a little better…and then perhaps I could give you a black eye."

Maybe, just maybe, I'd be with somebody else; not having to justify my act of insatiable greed.

He eventually stopped being a limpet, and like yin to my yang, circumnavigated the kitchen table as I walked anti-clockwise around its perimeter. He swiped his bunch of keys from the centre (how I hadn't heard their colossal jangle was a mystery…he must have spent five minutes meticulously laying each bronze and silver piece down purposely to spook me), and marched out the front door.

I let out a deep sigh, closed my eyes and leant against the kitchen sink. Clover, who had been dozing through this near-miss, tiptoed over to me, her wet nose and its affectionate rub as relief-giving as any teddy bear.

I guessed nothing had really changed since I'd been caught red-fingered by my mum, licking the topping off the trifle Grandma had lovingly prepared for Sunday tea, although I would have hoped that as an adult, a – heaven forbid – size ten-to-twelve, that I could pick and choose my own dietary intake.

At least I'd cleaned the house. He couldn't pull me up on that. Wet wipes were one of the best inventions of modern times for women like me. I'd zigzagged across the kitchen, removing all traces of crumbs, dog hair and grime. Even the dust magnets – bane of my domestic duties – were gleaming in the living room and study. True, he may have caught me in the act, but I'd felt strangely sanctimonious earlier on in the day that I was playing the role of 'wifey' very aptly.

My knees gave way to adopt a crouching position next to Clover. I hovered a while, stroking her golden fur as my thigh muscles quivered.

"No pain, no gain."

Isn't that what the ski instructors used to say when we were warming up before attempting the Olympic women's downhill in Austria aged just fourteen and totally underprepared? Was suffering really worth the sacrifice? 'Cos from where I was sitting, all I could see that I'd gained in return for my pain was the realisation I'd been institutionalised.

And yet, much as I dared to dream more and more of a life without his servile male oppression beating down, I was also aware of a fear I didn't know could even exist, a senseless hesitation: the fear of leaving him.

My job kept me suitably distracted. There was some horrible stuff going down. Everyone was stressed to the hilt and all Adrian seemed concerned about was fiddling with spread sheets while Rome was almost burning.

The Italian client's licensed character back-to-school products were late for the third consecutive year. The print run was a reprint of a previously successful laminated book that allowed children to colour in its pictures again and again; the black marker pen provided, being made with a special indelible ink. I had personally vowed to Simona Di Angelo and her Lego haircut, that all would run like clockwork this year.

"Here we go again." I sank my head in my palm.

What excuse was I meant to conjure up now? And these weren't the only books they were waiting for.

"It's only ink on paper, mate."

Every now and then the wisdom of Diana returned to keep me grounded. If only it was that simple. But this time it was ink and pop-up animals on paper. And not just any old pop-up animals either; pop-up animals paper engineered into the centre of the spread and thus very much in demand. No boat

175

on Earth was going to make a two week voyage from Singapore, up the Strait of Malacca, round the tip of India, up towards the Arabian Gulf, shimmying it along the Suez Canal, cruising through the Med between the gap separating Sicily and Italy's toe, making a last sprint for its coastal destination and home of fruit cake, Genoa.

I hadn't even noticed Daisy sneaking in earlier than usual, that she'd been snuffling into a steaming mug of something (undoubtedly caffeine-free) one minute, and nowhere to be seen the next. The pattern had repeated itself for half an hour already, with Daisy on and off her seat like a yo-yo every time her concentration couldn't be sustained any longer by staring vacantly at a computer screen. When I glanced across for what must have truly been the first time, I was stunned to see her sobbing quietly, eyes puffy and sore.

"He's left me." She slurped back sips of roiboos tea, whose string and tag swayed to reveal the irrefutably unsatisfying brew she was cradling with unsteady hands.

"I beg your…say what?"

"You know how Scott always had this thing…" she choked up and pulled a fresh tissue from her box (Daisy catered for everything – and I do mean everything – on her desktop), "…about starting a new life Down Under?"

Well no, this was definitely the first I'd heard of Daisy's boyfriend's 'Australian Dream'.

"…so, that's exactly what he's done…buggered off to Oz on a one way ticket," she finally managed to say.

Small brown puddles slopped across her desk, and tears rolled uncontrollably down her pale withdrawn cheeks.

"Here, this is the note he left. That's it, a six year relationship down the drain. See for yourself."

Unable to process it, I took the note from Daisy's trembling hands and then held her in my arms. She appeared to have eaten nothing in days and her skinny frame felt unusually skeletal. I was instantly awash with Bad Friend Syndrome.

My heartbroken colleague sipped cautiously at her rooibos again. What this girl really needed was a hot chocolate with all the marshmallow and molten dark chocolate trimmings to boot. And that was for starters.

I'll make my One Pot Chocolate Wonder cake tonight, I decided, before saying the only thing which even began to put any kind of context to this mess:

"Classic case of an early mid-life crisis, honey: it's not you, it's him."

It was always Him.

***

"I can tell you've been eating yet more cake, got a zit like a snooker ball pussing up there, eugh," my Him greeted me that same Friday evening.

I had started a couple of new rituals. The first I was ashamed of, no two ways about it. Every Friday night, as the working week wound up, I'd prolong my journey home with a weekend supermarket shop, methodically going through my list before heading to the chocolate aisle at breakneck speed. I'd grab the nearest box of delights: they were a present for someone, right? That's why I had to bury them under the vegetables in my trolley.

Back in the relative secrecy of my car, I'd make certain I was free of spectators and then scoff five chocolates in a row, hardly allowing the sensation to greet my taste buds. Once I'd revelled in the initial hit, I'd pull off, wait until I was on a nice, level, car-free patch of road, and devour what remained of the upper tray. The final part of the routine was once again to find a nice, level, definitely car-free stretch, wind the window down and hurl the shameful evidence – bottom tray of uneaten chocolates included. It sickened me, yet I had to psych myself up for the weekend somehow. Even if I knew he'd be out for most of it, there were always more occasions for him to lash out.

But this weekend was different. If I baked my One Pot Wonder tonight and refrained from eating it for two whole days to let those flavours mingle, then I'd be giving Daisy the most positive start I could to the next working week (of course there was always the very strong possibility she'd offer said cake around the office...of course refraining from eating the actual baked creation did not mean I was exempt from licking the bowl).

So yes, Daniel, yes, technically I had been eating more cake. Thank you for making that correlation between excess sugar intake and pimple. It's always so nice to be reminded that your past simply flows into your present.

Indeed, if there was one moment in time that followed me around like no other, it had to be the still-life episode: twelve year old Kate taking pride of place on a chair, atop a table for all to see and sketch at their leisure during art class. An excruciating hour of snickering and the masterpieces were complete. I then had the honour of perusing the offerings in a circulatory walk of shame as the cruel, pubescent tricksters watched on. Every one of my classmates' *Spitting Image* portraits showcased every aspect of my much despised features. Giant rubbery lips, bushy caterpillar eyebrows – ha, on some sketches they'd even been made into a mono-brow, moustaches, bristly legs and – as Daniel had kindly reminded me – spots the size of snooker balls. I was tarnished goods from that day on, officially marked out as territory. Had anything really changed?

The pain had welled deep inside. But the tears somehow stayed bottled up until home time, when a stash of yet more shop-bought tea-time cakes – courtesy again of *Mr Kipling* (who I can thank for the inauguration of my cake addiction), comforted me through loud guttural sobs; that and the one image of hope: the portrait that was lovingly sketched by Belle the hippie.

No, nothing had changed: same old victim, different role.

"Let's go out for a meal," Daniel said minutes later as a Quantum Leap version of him entered the room.

"Um...yeah...okay then, let's..." I said, and my fingers couldn't help but sweep across my chin to check if my beloved zit had time-travelled too. Alas no.

This sudden 'outing' would translate as a couple of hours of un-golden silence, of course; still, at least I wouldn't have to knock up a masterpiece – and wait for John Torode to give his verdict.

***

The second of my new rituals meant that most Saturday nights I would visit Lizzie for tea, cake (of course), trashy TV and chat/dissecting of emails. Much chat/dissecting of emails.

Lizzie had once been Henry's PA and she'd seen and heard it all when it came to his behaviour:

"Call Jamie Oliver in person, Liz, and book me up a private table at his new London gaff...for seven-thirty this evening...in the main restaurant at a push. Tell him I'll throw in a couple of our dot-to-dot books."

"The time is eleven twenty-four and thirteen seconds," the Speaking Clock would reply.

"It's not going to cut it, Henry. There are no empty tables. Jamie says dot-to-dots frustrate the hell out of him anyway..."

"But it can't be fully booked."

"Yes. It can."

"No it can't."

"Yes, it damn well can."

His landline came to the rescue, an hour passed. It seemed he'd forgotten. Lizzie got back to her in-tray.

"You'll just have to go to his better half, Jools, to sort this one out," he shouted across to her desk. "Tell them it's for Henry Boyle and it's urgent. Right, I've just been called for an important meeting by Adrian. Let me know as soon as it's done."

Twenty minutes later – he could wait, she decided – she entered the 'board room' in the basement, passing several troubled spirits on her way. She'd been born with a supernatural gift, and every now and again would freak her colleagues out with details of whom or what they'd had walk through them.

"Hey, way up. What's this?"

179

"My resignation."

Lizzie walked calmly out of the room (acknowledging the thumbs up of the old maid's spirit, who'd presumably endured a similarly challenging boss), left the building, and then realised she'd forgot to leave a parting gift.

The receptionist pretended she hadn't seen Lizzie re-enter as a former employee, or that she'd peeped around the doorway with a smile to witness her changing the stand details for the imminent Harrogate show…to a bouncy castle.

Now although Daniel blatantly resented Lizzie, she came across as too sensible to pose any real threat (revenge with inflatables aside). And he knew I was going where I'd said, because unbeknownst to him, I know he'd followed me to Lizzie's house on more than one occasion. However, the small market town of Somerton, whose biggest nightlife draw was the cosy Tudor pub in the opposite direction would have reassured immediately. Little did he realise the potency of ideas being exchanged.

Lizzie was Coffee and Walnut Cake, the ultimate listener; patient, self-less, the healing balm to a wound, and (mostly) full of good advice. Why hadn't I told her sooner; why hadn't I told anybody at all, for nine whole years?

"Daniel's been beating me for the past decade," I said as I bit into my scone.

One Saturday we decided to swap the TV for an earlier cream tea date in Cheddar. My declaration was met with a half fly-catching, half light bulb illuminating speechlessness as she tried to digest the shocking, although not totally unexpected, news: there had obviously always been something about Daniel, something her sixth sense couldn't quite get to the bottom of.

"But it's not like he's been doing it all the time…I guess, maybe twice, a handful of times a year? I don't know actually. It's all a bit of a blur to tell you the truth," I began in earnest to pour my heart out. I was officially one of those battered women – and men; a sad and sorry statistic who others lavished with sympathy.

When Lizzie finally found her tongue, the words were

exactly as I had envisaged.

"One, two, three, four, five, it's all the same, Kate. It only takes a once to 'accidentally' kill."

"I'll leave as soon as I've got my head together, I promise. It's just, you know, not that simple. There's the mortgage, household things, um…"

"Security can be an illusion."

There were other excuses too, but I knew they didn't count.

"And what exactly has he been doing to you?"

"I don't know. I mean, I do remember some of the instances. I get flashbacks and stuff; the beginning and ending, a punch, a slap, being dragged by my hair across the floor. But it's as if my mind has erased the middle bits."

I was unable to recall Lizzie's exact choice of words, though I knew they were spelling out just one. There was definitely another long and tangible silence, and the remnants of Lizzie's heavily-decorated scone slipped between finger and thumb as she no doubt imagined her friend in each of the violent predicaments I'd relayed.

Days later and I could still picture the way those perturbed hazelnut eyes widened over the rim of the willow-patterned tea cup.

Chapter Twenty-Four

"Why didn't you tell us sooner? We could've got you out of this mess by now."

Once I told Lizzie, Daisy and Steph were always going to be next.

"I suppose I've barely been able to believe it all myself. It's not like I have any visible injuries or scars, so how the hell could I expect anybody else to buy it?"

I could only look at the floor and tug at my earlobe. It was such a shameful thing to admit to anybody, particularly in my capacity as boss.

"Well, it's crazy to stay a minute longer, unthinkable," Steph cried. "I'll flatten him! You do realise I have friends of friends back in Swansea who can hire a hit man...or twenty."

We discussed the best tactics to flee; secret codes for the office if things were unbearable at home, pre-planned hidden meaning texts that could speedily be deciphered. Daisy even kept her spare room spare. Such a blessing to know there was refuge with a friend.

Meanwhile in the office, there was the co-ordination of four sales trips, as well as the secret quest to meet Hayden in Phuket at the end of the year, before which of course, I would have left Daniel. Absolutely.

I'd already dipped a toe in the Thai waters, giddily interpreting Hayden's reaction as a resounding 'yes' when he'd replied:

"Sounds like fun, and shouldn't be a problem to get the time off. I'll start saving my pennies then!"

The air was redolent with long distance romance, our attraction going full circle from passive written word to action. Maybe we could do this a few times a year, maybe eventually I'd move over to Singapore. This was all getting very exciting.

But everything came to a crescendo during the Frankfurt meeting. The show was but two weeks away and none of the new projects had been unveiled. As usual, every department – with the exception of ours – claimed to have too much to do to arrive on time.

I would certainly rather be picking the blackberries of my childhood, notching up the scratches on my fingers and gazing out at buttermilk bales of hay across the river at the foot of Grandma's orchard. Fast forward twenty years, who'd have thought I'd be sitting in a clammy underground cellar on the cusp of autumn instead?

It was a rare thing to be stationary in this little hub for long. Company meetings were few and far between. But I would regularly pass through on a sunny day, since the far end of the vaults opened out to a secret passage tunnelling beneath the main road to one of the grandest parks in the city. I instigated that tradition, another of my brainwaves to bring some fun to department meetings – and it hadn't failed to catch on. We'd recline in stripy blue and white deckchairs – our personal tribute to the production boys, whose flaws we'd mostly end up debating – amidst children playing hide and seek, and elderly folk sipping tea. In park life spirit we'd sometimes take our own flasks too. And of course cake.

Nothing could be tackled without cake.

Nobody would even notice we'd gone, except the receptionist, who'd given us the keys in return for a slice of Vicky Sponge. It was always the most productive of meetings, although we never wanted to go back. And then there was always the thrill of the door slamming firmly shut when we were still under the road.

I drummed my fingertips as we waited to see who would show up first. We all plumped for Adrian – it was his meeting – but amazingly and untrue to form, in waltzed Gary instead, stepping in and quickly back out again in his renowned hokey cokey, before realising he'd been foiled.

"Off on your tri-annual book fair holiday soon are you?"

he said with that boyish glint radiating from each of his hazel eyes.

"Four words Gary: where are my mock-ups?" said Steph chewing on the end of her biro.

"I rather think you'll find that's five," he said, taking an embarrassing number of seconds to do his mental arithmetic.

"I rather think you'll find mock-ups to be hyphenated," said Daisy.

Yeah, I thought that would shut him up too.

It didn't take long to figure out, once Adrian and the others had arrived, that there were going to be just five new series to present – none exactly exerting a siren pull.

Adrian had given us a budget to commission our own books, and swiped it back with the promise of product to replace it.

"Is that it?" I said with eyes on the brink of watering.

From left to right, Daisy and Steph looked just as mortally embarrassed at the idea of presenting this crap as I imagined I did.

"But these are the same books Sharon showed me months ago, full of content we've already sold. Do you think our customers are idiots?"

Adrian shrugged because of course he didn't do confrontation.

We'd worked so hard to secure the most fantastic line-up of meetings this fair, and for what? How could we even begin to compete with our rivals?

If ever there was a trigger to doing our own thing altogether, it was yesterday. I could barely contain my frustration. Adrian appeared to have undergone an overnight lobotomy. How could he believe he was showcasing the crown jewels? Not even his adaptation of chair to rocking horse could force me to smile. He landed hard on his coccyx to a deafening chorus.

"Well, that'll be meeting adjourned then," he laughed at himself too as he stood back up to shuffle his papers.

And where was the 'Sales Director' anyway? Shouldn't he have got off his arse and attended what should have been his meeting?

"D'you know what?" I said when it became apparent that my team were the only ones left sitting in disbelief around the table. "I think we actually are working for the Brothers Grimm."

"Whose tales they recount through chunkily and hastily thrown together compilations; the industry masters at churning out a slightly original version of another company's novel idea," said Steph, extending her arm as if reciting Shakespeare.

"I don't know why we expected this year to be any different," said Daisy.

Hayden aside, everything around me seemed to be plummeting fast from a once giddy height to the depths of despair. It wasn't like there had ever been bags of integrity, we were what we were: a pile-them-high-sell-them-cheap kind of a company. Still, what motivation there had been to do things at least a little better, with a slightly different spin, had vanished overnight.

**

"That's it, pack up your things."

It didn't strike me as a Eureka moment at first.

Harold, whose company frequently partnered up with the Boyles for special projects, came for one of his surprise visits one particularly fraught morning. As old school (and Madeira Cake) as they got, Harold had worked in the industry some forty years. He was well aware of our daily struggles, always on hand to offer advice, but even he had never witnessed the team quite as despondent.

"I'm taking you out for lunch. But we'd better disappear in phases: ladies first. Secure us a jolly nice table adjacent to the window at Browns. I'll saunter on behind. I've a little business to wrap up with Henry first."

We were only too happy to oblige and waited patiently for his tutorial.

"The twins have a very successful enterprise," he said an

185

hour and something later, raising his pinky in Etonian fashion as he sipped at his coffee, contemplating his words. "But – and it's a big but, to my mind – they are money driven. Now, I've been in this industry long enough to know that soon, that just won't be enough. There's nervousness in the air, a global recession on the horizon. Greed, coupled with the fear of losing everything, has reached a new level and believe you me, the bubble is about to burst."

I couldn't see where any of this was going but was eager to find out.

"That's where emotional intelligence comes into the game, and that's the advantage you have, my dears. You're in tune with what people want. You listen to your customers. Some of them are even your friends."

Harold looked from one to the other of his audience, as we all nodded our heads in recognition and support of his delivery. He took another sip of his coffee, straightened his tie, and gathered his thoughts.

"You do it for the love of the job, the connection with people, to promote literature, to make a difference – for money too, yes. But that is not your sole motivation…and that's what's so refreshing about you—"

"But…," said Daisy.

Harold put his finger to his lips and carried on.

"Your main issue is going to be financial, obviously…"

I sensed Daisy's habitual frown of lack and limitation.

"We've – you've – established that you have every skill required to run a business, as well as an enviable list of contacts and ideas. You also have that rare thing called 'camaraderie', well, from where I'm sitting anyway…"

Steph beamed at me.

"You do need to get excited about this, of course. But you mustn't let that excitement carry you away. Don't let it out-dazzle the fact that you need funding. This is where I can help. However, before we even start to put a business plan together, I need you all to take time out. We'll re-convene in the New Year, by which time I will expect you to have given this some serious thought. We all know you want to do it…"

I hope you got that bit, Daisy.

"…and that it will be an incredible journey, but what you have to be brutal about is the impact it will have on each of your lives. You all have very different sets of circumstances," he panned the table from one to the other, taking in our profound expressions, "so it's hugely important that you are honest with each other, and above all, honest with yourselves. Your income will take a mammoth hit. Are you prepared for that? Do you have significant others who can support you?"

If only.

"Righty-ho, I'm going to have to shoot off."

"Can I just—?"

"Sorry, Kate, my wife will be expecting me home early this afternoon and I hadn't quite factored this into my day. We'll catch up soon," he said rising and patting down his briefcase as if it were something of a ritual after a long public speech.

Harold kissed us on both cheeks, breaking with his usual convention and disappeared, leaving us dazed, and unsure of where, when and how to even begin mulling over our new apparent venture.

"On that note I think I'll get us in a stiff round of coffee liquors," I said.

Chapter Twenty-Five

"What are your intentions in Norway?" a short fairer than fair-haired customs officer had asked as he'd rifled through my belongings when I'd landed in Oslo. He ran his fingers over the touch-and-feel duck on the front cover of the row of books I'd neatly slotted face down onto the top of the sample bag, like Carol Vorderman lining up her numbers on *Countdown*.

"Tell you what, it's yours," I said handing him the fluffy mass-market curiosity. It worked a treat and he decided not to delve any further. Not that I'd anything remotely exciting to hide. Potty training and bogey books were about as avant garde as it got.

Three days of meetings later and I had to wonder the same: what was I doing here?

It was all well and good pretending this spot of loafing about at Oslo's harbour was sightseeing. But what it really boiled down to was procrastination. Two weeks into September and I should be making plans, at least starting to reflect on Harold's words. And then there was the small issue of the leaving Daniel thing.

But my feet seemed to take me to The National Gallery instead.

I knew Edvard Munch's infamous *The Scream* hung there, and though not an arty-farty type, there was a certain satisfaction in being able to say I'd seen all The Big Ones, just like I had with the travelling Gaugin exhibition in Stuttgart, as well as the beauties hanging in both The Louvre and Musee D'Orsay in Paris. I was kind of passing Oslo's collection, and it was on the way back to the snazzy *Radisson* – via my detour.

I began in earnest with the intellectual intention of studying every artefact and painting in depth. I read plaques and descriptions, letting it all sink in for future pub quizzes. But before long I was marching from hall to hall with the attention span of a child, desperately seeking Munch so I could say I'd seen the star attraction and get back out into the sunshine.

I knew when I'd found him.

The mood changed. Visitors' expressions changed. A melancholy solitude was woven like a tapestry through all of Munch's works as they hung in succession. Mental torment wailed through his palette. The queasy look on the green-faced girl of *Anxiety* spelt utter misery. It was enough to quicken my pace.

And then, there it was: The Scream.

I sort of recognised her. Funny that, because wasn't this meant to be a guy? But hang on. Wait a minute. Oh, bloody hell. I knew this person all right. My feet almost propelled me out the building in haunted panic, willing me to break into a sprint, just like Shaggy and Scrappy from Scooby-Doo.

But her gaze was magnetic. It was me. I was looking in a mirror. Munch had captured my fear on canvas.

I stepped back, shaking, teary eyed. If I continued to walk backwards, this figure would turn into a male. Like one of those holograms or optical illusions. I'd always been useless at working them out. But I wouldn't stand for this. That face had to change.

I turned to the other exhibits, feigning speechless critique until the trickle of heads had passed by. And then I turned back again. It didn't matter which angle. It didn't matter how many metres. The Scream was my fears made manifest.

Chapter Twenty-Six

At least I'd been sensible enough never to have introduced him to Morten. Oh, the insecurity it would have unleashed.

Daniel did come with me to Denmark once – and once only – on a day when his fury exceeded expectations. The journey to Heathrow was riddled with arguments. He didn't want me to drive; one thing for me to be doing the business, quite another for a woman to be behind the wheel. Yet neither did he have the conviction to navigate us to the airport, his sourness reaching its peak just East of Reading services when he'd seized the wheel.

"I'll finish us both off."

I wanted to engrave 'HELP' in the condensation of the window, in the vain hope that someone in an overtaking vehicle would make out the shaky letters, rescue me from my plight. But I knew that would only further exacerbate things. I guess I must have said something to make him straighten the vehicle, since I was still alive. Once again, I couldn't though, for the life of me, remember what.

Indeed, the steering wheel grab stunt had happened several times over the years, but all I could ever recall when I tried to summon the scene was the intense feeling of fear in those moments. The rest was lost in time. So curious the way he'd mangled my mind.

Hours later, sharing a beer with The Delectable One during a meeting whilst Daniel was safely relegated to the hotel, I wondered if Morten had ever done such a thing. Maybe his gorgeousness and charm were cover up for another smooth operator? But as he leafed through my latest of offerings in the bar, I knew that could never be. Hell no, I was an expert now. It was all about the eyes. And his met mine with the warmth and sincerity of a good man. His partner had better cherish him.

There was never any rivalling Copenhagen. It topped the bill as stomping ground for a new man. Just about every male seemed to be blessed with the kind of symmetrical features that blew a woman's mind – conveniently overlooking the minor detail that the female of the species also possessed Helena Christensen eyes.

I was feeling every bit the single female on this latest of visits. And where better to start than Tivoli? Perhaps, like Walt Disney, who cited the gardens as the inspiration behind his creations, I adored them too for making me feel part of a fairy tale; a place where bad things just didn't exist, and if they did, they'd be slain by a dragon breathing fire from its menacing snout.

And perhaps I adored Denmark itself because that air of *hygge* was everywhere I went. Even before I'd learnt of its meaning, I could already sense the infectious Danish art of blocking out the problems of the outside world to create a warm and cosy mood. It sounded too good to be true, but I intended to envelope myself in it completely while I could.

I was with Steph this time, since Morten wanted to think about dabbling in English language books too. Two damsels – at least it felt that way since we were walking past the Hans Christian Andersen-inspired Flying Trunk ride – in search of a decent eatery. I, of course, had been ogling the waffles. It beggared belief that Steph had uncharacteristically declined to follow their trail from the perfumed stand we'd just skipped by – so much so that I wondered if she was Daisy in disguise. We opted for pre-dinner drinks, in the hope they would be accompanied by nibbles, and soon got lost in the sheer escapism of the place; its tradition, greenery, lakes and fountains, flowers and parades; everything that celebrated life. Then, feeling a little playful, it was time to ponder the flotilla of rides varying in thrills and spills.

The ghost train whilst tipsy was fun we discovered. But the waltzers whilst woozy; waltzers that unexpectedly rose up into the air at an angle of one hundred and eighty degrees, they weren't so much fun. And since it was a low season 'school night', we were manually whirled with added gusto by the devilish guy in charge – even before the dreaded chariots embarked on their ascent. It took a worryingly long time to regain my balance.

In fact, you could say that something about my whole sense of perception changed after that ride. Paranoia crept over me. I had the strange sensation of being watched, although where in Tivoli's name that came from I have no idea. It was just impossible to shrug off the urge every couple of minutes to look over my shoulder.

I quickened my pace, only half-feigning hunger – it had been several hours since food, and we sensibly headed straight for dinner at a nearby pizza restaurant, completely missing the opportunity for traditional Danish fare, and downing as many soft drinks as possible to help wash every trace of alcohol out of our fragile systems. Tivoli wasn't all sweetness and light, after all. Wisdom was to be found sticking with the good old-fashioned horses.

"Talk about a wolf in sheep's clothing," I said as my still twitching hand tore off a wedge of Margarita.

"Why has mine got dill on it, Kate?"

"Dunno. Mine's okay."

"If I wanted grass on my tuna, I'd have asked for it," said Steph.

Once the initial rush of carbs had filtered into my bloodstream, I was bursting for the loo.

"I know it's slightly uncouth mid-meal, but I really can't cross my legs any longer," I laughed, and sped off, leaving Steph to scrape the remainder of said herb from her plate.

When I clip-clopped back into the restaurant, it was to catch the tail-end of some bizarre commotion or other taking place at the revolving doors. An elderly couple patted down their coats and straightened themselves up, I'd no idea what they were saying in Danish to one another, but they looked as if they'd been pretty jostled.

I made my way back to Steph and my pizza. She was bending to sort out a wayward buckle, something which seemed to be taking an eternity and so I munched on alone, knocking back large sips of water to compensate for our alcoholic over-eagerness.

Finally, she was upright again; pale and upright. So much so that she looked like she'd seen a ghost.

"Are you okay? You look a bit pasty all of a—"

"Yeah, yeah, I'm fine. I'm just…I think I need the ladies suddenly myself…"

Off she ambled in a most peculiar way. I could only put it down to the head rush of the fairground.

***

We were all smiles once again when we reached slithering *Strøget*, the world's longest pedestrianised street which sliced through the city. More daylight than their Scandi compatriots seemed to make for shinier happier people, even if the city lights were flickering on. We window shopped contentedly whilst commenting on the dress sense of the throngs.

Forget Paris, Milan and the rest. This was the catwalk. Copenhagen was me to a T. Things were quirky, interesting and naïve here. Clothes were unpretentious, had real stories behind them, rooted in Red Riding Hood and magic, pixies and wolves. And the Danes could do minimalist without being clinical or dreary. An effortless scattering of thrown together but thoughtful, earthy coloured items and ta dah, you had an instantly warm and enveloping montage, seducing the customer inside and taking them back to nature, camping trips and woodland schools. And so this endearing hygge wasn't simply to be found in the home, but in the fashion too. Shame the bikini range had finished though, I thought, as I daydreamed about my future beach romps in paradise.

As we strolled back to the hotel, and Steph caught her breath, my phone rang. Initially I panicked. I didn't need a showdown with Daniel right now. But then I flushed in recognition of the 0065 number.

Hayden.

My heart skipped a beat, not helped by the fact I'd just sunk my front teeth deep into an ice cream.

It was work related, disappointingly so: who cared about unit prices for sound chips? Since I was licking ice cream at the time, I fed Hayden a line or two to let him know; an image I could tell he found impossibly seductive since he was suddenly struggling to articulate himself. I couldn't help but smile. Clearly, despite his Very Best Business Attempt, I was still giving him the 'desired effect'.

The uneven cobbles beneath my feet caused me to totter like an airhead. I really hadn't expected to hear from him, and had momentarily forgotten all about Steph and her even slower snail's pace behind. She suspected something for sure.

"You two always flirt like that, do you?"

But I was giving nothing away.

The sensible but funky buildings lining Nyhavn expectantly awaiting the revival of the fishing industry that used to flank the quays, frowned down at me disapprovingly.

***

On our last night in Denmark we stayed at our former client, Ulrikke's, farmhouse. Tucked neatly away on the fringes of a little village just north of the city not far from beaches full of fine grassy tufts and mysterious Nordic blue sea, it was a *hygelig* gem.

In fact, indigo and blue were the anchors of Ulrikke's living room. A pyramid of logs welcomed us in, inviting us to take refuge in bucket seat chairs around the hearth. Our host pulled out some twill plaid blankets in case anybody was cold.

"Make yourselves at home, girls. Dinner will be a while, but I thought maybe you'd like to take a tour of the farmhouse, whilst I warm through the veggie tart."

"Ooh, yes please."

"Make it snappy though, we've got this lot to get through," Ulrikke said as she plonked a crate of red wine onto her reclaimed plank table.

Frank, the farm dog, sniffed at our heels, following us up the wooden stairs and into Ulrikke's office.

"Wow, Daisy would love this." I grinned as I walked over to the blackboard desk and picked up a chalk to scribble Ulrikke a message.

"Buy books, not candles."

"Kate, you can't write that, how rude."

"But it'll get her thinking. She used to be a good customer…"

"Yeah, until she walked away from publishing and set up a gift shop…anyway, we've got Morten now."

"Oh, purlease, will I ever hear the end of this, Steph?"

"Probably not."

The beagle with the slanting right-angled back led us out again and into a kid's playroom. The table and chairs and the bare bones were neutral, unassuming, and then wham: splashes of happy primary colours livened up the palette, covering walls from ceiling to floor.

"This is quite a place," said Steph as we followed Frank back down the staircase and into the kitchen.

"Did you do it all yourself?" I said.

"More or less," said Ulrikke with a touch of sadness.

She beckoned us to pull up a pew at the kitchen bench. Danish pottery and all its adorable patterns twinkled gleefully from every shelf and dresser.

"So, how went the meetings?"

We unanimously let out loud giggles. Ulrikke poured the wine and listened intently to Steph's account of Morten.

"Oh he sounds divine…You must introduce me to him next time. We can pretend you double booked the meeting." She winked.

"Nah ah, hands off my customer," I said.

"Spoil sport."

"Ah, mine as well now…potentially, anyway," said Steph, prompting everybody to clink glasses.

"Oh, Kate, do you remember the fun and games we had last time you were here?"

Steph looked intrigued as to the embarrassment that was

about to unfold.

"Well, she was staying overnight here with me after our meeting," said Ulrikke, "but she didn't turn up at the village station… Naturally, I began to get a bit panicked. I mean, the train system here in Denmark is safe and reliable, but it was eight in the evening and these little village stops are pitch black. So I just assumed she'd got off at the wrong stop and was stuck there on her own till daylight." She paused to light a candle, which was symbolic to say the least. "Anyway, I knew she'd actually got on the train as she'd texted me from Copenhagen. But despite sending her messages, I hadn't heard from her since. I was starting to feel pretty sick and wishing I'd driven into the city and picked her up myself instead…"

"So what happened?" said Steph.

"Kate, you can tell the rest of the story," Ulrikke said in a sudden high pitched voice on the verge of cracking up.

"I j…just don't know what it is with me…and trains," I snorted, unable to get my story out on the first attempt. "I think maybe all the station names sounded similar and the tannoy system wasn't working properly. Then I got talking to this older guy, who turned out to be one creepy pervert—"

"Ha, you always seem to attract them," said Steph.

I threw her an unimpressed semi-smile.

"Well, I just couldn't get away from him. He knew where I had to get off and it was like he was trying to get me to miss the stop so I'd end up having to go to his stop, which happened to be in the middle of a deep dark forest miles from civilisation." I shuddered at the thought.

"Ulrikke had explained to me that the journey took about forty minutes, so when I glanced at my watch to see it had taken an hour, I knew I was in trouble. Thank God I saw right through his plan and decided I'd do the sensible thing; stay on the train until I was thrown off. But then, hallelujah, a ticket inspector appeared. Creepy Pervert tried to make out I was talking nonsense, was really looking to get off at his stop, but I was having none of it. In the end, the inspector signalled ahead to the driver to slow the train down to a crawl, told me to get ready to jump out the door onto the passing southbound Copenhagen train in about three minutes." I paused to take a large slug of wine to ward off the shivers that came over me whenever I recounted these kind of close calls.

"I have never been so scared. I mean jumping out the doors from one – admittedly slow moving train – onto another train…it felt like suicide. But I did it. I was hauled up to safety by the guard on the other train and when I turned back to say thanks, my lovely, helpful northbound ticket inspector had disappeared. All I could see was a fleeting glance of a very pissed off face as Creepy Pervert realised he'd been defeated. Brr…" I hugged myself for a moment mulling it over. "I dread to think what he'd had in mind." I unfolded my arms from my chest and guzzled quickly at my drink.

I couldn't help but wonder if I was consistently putting some kind of a vibe out there?

It was far from the first time I'd been stalked.

The train thing had happened before with that weird Dutch guy who used to come into the supermarket I'd worked part-time at.

One day quite out of the blue, when Daniel and I had taken a trip to London, abraflippincadabra: there he was waiting in the carriage opposite the automatic doors as they opened to take us from Covent Garden to Hyde Park Corner on the underground, beaming with his I've-been-expecting-you face.

"Shit," Steph gulped her wine back as well. "Sounds like you had one lucky escape there, matey. It's put me off going on a train on my own at night – or with you."

"Anyway," I changed the subject, which was beginning to freak me out. "Maybe it's a daft question, but where's your husband? And I'm so sorry, I've totally forgotten his name," I laughed, feeling the blood return to my cheeks.

"Well, I'm not surprised with all these exotic customer names you have to remember," Ulrikke chuckled back. "Lars? Oh, yeah, I should have mentioned it. We've split. But

197

it's fine."

She walked to the worktop and flung the casserole dish to the back of the aga as if demonstrating it really wasn't so big a deal.

"Now, Steph, you are one of those veggies that eats fish, aren't you?"

The rise and fall of laughter simmered to a pin-dropping silence.

"Um, yes, I am."

"Oh no, don't go all quiet on me you two. It's all very amicable and was a long time coming. He's with somebody else; I have a new man in my life too. Well, on and off. A couple of them, in fact." She paused to chuckle. "It's all early days but I'm in love with the dating all over again thing, making up for lost time. We got together so young. It rarely lasts these days when that happens. There's a whole world out there, things to experience, stuff neither of us had got around to doing. We were married at just twenty-two. Can you imagine that happening now?"

"I'm so sorry, I'd no idea," I said.

"Well no, of course you didn't. Nobody did. The main thing is the kids are happy – we're all happy. I just bloody well wish we'd done it sooner." She smiled genuinely, pouring yet more alcohol into some tall glasses before handing them round on a circular tray.

So my instincts were right.

Last time I'd visited with Daniel in tow, we'd had dinner with Ulrikke and Lars next to the tall masts of the boats lining Nyhavn Canal. The four of us had been huddled, fighting the shivers beneath a quartet of outdoor heaters. Yet I had detected a flaw. Something between husband and wife wasn't right. Maybe only somebody in that same position could recognise their counterpart in another? It seemed I was fine-tuned enough to sniff these things out, no matter how hard a couple was trying to fake it.

And now here was a very different Ulrikke; a single, successful, sassy woman whose shop was going from strength to strength – stronger still if she'd buy some more books. She looked youthful too, as if the split had knocked several years off her.

Maybe my own life could be a *smorgasbord*, if only I'd let it. Ulrikke's spirit filled me with awe, if not a little envy.

"Anyway, how is Daniel? Any marriage plans for the near future?"

Steph coughed unnecessarily and rolled her eyes so they aligned with mine, with more than a hint at the fact I should have left him already. And then her head pinged back to her wine glass in an instant, as if she'd forgotten herself, and she couldn't seem to stop examining the havoc she'd wreaked on her chronically over-bitten nails.

"Based on what you've just told me, not until my mid-thirties," I said with an unconvincing smile.

Chapter Twenty-Seven

It took four attempts before Filpe – according to the name on his gold encrusted badge – would even take my order, let alone serve it. I guessed he'd sussed me out within moments, had seen my un-moneyed type before. He continued to lavish his service upon the gentry, returning every so often to his toadstool-shaped bar by the pool to faff about.

And later that evening there was more of the same from one of the pair of snobby English businessmen who'd taken up the gold-tasselled sofa opposite me in the 'day room'.

"Having a little bask in the luxury while the boss is upstairs, are we?"

"Ha," said his sidekick. "I'm sure he'll get off the phone from the wife soon, come back down to play—"

"I am the boss."

That soon had them decamping to the bar.

Why exactly couldn't a woman stay in Lisbon's Pestana Palace without being painted as somebody's mistress? I had never encountered such suspicion. Then again, an inexplicable neurosis had mysteriously, ridiculously descended upon me just like in Copenhagen. I put it down to Edward Munch and his masterpiece.

My feet had hardly touched the ground, and thankfully it had been time to jet off again; this time for the annual Portuguese trip, which strangely enough Daniel had been in remarkably good spirits about. Practically encouraging me, you could say.

"P'raps you could bring me back some of those *pasty di natar* things you're always raving about…"

They were hardly transportable. But if it kept him sweet in more ways than one, I'd try my best.

I usually made this trip in February, but had managed to convince Adrian there were a whole host of new business opportunities opening up at the moment. Brazilian editions had started to jump on board beefing up some of the print runs, too.

But no matter how I dressed it up, I was addicted; hooked on living life from another perspective, as far away from Daniel as possible.

As usual it wasn't the meetings but the landscape and cake that embedded itself firmly in my short term memory. The magnificent bridge that straddled the Duoro River; the kaleidoscope of tiles which adorned just about every building in the city – in all of the blues from cornflower to petrol, so unmistakeably Portuguese. Were they ever more dazzling than when camouflaging a washing line of denim? And yes, those *pasteis de nata* with their unforgettable eggy-ness and deep, deep vanilla! As for the heavenly chocolate mousse, it had become a longstanding lunchtime ritual with my biggest client in the city. But the chef still refused to impart her secrets.

Unfortunately, the Henry-like phrase "I've been chasing my tail to get this sale," was also engrained in my head, thanks to the guy seated opposite during the flight ceaselessly whinging to his female colleague.

Another unfortunate incident was bumping into Piers, of all people, at Oporto's airport.

My mouth was faster than my brain when I spotted him in his customary stance near the ticket desk as I was about to queue for a taxi.

"Piers Middleton? Is that really you? What the heck are you doing here?"

He was swigging on a bottle of Fijian water (which very nearly ended up removing my mascara, such was his surprise to see me), pacing to and fro, scanning the horizon as per usual to see who might be scouting for the cover of *Harper's Bazaar*.

"Kate!" he feigned delight so badly, eyes already skimming from me to his bulky silver watch and then the far-off departures board. "I'm here on a little business...you know, for the shoe company I'm CTO at now...off to Barcelona next, then um Milan and Paris. Gotta run," he said, ditching his posh water bottle in the bin, "fab to see you, looking lovely as always..."

And that was mysteriously that.

But all of this was a mere appetiser to the delights of Lisbon.

As time always dictated, I was sorry not to see much more than the cute mustard-coloured trams which gently nudged their way up the cobbled hills offering relief to weary legs.

Then again, I'd booked myself into none other than a lemon marzipan iced gem of a building which also happened to be a national monument. Wrought iron gates swung open obediently to reveal a long, winding, ornately tiled road, and the novelty of a porter in waiting. He opened the cab door, swooning over my bags before I'd even set foot on the red carpet. This was quite something, but definitely in keeping with the manner in which I could grow accustomed. And it got better. A scattering of rose petals adorned my bed. Had I missed something? Was Hayden waiting, ready to pounce from behind the dramatic, velvet, sweeping curtains?

Having had the good sense to keep the first afternoon free to 'prepare meetings', I changed into my bikini, covering the lily white bits in a sarong so long it could wrap around a bus. It was also probably best I stayed out of the room. All this décor was lovely, especially the coving that looked like it'd been piped onto a cake, but I was petrified of breaking something.

"Okay, I can't put my life on hold any longer," I said aloud as I checked I'd double locked the door (Munch's image had woken me yet again in a cold sweat last night).

"I'll discuss it with myself tonight over room service, come up with a plan and stick to it this time."

And with that, I determined to erase Daniel from my mind for the afternoon. The pool was too beautiful to have him contaminate the view anyway. I reclined on a fabulously cushioned lounger, not too far from the water's edge so I could dip my legs in relative style whenever I felt the call. Perfectly manicured toenails were the only thing missing as I glanced down past a double chin to my feet; that and a cocktail. Filpe had better be bringing it soon.

But now I'd stopped rushing; now the sound of airliners had trailed off into the cloudless Portuguese sky, I couldn't help but reflect already. These trips were more than just business, more than just escapism too. They were little voyages of self-discovery, each giving me more belief than the last that I really could break free from Daniel's spell.

As I peeled away the layers of fear, the real Kate was emerging from a lifelong cocoon. This amicable solitude was a good thing, for with it, came the realisation that I didn't want to keep living parts of my life in inverted commas. All of it could be like this, every day, a life free from persecution, belittling, ridicule and physical harm.

So why was I still living two separate lives; lives which had become so blurred, so jumbled?

Now I was seriously thinking of leaving the company too. After all my years of hard work and sacrifice, I'd be relying solely on my credentials. Would they be enough? What if I took the wrong turning at this crossroads that loomed ahead? Taking this risk could land me right back where I'd begun: at the bottom of the social heap.

Was I really prepared to sacrifice the loss of income for something more austere? I enjoyed the finer things in life, felt entitled to them after all those years with my head in a book. I didn't want to drive about in a safe run-of-the-mill creation of a car, just like everybody else, or worse still, in something ramshackle and archaic. Maybe that suited some. I supposed if my teenage years had been different, I might share in their contentment. But I'd struggled so much, worked too hard to simply throw it all down the drain on an ill-conceived whim.

I was a Somebody in the position I had. And I knew how it felt to be a Nobody. I was terrified of going back.

Above all, I had a point to prove. And that adrenalin rush from pulling into the local petrol station in my expensive set of wheels, flicking my hair and flashing the plastic in front of my perpetrators past was, frankly, too addictive.

If I lost that people could say things.

But what could they say about somebody who drove a ruby-red Audi convertible, shopped at the high-end of the High Street, travelled the world, had her hair done in the best salon in Somerset – other than they were jealous, they'd been wrong to judge me by my schoolgirl cover?

Nowadays, I liked what I saw – most of the time – in the mirror. But those looks didn't come without the best cosmetics. It took money to keep up the façade.

But I couldn't go on like this, living off the perks I was skimming alone. I spent so much of my life at work, that somehow, selling products I didn't believe in seemed immoral. There was a bridge from my head to my heart. Had I enough belief, enough bottle to be a pioneer and cross it?

I decided to start studying the traits of those who had. It was the only thing I could do; the only way I would know if this is how it felt before the big jump.

I'd start with Oprah…and Richard Branson. Inspiration didn't come much bigger than that.

***

Dressed in a crisp white sleeveless shirt and gunmetal pencil skirt with matching jacket, accompanied by some seriously chunky bling – fake, but good fake – I made my way to my first meeting the next morning.

Eduardo was as debonair as ever.

"You look wonderful, darling, simply divine."

I knew I had to act fast. I bent down to unzip my case on the floor, squeezed as usual between the antique chairs and table which made up Eduardo's 'office', and gathered as many books as possible. Not easy with small hands and awkward-shaped thumbs.

Eduardo sat in his regal leather chair watching on.

"Well now, let's put those away and go out for a nice lunch instead," he said no sooner had I heaved a pile onto my lap like an over-eager *Jackanory* presenter.

Bollocks. Once again I hadn't been quick enough. How could I resist though? I knew the drill by now.

And so to Restaurante Maria and the dark soothing space where pre-lunch drinks were always served before we were shown through to our customary table like a couple of dignitaries.

The ritual of ordering was an art. Two lone souls in a restaurant, a four waiter per table affair, silver cloches, and most importantly: a cavalcade of dessert on wheels. For once I really couldn't make a cake decision.

"Have one of each of the puddings."

"Eduardo, I can't, it's too much." They looked so delicious. But such a thought was beyond pig-greedy.

"Nonsense, I insist." Eduardo frowned at me as if I was being absurd to even contemplate turning down food of this calibre.

"Well…um…okay then, if you put it like that."

He basked and glowed in pleasure. His observation of a woman eating, savouring every mouthful, was poetic. Eduardo expected me to satisfy my appetite without judgement. He wanted me to shun the fat and calories. To hell with them then!

The whole world lurched at me in that moment. Yes, I realised life couldn't be like this every day, not really, but Eduardo was a man who opened doors, stood to welcome a female and seat her at the table (as much as that would have narked somebody like Steph), rising again at the end of a meal to wrap her coat around her: one of the last remaining true gents of publishing, a very rare breed.

"Now, you must have some Madeiran cheese and biscuits."

"Thank you, yes, you know…I think I just will."

***

Emboldened by my growing assertiveness, I checked out of the hotel, lodged a complaint about Filpe, demanded a discount on the bill and returned to a precious empty house. Daniel was working late at the farm followed by his YF meeting.

"I'll leave after Frankfurt. There: I've said it."

In the same way a dieter needs the time to be perfect, continuity was crucial to meeting prep. I put the rough outlines of a plan into place, I ummed and I ahhed. Some days doubt crept upon me. Was I really strong enough? Where was the safety net?

But even the media was screaming out at me before it really was too late. I would switch on the radio and a debate about domestic violence would be raging full throttle, airing the misconception that an abusive relationship is violent all the time.

Days later, I chanced to stumble across an article in a newspaper, addressing the *hidden taboo, silent crime*. A day later again and an EastEnders plot mysteriously reached its culmination, featuring a woman who was being tortured with an iron in her own kitchen by her husband; the man who was supposed to love her.

Unlike this poor fictitious woman, I had my independence. That was the craziest thing of all. My job and the salary it provided, my skills, my qualifications; they would always be there. I was the pin-up of self-sufficient. There were other women out there who had given their careers up to stay home and raise the kids, women who no longer had a stream of income or viable means of escape. Those women would have given anything to be me. I had to do it for them as much as myself. Even living in a bedsit with all of my worldly possessions in one room would have been a retreat.

One day I booked myself in for a tarot card reading. To be honest, it was about time. How can anybody living in Glastonbury not take advantage of the myriad mystics on their doorstep?

Except this wasn't any old set of tarot cards; these were Glastonbury Tarot cards (I mean I hadn't known they would be, but I suppose it made their message all the more relevant, right?).

206

I was nervous as hell, until Jenny greeted me at the front door of her home near The Chalice Well, reassuring in plain clothes.

"This isn't ouija boarding or clairvoyancy or anything like that, relax love. I could sense the foresty dark green of your aura even before you rang the bell." She smiled before leaning in to kiss me on the cheek as if we'd known one another all our lives, then led me in to her tiny mid-terraced house. "Take a seat...I'll fix you a tea – you drink normal builders' I presume? I'll bring the cards through in a jiffy and cut them up. All we'll be using is your intuition and that's it."

She disappeared down the rabbit's warren which joined sitting room to kitchen. "You'll choose the cards that speak to you most right now, but whether you follow their path or take a new one is entirely up to you, so nothing's set in stone," she raised her voice above the clinking of the china I could see her laying out on the draining board.

"Okay, yeah that sounds good," I said, picking at my nails as I scanned the books lining her walls which catalogued everything from Pranic Healing, to Tales from the Ancient Isle of Avalon, and Rune Stones, to Macrobiotic for Life.

It turned out Jenny was right. I opted for the three card reading and the images it brought forth were as relevant as any that could have been randomly picked. I knew that all the more so after she let me study the others which made up the pack.

"Interesting, very interesting." She turned the cards I'd selected one by one and concentrated on their message.

The first card was the Seven of Swords: boundaries.

"So this is where you are at the moment," said Jenny. "The goalposts of your current relationship are stifling you, to the point that it's impinging upon your own sacred space. It's time to go within, follow the messages from your higher self and make your perimeters very clear to significant others..."

The second card was The Chariot. It depicted a woman with a flowing mane of brown hair and a green cape sailing away from Glastonbury Tor in a boat. It was my situation captured with the strokes of a brush. And there wasn't the slightest hint of trepidation to be detected in this woman's face. In fact she was radiant, smiling. She knew where she was going, and yet she didn't know where she was going. All she felt was freedom and that was the only signpost she needed.

And the final card was the Five of Staffs: empowerment; a thunderbolt of lightning zigzagging to the ground and a shaman standing against a very dark sky.

"Wowzers," said Jenny. "Just look at the pattern here. Everything's flowing wonderfully… Okay so the Five of Staffs is truly one of the most powerful cards in the Minor Arcana. It's telling you that you've grown in awareness of your inner power and now the only thing you need in order to turn your life around, is sheer self-belief. If you believe it, you will see it come to pass…"

As if all of that hadn't spelled it out clearly enough, I decided to purchase some angel cards and Native American animal cards too, whilst affirmation cards and aspirations were pinned all over my visualisation board in the office. I was beginning to know how it must have felt to be one of those poor OCD people who lock the door several times: double checking, double-double checking and triple-double checking. Still the fact remained: everything I did, no matter how weird or whacky, great or small, came back with the same unmistakable message: something greater is out there, time to go.

Finally, the mathematical equation no longer balanced. The fear of staying was greater than the fear of leaving.

Chapter Twenty-Eight

"Do you realise the Greek word for single is the same as the Greek word for free?"

Daisy delighted in sharing this revelation as we gave in to some much needed gin and tonics. Shoes had been removed and we were even massaging the balls of our feet on the Maritim bar's carpet – more than a little disgusting when one considered the kind of things that had been spilt on it over time.

"And how did you discover that little nugget of trivia?" said Steph with more than an undertone of criticism.

"Stavros, my Greek customer," said Daisy as she finally removed her ski-style owl head wrap. She tugged on the tassel ears sensing an impending heckle.

"Ahh, Horse Tail Guy, the one who fancies you."

"It's a pony tail," said Daisy.

"But you don't deny the attraction…and it is a horse tail, Daisy. How can something that long and tangled be called a pony tail, for goodness sake?" Steph was in one extreme grump. Frankfurt wasn't her show and she'd never really taken to hanging about looking unimportant.

We were celebrating the end of our last day of meetings in traditional fashion, and without the men. The three of us had descended upon Frankfurt a day early for the obligatory set-up of the stand and here we were again at the end of it to do the same in reverse, whilst the others made their annual excuses.

The usual passage of cold air had blown into the gargantuan halls as we'd battled a week ago to slot buckled shelves into place. If you weren't up and at it by sunrise, you could expect another company to have pilfered any perfectly formed specimens from your stand – replacing them with their deformities by noon. Those who arrived late found themselves hammering unruly metal in desperation, unable to display their wares, crying into polystyrene cups of Cava.

Set-up day was also notorious for ogling eyes, mainly the vice of certain males of the species, who couldn't resist copping a load of a female's pert backside, or a glimpse down her low cut top. I learnt quickly having worn a medium coverage vest in 1999 that only a T-shirt neck line would do. And the women were just as indulgent. Goodness knows I'd scrutinised a few stand maintenance guys over the years.

In contrast, once the fair was in full swing, perspiring bodies wilted onto stands. Men struggled to contain their bodily secretions in heavy duty suits and windpipe restricting ties, whilst women got away scot-free with sleeveless dresses and the sheerest of stockings. The over-enthusiastic exhibition staff, kitted out in insanely warped costumes, would pounce on passers-by with leaflets that would be tossed straight into the bin. It was the one area where the systematic organisation of the *Messe* and recycling objectives of the German nation failed miserably.

In all others, the perpetual vigilance of the book fair staff could not be faulted. The giant car parks functioned with military precision. The cloakroom attendants required a degree in seven languages and the philosophy of organisation. And the crew who scanned the bags upon arrival at the halls, tipping my underwear and moustache bleaching kit all over the table at the entrance for all and sundry to see in case I had an explosive device inside, they were beyond impressive.

Of course people had already begun to trip into stands, usually on account of one too many daytime drinks. Banana Man (so called after he'd caught a glimpse of Diana in her infamous black leather pinafore – and had skidded, as if on a banana skin, crashing into the front panel of our stand, knocking down all of the signage) was still doing the rounds, tirelessly trying to flog advertising space for one of the less prestigious publishing magazines.

Stand parties were in full swing too, even if it was only Wednesday. I loved the way hangers-on effortlessly blended into the hinterland, quaffing free supplies of booze and food, negating the expense of dinner.

Even on the first day of business, the morning stroll into the fair had been particularly dull and uninspiring. Fog and rain descended on the city, as was so often the case mid-October. No wonder Heidi had been homesick for fresh mountain air.

Amidst the sniffles and sneezes, I could see my own breath leading the way as I powerwalked to keep up with the others, who were all better equipped in the leg length department. There was something so depressing about the arrival of this fair; a sure sign that winter was snapping at the heels with chattering teeth just around the corner, and if I didn't follow through with things, another Christmas spent with Daniel.

I supposed there was beauty to be found here too. You just had to know where to look. The green spaces were only really marred a little by the distant banking empires and crisscross of jet trails. Even in the heart of the city, the dangerous-when-tipsy tram tracks looked so pretty covered in their lush velvet grass. Frankfurt, dreary old Frankfurt made me feel powerful, in control and secure. Life was orderly. One knew where one stood. When I looked at my life through the eyes of this city, being with Him didn't make a scrap of sense.

"Be done with him. Get out now while you still can," the iconic pro-socialist giant man with the hammer outside the book fair seemed to roar in the wind.

D-day was looming. I'd even set the date. There was the small matter of informing my brother, who would be instructed to arrive at 11am on Saturday October the 25th with his car. Then my real life could begin.

I never entered the fair unscathed and wasn't about to do so now. A cackle of foreign gents echoed behind me as I caught the point of my red patent heels in the rubber matting. I hobbled on one foot flamingo-like, attempting to free my beautiful shoe and yelp to my friends. Heaven help me if we ended up going straight out for dinner in Sachsenhausen later with its maze of cobbled streets.

The familiar and the quirky brought a smile back to my face as I clip-clopped along the ruby-carpeted aisle of Hall Eight, which had been vacuumed to perfection.

Show time.

I hoped against hope to arrive before the Boyles, putting paid to any last minute straightening out of our decorative efforts of the day before. It always happened. Fortunately this year our stand neighbours had succeeded in kidnapping Adrian to run through a slideshow of their grandkids, whilst Henry had been commandeered by a dutiful book fair employee who was adamant that only half the stand cost had been settled:

"You will accompany me to the office now, or we dismantle your booth."

But the part of the day that had made me wince above all others, had to be the visit of the sultry Mexican beauty. She'd been studying the new and exclusive 'board game' section of the booth. Once Henry thought he'd sufficiently captivated her by perching on the table, putting that overworked cheesy wink and grin combo into practice, and giving her the life story of the company's formation, he'd then straddled himself in a wholly inappropriate manner across a chair, arms folded and rested on its back with the poise of a Cossack dancer. At least his Hawaiian-patterned shirt and the unsightly hairs protruding from it had been hidden. But he'd then embarked on a full-blown kingpin-cum-revolutionary speech:

"We can put anything on any design on any board game you know, yeah, that's right – aliens, fairies, wizards with a similarity to Harry Potter, googly-eyed animals that put you in mind of Disney but aren't quite up to scratch illustration-wise, blah, blah, blah."

Caught up in my meeting, I could make out his disturbing silhouette rocking about on a chair, entranced by this femme fatale and her immaculate fuchsia nails, in danger of falling backwards and jeopardising any business with anyone.

I had been brimming that morning, simmering over with anticipation as to who would buy what. Silly really considering we only had five new titles. But the buzz of a book fair produces a certain kind of magic, glossing over the imperfections of everyday life.

In some companies, the same old editors greeted us. For every small independent business, there were the usual suspect lethargic corporate beings, drilled to perfection about what they mustn't buy; creativity hampered by a job description.

In others, like the big multinationals in Paris, there was a constantly high turnover of staff, making it virtually impossible to get a foot in the door. No sooner had you struck up a rapport with one editor, than another showed their face and it was just like sliding down a snake in one of Henry's unoriginal board games.

Contacts old and new still requested one sample of everything, probably to supply their bookshops. And samples mysteriously disappeared, no doubt being swiped and imitated by competitors.

Then there were Gary and Sebastian, who'd resumed their double act and seemed to be incessantly snapping away at rival stand exhibits, presumably to report back to the twins with 'new ideas' to copycat. Any and every time I left the stand for a sneaky loo break or to queue for the dreaded delights which constituted the *Imbissstube's* idea of food, there they were over one of my shoulders, mobile phones in hand.

And then there was Jake. I wondered if I'd missed an entire episode of my life. What started as a little harmless flirtation in Bologna, had suddenly – in his head anyway – turned into the Freedom of the City.

An evening later when we found ourselves a little too cosily seated at the same table in The Maritim bar – again – he'd permitted himself to rub his hand up and down my thigh. His promiscuity made me squirm, particularly as I was sitting next to Henry at the time, thus the placement of those probing fingers could have had some interesting consequences.

One thing was for sure: it was all becoming a little too footloose and assuming. I wasn't sure what our unofficial entanglement was all about. He repulsed me whilst making my heart flutter. My wicked side wanted to mount him. Yet my sanity prevailed. I knew I would feel utterly sick in the morning.

And then there was Martyn.

"Oh. My. Word, I could have eaten him there and then," said Daisy, even permitting herself a squeal. "I've no idea where he came from and why of all the women at the fair he made a beeline for me? But I'm not complaining...he's taking me out when we get back. We're going to have a night at the theatre in London."

I was pumped that the show had ended on such a high for her. She had only secured herself a date with one of the UK publishing industry's hunkiest of males, Martyn Bostock. He'd rocked on to the stand for an impromptu meeting and spotted Daisy alone. From thereon in they'd been inseparable, causing him to miss several of his meetings, whilst Steph and I had scurried around covering for Daisy's. But it was worth it. She had such an infectious sparkle. Her zest for life had returned. This was her moment, and not even my concern as to how my own personal next few weeks would pan out, could overshadow my happiness for my friend.

It was just a date, true. But it signalled so much more. Daisy was looking to the future. And more importantly, she was living life in the present. Scott really was history.

As for me, I may have dreaded the banality that the return to normality brought with it, but something had happened to me this year too. No, I hadn't shed my clothes for Jake, thank God. But I had started to shed my skin. I needed to capture that energy and keep a hold of it when I was packing up my belongings and stashing them into Simon's car.

It dawned on me now that I'd seen so much of this lack of fulfilment precisely here over the years, and not just my own.

People didn't just come to Frankfurt for work. They came to pretend. People offloaded here. Then back they went to the monotony of their marriages, or their lives of limitation.

This hub of bodies briefly, momentarily, crissed and crossed like a busy international airport. But even at the end of the fair, the traces of their energy were still there; the echoes and promises of all manner of verbal and optical agreements.

***

Once again: thank the Lord for follow ups. I might be back in Glastonbury, but I also had the perfect excuse to spend more hours in Bristol, working later in the office. And thank the Lord the text from Jake had chimed its merry way onto my mobile when I was twenty-eight miles from home. How had he got my number anyway? Only a fool would have given it him. An hour and a half later and Daniel could easily have read that somebody had taken it upon themselves to refer to me as 'sexy'.

I deleted it.

But the thought of a date and a little bit more, I just couldn't erase it. It was too easy to arrange. All he'd have to do was check us into a hotel in Bristol when he was next down visiting a client.

I could always pretend I had to take my own customers out, was kipping at Steph's.

My head was spinning with Hayden. I didn't want the fuss of Jake. But just for the novelty, I did put forward a proposal in an email.

He replied back immediately to say he "surely would."

Chapter Twenty-Nine

"That cow's been at it again," Jason panted, still in disbelief at whatever whoever it was had done.

He was covered in sweat and agitation as he pressed the play button on his Dictaphone, something I'd no idea he carried about him.

"She'll be the downfall of this place, Her Upstairs...letting customers pay by Bill of Exchange in the twenty-first century...not chasing up their debt...her and her fancy heels and dresses, flaunting herself about like a prize-winning floozy. P'rhaps that's why the Belgians put in such big orders...there's obviously something else she's selling..."

Sharon was blaming me personally for the demise of the Belgian client who owed us so much money. And Jason, who happened to have the means, had cruelly documented the evidence on tape.

Like a bog standard attempt at a Custard Tart that's failed miserably in the wobble department, his heart was undoubtedly in the right place. Still I would rather not have known, and something told me there was fuel to this chitchat.

Bam!

A sinisterly entitled PAYMENT SITUATION email pinged onto the screen before me in the kind of bold capital letters that screamed trouble off the Richter Scale: Boekerij Gordon had defaulted on payment again. Sender was Rupert, and I knew this meant a trip to Bruges like yesterday. What a hideous voyage, not least because I doubted I'd be going alone or that I'd get to factor in a chocolate-making workshop.

Business with Wim had been a dawn of superlatives. And nobody but me had thought to question the vast quantities being ordered by The Netherlands. It wasn't as if these were licensed character books. There were no distinguishing mice adorning them. Yet eighty thousand copies were regularly being reprinted per series. And so it seemed, they weren't being sold on to the bookshops, supermarkets, petrol stations and kiosks of Belgium and Holland at all, but hoarded in a squirrel's dray somewhere deep in the suburbs of Bruges: a rich harvest of literary pickings to ensure survival of a deep dark winter.

"Well, this is all getting a bit too much now," said Daniel. "Are we in a relationship or not?"

Officially, we were, for I still hadn't managed to overcome the blasted P word. My head would conjure up nothing but reasons to delay.

"It is crap timing, I know. But it is what it is: we're owed several million and I am the sales person for that cli… customer…I can hardly get out of going."

"Yeah, yeah whatever, always an excuse," he said slurping down his cuppa before work. "I don't know why you don't just be done with it and live in Europe to save all this dilly-dallying about and messing me around. Several million? What a crock of shit. You aren't selling stocks and bleedin' shares, they're kid's books, woman…"

**

Adrian squinted, feigning study of the real stocks and shares. I'd put money on it that he'd be reading a tabloid of a certain name on the way back, a surreptitious peep at page three when I wasn't looking. He sipped cautiously at his hot cuppa as would only a Gent on a British Airways flight to Brussels. Meanwhile, Rupert caught up on sleep. His presence would be a sure sign to the customer that She Sells meant business; that the expectation was for Wim to put a plan into action and fast. And I felt remarkably cosy in my grey cardigan with oversized fabric flower brooch.

I had a cardigan for every occasion; the days when you just wanted a bit of arm out and it was springtime sunny, the super freezing chunky knit days, the baby doll shrug cardigan to finish off an outfit and keep the summer evening chills at bay, and the boyfriend style (perfect if you had one like mine) – long enough to skim the thighs, cover the rump and streamline your figure. But today was a day for The Reassurance Cardigan.

Wim's wife greeted us cheerfully two hours later, her multiple mini-braids swaying to and fro like one of those pendulum desk ornaments I used to gaze in awe at during childhood doctor's appointments.

"I had it done in the Dominican Republic last week," she said with a big grin. "Do you like?"

"Ooh yes, it's very pretty," I said. "How long can you leave it in? Is it easy to wash?"

"Nice to know Wim still manages to keep you in style despite owing me millions…"

She scuttled away after Adrian's remark, returning with a tray of instant black coffees, and a husband who trailed sheepishly behind.

"Hellooo, so lovely to see you all: sit down, sit down," said Wim.

I frowned. He was my client and he hadn't as much as looked me in the eye. I'd just as well go out in the kitchen with his wife and swap notes on the Caribbean, or flirt with some of the warehouse guys.

***

"So, that's that sorted then: toast."

"You really believe he'll stick to the payment plan?"

Two hours later again and I peered dubiously at my what-could-only-be-described-as-a-tankard of beer. I never usually drank the stuff, but just occasionally, on a sunny afternoon in a European square when you were marooned with men of a certain rank and file, it had a kind of appeal.

"We have to, Kate," said Rupert. "Adrian, I think you did a marvellous job in there today." Cue manly slap on the back. "Now all we need is for Wim to comply with our plans for re-sale of the stock – that and the settlement of the debt, and the establishing of new customers here – and we'll be back to business in The Benelux."

Adrian's eyes flashed at the hint of profit and the fizz of his Belgian speciality beer, the aptly named *Brugse Zot*, which he'd zero idea translated as 'Bruges Fool'.

"Did you know that each beer comes with its own glass in Belgium?"

"Really? Fascinating…"

The sandwich board advertising plump Belgian waffles, now that was something to behold.

"Fancy another?" Adrian gasped after wiping the remnants of his amber nectar from his chin with the back of his hand.

Where had he put his first? I'd just about managed a couple of sips without the bubbles flying up my nostrils.

Rupert obediently beckoned a waiter.

Adrian ordered an extra beer for everybody; ignorant of the fact my glass was still full. Then he eyed up the giant, plastic, fake cone of chips outside the eatery.

"Oh and a large plate of French fries…"

The waiter glared.

***

The last time we'd seen the company to which we were en-route was during their very spontaneous visit to Bristol. Adrian had insisted I invite them over to discuss becoming 'major partners' in the Benelux market. All a bit pointless really when he'd instructed me to continue selling the new titles to Wim. A lunch appointment in the hotel down the road had been arranged and unusually, the She Sells contingent had all turned up on time, even Adrian, who a quarter of an hour later, rather than greeting the potential business partners with a polite handshake and small-talk about the warm spell of weather, announced waywardly, "you're late!" accompanied by his customary teenage giggle and everybody else looking at their shoes.

Fries devoured, we'd deposited Rupert at Bruges' central

219

station to board his train back to the airport. The mood felt calmer now, lower key. No, I wouldn't go as far as to say this would be a buddy-style trip. Yet the ambiance minus Rupert somehow felt like that shared between mates.

"We're here," the taxi driver announced as he pulled up outside a row of very domestic looking buildings.

"Are you sure?" I said. "I mean these look suspiciously like houses to me...the company we're meeting with is pretty medium-size. I don't think it's operating from somebody's living room."

"Lady, you gave me the address. I've driven you there. Mission accomplished."

"Can't you call the number for us?" Adrian offered up a crumpled piece of paper. "Here."

"That's looking a little like an email from Henry," I said.

"Oh, yeah."

"I'm not a receptionist, guys. I can take you back to the hotel, or you can get out here."

"Okay then. Here it is. Thanks for your help," I said, "most kind."

"Yeah, thanks for your help. You won't be getting a tip," Adrian sneered.

"D'you maybe want to say that after he's unloaded our sample bags from the boot?"

Bags dumped, passengers stranded, the driver sped off.

I approached number 131 with Adrian shying away just behind me, and knocked uncertainly at the door.

"Oh no, there's no company here," answered a forty-something woman, hair up in curlers, toddler welded to her dressing-gowned hip. "But you're welcome to come on in. We get this happening all the time," she laughed.

I wasn't sure I'd have such a sense of humour about two randoms constantly turning up on my doorstep when I was half-dressed.

We sat in silence as Trudie – she'd introduced herself whilst prepping a bottle of formula milk and some pureed swede – flitted about packing the little boy's change bag.

"This is so very sweet of you," I said.

"Oh it's nothing. I'm heading out that way anyway for a play-date at the park," she giggled again. "If you can't help a stranger with a lift in a time of need, who can you help?"

I was careful to avoid Adrian. His eyes were scanning every corner of the room in a nervous display of not knowing where to look. If I met them I was sure to crack up at the preposterousness of it all.

Half an hour and a bizarre offering of rusk biscuits later: "They're good for the constitution, full of vits and minerals," Trudie said as Adrian bit into his, we were deposited outside the Wholesale Books of Bruges headquarters.

"You're late!" said Joop van Outen, raising a set of the bushiest eyebrows as Adrian outstretched his hand to be shaken.

***

I was a little apprehensive about being holed up in a hotel overnight with Adrian, admittedly, especially after Steph's Caribbean debacle. He'd apparently finally succumbed to her feisty beauty, knocking on her door for an attempted midnight cuddle during their 2002 export sales trip. But I also realised this was a great opportunity – much like the way Daisy and I had secured that Spanish language trip to Granada last summer – to print out a request for a pay rise, wait until he'd had enough beer and then get him to sign it.

It was also rather sad the lengths I had to go to achieve a well overdue rise in remuneration. And I supposed the very reason we were in Bruges hardly made it the appropriate time and place.

Sitting at a far-too-small table outside a heavily *moules*-influenced café, I tried to pretend I hadn't spotted the accordion player in the background.

"Muscles, is it?" Adrian said. "Or maybe madam fancies some muscles? They also have muscles. Or you can order some muscles."

"Crikey, Adrian, I can hardly contain myself. You're so original tonight."

221

"Ah, lighten up, Kate. All of this Wim stuff is sorted. And thanks to my patter with WBB earlier, we have them ready and waiting to suck up the dregs." He smiled, turning slightly to cock his head at the street music.

I cringed. What a way to talk about customers. And as for that musician, couldn't he just do one?

But the impossible intimacy of the seating arrangements and the wedding-style flower baskets draping from the window sills only served to lure him in. I longed to take refuge in the praline-filled window of next-door's chocolate shop. This was getting dangerous. And then I remembered: I wasn't Steph. He'd never shown me any signs before, no reason he should start now, just because there was beer and Flemish folk music.

Accordion man stopped and offered up his hat for some tips. The waitress served us our moules curry. That was close. We both tucked in. I hadn't realised how ravenous I was until the steam from my bowl wafted up to my airways.

Before I even registered the music had re-started, I shuddered as a large hairy brunette vision pushed the concertina folds of his instrument back together in defiance and made undulated dance moves towards Adrian's back. He was accompanied by a man with a basket of red roses, whose eyes spoke of romance, sparkle and starlit dinners under a velvet sky. He waved a single stem in front of Adrian's face, rolling his head and shoulders towards me.

"No, no, we're just colleagues," said Adrian. He cowered in his seat, unsure of what to do with the forkful of rice that was midway between his bowl and mouth.

Even though I sensed the growing expectation of the diners surrounding us, I couldn't help it. I just had to pretend otherwise. It wasn't every day you got to make your boss squirm.

"What do you mean, honey? That's not what you said last night. You told me you loved me to the moon and back…and now you won't even buy me flowers?"

Adrian coughed rice across the table. Oops. Maybe I shouldn't have taken it so far – even with the drink. This would be a bit of a painful memory for some time to come. He dipped his hand into his pocket, pulled out a note, selected a rose and passed it to me with a puzzled smile.

When the embarrassment had settled, and his plate was almost spotless, Adrian opted to converse once more.

"Well, I wasn't quite expecting you to do that; my wife maybe – just a tad embarrassing. You're a strange one, you. Quiet as a mouse, but get the drink into you…"

I laughed.

"Is that a compliment? I'm not that reserved."

"But you're happy with your boyfriend, aren't you? Few years and you'll be married up, couple of kids…"

What? Where did that come from?

His statement lingered like a bad smell. I couldn't look at him, much less answer, and even much less continue with my moules.

"He's ah, he's just got us three more hens. That's more than enough for me to contend with right now."

Chapter Thirty

I could sympathise with the vacant soul-less stares of the Red Light District's women. As they painted their nails candy pink and read Dutch literary classics, patiently awaiting their next assignment in the neatly lined up gabled houses, I had to acknowledge that I too, was still living a similarly numbing existence. October had come and gone and the only packing had been for Amsterdam.

"Do you think women's rights have ever really moved on?" I asked Steph. "Or are we as humanity holding on to some kind of nostalgia? It's the oldest profession in the world, isn't it…?"

Somehow, even as two women who were beginning to feel a little out of our depth, the further on we strolled, the more this visit was becoming imperative. The glow of old-fashioned street lamps reflecting in the canal made for a truly romantic setting; somewhat ironic for a part of the city that wasn't exactly renowned for fluffiness. And after getting lost visiting a client in the labyrinth that was The Hague, fearing we'd never find the hire car again, even being here in the evening brought its own kind of odd relief.

Although not long back from Bruges, a visit to catch up with the Amsterdam publishing scene – which jammily coincided with Steph's holiday choice – had been a long time in the planning. All of the towns and cities basked in the light made famous by Dutch landscape painters, had merged into one seamless drive on the open road as we darted about to my clients. It had been no stereotype to wonder at the flatness of it all, grazing on *Speculaasjes* – Dutch windmill cookies – as we ungratefully sped past yet another windmill, and yet another rectangular strip of poker-straight tulips. The evening's meander was the perfect reminder that I was, in essence, free.

"Any news yet on Wim?" said Steph with a frown which suggested she already knew the answer.

Ah Wim. He'd already started defaulting on the new payment plan. And my mind was so far away from work that I forgot to formulate a response.

"A Euro cent for your thoughts, Kate?"

"You really don't want to know."

"You're still up for the exit, aren't you?"

"Which one?" I said catching the scene in the flashing light bulb studded windows again.

This was ridiculous. I did have a choice. Whereas some of these poor souls, well, they could have come from my kind of situation; maybe one that was amplified to the level of severity that the battery occurred every day. But that had to start somewhere, had to escalate from some sort of beginning.

"It's depressing, isn't it, seeing these women like this…"

"Drink, drugs, trafficking, abusive families: happens everywhere, just here prostitution somehow seems more acceptable," said Steph.

And then there was Anne Frank. When I took the horrors of Anne's story on board, even if I'd only ever sailed past her house, how could I justify suffering any longer? It was, as Steph had rightly told me two months ago, insanity to stay a moment longer.

"I think I'm done with the crimson lights now," said Steph. "Shall we go find a bar? Not sure I'm up for a café though." She grinned.

I had a speedy flashback of my adventure on the bus with several lumps of potent *Squidgy Black*; Sarah Snelling, *The Orb* on my headphones, a failed attempt to jump on a *Debenhams'* escalator to sleep it off in the toilets on the top floor, and an ambulance.

"No, not for me either." I waved the very suggestion away with the back of my hand.

As was often the case, a few drinks with Steph turned into

225

many more.

"You know how karma isn't working nearly fast enough," I said, "and how much stress all this stupid unpaid Belgian debt is creating—"

"Am I thinking what you're thinking?" said Steph, one hand circling the remnants of her Vodka and coke with her straw, the other fiddling with her brand new phone with built-in camera, which she'd barely stopped touching the whole trip.

"I think that means we're both in agreement," a wicked smile lit up my face.

I delved into my laptop bag and revealed a bundle of suggestive posters.

It was a hopelessly childish but fabulous idea of Daisy's (how she'd let her hair down since Martyn B). She'd even offered to put the design together and make the photocopies.

Steph and I were soon in our element, running around the city, hanging pictures of the hunky muscle-clad guy, who could be reached on Wim's mobile, on the pub doors, toilets and bike baskets of Amsterdam. The thrill of doing something so feral was exhilarating, even if it didn't exactly cast me as model boss. The dynamics of my department were governed by friendship and creativity, I reminded myself. And these little outlets of fun kept me sane, especially when all was carnage at home.

Mayhem morphed into drunken calm. We headed to one of the main shopping streets where upright youths sped past us on bikes like a stream of puppets, reminding us how much we and the rest of Britannia slouched.

"So, should we stagger departures?"

"Or screw She Sells up royally with one mass exodus?" Steph chuckled.

Flower sellers were just starting to shut shop; their blooms still pristine. Amsterdam was such a city of contrast. Before long we were wandering through streets littered with the dreariest of re-funked social housing and edgy raw Bristolian street art. But perseverance paid off, leading us back to canals full of fetching town houses, where pocket-sized national airline blue cars framed the canal side, some parked precariously close to the water's edge as if contemplating ending it all.

They reminded me of Daniel. And that wasn't good.

***

Simon did pick me up, true to his word. It was a swift operation, pre-planned to perfection to coincide with Daniel's absence – except I had only packed enough clothes for two days.

"What about your mortgage and the house and all your joint possessions?" said Mum as we tucked into the fortnightly Sunday roast.

"I think she's nuts too," said Simon. "You're lucky to have him. The world's full of tossers, I should know, I'm one of them. Daniel bloody adores you though, anyone can see that. I just can't believe he's been knocking you about. It's not like you've ever come over here with strangulation marks on your neck."

"It's probably just a phase," Dad agreed. "Didn't we go through that, love," he winked at Mum, "the seven year itch thing?"

No sooner had I digested the last spoonful of apple crumble and custard, than Simon coaxed me back into his turbo exhaust Fiesta to return to the compound, head down; a prisoner back inside after compassionate leave.

Chapter Thirty-One

"Crikey," Steph bit her lip and lowered her head, "I'm not sure if this was me or you?"

She handed me the Dutch speeding ticket which had landed on her desk that morning.

Normally, I would have sworn it was indeed Steph who had put her foot down on more than a couple of occasions, but who cared? Nothing much mattered anymore.

The rest of my Sunday had been spent looking in longing at the verdant pastures surrounding my Rapunzel tower; the lush green I'd had a quick taste of, but had then become pathetically fearful of, running back to my captor and all that was familiar. Glastonbury Tor had stood fiercely proud, guarding her hill with her palpable authority. Even from afar, I was in awe of her independence, her stature.

Feeble bitch.

That's who I'd become. I couldn't blame my family either, much as they frustrated the hell out of me; The Showman had succeeded in brainwashing us all.

I couldn't even meet my reflection in the mirror before work that morning; had scraped my hair back into one of those trendy half-pony tail, half-bun things; strands poking out everywhere. They didn't suit me. I didn't care.

He'd sat in the rocking chair of the spare bedroom, clutching at a pillow, weeping like a little boy, telling me he didn't know what he would do if I left, couldn't be held responsible for the next chapter. Well, that would just have to be the chance I took – when the moment was right again. I should have trusted myself to keep running. But he'd made me feel so much pity, and then there was the loss of the money. Once I'd slammed the front door shut, reality hit hard. Try as I might, I couldn't quite face living on my income alone yet. Not for a few more weekends, anyway.

They said it was always the quiet ones who took their own lives; the ones who didn't keep banging on about it. I had to convince myself of that, I had to believe that the very fact he was always bringing it up meant he'd never really act upon it.

"I need you. You're the only one who can make me get better."

Wasn't that just the classic narrative, the glue that kept me bonded to him for so long? If only I could throw a bit more love and a bit more patience his way, give him just one more last chance.

If only. If only. If only.

"I'll change, get counselling." His eyes lit up, he must have thought this couldn't fail to win me over. "We could go together," he said, as if I was somehow part of the problem. "I can't bear life without you. I'm nothing without you."

Just one more trip away, just one more fling. That would inject the last bit of confidence. I'd never had a fling on a sales trip, it was about time.

Yes, I liked this excuse better. There were bound to be questions from those I'd informed about the weekend's planned escape. This was more credible to the prying outsider, more moral somehow.

Of course, I'd keep it zipped about the sex.

Chapter Thirty-Two

Conk, conk, conk, splurt.

"I don't flaming well believe this! Noooo, don't do this to me. Oh, you little…"

I swerved myself and my Audi into a tiny layby on the A38. I was half a mile from the airport, as well. Half a mile! But it was too far to walk with two cases. And I couldn't just abandon my cherished motor. Why, oh why couldn't this have happened in the car park, or on the way home?

It was an *RAC* miracle that a short while later, the macaron-clad bakeries of Paris beckoned, displaying their rainbow-coloured backgammon sets of mouth-watering deliciousness in every shade from pastel peach to grass green.

Daniel refused to pick up the car. I would have to somehow sort out the logistics from France. I supposed the fact I was away for The Carnival hadn't exactly helped win him over. He didn't like to go out much, but mid-November was an exception.

"You know how important it is to me, it's a family tradition what with Sissy having been Carnival Queen three times," he'd said.

"But once you've seen one float, you've seen them all. My absence doesn't need to upset your plans. You can still have fun with Hannah and your mum. I didn't plan it this way. Saturday's flights are fully booked."

"What a thing to say. Have you no idea how much work those clubs put into making their creations?"

The commotion on Glastonbury's Carnival night was just too much for some. Fights spilled out onto the roads, into the pubs and onto the unsuspecting doorsteps of houses, as some

of the locals took on the personas of other-worldly beings –
in costume or not. This was testosterone's excursion of the
year: armies of teens and twenty-something males on their
annual mission to instigate war.

The heavenly smell of candyfloss and fried onions would
fleck the air. Even I couldn't deny that just about anything
could happen under the spell. It was the one night of the year
where Glastonians could be whom they wanted and do what
they wanted – well, notwithstanding the festival.

One year my friends and me had got so pissed on Malibu
and lemonade, that when we'd seen our old Science teacher
in the throngs, I'd uncharacteristically yelled:

"Oy, Penfold!"

Mr West had been our Head of Year, the one who'd taken
it upon himself to grant me detention for a certain tomato
throwing incident, taking place after my epic Corned Beef
Hash Smash. He also bore more than a striking resemblance
to the mini-me from the cartoon, *Danger Mouse*.

I'd been concurrently glancing down at the technology
room from the home economics classroom (where a certain
Tim Franks might just happen to look up at me, because in
my head, of course he was as madly in love with me as I was
with him) whilst removing said pièce de résistance from the
oven.

Smash…and cue mahoosive piss-take from a couple of
nerds who were even lower down the pecking order than I
was.

The audacity!

Naturally, pelting leftover cherry toms out the window at
said foes at lunchtime (with no clue they would later douse
themselves in conveniently squeezy ketchup sachets courtesy
of having a mum who was dinner lady), was a recipe for
disaster. And so it was that I set myself up good and proper.

That hadn't been a good day. In fact it had turned into a
classic raiding-the-cupboards-for-shop-bought-Cherry-
Bakewells-in-floods-of-tears kind of a day.

I blinked away the tangents of nostalgia and brought my
focus back to the job in hand. I was en route to a meeting

with a publisher who was based on an industrial estate some ways outside the city. He'd bought reams from me over the years, despite being one of the least *charmant* of my French clients. So I was happy to get this one out the way.

The backseat taxi window framed moments of Parisian life. Those first peeps of the city were always whimsical. Boutiques advertised an abundance of *objets* for sale; pretty cottage garden flowers here, vintage mannequins peering demurely out of equally vintage fronted windows there. An old-fashioned bread truck jutted out from the kerb, offering passers-by a wistful view of its baguettes snuggly balancing on top of one another. And Parisiens made their way home after a day in the office/café/museum/shop.

"*Je suis ici pour un rendez-vous avec Pascal Boucher,*" I finally reported to the receptionist.

"*Ah, oui, il m'avait laissé celui-ci a vous donner, madame,*" she grinned pushing her specs higher up the ridge of her nose as she passed me Pascal's scribbled apology: an urgent meeting had cropped up in Nantes.

"*Il aurait du m'appeller,*" I screamed back at her.

What a waste of sixty Euros. And now another sixty for the return, all just to be given a piece of paper. Why hadn't he called?

I ran out to flag down the taxi. But it was too late.

"*Putain de merd.*"

I'd put money on it (if I had any left) this was revenge for the Boyles refusing the discount for those faulty sound chips from the Halloween book (sounding more like a sweet bleating sheep than an evil Count Dracula).

***

I still couldn't quite bring myself to 'do' dinner alone. Even the understated elegance of menu typography couldn't persuade me otherwise. So much for a sales trip one night stand, how exactly was that supposed to manifest?

I stopped at the window of a *chocolatier* instead, pondering its offerings. I really should take something back for Daniel but the salted caramels spoke only to me. And so I bought a box, making short work of them as I strolled to Notre Dame – it's not like he'd have appreciated the chic packaging anyway.

Wouldn't it be amazing to come here with someone like Hayden? Smitten, besotted, romping from dusk till dawn, stopping merely for dinner and a promenade past the Eiffel Tower, then back to it. There could be no greater memory than that of a romance in Paris. I wanted it badly.

I turned back on myself and headed for the comfort zone of the room-service menu. The safe dark colours of the Parisien women buzzed up and down the boulevards, another reminder that I had failed to dare on the dining front. Whilst undeniably glam, they also seemed to be in constant mourning – a sombre, limited palette of colour that equally summed up my relationship (and current mood), begging me to ask myself why I dressed in such a ground-breaking red coat only to lock myself away with a bland *Novotel* risotto and the remote control?

***

A Paris haircut, manicure and pedicure had become something of an in-between meetings tradition, and on my last morning in the city, I knew it was the boost I needed for last night's chickening-out, the absent-from-Carnival guilt which lay waiting at home, and my final meeting: The Biggie, Gerard Le Croix.

His suggestion: *Café des Editeurs* was the perfect backdrop, being venue of choice for the French publishing world since way back when. The pulse of Paris truly centred on these hidden bistros and cafés, rather than the museums packed to bursting with tourists.

Whilst it may have been the height of sophisticated European café culture, it was also the ultimate squeeze when you had a large trolley bag stuffed to the hilt with book samples. Try as I might, I could never quite pull off the look of elegant businesswoman for long, and invariably ended up looking more like a heffalump of a 1960s travelling salesman. One foot would be stretched behind the case, the other straddling it, hopelessly trying to balance in a skirt that was edging its way up my thighs, just to pick up the cumbersome things, paving the way for that most uncomfortable of moments where two relative strangers bend down to fumble for the same squeaky board book, praying that they won't accidentally touch one another inappropriately, or the sound chip on the pig's nose.

"Can I ask you, Gerard, how did you get started?"

I wasn't sure if this was appropriate. But I sipped my coffee expectantly. Gerard didn't know the twins. I was sure I could trust him.

"Me? I just decided one day that I was doing zee job of everybody in zee company where I worked. But of course, I wasn't getting paid for eet." He paused to laugh, stirring his coffee idly, and I joined in in recognition.

"Zee bottom line is, you 'ave to sink or swim and that is all there is to eet. You do eet, or you don't do eet – and if you don't do eet, nothing will ever change."

And so it was that Paris corrected my autopilot: I knew it. The city knew it.

I stood tall and proud, virtually sailing down the street to the taxi rank, looking the world and all of those in it in the eye. Self-worth propelled every step. I was sure if I put my hand behind my back, I'd find a large clockwork key planting in me an unwavering determination.

I was first in the queue and finally my ride pulled over. I slid my shades on top of my head to talk to its driver.

A sad and hunched over twenty-something-going-on-seventy-something, spotted my cases and asked me the obvious through the window.

"*Oui, Charles de Gaulle, s'il vous plaît,*" I said, letting him take my things as I settled into the back of the cab for the journey to the airport and my new life.

Unbeknownst to me, Fabien, the taxi driver was in a dark place. Oh for fuck's sake. Why did I have this tendency to attract psychotic men with deep-seated problems?

234

Fabien was desperately miserable, had recently contemplated taking his life, he told me, at which point he also placed his foot down harder on the accelerator, overtaking vehicles of all shapes and sizes on Paris's motorway.

I gripped tightly at my handbag, as if that would make the slightest difference, and then opened it in a panic, searching for my inhaler which I rarely used, but never travelled without. I didn't want to draw attention to myself and the urge to hyperventilate hadn't quite descended upon me yet. Instead I squeezed my medication reassuringly in my hands and applied extra pressure to my imaginary brakes.

Funnily enough, the idea of a meal alone didn't pose such a threat anymore.

How had it come to this; that he was working up to ninety hours a week to pay for a taxi of his own, and then what? He was pleading with me for the answer. But he was hungry for love too, in desperate need of a woman.

"*Et où est-ce que je peux trouver une femme qui supporterait ça?*" he demanded of me.

I wasn't sure where he could find this mystery lady either. But I needed to come up with a solution unless I wanted to end my days in a mangled wreck. Don't think of Diana and the paparazzi. Just don't. I shivered then quickly pulled myself together. I could turn this around. I wasn't prepared to be at the mercy of yet another man.

I wouldn't fob him off. It was important to acknowledge his pain, make him feel justified in his grief. I tried the 'you are young you have plenty of time' route. But he punched his fist into the air exclaiming age was but a number, he felt ready to fall into his early grave.

"*Non, non, non,*" I cried.

The speed at which he was bombing down the A3 was insane. There was nothing else for it. I had to concoct the impossible. I thought, and I thought fast.

"Okay, so there's this famed crystal from a shop in Glastonbury, the town where I live," I said *en français*, having no idea if my story was true. "And it brings

235

everybody who possesses it great luck, abundance and most importantly, the love of their life. I will send it to you."

He told me he hoped I was right since he wasn't sure how much more he could take.

"I owe you another one," I muttered to whichever guardian angel had protected me today.

When at last Fabien stopped the taxi outside departures, I didn't know whether to laugh or cry, and then he asked me for a kiss.

"*Ah non. Je veux dire, je veux bien...*" I lied "*...mais ce n'est pas du tout approprié.*"

I was a client after all and the right woman was out there for him in Paris; ready and waiting, I reminded him. He just needed to believe. Then in time she'd reveal herself.

***

Hannah's car was parked in the drive when I arrived at the cottage.

Then again, like Princess Diana, I'd learned early on that there were three in 'this marriage' too. She rolled her eyes at Daniel, as she stirred what smelt like minced beef in purposeful circles. So, now in my absence, he'd started pulling in the troops.

I accepted some time ago that she (and Daniel's mother) despised me, didn't find me to be a favourable enough match for His Royal Highness. A glass cupped against the wall had taught me that much.

"Grumpy Moping Cow," they'd called me. And "Mouthy Bitch," on account of all the arguments I had allegedly started in his bedroom which resulted in the broom thumping the downstairs ceiling, reminding me to turn the volume of my screaming down.

"Well, you know what that Silly Mare can get like..."

I was desperately ashamed for eavesdropping, and therein was a lesson to be learned. But I was glad I'd done it too, because at least I knew. I was never under any illusion. It would never have done any good for me to run to them for help when Daniel had beaten me in the past. They'd have laughed me out of town.

Don't get me wrong, they'd had nothing but praise for me in the beginning – ever the mistresses of enticement:

"You're so good for him."

"You make him so happy."

"You make such a great couple."

"You're so much better for him than Stella."

Because when it came to Daniel, it was always somebody else's fault.

"What would you like for pudding?" said Hannah, whose cake definition had long escaped me, and I realised now was categorically Beetroot Cake. Oh, but not Chocolate Beetroot Cake. The kind I mean is the lame slice that can barely hold itself together for excess rice flour and wheat germ collapsing onto your plate, served up in a depressingly organic café which you will never again make the error of thinking purveys anything remotely similar to cocoa.

"I can warm you up some rice pudding. Or would you like one of these steamed puddings that I found in the back of the cupboard – with some custard maybe?"

She grabbed at the tins which had been pushed to the back of the shelf, blowing over their tops with eyebrows whose arc hailed from a comic strip.

"They're a bit dusty."

"I'm not surprised," he said. "That there cupboard hasn't seen a duster since the day it was manufactured. None of 'em have."

Brother and sister continued to refuse to register my arrival, or show the remotest concern as to how I'd actually got home without my own transport.

Hannah headed straight to the drawer by the sink, no doubt to deliberate about the lack of cleaning cloths of any description. I swear Clover winked at me in moral support since tribalism had reached new heights.

I marched out of the room, heaved my cases onto the bottom step of the stairs and proceeded to drag them unaided to the top. The noise was hideous. I was surprised they hadn't both sped across to check I hadn't dented Daniel's precious oak planks.

When I re-emerged in the kitchen a short while later, stacks of tins and jars were lining the worktop like a fairground rifle range. Hannah scrubbed at their tops with unparalleled martyrdom. Then again, she was an expert. Not so long ago she'd helped re-thatch the roof, revealing toned and bronzed abdominals in hot pants, which of course had nothing to do with the fact Big Brother had just bought her a brand new car...or that she was getting to stand on scaffolding in full view of the passing traffic. All those carefully constructed hours at the gym paying dividends.

I tried to suppress my temper as I switched on the kettle, knowing no good would come of sisterly war. That was until she started trawling through my baking ingredients, spilling the very difficult to come by fructose all over the floor.

"If you're feeding these sorts of things to my brother on a regular basis, you really shouldn't be." She frowned, squatting to sweep piles of glistening crystal into the dustpan. "I'm prepared to overlook it this once since somebody needs to make sure he eats a hearty square meal, but it wouldn't help him or anyone to stay fit and healthy in the long run." She paused to eyeball me up and down. "If Daniel wants a treat, there are some very good low fat diet bars on the market—"

"Pumped with chemicals, that's right...ever heard of aspartame or phenlyllanaline? Really good for you," I said.

"I'm just trying to help keep the house in order, Kate." Hannah failed miserably at masking her smirk. "Daniel works so hard and such long hours. You really need to start pulling your *weight*." And now that smile widened rapidly.

"How dare you," I pulled the brush from her hand and pointed it at her with an embarrassingly shaky hand as if I were in possession of a machete. "Go and sort out your own home, you contemptuous cow. Oh, I forgot, you still live with Mummy."

But before I could act upon the spontaneity that next popped into my head, Daniel burst in from the garden.

238

Nice one, Sissy.

He lunged at me, pinning me roughly against the wall.

"See, this is how he treats me when nobody's looking," I shrieked.

I shouldn't have.

My mind raced with flashbacks of hands clasping my throat. As soon as he had me on my own, he'd throttle me for this, and that really would be it. I'd been warned it was coming, and like an idiot, I'd hung around for more.

Hannah looked unnaturally alarmed. She glanced sideways at me with an expression somewhere between guilt and fear, then fled the house, accelerating seconds later boy-racer style in her brand new Renault Clio, as the hatred in Daniel's eyes grew, and his body pushed me harder against the cold bricks of the wall.

"You're hurting me. Please let me go."

"I haven't even got started," he said with a perverse smile.

"I appreciate all Hannah has done, really I do. But I'm back now. I can make up for lost time."

"You think that will make me forget the way I just heard you threatening my flesh and blood?" he said. "She was clearing up your mess, making up for everything you lack, she's one hundred times the woman you'll ever be; you lazy fuck."

I stared in a helpless daydream at the scuffed toes of my boots.

I was one pathetic mess. And how could Hayden be my salvation when he lived halfway round the world?

But Hannah would be back to rescue me any moment now, surely? Maybe even with the police.

"Sorry," I whispered. It wasn't entirely creative, but it was all I had left.

I breathed a quiet sigh of relief as he released his hard grip from my chest, slowly at first and then he tore himself away from me. I caught his look of contempt and he spat – it seemed to be his trademark now. Saliva showered across my left boot.

"You're going cuckoo, cuckoo," he laughed demonically

and then a look of renewed determination painted itself across his face and he came back for seconds, thrusting my head against the hard exterior of the walls. His hand cupped my chin and twisted my head Rubik's Cube style, embarking on a slow but painful scrape along the rough crags of brickwork. I tried to hold my breath until it was over.

"We'll need to get you in a straightjacket, check you into the nuthouse tomorrow."

Yeah? Well, that'll be your final insult.

I had no idea of my thought's timing.

It was the most imperceptible of ruffles and groans, that's how it started, but I sensed its energy building in intensity and purpose. A scuttle so precise, so evidently thought through, became a silent yet athletic leap, revealing to me (and me alone) four legs and a defiant tail, soaring, gaining in height and speed until they clamped at the shoulders of the man who was crushing my cheek.

But my comfort felt short-lived. In as much as I adored that dog for saving my life, I feared she'd pay heavily at the cost of her own.

The noise that came next was a deafening yelp whose years of bottled up anguish and maltreatment knew no limits. Clover was a lioness who knew where her loyalty lay. Instead I prayed she wouldn't rip into his flesh as he toppled back and swiped for her, missing completely, stumbling and knocking his head on the corner of the table – and still she clung to him, her grip masterly and unyielding.

How a portrait can change in the space of twenty seconds.

I didn't dare blink in case this image before me should expire, the watercolours bleeding into wishful thinking. But Clover growled with an incessant ferocity. He'd never seen her like this. I'd never seen her like this. But I'm sure this beautiful soul had mentally rehearsed these moves over and over: day after day, night after night. Between the two of us, she and I had endured a collective of scrapes and lashings which she had decided she wouldn't let him forget.

He tried to calm her with a gentle patting motion which set her teeth on edge. She threatened to snap at his fingers and so he retreated, and still she kept her paws either side of his hips. His eyes were a frightened boy's as she howled and he waited until this was over.

I slunk against the wall, one hand assessing the damage to my face, which felt like it had been attacked by a cheese grater, and slipped further to the floor sensing this could take a while. Normally it would feel like a very bad idea, exposing my torso, head and shoulders to his boots, offering myself up as a target. But something about the dynamics in this house had changed in a moment of divine intervention. Clover was not letting go.

"All right, girl, let me go...I'll get out the house, let you calm down a bit...give you some space."

His eyes, the whites of which were shot through with a tangle of terrified red, met mine. And for once I held that stare, long and hard, in the sweet realisation the battle was over.

***

Unworn clothes were put into piles on the bed, ready for their imminent charity shop drop. Clover seemed only too pleased to help. I've no idea how long we sat there side by side on that cold kitchen floor, dazed at his swift disappearance after I'd beckoned her my way; ears still ringing from the assault of the exhaust on his van. But eventually we sprang to action, neither of us able to exit the building fast enough.

Then something caught my eye...and Clover's nose on the bedroom floor. The shard of dusky light from the south facing window revealed a perfect brown sphere tucked just out of reach beneath the dressing table. With the aid of a coat hanger, I flicked it out. The solitary Malteser swirled across the floor some eighteen months to the day it had orbited in the air. It nestled into a groove reminding me for the last time how useless I was at cleaning, its whirlwind spin coming to an impulsive halt, the definitive sign to leave him, followed by a canine crunch.

There was nothing to loot – a couple of cases, and when I'd crammed what I could into those, a few plastic carrier bags besides. The physical extractions of a lifetime with Daniel fitted conveniently into the boot of my car: clothing, toiletries, a few books, the full length mirror and the bathroom scales.

I couldn't quite bring myself to deprive him of the nourishment provided by my baking equipment. At least they'd give him some kind of a head start.

Clover sat by my side in the front of the car. Lizzie would meet me in the layby in twenty minutes, whisking her off to her new life; just as we'd pre-planned she would when I'd finally stopped my procrastination. Much as I wanted to keep Clover, I knew this was for the best; a room in Daisy's small city apartment was no place for a Labrador.

I never did get round to sending Fabien the crystal. I hoped he hadn't done anything stupid. I hoped, like me, he had finally woken the hell up.

Chapter Thirty-Three

In the days and weeks that followed, things couldn't have been more ordinary if they'd tried. Hayden hadn't pledged his undying love from the top of his skyscraper. Okay, so I hadn't exactly told him I'd left Daniel. But surely intuition alone told him I was shiny and new. It wasn't that he'd stopped flirting, the emails were still pinging forward and back, but things weren't moving up a notch nearly fast enough.

All right, I confess, someone else had intuitively realised I was officially free. It turned out Jake would be paying Bristol a visit in a couple of days, staying in that antithesis of a lustful backdrop, *The Travelodge*.

One word and one word only sprang to mind: cheap.

He was cheap. He thought I was cheap.

He could flaming well forget it.

I was tired of the chase. Above all else, I'd invested everything into Hayden anyway. As far as I was concerned, we were meeting in paradise next month, regardless of the fact he'd not mentioned it again. I'd sent him a print-out of the reservation for the exclusive 5 star hotel – in case he should arrive there first. I'd even booked his flight from Singapore for a bargain price – in case he was too busy to look into it. And I'd express mailed the ticket over to him. So of course it would happen. He was just being a typical guy, reigning in his excitement.

Chapter Thirty-Four

"You'll be holidaying in Phuket alone."

At first I assumed he'd been too ashamed to mention that he and the infamous Geraldine, were still a painful item; that he'd not yet managed to find the antidote to her poison.

"I see...you forgot to mention her, silly you. She obviously means the world to you if you feel the need to discuss your sexual desires with me on a daily basis." I tapped away at my keyboard in embittered passion. I knew the danger of replying to anyone about anything in full-on rage when it came to email, but this cold-hearted revelation deserved nothing short of my wrath.

"You're just scared of the reality," I continued, dictating to him the workings of his mind, "scared you might not live up to the image you've created. Do you even realise I've fallen in love with you, so none of that actually matters? Please, just give us a chance."

I hated myself for begging but logic had long escaped me.

"Let's go out for dinner when you fly over for Christmas. You at least owe me that much. You knew I'd booked up an expensive hotel for three nights in Thailand because you told me you were saving up to come and meet me...not to mention the fact I've paid for your flight. I believed you. Why would you say that if you had no intention? What was this all about, if that wasn't the plan?"

And then I descended to the kitchen below, pacing moodily while the kettle boiled me a magic potion. Daisy and Steph greeted me warmly as they offloaded identical quinoa salads into the grubby fridge. I was so engrossed in my next round of ammunition, so enveloped in suffering that I hadn't even answered.

I should never have left Daniel. The devil I knew was right: nobody else would have me.

A solitary, bold, unread message welcomed me back to my desk. I knew how he operated – at least I thought I did – he'd want to have this all wrapped up in a jiffy so he could wave away the guilt, hit the pub later, and have a laugh about it over a beer with his ex-pat cronies.

"Stupid little jumped-up English bitch. Why would you give any of this up to be with her when you're surrounded by the most beautiful women on the planet?" They'd fall about in fits.

"No way, Kate," he'd matched my reply within minutes. "I'm coming to the UK to see my family. That's it. I'm not coming back for you. It's never been about you. You don't even come close to figuring into my plans…or my life in general for that matter."

My heart sank. I tried to ignore the rise of the lump in my throat, the heat of the tears building up in my eyes.

"I don't have time for you, never will," he continued. "Now, we're not going down this road any further and whatever it was, it is well and truly over O.V.E.R. I'm sorry for your over-exaggerated feelings, but I don't control your screwed up thoughts. I had no idea I'd had this effect on you. They were just a few over-excited emails, a bit of fantasy to make the working day a little more fun. That's all. Regards Hayden."

"That's all?"

Daisy and Steph swivelled in bemused harmony in their chairs.

"And since when has he ever signed an email off with 'regards'?" I said, unaware of my audience. "The bastard: he's conned me good and proper."

My stomach was on the verge of emptying its contents, swamped by a churning nausea. With no idea where I was heading, I slammed as many files and pens as I could gather down onto my desk before bursting out of the office. My very last hope was that the brittle wintery wind would snap me out of this nightmare, so I would find myself back under

245

my cosy duvet, thankful that it was all just a bad dream, the alarm hadn't gone off yet, and my day hadn't even begun.

"I am out of here," I screamed, fearing I was losing my mind as well. I marched with purpose, fuelled by anger. I needed a shop, any shop.

What must they be thinking up there? What kind of a manager behaves like this? That's the last damned time I mix business with pleasure. I hoped in vain they'd assume it was something to do with a shipping drama. It would be completely out of character, more of a Steph operetta, but it was kind of mildly plausible – at a push.

My credit card was several hundred pounds heavier when I returned laden with posh pastel paper bags. And now I had the unenviable task of explaining myself to my colleagues, who were evidently shocked.

"I thought we shared this kind of stuff," Daisy clearly felt especially left in the dark since we were now flatmates. "I can't believe I hadn't picked up on this. I don't think I've even detected a blush."

"I knew you'd tell me I was crazy, on the rebound...and... and I didn't want you to be mad at me for putting any of our jobs on the line," I said in-between sobs. "I feel like such a fool."

Tears streamed down my cheeks. I quickly felt the shame of their burning and dabbed at them without the aid of a mirror, smudging what was supposed to be waterproof mascara, but hardly caring if I'd turned into a sad panda.

The window cleaner popped up outside, making us jump. But even I, who would usually find his monthly appearance a hilarious affair, since it never failed to catch one of us unawares, couldn't erase my frown.

"What an absolute rotter he's been," said Steph, arms holding me tightly. Then for fear of the window cleaner misinterpreting her, she shouted: "Not you, sorry, you've joined us at a bit of a heart-to-heart."

He waved his cloth signalling no offence was taken and continued to remove the pigeon poop from the outer panes.

"Hmm, I can think of stronger words," said Daisy joining

the group hug. "Of course we're not mad at you. I'm sure we'd have done the same in similar circumstances…"

I wasn't meant to see her roll her eyes heavenwards to Steph, who mimed back at her to stop it.

"…just not with him. Kate, what possessed you? Not only is he a Bad Egg, he's an Ugly Bad Egg. I mean that hair!" Steph glanced at Daisy again with a don't-make-it-any-worse-than-it-is grimace.

"Did I miss something in Singapore a couple of years ago? Like did you two cop off when I was looking the other way? Come to think of it, I do recall an excessive amount of banter when he called you in Denmark that time. But still, I'm just a little confused here."

"No. Nothing happened in Singapore. I felt some sort of attraction, could never figure out why. Got the same vibe from him too, but that was as far as it went—"

"Mate, has it escaped your notice just how flippin' gorgeous you are? You don't need a Hayden. You can do so much better than that, in personality and looks, Daisy's right. Come on, you've just left one bad relationship, don't go trying to track down another."

"Actually," I sniffed. "We've both been as incorrigible as each other."

"Hey, don't go all mushy on him," said Steph. "Just you wait until he drags his sorry arse into this office. He's a wanted man, dead or alive."

I was so thankful for their concern and care, it could have gone the other way after all, but I knew only I could put this right. I'd got myself, and inadvertently my team, into this mess, now I had the Herculean task of getting us out of it.

It was just as well Daisy and Steph were my friends, my Dear Friends at that. Anybody else could have used this as ammunition to get me fired. It didn't take much to check servers, emails, that sort of thing. And if they had got rid of me, how good would that look in a reference: 'good at her job, but really can't be trusted around the men'.

I'd had a really lucky escape and I knew it. But my will was defied and my desires utterly frustrated. I curled into a snowball, willing the festivities to pass me by. And this had to be the first December that I'd declined to partake in Daisy's organic chocolate covered marzipan. Now I would be all alone. All alone at Christmas was not a good place to be.

His words gnawed away at me. I was angrier than I knew was humanly possible. Was it a bet? Were there other people 'in on it' in the office, making a little money on our saucy exchanges? I had to hand it to him: he was a damn good actor. I'd fallen for it all right.

***

The morning of his flight to London, I wondered if karma might lend me a helping hand in the form of a tempestuous storm, gathering in strength as his plane prepared for descent over The Wash.

"It only seems fitting to wish you the bumpiest landing of your life, and a flight filled with colon-cleansing clear-air turbulence. ps. Now things are strictly professional, I expect my department to continue receiving priority treatment. We still demand outstanding service and for our clients to be looked after appropriately. If you'd rather instigate some changes so that we have a new point of contact, that's fine. In fact we'd much prefer it."

He emailed with a new generic heading, deleting all traces of the past.

"I'm sure we can remain professional, Katherine."

Huh, so he was being careful now.

I deleted every one of his messages after offering them up as further proof to Daisy and Steph. I'd picked them apart enough these past few months. They were nothing but a tease to me now.

"I still don't understand why you find him remotely attractive?" Daisy laughed, trying to cheer me up.

I sat slouched at my computer. I knew he was in the building by now, could somehow sense his presence.

The Thrills' *'Let's Bottle Bohemia'* CD played quietly on my *Apple Mac*.

248

"So if I betray you, you won't be the first, I won't be the last…"

I fast-forwarded to the next track.

"Now I don't mind if I hurt you, if I hurt you, if I hurt you and leave the guilt behind…"

And the next.

"Not for all the love in the world, no not for all the love in the world."

I ejected the disc and tossed it into the bin.

***

"Th'ick Hayden kid's downstairs, girls," said Jason as he fished his teabag out of his mug with a pencil and put it back behind his ear. "What a tosspot. Thinks he's Richard flamin' Branson that one…"

We were gathered in the kitchen queuing for the kettle, thanks to Jason forgetting to set the heating overnight.

So here he was all right, wrapped up like a present with a bow on top for his family's Christmas. How thoughtful of him. He couldn't even be bothered to arrange his flights to coincide with the office party, which had only taken place four nights ago. I don't think any of his colleagues matter much to him, I tried to reassure myself. We're all just Cash Cows to keep that salary of his flowing.

Most of all, I was seething that he hadn't the decency to come upstairs to say hello to the others. They worked with him day in and day out. It was so rude. Daisy had never even met him face to face.

'I think we need to clear the air,' I texted him later. 'Why haven't you introduced yourself to Daisy? You wouldn't have behaved like this if what happened hadn't happened.'

'Ok, agreed,' he replied surprisingly quickly.

Huh, he's only petrified of me embroiling him in murder on the production floor.

'Can meet 4 quick 1/2 hr super quick drink @ RL.'

'RL? Where's that?' I replied.

"Can't he be precise?" I said to Daisy who was anxious to

249

finish her To Do List which I'd already delayed by several hours. "I mean it's blatantly obvious I'm going to have to go back to him to double check in case he's waiting in one place and I go to the other." I tutted, secretly revelling in yet another opportunity for critique, and popped the last of the champagne chocolates from the box that Harold had brought us onto my tongue; wondering how we'd ever be ready to reconvene with him and the banks in a matter of weeks.

'The Red Lion, where else?' he batted his words back at me.

Damn, I should have seen that coming, and now I was furious I'd appeared to invent excuses to keep the flow of conversation going. He'd so planned that.

***

Daisy, Steph and I camped out in the Italian bar. It was just over the road from The Red Lion, the perfect spying den. We sipped on Chianti, faces pressed to the window, checking my watch every half a minute, on the lookout for a flash of that distasteful puffy gold body warmer, illuminating the cold streets of Bristol.

"He's standing me up, after all this," I said, in a mixture of disbelief, self-pity and rage.

"He's running scared, honey. You looked fabulous today. It's made him realise what he's lost," said Daisy trying to reassure me – one of many patient attempts that day.

"But he didn't even see me today."

"He may not have, but Gary, Sharon, Adrian…"

"You're clutching at straws now."

"You'd be surprised, they're sure to have filled him in—"

"There he is," said Steph. "Off you go, darling. And good luck, not that you'll need it in that dress."

"No."

I gripped my glass as they both tried in vain to hide their exasperation.

"I won't. It's about time he knows how it feels to be stood up. I'll go in ten," I smiled to myself.

"Okaaay," said Steph. "But let's be sure you catch him and he doesn't run off somewhere else after all the crap he's already landed on you. You deserve an explanation so let's make sure you get it."

Leaving just thirty seconds to spare before I'd delayed him by exactly ten minutes according to the calculations of my watch, and feeling aptly fired up, I fled the bar. Once outside I paused beneath the shimmering street lights, reflecting the earlier downpour on the surface of the road, to regain my composure. The former torrents of rain were now little more than a barely audible patter and quite the refresher I needed after the hustle bustle of Dalgarno's.

I couldn't see him at first, but I was certain he was still in there somewhere – no doubt propping up the bar, slaking his thirst, restoring his 'bottle'. We'd been like a vigilante, studying his every move from afar, and unless he'd exited out some back alley fire door, there hadn't been another sighting of a human firefly.

I edged my way through pre-Christmas party gatherings. Someone pinched my backside, and I turned to make an educated guess as to the perpetrator, giving him my best sharp elbow.

"Fair enough," he said.

Yes, I felt in character now: The Bristol Bitch.

And there's my prey, there he is waving his pathetic Singapore Dollars at the bar.

With feline prowess I snuck up on him.

"You're in Bristol now; you can put your stupid Monopoly money away."

He seemed a little rattled that I'd caught him unawares, but appeared relieved that I'd spoken the first word.

"So what are you drinking tonight?" he said with all the interest of a teenager caught up in politics.

"Whiskey and orange, on the rocks," I said looking straight at the bar in a bid to appear aloof, more interested in striking up a conversation with the libertine male behind it.

"Whiskey and what? What kind of a drink is that?"

His nervousness was so palpable that it shook his voice. I

251

meant business and he knew it.

"Whiskey with orange juice, please. Not cordial or squash, juice. You should try it some time. Really hits the spot," I said, messing up my attempt at appearing nonplussed. Slapping him was all I could think of doing right now. He didn't seem to have a clue how much he'd betrayed me.

He delved into his back pocket and pulled out some crumpled Sterling notes, trying to decide which passed as the corresponding amount.

The barman served him both drinks and when Hayden handed the strongest of the measures to me, I noted he was careful to avoid any brushing of my skin leading to a potential electrical surge.

How futile, after all those emails of longing, revealing the things he wanted to do to me.

He found us a lone table, something of an achievement in the tightly-packed bar. All around us people chanted, laughed, and generally revelled in jubilant mood, the volume of which made it difficult to have any kind of conversation. But who could blame them? No more work for a week or so. Christmas, which seemed to arrive frighteningly earlier each year – at least in the printing industry, was finally here.

I removed my scarlet coat to reveal a figure-hugging Christmassy-green dress that tied enticingly to the side of my ever-decreasing waist. I sensed his breath was ever so slightly taken away, but then he quickly summonsed a stern look.

"No point making yourself comfortable. I've people to get back to."

I mentally retracted the knife from my stomach.

"It's a warm, air-conditioned bar, Hayden. Of course I'm going to take my coat off. I'd prefer it if you did the same. That thing you're wearing clashes badly with your skin."

I. Am. On. Fire: keep the quips coming, Kate.

Things were turning so sour already. But he'd chosen to set the tone. I was merely giving as good as I received.

"Listen, I have no idea why you got the crazy idea you got about us."

His emphasis on that little word made it clear it was nothing more than a girly invention on my part.

"It was just a bit of fun," he said, making it known that I was seriously dislocated from reality. "A bit of banter that very clearly got misinterpreted...and you're meant to be the linguist."

He swigged at his lager.

"I have somebody special in my life and I'm really happy with her. I live in Singapore for heaven's sakes. And you're living in cloud cuckoo land if you thought I'd give any of that up to come back here. Now let's just put this silliness behind us, forget it ever happened and move on—"

I stared at him, unable to process his words for a second or two, and then let the drink do the talking.

"Firstly, I never expected you to move anywhere, okay: let's get one thing straight; just because I have...I mean I *had* feelings for you; they were never a flaming marriage proposal. But it does tell me all I need to know, that you're all mouth and no trousers, not half the man I thought you were."

He raised his eyebrows in alarm and I took a quick sip of my drink.

"Secondly, you might be able to put this silliness behind you. And maybe that's a man thing, some sort of denial tactic, but I can't. You're an idiot, Hayden. You made me leave Daniel."

It wasn't quite true. I would have left even if there was no chance of being with him. But he'd embarrassed me. I was bitter and I wanted revenge.

"Look, I've said it already and I'll say it again, we're not going down that road anymore," he shouted with a passion I hadn't seen before.

All out of words, I wanted to put the miles back between us. I decided that adequate payback for now would be to portray him as the small, pathetic, hopeless creature he'd just made me feel like in a pub full of revellers.

"You know what? You are unbelievable, ugly and unbelievable," I yelled at the top of my lungs. "What excuse

253

for a man does that to a woman in my league?"

There, his audience could make of that what they would.

Hand on hip, I drained every last drop from my unfathomable drink, and, as if I were calling time on our marriage, I abandoned him there and then.

Oh, that felt good.

Such short-lived revenge may be, but to see that face, a sad flustered mess not knowing where to look, that was priceless.

Daisy and Steph greeted me expectantly, not knowing at all what I'd just run from. They ordered a final round and took me to dinner.

"Look at me. Would you have done what he did? I mean, I know you probably aren't single, you are rather a dish. But if you were…"

I was the height of mortification acting up to the waiter. But this sad routine had to be played out tonight. Tomorrow was another day and a fresh headache.

***

Christmases past had willed me back to the office. Hour upon hour had been spent wishing the drudgery of festivities away – anything to escape the fact I was curled up on the sofa with a man who could break my legs off if I said something out of turn.

What a contrast this year. I was dreading the return to work. The sober fact of the matter was, I had taken things beyond what could be described as far. I couldn't even recall my choice of vocabulary that fateful night; all I knew was I had spectacularly insulted Hayden. There was little more I could do except hope that my outburst had given him temporary amnesia too – at least until we could establish some kind of civility. The dynamics of our relationship – even pre-email affair – were well and truly over. I knew it had to end at some point. Even in my fairytale state of mind, this was always on the road to nowhere: he was right.

I was in a lovelorn, rain-clouded world of my own where

the days, half-eaten by darkness, matched my absence of joy. All the while those around me were gift-wrapped in a holiday season bubble of celebration and goodwill. Mustering a smile was beyond painful and I never knew when I would suddenly have to run to the loo for a hearty cry.

Once I'd ingested about as much television as I could take during the long yuletide week with my family, evenings were spent retreating to my old room, trying to re-direct my life from the perspective of yet another spiritual book. My latest read promised potential. Only slowly at first, but then I sensed the overcoming your fears page-turner (which had won a number of awards) was building up to its punch line.

And then there it was: 'Do the thing you want to do, that you just don't think you can do. Just do it'.

Several restless hours later (mostly spent heaving the thick duvet on and off, wriggling and striving to get comfortable in a pre-menstrual dilemma) I tiptoed across to my laptop, pulled my dressing gown around me and proceeded to construct – and send - an email of apology.

There was no reply. I hadn't expected one.

Chapter Thirty-Five

"Agghh," I searched desperately for a chink of light, heart thudding with no idea of where I was until my left arm flailed at something that resembled a lampshade and I managed to switch it on, exhaling deeply as I came to, realising it was just a dream; Daniel hadn't locked me in the house.

I had been feeling utterly lousy, not just bogged down with the usual welcome to the New Year sniffles, but an emotional wreck. What a start to January. I officially inhabited no-woman's land. Unsure of where I was going both privately and professionally.

A hare-brained idea popped into my head one bleak rainy morning. I tried to brush it away, dismiss it as another of my eccentric schemes, but it just kept coming back. With a vengeance. Much like the boundless signs I had seen to leave Daniel, the word 'Singapore' appeared in writing or conversation any and everywhere I went.

On a particularly washed-out afternoon, when the mournful clouds promised nothing but even more inky grey days ahead, I found myself in the travel agents booking a return flight to that very destination.

"I can't believe you've spent all that money. Don't give him the satisfaction. You've done nothing wrong, remember?"

"Truth is we're equally to blame, Steph. I know what I did would have smarted. I have written – and said – some extremely lowlife things. And of course he'd pretend they didn't touch the sides, but I know all too well how words can sting, how they stick around long after they've been uttered. Gosh, I'm sounding literary today," I chuckled, trying to get the others to see the comical side too.

But Daisy and Steph's wooden expressions remained etched across their faces.

"If you, Daisy, and I didn't work with him on a day-to-day basis, there'd be no need to go to these extremes. But we do. And none of this is your fault. I also need proper closure now, a chance to move on with my life. I can't start a New Year off like this. It's not healthy – we need to put it to bed."

"Yeah, well, as long as that's the only thing that's being put to bed after all of your shenanigans, madam. I just hope you know what you're letting yourself in for, raking it all up again like this. Promise me you'll stay safe, report on how things are going."

It was comforting to know that Steph really did care.

***

Of course I didn't have the remotest outline of a plan. I figured the million dollar idea would 'come to me' between now and touchdown in Singapore.

It didn't.

And so I jumped on a harbour cruise instead. Procrastination, my old friend, weaved me through the junks, barges and tugs. And a local lady motioned for me to join her at a table on the bottom deck. She painted my name in Chinese characters in exchange for a couple of Dollars. I held the finished article close as I watched the forest of emotionless skyscrapers pass by. How I wished I could match their not bothered composure.

"It's a man, I can tell," the little lady almost sang back down the boat. "Do what you have to; then come back in the evening. It's magic show here. Lights make you happy again, all become clear in life."

She chuckled as if she had once been there herself, and then turned to walk to the top deck. I was just as confused as when I'd boarded. But she was right: no time like the present to take the plunge, get the craziness out of my system and move the hell on.

***

I did feel pathetic for cracking open the miniature mini-bar whiskey once back at the hotel. But a sip or two provided the final push I needed. Nervousness somehow completely abated, I left my room with a handwritten note in my hand.

"Can I ask where you're going? You look sensational… hope you don't mind me saying," the dashing American tourist in the lift – dashing with the exception of the 'fanny pouch' – affirmed to me how good I looked.

A block away from Hayden's office and the girl cleaning the toilets of McDonalds was repeating the same mantra, as if she also secretly knew what I was up to. But this mission was starting to feel like torture again. If only I'd thought to bring a hipflask. Now I understood Gary's hokey cokey dance.

C'mon Kate.

I triple checked my reflection, on the verge of hyperventilation. You've done stuff like this before – without alcohol.

It was true. I had scripted ludicrous phone calls to boys. Like a very long time ago and in the phone box. And okay…I usually got my best friend of the moment to read them out in exchange for a few Rhubarb and Custards. But still.

I put one hand in my pocket and walked back into the flurry of street life. Quarry Suite's wealth stood tall like a modern-day Goliath. David held her breath and entered the skyscraper.

***

A delivery guy marched up behind me, ushering me forward to the door.

"Oh no, after you," I said, hanging well back.

The pillar at the end of the corridor made the perfect spying post. It wouldn't be wise if one of the other office staff detected a mad woman loitering around. I dithered for a moment. Could I really bring myself to do this? It had all been an adventure, I'd brought myself this far. That was admirable, verging on crazy enough. Surely now it was best to do a runner before it all got out of hand?

"Just do it. You're here aren't you? Slide the envelope under the door! How hard can it be?"

The Voice had returned.

Having knocked her back before (and look how far that got me), I knew I could trust her this time. Autopilot took over my bodily functions. I tiptoed up to the glass door of the office (fortunately everyone must have been at their desks), slid the note beneath it and walked away. Fast.

Ha, this was acting, Miss Lacey.

Half an ear was cocked out for a 'Kate, I love you' cry echoing down the corridor, straight to my heart. But it didn't come.

Ah well, there was still the train station scenario.

I'd played that one over and over in my head, like some kind of dramatic movie scene. Hayden would call after me, give me an extremely delayed kiss and sweep me off into the sunset on a motorbike, despite the fact he didn't actually have one.

But as I left the office block further and further behind, waited at the MRT and then boarded the next train, it was clear that one wasn't going to come to fruition either.

Could the soundtrack of Natasha Bedingfield's 'These Words' please now kindly dislodge itself from my head?

How was I supposed to contain the choked up tears of my life as I had recently come to know it, being well and truly over? This was – if I acknowledged the wellspring of feeling embedded deeply in my subconscious – my absolute last ditch attempt at making him realise what a mistake he had made.

But it seemed the only error being made here was the colossal amount of cash I had parted with. I could have just put a stamp on the damned sorry note and been done with it.

I made my way across to Outram, the district I'd become familiar with during my visit with Steph. There was a cosy looking coffee shop that would be the perfect location to gather my thoughts of defeat over an iced moccachino – and fret that I had completely freaked him out now I had turned into an international stalker.

A brief trail around the outdoor street markets rounded off my wholly unsuccessful day. I headed back for my hotel, unsure of how I was going to spend the next thirty-six hours.

I took a shower, whatever the time of year, Singapore's humidity was relentless. The see-through glass steamed up and I belted out a string of *Coldplay*'s most depressing hits. Then through the rush of droplets overhead, and the break for the instrumental bit, I thought I detected something else. I stopped my vigorous shampooing, flung open the door, almost slipped on the soap, tripped instead on the shower gel and fell into a heap on the soft-carpeted floor.

"What are you like?" said the husky voice on the other end of the mobile.

It was the last thing I'd been expecting. And it felt very wrong to be talking to him stark naked.

"Look, hang on. I really need to grab a towel."

"Well, um, I didn't quite mean to time my call like that," he said clearly flustered at the image, having determined never to look back.

I bundled myself into the complimentary dressing gown instead.

"I'm decent now," I said.

"Okay," he paused briefly, "I have a football match…near The Hotel Majestic as it happens. Why are you staying there anyway, Kate?" he almost screeched, "there are much more hip and happening places to stay in this city, you know."

"I just liked the look of it," I said, not quite sure why myself.

"So, the options are: we can either meet for a quick drink this evening after the match. I'll come to The Majestic, we can have a quick drink in the bar…"

I wondered how many times he would insist on emphasising 'quick'.

"Or, you could come to the office tomorrow, say seven and we'll go out for a quick drink after I've finished work: up to you."

I hesitated. Was it a trick question? If we met at mine tonight, well, that was a little inappropriate perhaps. No, that wouldn't have done at all. I was here to patch things up, apologise; get over it.

"Tomorrow sounds fine. I've actually got other plans tonight."

First I've heard of them, I smiled, delighting in my announcement.

"See you tomorrow then, enjoy your evening."

My teeth chattered as I lay the phone on the bedside table.

"Well, that's perfect. That's ideal," I told the four walls surrounding me as I finished drying off. "I'll grab some street food tonight, early to bed and then a full day shopping. Maybe a Singapore Sling at Raffles if time allows."

The little lady was right. The guidebook also said the most magical time in Singapore is at dusk, when the city is bathed in neon lights, a party about to get started. But the cinematic beauty washed over me. I had more important business to attend to right now; the trek to Quarry Suites tomorrow to apologise to my own quarry. Well, former quarry.

***

It was uncanny being back in the show room. I could have gone straight into character acting out any one of the scenarios we'd exchanged. In fact that would have come as second nature. I wasn't pretending to be somebody I wasn't, unlike him.

But I determined to stamp it out of my thoughts.

He was alone when he opened the door and that threw me, making my earlier forbidden thoughts daringly tempting, lest his over rehearsed non-committal expression gave them no room for further contemplation.

"I'm finishing up a call. Take a seat."

Twenty minutes later we walked side by side in oafish silence to wherever it was he was taking me. I struggled to keep pace in kitten heels.

"I'll need to stop at the cashpoint," he said without really

261

looking at me.

I propped my flagging self against the wall outside the bank and waited. January was hardly as balmy as August in this city, but my sweaty upper lip told a different story. I was glad for the opportunity to wipe it undetected with the back of my hand.

This whole thing was so surreal. I wished I'd downed another drink before leaving the hotel. I was far from alcoholic, but in these situations something to take the edge off was a must. The effects of that Singapore Sling had worn off far too quickly.

Both of us remained without words as he led me across town to his bar of choice; presumably a place unknown to his better-half and anybody who associated with her.

"Table in the corner seems to have our name on it," he gestured once we'd arrived. "You take a seat; I'll get in the drinks. Don't tell me, whiskey and orange—"

"Actually, I'll have a Campari and orange – if they do it."

He frowned and shook his head.

"Hey, I could have insisted on blood orange," I said as he made for the bar.

He returned armed with two glasses and a subdued smile suggesting this was indeed going to be a short-sharp-to-the-point kind of drink: business, definitely not pleasure.

"So how's the sightseeing going?"

"I've mainly been shopping to be honest. But I did squeeze in a trip to Raffles this afternoon. Geez, the tourists…and the over-inflated prices…" I picked at my nail so hard under the table that it started to draw blood.

"Know it well, Kate; routine for me whenever I get visitors."

"I took a lovely selfie there. Wanna see it?"

He didn't seem to catch that bit. Why did I have to say that anyway? What a stupidly embarrassing thing to say. As if that was even a word.

"…other than that, I took a harbour cruise, met a wise old lady; did more shopping in the markets. You know, the usual." I started to pick at another nail and then remembered

I was wearing white jeans.

He seemed pensive.

Natalia Imbruglia's *'Torn'* came on. I fast forwarded through the lyrics and found myself standing.

"I um, I just need to visit the ladies. Shall I get the menu on the way back? Do you need a top up?"

His eyes glazed over as I stood before him and my confidence returned. But then it was a powerful song. Yes, it might serve him well to take heed of Nat's words.

"Food, no, top up, yes. Same as before please."

What a bugger, I was starving. No way was I eating on my own though. This was nerve-wracking enough.

Reflection checked. Perfect. Nothing more I could do but see the evening through now. I took a deep breath and made my way back to him.

"Look, I really am genuinely sorry...for the part I have played in all of this," he said as I approached.

"Oh, it's okay," I said as if he'd no more than trodden on my toe, "water under the bridge and all that." I waved my hand to dismiss the best part of last year.

But it seemed that first beer was the prelude to the truth. Maybe he should have eaten first. This wasn't at all what I was expecting.

"I'll never leave this city," he'd said it in Bristol and now he was saying it again, before taking a giant gulp of his pint and aiding it down with a vigorous and repetitive nod of his head. It looked painful. "I'll never go back to the UK."

Singapore has made you, I know.

This city had made him. She'd given him all the tools; all the material goods, and all the ladies. Without her he'd simply fade into virtual nothingness. I sure as hell wasn't going to try to compete anymore.

He laughed aloud suddenly. I hoped he couldn't read my thoughts because he'd have bitterly disagreed.

"By the way, that email you sent me...I really did have an awful flight. You should be careful what you say. I was even a little scared you were in possession of mystical witchcraft type powers hailing from Glastonbury and all. Everybody

263

was clapping hysterically on landing."

"Good," I said, and I meant it.

"I'd have loved to have followed through with you, Kate. You know that," he said flipping his beer mat as if to play down his confession. "But ultimately, I just couldn't trust myself; me here, you there. Me surrounded by temptation…"

Hang on a minute, temptation does exist in Europe too.

I remained verbally opinion-less, best let him carry on and get it all out.

"I just couldn't trust myself," he regurgitated his words again, tripping over and over himself with his mazy explanation, "and that wouldn't be fair to you."

It was an admission that there had been feelings on his part, for sure. He just wasn't prepared to act on them. But I wasn't going to be anybody's backup plan. I listened and listened and though I surely knew my mind was becoming intoxicated with my fourth Campari mixer, I saw it as clearly as I needed to.

He was not The One.

How could I have ever thought about sharing my life with this man? He couldn't have been anymore East End boy to my West End girl. He would never be one for spontaneity. He lived his life with his head, every part of it. Whilst I had just learned how to do the exact opposite, something I was under no circumstances prepared to unlearn.

"It's okay, Hayden. You don't need to explain anymore."

All I wanted to do was limp back to my hotel room – ever so slightly disappointed – and sleep, then sleep some more, waking as a new woman, free of the mind games. But he had saved my life, of that I could be certain and for that I'd be ever grateful. Like a cat with nine lives, I'd hovered at eight and a half for too long; next time Daniel would have killed me.

My stomach growled as he repeated himself again. It'd been hours since I'd thought to put any food in it.

"I'm starving. Are you sure you won't eat?"

"No, that would make it a date. And we're not on one of those."

"Well then in that case, I think it's probably time to go."

The Japanese businessmen, who politely lined the bar as we'd entered, were still drinking – not in such a neat row anymore. Hayden chuckled at their oblivion, muttering something along the lines of:

"It's not meant to be, well, not in this lifetime anyway."

Pinpricks of energy lit up the sky as we stepped outside. He leant in to kiss me softly on the cheek, the warmth of his lips lingering a fraction of a second longer than was strictly necessary.

"Bye, Kate."

We waited standing a sober distance apart.

A swarm of taxis appeared as if by magic, pulling up next to the curb. So did a lone figure toward the end of the taxi rank fringing the bar, one who looked so suspiciously like Daniel that I thought it futile to do a double take.

Hayden opened the rear door of the nearest cab. I climbed in whilst he directed the driver to my hotel. I fixed my gaze unbendingly on the road that lay ahead, resolutely so as distance and speed left Hayden behind, to do whatever it was he was going to do with the rest of his life.

We rounded a corner. A giant beer advertisement seemed to support my decision.

'Never settle for less'.

Fighting back the welling tears in danger of forcing me to break out in a fit of painful sobs, I determined to re-compose myself. And then there it was again, a perfectly framed affirmation, reconfirming the way ahead as the taxi rounded yet another hairpin bend.

'Never settle for less'.

"The world needs more billboard signs like that," I shared my insight with the taxi driver and blinked away my watery eyes.

"Yes, good beer that make," he said.

And then something did tell me to look back. Not to check if Hayden was in fact sailing on the back of us with a skateboard like some kind of budding Michael J Fox, but call it instinct, I just knew something sinister was going on.

Chapter Thirty-Six

It was him. I knew it from the millisecond the feeling had entered my psyche. Daniel was trailing behind us in that very Singapore cab.

There was no time for how or why. No time to try to convince myself that the silhouette in the vehicle practically touching our rear was his international lookalike – since he had eternally been petrified of flying anywhere more than four hours away.

Everything slowed down into a disorienting fug. The driver sensed my unease and began to fire questions at me:

"Are you all right, lady? Have you forgotten something? Did you leave your purse behind?"

"I'm…no, I'm fine. It's okay, really…"

But it wasn't. My heart was beating faster than I knew was humanly possible, whilst my fingers took on a life of their own, frantically searching for Hayden's number.

He beat me to it, his incoming text screaming concern:

THE GUY IN THE CAB BEHIND IS AFTER YOU. GO STRAIGHT TO FREDDIE'S IN OUTRAM AND RUN FOR IT. I'LL BE ALONG AS SOON AS I CAN X

A kiss? Now?

My hands were shaking too much to reply, and I really didn't want to let on to the driver that we were in a movie car chase. The faster he sped, clearly the faster the cab behind would pursue.

"Actually, I um…need to go somewhere else instead. Yeah, take me to…" and I pulled out the scrunched up address which I just happened to have in my bag "…this address on Pearl Bank Road."

The driver looked in his mirror either suspiciously at me,

or the proximity of the taxi behind, sped up and nodded his agreement.

The rest of the journey was a very long blur. If I looked over my shoulder I was afraid the evening's consumption of alcohol (and no food) would end up doubling my bill. Just as focusing on a seat back in a plane that is banking and tilting, offering more than a panoramic view of ocean and sharks, is the quickest route to regaining composure in a 747, so is the sweaty and battered leather casing, complete with panel of indecipherable prices, when you are being pursued by a cab whose driver has presumably been promised quadruple the fare to jump red lights and glue itself to your bumper.

After what felt like hours, much tapping of feet and knocking of knees complete with flurries of (presumably) Malay swear words of the most uncensored calibre, my cab screeched up to the familiar hill that doubled as the skyscraper's driveway first, followed immediately by Daniel's.

Admittedly, Hayden had to think on his feet but this executive plan of his was about as flawed as they came. Trouble-shooting for late vessels and last-minute board book print runs may have been his forte, but when it came to devising an escape route for a woman being trailed by her former abusive partner, he was clueless. There was no sign of Freddie. Instead my driver, who was now understandably eager to be paid, tipped for his troubles and on to his pending airport assignment, had been shoehorned by Daniel's.

"Please would you mind waiting just a few minutes... thank you so much, I can pay extra, I—"

"I have no time for this," he yelled over my pleasantries. "If I knew you'd get me trapped, I'd have made you walk. I'm running a business here, lady."

I didn't dare look out of my backseat window, but the clunk of the locks told me the driver was about to take me hostage in a most unfriendly turn of events, either that or Daniel was approaching us fast.

My palms were damper than damp. My heart could have rivalled anybody's cardiac arrest. A blanket of fear threatened to suffocate me and I had no idea what to do next. My phone pinged. It was Hayden again.

I'M COMING. FREDDIE WILL HAVE HIT THE PANIC BUTTON IN RECEPTION BY NOW, POLICE WILL BE THERE SOON. STAY CALM – DO NOT DREAM OF LEAVING THE TAXI.

That particular set of instructions, meaningful as they may have been, was all the motivation I needed to take care of this myself. I fumbled around in my purse, paid and tipped the driver, assured him I'd have the driveway unblocked in moments if he'd allow me to step out the cab, and then I stood before Daniel, eyeballing him up and down in the dark, a cowgirl in a spaghetti western. And perhaps a very foolish one, for he may well have carried a fully loaded gun.

He reached into his rucksack and that was when the idea of a reality check seemed like a good one, despite my tipsiness. Except instead of revealing a weapon, he clutched at a bunch of what appeared to be glossy prints, in a hodgepodge of shapes and sizes.

Instinct told me to step back, and as I did, he tossed a confetti of photos at me. Like something out of a celebrity paparazzi spread in OK magazine. Some landed face down, illuminated beneath the outside lights, most framed a 'guilty party' of male and female couplings; the female being me.

Me and Eduardo leaving a posh Lisbon restaurant.

Me and Gerard sharing coffee in Paris – somehow, heaven only knows how the snapper had managed to pull it off – gazing intimately into one another's eyes.

Adrian handing me a red rose during a cosy dinner for two in Bruges.

And then a second snap of us beaming cheesily at an accordion player.

Me looking suspiciously like I am chatting up Filpe, the waiter in Lisbon whilst wearing a bikini.

Me and Jake sidled up extremely snuggly (Henry conveniently cropped out of the shot) in Frankfurt.

"You drove me to it, you drove me to all of this, you flamin' whore."

In the corner of my eye I detected Freddie slide through the narrowest of gaps from the main doorway to the building. He loitered reassuringly in the background but couldn't deter me from smouldering and trembling all at once. It was like this was happening to somebody else in a film, a far-fetched and outlandish script I had accidentally walked into. Yet I had also reached the point where absolutely nothing surprised me when it came to Daniel anymore. Not even this.

Hayden's cab screeched up the driveway and out he leapt – an action hero who never missed his call to save the day. He sprinted all of five metres across to me.

"What the hell are you playing at?" he shouted at Daniel with a sudden authority that would have served him better a few years ago with Geraldine.

I removed his hand, which had worked its way around my waist in some kind of show of protection, as a medley of cabs reversed, circled, revved and smoked their tyres collectively in one head-turning blast.

"No, you're decidedly not my knight in shining armour. Thanks for the tip-off to come to Freddie and all, but..." and frankly I couldn't believe I was coming out with this perfectly scripted Steph-style spiel "...there's really only one man here, and that's Freddie."

Freddie grinned. Hayden retreated reluctantly toward the skyscraper's base. And Daniel just kept on throwing his snaps to the ground as if he were a croupier dealing cards.

I stooped to pick some of them up incredulous at the lengths he had gone to.

"How?" was pretty much my only question.

"You couldn't have acted alone." I shuddered, thoughts running through my head as to potential accomplices.

"I had my help," he smiled.

"Yeah, I'll bet. Well, I'll doubt it was Hannah...or your mum...nor your Young Farmers posse. Most of them wouldn't as much as leave Somerset, let alone jump on a plane. And in any case...the people in these pictures are mainly clients."

"Ooh, you don't know a lot, young lassie."

269

Even here, on the other side of the world, he had to insist on the broadest and most uncomplimentary of linguistic performances.

"Magic Mike," he said, eyebrows raised.

"I beg your pardon? You mean that cretin from Young Farmers?"

"Spot on, babe, spot on," he grinned, "you see young Mikey, well, he knows Lady Peacock...preeety well, being her nephew and all—"

"Come again?"

"He means Sharon, Kate. Who else? Now this is all starting to make sense, isn't it? She's hardly your number one fan...especially when I recall the stuff she said prior to your trip over here with Steph a few years ago..." Hayden inched forward "...and the way she's been banging on about you... and the Belgian debt these past—" and then retreated again, realising he had said too much.

"She what?" My eyes were laser beams, probing his, wondering who else had been privy to the recording Jason had shared with me. "Why would she be doing that?"

"It's nothing, forget I said it..."

"Oh and your best bud Steph's been helping out too," Daniel stole the conversation back.

Wow. That was unexpected.

"Steph? Never."

"Oh yeah," he was shaking with nervous excitement, "Lady P was offering good money for some of these shots." Daniel smirked as he laid the final offerings across the ground and kicked a particular snap of me pinning up a poster of a six-packed 'Wim' in Amsterdam. "Money talks... although...Stephanie did need me to kick her arse whilst you were conveniently in the bog in a certain pizza shack in Copenhagen."

"I can't believe she'd stoop so...I get it, that's what the fancy new phone with the camera was all about—"

"Don't be too hard on her, Kate. Put yourself in her shoes. Look, I'm going to square with you: I knew some of this was going on," said Hayden. "If I don't come out with my version

270

of events, then you'll only hear it from someone else grapevine-style…I've known for a while she was trying to get you sacked—"

"Excuse me?"

"Haha, not so much Ken to yer Babie now is he?" said Daniel.

"Just butt out, mate. You haven't got the foggiest what you're talking about—"

"Yer? Come here and say that and I'll ram this down your throat." Daniel made a fist and waved it about like an over-eager trainee with a machine gun.

"Stop it, the pair of you. Let him finish, Daniel. I want to hear this and it had better be good."

Hayden took a deep breath, grappled for his cigarettes in his back pocket and sparked up, inhaling greedily.

"Well…I'm waiting?" I kicked about at some loose chippings, somehow resisting the temptation to lob them at both of them.

"Okay. The long and the short of it is…" he flicked ash to the ground before taking another heavy puff, "she's been blackmailing a few of us, myself included…to set you up in unprofessional circumstances—"

"You are joking?"

"He's not," Daniel said with a laugh.

"Gary, Piers, Sebastian, Steph, your ex…she tried to get Sid on board too, but he refused," said Hayden.

It was at this point I thought that my eyes would literally bulge out of their sockets.

"Why? Just why? What an evil, conniving—"

"Yes, she is. But it was business. How do you think half of Singapore works? This is everyday shit we're talking about: backhanders and corruption. Scare the likes of Steph, who's hardly rolling in it and you're on to a winner. Gary's a soft touch too, as we all know; Sebastian has too many skeletons in the closet to say no…and Piers is easily won over with a brand new Rolex. The woman's got cash coming out of her ears. She doesn't like you. She'll stop at nothing to get you out."

271

"Yeeep," said Daniel, tightening the cord and toggle on his rucksack, "all my bingo numbers came in at once when I hooked up with Mikey…didn't take long for us to put two and two together. I've never trusted you," he paused to spit sideways, "not from the moment I had the misfortune of courting you—"

I turned to Hayden, hands glued to my hips.

"So why didn't you—?"

"I know what you're going to say. Why do you think I wouldn't go on a date with you at Christmas? Why do you think I cancelled out on Phuket? I didn't want you to lose your job. You've no idea who was on your trail. Well, you do now."

"And your girlfriend, she's real…or a cardboard cut-out?"

"She's real, yes, I'm afraid so." Hayden looked at the floor. "I wanted to come clean about everything sooner…but it would have seemed too outlandish to be believable. You'd have gone straight to Henry and Adrian…and that would have backfired badly."

"And not just for me, huh?" I winked and threw him a sarcastic smile. "Well good for you, Hayden, for breaking with tradition and putting yourself first."

"I won't leave it like this." A silent until now Freddie stepped forward, slowly at first and then quite decisively. "You are not safe in this city, Kate, with this psychopath on the loose. He probably knows where your hotel is and everything. Time we called in reinforcements."

Daniel dropped his rucksack in voluntary defeat, raised both arms and lowered himself to the ground as if bowing to Mecca. It was truly breath-taking; pitiful, comedic yet breath-taking. For in so doing, here was his acknowledgement to the outside world (well Hayden and Freddie) as well as his victim, that nothing, not one fraction of time over the past decade had been manufactured in my mind.

I am not sure how any of us expected this scene to end, but he needed help, he needed therapy. Much as it momentarily whet my appetite, the harsh and the stark of the Singapore police force, like the notion of putting stem ginger in a cake, wouldn't make anything right. What Daniel needed was self-love, to start his own journey of healing. But he'd be taking it alone. I stooped to my handbag and pulled out a book.

"The only condition upon which I will refrain from pressing charges is if you read this. And I mean really read it. Cover to cover. Then start looking for love in all the right places. None of which are me."

"Thanks, babe, I mean Kate." He took the Self-Help book from my hand, and even in my crouching position, I noted the glassy eyes; eyes on the verge of letting it all spill out. "It's really over now, right?"

"Yes, it really, really is over. Don't keep doing this to yourself, Daniel. Get yourself better, fix your mind, make peace with your demons and, because I really can't put any finer a point on it...move the fuck on."

I felt I had grown several metres above the two of these men as I stood again; condescending, perhaps, but in their own unique ways, were either so very different to the other?

I crossed the driveway to Freddie, taking his hands in mine, hoping against hope he'd be able to cancel, at the very least postpone the cops' imminent arrival.

"Couldn't we just organise Daniel a taxi to the airport and insist that he takes the next flight home?"

Freddie's lips quivered as if stifling back a full-on rumpus of laughter. That was the moment I realised he'd been lying. Panic button indeed! No wonder this felt like a movie scene, Freddie had us as convinced as Ewan McGregor playing Nick Leeson in *Rogue Trader*.

I turned to look at the shadow of a man who was attempting to pry his photographic evidence off the gravelly driveway.

"You won't get anywhere without nails," I crouched to retrieve them one by one, taking the bobble from my hair and binding the prints together.

"These stay with me...until I get to a paper shredder."

Chapter Thirty-Seven

It didn't matter that as I checked-in for my flight back to England at Singapore's Changi airport, I found that I hadn't arrived quickly enough to secure my preferred window or aisle seat. The middle would do fine.

It didn't matter that in a vision of hilarity (and utter cheek since I had funded it), I spotted a gorgeous early twenty-something woman with jet black hair and skin made of alabaster, the tiniest of waists, dripping in designer clothing and clad in towering heels on the arm of a certain male in a puffy gold body warmer, waiting in line for Thai Airways' 20:35 departure to Phuket via Bangkok.

It didn't matter because the seeker had found.

She'd only gone and stumbled upon The Holy Grail.

It was such a modest uninspiring cover for a work of non-fiction that delivered the essential truth about life. But from the very first word, I was transfixed by the book I'd bought at the airport. I barely moved on the long flight home – bar the odd round of stretches to avoid Deep Vein Thrombosis – immersing myself with this sudden knowledge of a certain governing Universal principle: The Law of Attraction.

Apparently, it had always been there! So how exactly had I missed this? And not just me…how had everybody missed this? Was everybody else equally unaware?

It was as if my whole past collapsed in one magnetically synchronised spiral of events. Now I got it. Now I could see the way my thoughts about myself – my longstanding role as the victim of my life story – had continued to attract more and more unjust situations.

Yes, as it transpired, I'd been in control all along.

I'd only been and created all of it through my imagination,

every little and not so little thing, from the laughter in cahoots from my peers at school as they scrambled to avoid sitting next to my underdog self, to all of those spiteful and loveless attacks from Daniel.

From the bizarre and random episodes of being stalked by strange men, to being paid a pittance by my employers; and now there was Sharon and her 'Operation Follow Kate around the Globe' to add to the mix.

In kestrel vision, I viewed the map of my life from above, observing the links between my childhood feelings of inadequacy and every event that didn't please me. Life had followed me, always. What I'd given out in word, thought and deed, as accurately as a boomerang, I'd damn well received it back.

I'd grown ever more terrified of Daniel, so he had to keep abusing me. I'd become sour and vicious toward most of the people I worked with, so they had to keep provoking me. This wasn't just spiritual, it was scientific. Quantum physics in action.

Would he have apprehended me at all as a teenager if I hadn't been so vulnerable? The answer was a categoric 'no'. I saw it so clearly that I even forgave him. And I mean truly forgave him during that flight. All he'd done was sniff me out as the perfect target to offload his emotions; someone to enervate slowly but surely. I'd made it so easy for him when I was radiating all that negative energy.

But maybe it had to come to this moment. Maybe it had all been leading to this. If somebody had presented me with this theory a couple of years ago, I would have probably recommended they think about a stint in a mental institution. The student was finally ready. She'd completed her elementary course in Self-Help and now the teacher had appeared.

As I read on and on with fascination, increasing my understanding of the real way the world around me worked, the simple fact of the matter was, if only I'd aligned myself with rightful thinking, if I'd adopted a loving approach to everything and everyone, given gratitude for the things I had, and conjured up positive images in my mind, instead of fearing just about anything and everything, well, things would have been very different.

But no regrets, dredging up the past was only going to create more of the same. I knew what I wanted and now I had the key to make it happen. Nothing would ever be the same. Wobble and falter I might, but with this knowledge I could quite literally change my world.

How ironic, The Genie in the bottle in those Aladdin books I'd been selling to my clients had been screaming this out at me for years.

First stop: visualisation of setting up our own company.

Chapter Thirty-Eight

Six months after swapping office for oven, Steph and I opened up our *'Cherry on the Cake'* Bookshop Café. Bristol was buzzing about us. Oh, in a good way, I promise. And Daisy was having second thoughts.

But first I guess I ought to rewind a little. I didn't exactly manage to get a word in with Harold all those months ago when he'd taken us out, to explain that actually, setting up a clone of She Sells was definitely not what we had in mind. Well, what can I say? Law of Attraction did its thing all right. When we next met, Harold was won over immediately by our slightly alternative business idea. Not only that, but he gifted us – yes, gifted us – the deposit on our premises…in return for a guaranteed window seat and free coffee, cake and bestseller whenever he happened to be in the city. It was a deal clincher and we were only too happy to oblige.

And then there was the not-so-small matter of Steph's betrayal. You may well wonder how I came to forgive her, to trust her again. But the truth is she was the easiest person to excuse. After all, I'd been there, done that and worn not so much the T-shirt but the puppet strings, several times over, when it came to Daniel and his tricks. She'd panicked about her job (Sharon was pulling a lot of invisible strings herself) and she – and she alone – had a hefty rent to find for her flat every month. Ultimately (despite saying she'd flatten Daniel), he was too cunning with the manipulation. Which, in a schadenfreude-like way, made me feel slightly better about my own escapade with him, and so it was that we hugged quickly and made up, vowing never to let a man come between us again.

As for Lady P, as you can imagine, she was the trickiest to condone. Yes, that one took a few weeks, and a hell of a commitment to daily meditation. But finally I realised she was just one of many Spiritual Button Pushers, the kind of people who take us to the edge; those who, in the end, we learn just about everything from when it comes to the importance of love, positivity, and accepting others Just As They Are. The fact is, had I owned my vibration, she could never have touched me.

And would you believe it? One evening Daisy handed me an envelope, addressed to me at my former workplace:

Dearest Kate

Please read this before you burn it, I promise I'm not about to stalk you (again). This is just a note to say 'Thank You'. 'Cos how right you were. I needed to put a few demons to rest as it turned out. In other words, cheers for the book you gave me in Singapore that embarrassing evening. Too many people scoff at these Self-Help guides…and so did I used to. Ironic really, 'tis those who make fun of them who could probably most do with their advice.

But I digress.

There's a lot of stuff about my past that I kept hidden from you. Without making too fine a point about it, well, Uncle Ted used to knock me about a bit when I was a kid. I say 'a bit', but before long the knocking got harder, more frequent, more terrifying. And well, I guess just like the bullies at school are often those who are picked on by older kids, or their own parents…I've gone through my life (and I hang my head in shame for it), doing the same – just to the opposite sex.

Why do I still work for him I bet you're wondering? 'Cos he signed his farm and the land over to me in his will when I turned 18. It was his way of making it up to me I suppose. Christ, he wouldn't dare lay a finger on me once I became a fully grown man, or be strong enough to. And so when I look at him…much as I've wanted to swing for him on many an occasion for what he put me through, I just can't. 'Cos all's I see is a sad, tired old man. A man full of regrets, a man who pays the price over and over for the way he beat me. It's like looking at my mirror reflection.

If only my own father had stuck around it would never have happened of course, but what could Mum do when she was a working single parent without childcare? Sissy and I had to go to the farm. The only saving grace is he never laid a finger on her. My God if he'd dared! But those were the days when Aunt Lil was alive, albeit wheelchair bound after her 'fall' from the top of the stairs. I was there when that happened, Hannah too, though thankfully she'd have been too small to remember. I'll never forget the look in his eyes when he realised what his shove to get past Aunt Lil as she was dusting the banister had done. But anyway, no point reliving that flashback all over again, besides, Hannah was always in the house or the garden with her, safe from harm. Whereas Uncle had me breaking my back since I were knee high to a grasshopper; cutting the peat blocks and laying them out neatly, hands covered in earth – I'd still be picking the dirt out from under my nails the next day at school. And I wasn't too much older when he had me cleaning out the pigsty and gathering the windfalls to make cider.

I'm off on a tangent again, I know. It's just there's so much I want to say to you. The counselling is really helping – did I tell you I signed up for it in the end? I can't say it were all my idea. Even after reading the book. But Hannah, well, she never spoke to me for weeks after she saw me go for you that day in the kitchen. And when she did it was to tell me she'd booked me up for some 'therapy'. Actually, she even paid for it. I know you two were never the best of friends, but deep down she was fond of you. I know I often treated her better than you when we were together too. It's what my counsellor refers to as a 'protection mechanism' you see. The lashings I got

279

as a boy affected me so much subconsciously, that I'd do anything to protect her... 'cos I was scared Unc would start on her next – the counsellor thinks that's why I treated you like a housewife too...all those years of seeing him make Aunt Lil do all the domesticated chores.

But anyhow, although there are a fair few sessions to go...and a whole host of other things we're getting to the bottom of, I just wanted to say thanks and sorry, then let you get on with your life, as I will with mine.

I mean I'm not sorry I met you...or for the times we spent together. We did have some fun now and then, didn't we? I hope you'll remember the good times now, forget about the bad. Because I really am sorry about the rest.

You've changed my life, you know. I'm even trying to let my hair down a little bit – and you'll laugh at this, but Hannah's talking about taking me to New York next month. So let's see what all the hype's about!

Oh, enclosed is some money: your half of the house. Yes, I've had to re-mortgage it to do this, of course, but it's only right. We may not have signed any agreements, but 'one day,' to quote Del Boy Trotter, 'I really will be a millionaire!'

So take this, and be happy and luckier in love and life than you were with me. I get a feeling – call it my 'inner voice', that the future is very bright for both of us now we've learnt the lessons the Universe needed us to.

Daniel x

"Daisy...uh...does your drinks cabinet extend to whiskey by any chance? No need for orange, I'll uh, I'll have it on the rocks."

***

"Couple of businessy toffs out there," said Becky, our latest waitress recruit. "One wants the Peach Pie with vanilla pod Chantilly. The other's having the *Nutella* and Banana Cheesecake."

That didn't sound very 'businessy'.

Curious, I peeked through the crack in the kitchen door to see what looked suspiciously like the back of Sid and front of Piers sat before a pile of paperwork, biros tucked behind their ears.

"Well, I never…"

"Somebody you know?"

"Go and find out what they're reading."

Becky disappeared and I got back to baking my Lemon Meringue Pie. Steph's usually turned out better; she was infinitely lighter-fingered. But it was my shift today and my determination to beat those egg whites at exactly the right angle was definitely paying off.

The doorbell tinkled notifying us of new customers.

I just couldn't believe how busy we were. This was the kind of success dreams were made of. It was corny perhaps, but true: when you did what you really loved, money just had to follow.

"Crikey, there's a whole gaggle of blokes in there now…and a token woman," Becky said elbowing the kitchen door open with a tray of empties. "I've had to push tables together and everything."

"What, you mean more male customers, or more males of the Sid and Piers ilk?"

"More males with Pinky and Perky," said Becky. "Oh and yeah, the books: *Pride and Prejudice*, one of them, *Men are from Mars* the other. I best go back out front and hang around for their orders."

I couldn't resist peeping again to see not only Sid and Piers, but Gary, Sebastian and Sharon besides – hang on a minute, this is starting to look extremely suspect – and finally my gaze rested on a laptop screen showcasing none other than Hayden, via that newfound wonder, Skype.

My ears pounded with a whirring sensation. My heart was a racehorse. I had to pace the kitchen several times before I could feast my eyes again on what I thought I had seen.

Meanwhile, a meeting had commenced.

"So, first of all thanks guys – and girls – for showing up. I know we've all risked a lot to see this through over the past couple of years...but a few more weeks and we'll finally have everything signed and sealed, and our baby, our very own company, will be legal and kosher," said Sid.

"It's not been easy for me at all," said Sharon. "You've no idea how difficult it's been sneaking around behind the twins' backs. If it wasn't for M&S and nursery, I'm not sure what kind of excuses I'd have come up with."

"Yeah, we know, Sharon. It's been tricky for all of us," said Hayden reclining in his seat, hands propped behind his head as if re-enacting his holiday on that Thai sun lounger. "Just because I'm on the other side of the planet, doesn't mean I don't feel for you all. I know whenever I call up Gary he has to sneak off like he's having a barney with his girlfriend."

"Sometimes I am," Gary said. "The stress this is putting me under is too much to bear. My only let up is that we now have one, rather than three moaning bitches on the top floor asking me for samples...but Daisy's so swamped under now, even she forgets to chase."

A thunderous round of laughter ensued.

Life is full of moments, precious snapshots in time: speechless mouths, astonished eyes, and burnt Lemon Meringue Pies.

Kate Clothier's greatest career triumph – irrespective of the sales, the travel and the impressive client database – happened on an inconspicuous Wednesday afternoon at a quarter past four.

And for once I didn't check my reflection in the mirror, chiefly because there wasn't one. Well, not in the kitchen, anyway.

Having overheard the conversation playing out in my café, having listened to my flatmate recount her days of stress and toil without a hint of a pay rise, having asked only that morning for a little help from the Universe, having messaged Steph to 'get her arse in here now', I knew exactly what had to be done.

"Inspired action," I whispered.

"You what?" said Becky knitting her brows.

"Watch and learn."

I walked to the front door, Steph pushed it open from the other side and flashed a coy smile, having presumably realised the golden opportunity we had laid out in all its afternoon tea and cake glory in front of us. Not only that, but she clicked her fingers and Jason poked his upper half through the doorway too.

"Don't anybody be getting any silly ideas now," he said with a hearty chuckle as he stepped inside, shut the door firmly behind him and folded two seriously butch arms.

I tucked just behind him to put up the 'closed' sign.

And there it was. Or rather there they were: a cluster of saucer-eyed souls who had come together in perfect universal orchestration to create one of those sublime historic moments.

"Well, well, well," I said with quite possibly the largest grin I had ever known myself capable of. So large in fact, my jaw muscles were threatening to keep it there. Not that I'd have minded. I was in my element, for I just knew how the dialogue would play out, had foreseen the conclusion of my words before they'd as much as spilled out in real time.

It was a done deal.

"Kate? Is that you?"

Hayden looked incredibly small, as if he'd just seen someone from a past life.

"Indeed it is," I said, patting the sides of my aproned hips so that flour fell all about them in a snow storm. "Welcome to *Cherry* on the Cake Bookshop Café," I said, winking at Hayden specifically. "And in the words of Silvia, 'what a pavlova we have here before us'.

Nobody said a thing. Pretty obvious really that the floor was all mine.

"Interesting conversation of yours I've just been

listening in on. I say listening, but of course the volume was so loud that I had no choice but to record it as well." I waved my mobile phone in the air.

"So…here's what's going to happen if you want me to keep schtum."

Sid squirmed, chewing his lip as he had in the Bolognese Battle; Sebastian covered his golden locks and buried his head in the Cath Kidston table cloth, the others were statues.

"Ms Peacock: you are going to insist Daisy gets an immediate five figure pay-rise."

"Um, okay, Kate," Sharon swallowed air, "will do."

"By end of play Monday morning…in the words of Henry."

"Sure thing, no probs."

"And after that you are going to reimburse myself and Steph—"

"I beg your pardon, I don't quite understand."

"Oh, that's okay, I'll fill you in: you see it goes a little something like this…all those hours of Gary pissing about with your little side line – that I am sure you'd still like to come to fruition; all those hours of you pissing about shopping in Clifton's finest stores; all those hours of refusing to help produce us any books…well, you see, they cost us sales. And those sales cost us a pay-rise. I'll be wanting that money back now, for our expansion plans," I said rubbing my white powdery hands together. "Dig into your investments, Shazzer. I'm sure you'll find you'll have those with me by hmm…end of play Monday morning as well."

Sharon began to sob.

"Oh come on," I patted her on the shoulder. "I've let you get away rather lightly for your recent activities, fair's fair, it's not like you can't afford it."

"Erhem," came a deep noise from the doorway.

"Oh yes, and the pay rise thing…you'll need to extend that to Jason as well," I said.

"Ah, Becky, I think they could use a couple of refills

of tea here," said Steph to our stunned waitress.

"Oh, and as I'm feeling in a decidedly good mood, let's get them all a slice of today's special too: Kate's Ultimate Berry Pavlova. My treat though, that one's on the house...Hayden, I must apologise though," I said as I moved closer to the computer screen, "we're all out of Cherry Bakewells."

It was at this point that a paler than pale Hayden fell off his chair and if I'm not quite mistaken, appeared to mutter into cyberspace:

"It is...ah...as they say...always the quiet ones."

Fantastic Books
Great Authors

CROOKED
CAT

Meet our authors and discover
our exciting range:

- Gripping Thrillers
- Cosy Mysteries
- Romantic Chick-Lit
- Fascinating Historicals
- Exciting Fantasy
- Young Adult and Children's
  Adventures

Visit us at:
www.crookedcatbooks.com

Join us on facebook:
www.facebook.com/realcrookedcat

Made in the USA
Columbia, SC
27 September 2017